A CHRISTMAS MIRACLE

BY
AMY ANDREWS

REUNITED WITH HER SURGEON PRINCE

BY
MARION LENNOX

10658571

MILLS &
BOON®

Amy Andrews is a multi-award-winning, *USA TODAY* bestselling Australian author who has written over fifty contemporary romances in both the traditional and digital markets. She loves good books, fab food, great wine and frequent travel—preferably all four together. To keep up with her latest releases, news, competitions and giveaways sign up for her newsletter—amyandrews.com.au/newsletter.html.

Marion Lennox has written over one hundred romance novels, and is published in over one hundred countries and thirty languages. Her international awards include the prestigious RITA® award (twice) and the *RT Book Reviews* Career Achievement Award for 'a body of work which makes us laugh and teaches us about love'. Marion adores her family, her kayak, her dog, and lying on the beach with a book someone else has written. Heaven!

A CHRISTMAS MIRACLE

BY
AMY ANDREWS

MILLS BOON

All rights reserved including the right of reproduction in whole
or in part in any form. This edition is published by arrangement with
Harlequin Books S.A.

This is a work of fiction. Names, characters, places, locations and
incidents are purely fictional and bear no relationship to any real
life individuals, living or dead, or to any actual places, business
establishments, locations, events or incidents. Any resemblance is
entirely coincidental.

This book is sold subject to the condition that it shall not, by way of
trade or otherwise, be lent, resold, hired out or otherwise circulated
without the prior consent of the publisher in any form of binding or
cover other than that in which it is published and without a similar
condition including this condition being imposed on the subsequent
purchaser.

® and TM are trademarks owned and used by the trademark owner
and/or its licensee. Trademarks marked with ® are registered with the
United Kingdom Patent Office and/or the Office for Harmonisation in
the Internal Market and in other countries.

Published in Great Britain 2017
By Mills & Boon, an imprint of HarperCollins*Publishers*
1 London Bridge Street, London, SE1 9GF

© 2017 Amy Andrews

ISBN: 978-0-263-92670-5

Our policy is to use papers that are natural, renewable and recyclable
products and made from wood grown in sustainable forests. The logging
and manufacturing processes conform to the legal environmental
regulations of the country of origin.

Printed and bound in Spain
by CPI, Barcelona

Dear Reader,

This book was born from a couple of different sources. I'd had a plot percolating in my head for a while, about a woman in desperate circumstances who rescues an old man from some thugs and ends up becoming his companion. But it was fuzzy and indistinct. Then I was challenged to write a bearded, tattooed, motorbike-riding doctor and the two ideas started to coalesce. Suddenly these two separate entities became one, and Reid and Trinity's story bloomed like a hothouse flower.

In many ways I knew Trinity and Oscar, her five-year-old son, intimately. Having worked as a PICU nurse for over twenty years, I've looked after many premature babies with long-term respiratory complications and their parents.

Reid, however, was a different story. Sadly, my experience with lumberjack-looking dudes is limited to research on image sites and Pinterest. But I knew his heart. I knew his mile-wide streak of honour and his innate sense of justice. I knew his deep and abiding love for his grandfather. And I knew he was perfect for Trinity. The kind of guy a woman like her—mistrustful, suspicious, wary—could depend on. The kind of guy who would open up his home to a stranger and not expect anything in return.

I absolutely *adored* giving Trinity and Reid their HEA.

As we immerse ourselves in the festive season I ask that we all spare a thought for people, like Trinity, doing it tough. And perhaps also consider the many ways we can reach out and make things a little brighter for someone less fortunate.

Wishing you and yours a happy and safe holiday season.

Love,

Amy

For Sam Walmsley from the London HMB office, who
wanted to see a tattooed, bearded, motorbike-riding doc.
This one's for you!

Books by Amy Andrews

Mills & Boon Medical Romance

Visit the Author Profile page
at millsandboon.co.uk for more titles.

CHAPTER ONE

TRINITY WALKER WAS having a bad day. In a life that had been punctuated by bad days, it was a drop in the ocean. Sadly, they were beginning to have an accumulative effect.

She was twenty-four years old but she suddenly felt ancient.

She'd just needed three more days. Come Monday her government payment would be in the bank and Oscar would be walking through the school gates for the first time.

She could finally get some order to their lives.

Regular child-free hours to dedicate to a job that would bring in regular money for things like rent instead of relying on government support and a variety of other dodgy alternatives.

Couch surfing, shonky hostels, single room rentals in share houses and the occasional night—like last night—sleeping rough in her ancient Mazda, was no life.

Not for her or her five-year-old.

Every now and then she'd get lucky and land a job with some form of accommodation attached. A room, sometimes a small flat or bedsit. It never usually lasted though. More often than not it was Oscar's health issues that ended the job and therefore their housing. Yesterday it had been Terrible Todd.

Her big, ugly, bearded, tattooed boss who drove a motorbike and reeked of cheap cologne and engine grease. Todd had announced that he did, after all, want her to pay for the accommodation.

Just not with money.

He'd felt they could come to an *arrangement*. She'd walked.

Bastard.

Bloody hell, why even bother with a permanently stressed-out, exhausted single mother who wasn't even that much to look at? She was five feet four, her long dark brown hair was so fine it hung limply down her back and she was somewhat on the thin side.

And not the sleek, glowing, deliberate thin of a catwalk model. The stringy, wrung-out thin of a woman who'd been stressed and struggling to make ends meet for the last five years. She'd *used* to be passably pretty back in her size twelve days, but even a fairy godmother would baulk at Trinity's current state.

Hell, it had been so long since she'd even thought of herself as a sexual being it always surprised her when someone else did.

Someone like Terrible Todd.

And here they were. With nowhere to go and no money to pay for anything much until Monday. Homeless again.

Homeless.

The word cast a sinister shadow as a cold hand crept around her heart. Fear over the welfare of her child, always present, threatened to overwhelm her.

Seriously, when was she going to ever catch a freaking break?

Maybe she could impose on Raylene again for the use of her couch tonight. Just one night. They could go after dinner and be gone by breakfast so Raylene, who was also doing it tough, wouldn't have to feed them.

'Look, Mummy! Look at all the ducklings. They're hungry.'

Trinity broke free from the sticky tendrils of anxiety. She was sitting on a park bench about two metres from Oscar, keeping an eye on him near the pond's edge, but had mentally tuned out.

'Yes, darling.' She smiled.

Her own belly growled in hunger as she also smiled at the old man standing next to her son at the pond's edge. He'd brought the bread with him about ten minutes ago and Oscar had followed him from the slippery dip like the freaking Pied Piper.

The elderly gentleman had said hello to her and had looked down and smiled at an eager Oscar as he'd asked the man politely if he could watch him feed the ducks.

'Watch me?' The old man's fuzzy eyebrows had drawn together before he'd given a hearty belly laugh. 'Goodness, young man, you can *help* me.'

Oscar had beamed and for a moment, Trinity had almost burst into tears. It was utterly ridiculous. She didn't cry. She was not a crier. Tears didn't put a roof over her kid's head or food in his belly. But she was feeling so damn low after her brush with Terrible Todd, such a simple act of human kindness had restored her faith in people.

She thought the elderly gentleman might be about eighty. There was a slight stoop to his shoulders and his clothes hung a little as if he might have lost some weight recently but Trinity could tell he once used to be a large man.

A giant next to Oscar that was for sure.

Her heart filled with love for her little guy. He was everything to her. Her stars and moon. Her reason to keep striving, to wake up every morning and eke out a survival when everything seemed so hopeless. A dear little boy who had changed her life.

Who had saved her from a life going nowhere.

It made her sick thinking about the number of times she'd nearly lost him. Born at twenty-six weeks, with tiny lungs and a major heart condition, he'd had an uphill battle. Six months in the NICU including two major heart operations. Another three months in the children's hospital until he was finally discharged *home* on sub-nasal oxygen. Then the next few years being knocked flat by every cold and flu bug going, in and out of ICU.

Trinity had been scared out of her wits for nearly five years.

Although he hadn't been sick for over six months. She hoped that it was a sign and not just flu season being over. That he was finally growing out of his chronic lung condition as the specialists had predicted, that his lungs were finally growing big enough to cope.

She really hoped so. He'd frightened her out of nine lives already.

A group of three teenage boys who should, no doubt, have been in school, were climbing all over the play equipment behind her. They were far too big for it, laughing too loud, talking too loud.

The bread all gone, Oscar ran back and started chattering at her, his voice high and excited. The old man walked by, nodding his head at her and saying, 'See you later, alligator,' to Oscar who laughed as if it were the funniest joke in the world.

'In a while, crocodile,' he called out after the man's disappearing back, hopping from foot to foot.

Trinity smiled, pulling his skinny little body hard against hers. His wispy white-blond hair tickled her face as a lump rose in her throat. Just three more days.

She could do this.

A shout interrupted the hug and they both turned to investigate. The teenagers had bailed up the old man. They were shoving him none too gently from all directions and the old man was not taking it quietly.

'What are they doing, Mummy?' Oscar said, anxiety trembling through his voice. She'd heard that anxiety too often during his hospitalisations.

The man stumbled and almost fell and a surge of red-hot fury flashed through Trinity's veins. *How dare they?* This was a suburban park in a reasonably well-to-do neighbourhood—it was safe. That was why Trinity had chosen to pull the car up here last night. They were nothing but thugs.

'Stop it,' he said, his voice strong and angry. 'You have no right to do this!'

'We can do whatever we want, old man.'

Trinity's heart hammered as rage took hold. Yes, these guys and the Todds of the world always thought they could do whatever they wanted.

She looked around—there was no one else in the park. *She was it.* Her pulse skyrocketing, she set Oscar down on the bench beside her. 'Darling, I want you to stay here and don't move, do you hear me? Stay very still.'

His little fingers clutched her forearm. 'Like when they give me the drips, Mummy?'

Trinity hated that so much of her son's young life had involved needles and doctors and hospitals and pain.

It fuelled her anger.

'Yes.' She kissed his forehead. 'Exactly like that. Mummy will be back in a minute.'

She rose then, covering the distance quickly. *'Oi!'* she yelled. 'Stop that right now.'

The three teens were clearly startled enough to obey as she stormed up to them. There was thunder in her veins and lightning in her eyes. She was furious but there was a clarity to her anger as skills from a distant time in her life surfaced again.

These guys had chosen the wrong person to mess with today.

The guys laughed when they realised from whom the demand had come. 'Oh, yeah?' the beefiest one sneered at her. 'What are you going to do if we don't?'

'I'm going to put you on your ass.'

The old man looked bewildered, his white hair mad-scientist-wild. 'It's okay, my dear,' he said, a gentleman to the core despite his confusion.

There was more hysterical laughter before it cut out and sneering guy locked gazes with her before giving another, very deliberate shove, right in the middle of his victim's chest.

'I say!' he objected, his voice quivering with outrage, causing more laughter from the moron gallery.

And an eruption inside Trinity's head.

The rage she'd been trying to keep in check exploded in a blinding flash. She grabbed the hand of the beefy guy just as he was about to push again and in one swift, practised, if a little rusty move he was on his back, his arm twisted painfully in her grasp, her foot jammed hard against his throat.

His friends' eyes widened as he gurgled on the ground, clutching at Trinity's foot with his spare hand. A second or two passed before either moved, then one of them puffed his chest out and lunged. Trinity was ready for him, landing a solid blow to his solar plexus with one efficient chop, dropping him to the ground.

She cocked an eyebrow at the third guy. 'You want some?' she demanded, her voice icy. 'Get out of here, now,' she snapped, giving an extra little twist to the guy's arm before removing her foot from his throat. She pulled her phone out of her pocket. 'I'm calling the cops.'

The three guys didn't wait around; they scarpered.

It was only then Trinity realised how fast her heart was beating. Automatically she turned back to Oscar, who was watching her with an owl-like expression, his big eyes huge and unblinking.

She rushed to him, her hands shaking as she scooped him up. 'Mummy, you were like a superhero,' he whispered, his voice reverent.

Trinity laughed. A kid who spent three quarters of his life in hospital had seen a lot of cartoons and the superhero ones were his favourite.

'C'mon,' she said, 'let's go and check on your friend.'

She turned around to find he'd walked away and was almost at the road near where she'd parked her car. He walked hesitantly though, looking around.

She put Oscar down and they half walked, half jogged to catch up. 'Excuse me,' Trinity called. He didn't answer. 'Excuse me, mister?'

The old man turned around, his face blank until he saw Oscar. 'Are you okay?'

'What?' he asked, ruffling Oscar's hair. 'Oh, yes, thank you, dear. I just…' He looked around him as if he didn't know where he was. 'I'm not sure why I'm here. Do you know where I am?'

A spike of concern knitted Trinity's brows together. Had the incident with the teenage boys traumatised him? They hadn't physically hurt him but she couldn't blame him for being shook up.

'It's Monno Park,' she said, laying a gentle hand on his arm. 'You came to feed the ducks.'

The man stared at the pond for long moments. 'Oh. Did I?'

'Do you live around here?'

The man glanced at the park around him and the houses on the street opposite. 'I…think so,' he said, his big hairy eyebrows beetling together.

Trinity was really worried now. Maybe this wasn't a re-action to his confrontation with the thugs; maybe he wasn't of sound mind to begin with? Maybe he had dementia? Had he wandered or...*escaped* from somewhere?

'Is there someone I can ring for you?'

'Oh, yes.' His face brightened. 'My grandson, Reid Hamilton.'

'Okay.' She nodded encouragingly. 'Do you know his number?'

His expression blanked out again. 'He works at Allura. The veterans' hospital.' He stood taller. 'He's a doctor.'

'Right, then.' She smiled. Not even dementia, it seemed, diminished a grandparent's pride. She felt a momentary spike of envy at that. 'I'll look it up.'

Trinity wasn't at all confident as she rang the hospital and asked for Reid Hamilton. If the man had some kind of dementia, who knew if the information was correct? She might need to ring the police, after all.

The phone picked up and a male voice enquired who was calling, then informed her Dr Hamilton was with a patient. Trinity was relieved that she was on the right track. 'It's about his grandfather,' she said. 'I've found him wander-ing in a park. I'm sure he'll want to know.'

'One moment.'

Trinity smiled at the man, who was watching her in-tently, rubbing his creased forehead as if it would help clar-ify things for him.

'Hello? Who's this?'

Trinity blinked at the brisk voice. There was an author-ity to it she doubted few messed with. But she was over boorish men. 'Is this Reid?'

'Yes.' The impatience in his voice could have cut dia-monds.

'My name's Trinity. I think I've found your grandfather wandering around in Monno Park. He seems a little...'

she dropped her voice, not wanting to hurt the man's feelings '…confused.'

'Goddamn it,' the man cursed, low and growly. 'I'll be there in fifteen.' And the phone cut out in her ear.

The low rumble of a motorbike engine always put an itch up Trinity's spine and today was no different as, fifteen minutes later *exactly*, a big black bike pulled up at the kerb not far from where she, Oscar and Edward—he'd asked her to call him Eddie—were standing.

'Ah, here he is,' Eddie announced with palpable relief and obvious pleasure.

Trinity watched as the guy on the bike, dressed in top-to-toe black leather, dismounted with a long-legged ease that spoke of many hours in the seat. His helmet was a sleek black dome—gleaming and aerodynamic.

A little hand tugged at her pants and Trinity glanced down at her son, who was even more bug-eyed than he had been witnessing her drop two beefy teenagers to the ground.

'Mummy,' he whispered. 'It's the black Power Ranger.'

Trinity almost laughed—he did look very Power Ranger-esque in his boots, leathers, gloves and helmet. But then he took the gloves and helmet off, unzipped his jacket and completely destroyed that theory.

Reid Hamilton was more lumberjack than superhero. He certainly looked like no doctor she'd ever met and she'd met many. He had endless blue eyes, a wild mane of dirty-blond hair, pushed back off his forehead, and a full, thick beard that was neatly trimmed rather than long and scruffy. He was big and rangy like his grandfather and she could just make out tattoos on the backs of his hands.

'Hey, Pops,' he said, smiling at his grandfather as he strode towards them. When he drew level he enveloped Eddie in a big bear hug, holding him close for long moments before clapping him on the back a couple of times in a very manly demonstration of his affection.

He pulled back and flicked a glance at Trinity. 'Ma'am,' he said.

Trinity, who despised everything to do with beards, tats and bikes and hadn't had an orgasm in five years, almost came on the spot.

CHAPTER TWO

THE NAUSEATING SLICK of adrenaline that had been threatening Reid on his ride from the hospital dissipated instantly at the sight of his grandfather. Pops looked pleased to see him and there was strength in the old man's arms as he returned the hug. He seemed to be in good shape.

But clearly Reid was going to have to get someone in to care for him in the mornings while he worked now he was becoming more mobile after his fractured neck of femur. Or at least keep an eye on him. This was the third time he'd wandered. Reid had figured with the cricket on the television nothing short of a bomb would shift his grandfather from the living room.

Obviously he'd been wrong.

'Thank you so much for ringing,' he said to the woman who stood staring at him with a mix of unease and something akin to distaste on her face.

He was used to the look. A lot of people didn't trust dudes who rode bikes and had tats. And, God knew, some of them had reason. It didn't usually bother him.

For some reason, with her, it did.

She was probably a foot shorter than his six-foot-four frame and holding on tight to a kid's hand. The boy was skinny with hair as white and feathery as Pops'. He craned his neck, staring up at Reid all goggle-eyed.

'No problem,' she said. Her voice was cool, her expression tight, but, even so, two full, sensuous lips drew his gaze. There was an intriguing set to her jaw. Something told him this chick had gumption. 'I'm just glad it all ended well. I was worried.'

'You were?'

She started as if she'd said too much but she recovered quickly. 'Yes.' It was prickly and defensive.

'Are you a Power Ranger, mister?'

He dragged his attention from the woman to the child. His voice was small but it rang clear, full of awe. Reid laughed.

'Nope, sorry, little dude. But they are my favourites.' He presented his fist to the kid, who bumped it enthusiastically with his own pale, puny one.

'Mummy fought off the men who were being mean to Eddie like a Power Ranger,' the kid said conversationally.

The words were like a punch to Reid's abdominals. He glanced sharply at the woman who until a minute ago had been a complete stranger.

'Shh, Oscar,' she dismissed, shaking her head at her son, her cheeks flushed.

Instincts that had kept him alert and alive in the Middle East on two tours of duty went into overdrive. His scalp pricked. 'What happened?'

'It was nothing,' she insisted, her gaze darting to the nearby car.

Reid glanced at his grandfather, who was smiling blankly. Clearly he'd forgotten the events already.

'There were three of them and they were all pushing Eddie and Mummy threw one on the ground—'

The kid let go of his mother's hand to demonstrate, making a *pshwoar* noise as he lunged with his legs, dropping an imaginary person in front of him.

'And then she karate-chopped another one.' The kid

sliced his hand through the air with a *hai ya*! 'Then she told them to leave and they ran away.'

Reid blinked at the revelations. He believed them. Not because the kid was so convincing but because the woman wasn't quite meeting his eye. 'Really?' he mused, lifting an eyebrow in her direction.

'They were just teenagers. Anyone would have done the same.'

Sadly, Reid knew that wasn't true. Over a decade in the military had taught him that most people did nothing. But not this woman. This woman had taken on *three* people—guys—in defence of his grandfather. He took a moment to look a little closer at his grandfather's guardian ninja.

She wasn't exactly big and strong. There were fine lines around her eyes and on her forehead and he thought she might be about thirty. She didn't look tough, especially not with a mouth that could have been perfectly at home on a catwalk model.

She looked…tired.

But he'd definitely picked up on an inner resilience. The kind that people in war zones displayed. And he knew enough about the world to know that war zones came in many guises.

What kind of war zone had made her so tough? Crappy childhood? Dangerous relationship? He slid his gaze to her left hand. No ring. Not even a white line or indentation where one might have been.

Not that lack of tan line meant anything necessarily.

But he had a feeling in his gut about her. Something told him her resilience had come from bitter experience. And Reid always went with his gut.

'Reid,' he said, reaching out his hand.

She eyed it warily before slipping her hand into his. 'Trinity.' She shook briefly—firm and sure—before quickly withdrawing.

'And you're Oscar, right?' Reid said, turning his attention to the kid.

Oscar nodded and held out his hand for a shake. Reid smiled but obliged, shaking the kid's hand. Also firm and sure considering he looked as if a puff of wind would blow him over.

He glanced at the woman. 'Well, *Trinity*, it seems I am in your debt.'

Her eyes, tawny brown with flecks of amber, widened as she drew Oscar closer. Most women he knew would have flirted with him over that but she looked as if she wanted to bolt.

'No, of course not,' she dismissed, her gaze darting towards the car again. 'It's fine.'

Reid frowned. 'Be that as it may, how about I take you guys out to lunch as a thank you?' He checked his watch. 'What d'you reckon, Pops? You hungry?'

'I could eat a bear,' he said. He made claws with his hands and gave a little roar for Oscar's benefit. Oscar giggled.

'No.' She shook her head. 'Really. I don't need to be thanked. C'mon, Oscar.' She reached for his hand again. 'Say goodbye to Eddie.'

'Oh, but I want to go with Eddie and eat a bear.'

The kid looked as if he could do with a bear-sized meal. So did she. 'Sorry, we really must be going. We have plenty to do today.'

Oscar's eyebrows practically hit his hairline; he was clearly surprised at the announcement of such a full day. Reid suspected that was because there wasn't one. But the kid didn't push, just sighed and shuffled over to Pops.

'See ya later, alligator,' he said, his voice chirpy despite the resigned slump to his shoulders.

Pops stuck out his hand and they shook. 'In a while, crocodile.'

She said a quick goodbye too, ignoring Reid as she bundled her son into his safety seat in the back of the car. It was possibly the oldest car Reid had seen in a long time—about thirty years if his guess was right. Back in the days when cars were heavy and solid and *not* made to crumple. The paint job was faded and peeling around the edges and there were several small dings in the panelling where rust had invaded like cancer.

He'd noticed it parked here yesterday afternoon as he and Pops had gone for some fish and chips at Bondi. It had still been here on their way back last night. And as he'd left this morning.

It was rare to see bomby old cars in this street. Reid doubted there was a car in the entire neighbourhood that was more than three years old. He glanced inside as Trinity buckled Oscar in. The car was bulging with black garbage bags. On the back seat, in the foot wells and along the back dash. It was a similar situation in the front, the passenger seat and foot well crammed with plastic bags.

It looked as if everything they owned was in the car.

His scalp prickled some more. He was starting to get a very bad feeling about Trinity's situation.

She backed out of the car and shut Oscar's door. 'Good-bye,' she said, the cheerfulness forced as she smiled at Pops and flashed him a quick glance of acknowledgement before sliding into the driver's seat and pulling the door closed. Her seat belt was on quicker than he could blink.

Reid almost laughed out loud. This was a first. Women didn't usually object to spending time in his company. Not even the tats turned them off. In fact, these days, that usually drew them like a magnet.

But this chick couldn't get away from him fast enough.

Before she had a chance to escape, he knocked on her window. She shot him an impatient look but rolled the window down. 'If there's ever anything I can do for you.' He handed over his card. 'Please don't hesitate.'

She took it to be polite but Reid had no doubt she'd toss it the first chance she got. He'd known her for fifteen minutes but he already knew that. She reminded him of some of the village women he'd met in Afghanistan. All he'd been able to see of them were their eyes but they'd told him plenty about their relief and resentment.

'Thank you,' she said and rolled the window up.

She jammed the key in and turned it. The engine didn't roar to life. In fact the only sound coming from the front of the car was a click. Her knuckles whitened around the steering wheel as she turned the key again. And again. And again.

Click. Click. Click.

She undid her belt and Reid took a step back as she opened the door. 'It does this sometimes,' she said, her face tight as she reached down and pulled a lever before exiting the car. 'It's a battery thing.'

It sounded like a starter motor to Reid. He'd tinkered with enough engines in his life—cars, motorbikes and military vehicles—to know the sound of a dead one. Although if the battery connection was dodgy then that was possible too.

She walked to the bonnet and slid her fingers under the lip, lifting the heavy metal lid. Her biceps tensed beneath the weight of it as she secured it in place. Reid joined her. The engine looked as old as the exterior. None of the clean, sleek functionality of a modern engine. Just a greasy, blackened chunk of metal with years of built-up grime and neglect.

His arm brushed hers as he peered into the mess. He didn't miss her sideways step as she tightened all the battery terminals.

'That should do it,' she announced as she unlatched the bonnet and clicked it shut, giving him a wide berth as she all but sprinted into the car.

Reid stood on the footpath next to his grandfather as she tried again.

Click.

Click. Click. Click.

'Sounds like the starter motor,' Pops said.

Reid smiled to himself. His grandfather was getting more and more forgetful but, a car enthusiast from way back, those memories were still fresh and vivid. 'Yes.'

He strode over to the car. Trinity, gripping the wheel, appeared to be praying for it to work. He knocked on the window. It was a few seconds before she acknowledged him with a straight-out glare. But she rolled the window down anyway.

'Sounds like the starter motor.'

She blew out her breath, staring at the bonnet through the windscreen. 'The starter motor.' The lines on her fore-head furrowed a little deeper.

Reid crouched by the car door, searching for the right thing to say. A wild animal was always at its most dangerous when it was cornered. And that was how Trinity seemed at the moment—wild.

'I've got a mate who's a mechanic. He'll fix it pronto.'

She seemed to contemplate that for a few seconds. 'Do you know how much it would cost?'

Reid shrugged. 'A few hundred dollars.'

She looked away but not before he saw the quick flash of dismay in her gaze. Her knuckles went so white around the wheel he was worried they were going to burst through her skin. He knew in that moment Trinity was just barely keeping her shit together.

'I can pay for it.'

'No.' She shook her head vehemently.

Reid put his hands up in a placating manner. 'Just hear me out. I said that I owed you and I meant it. Let me do this for you. As a thank you. I can arrange it right away and give you a lift home.' He flicked a glance to Oscar sitting quietly in the back seat as if he was used to such breakdowns. 'What do you reckon, little dude?'

'We don't have a home.'

Reid blinked at the matter-of-fact revelation as Trinity admonished her son with a quick, *'Oscar!'*

He glanced at the interior of the car, packed to the rafters with bulging black garbage bags. He'd suspected as much…

'Ignore him,' she said, her laughter so brittle he was surprised it didn't shatter into pieces around her. 'Kids say the damnedest things.' Her gaze was overly bright, the smile plastered to her face so big it looked painful.

Reid didn't know why fate had landed Trinity and her son in his lap today. But he was standing at a crossroads. He could take her assurances at face value and walk away. Or he could step in. As she'd done for Pops earlier.

Reid was a big believer in fate. His faith in any kind of God had been destroyed a long time ago but he'd seen too many incidences of people being in the right or wrong places at the right or wrong time to dismiss the mystical forces of predetermination. Trinity and Oscar had crossed his path for a reason and if he could help them in some way, he would.

Part of his job was advocating for homeless veterans— why wouldn't he afford these two the same courtesy?

'I'm going to call my mechanic friend. He's going to come and pick your car up. Then you and Oscar are going to come to my house where we can talk a bit more.'

'Oh, no, we're not,' she said, the plastered smile disappearing, a determined jut to her chin.

'Trinity…' He didn't know why she was looking a gift horse in the mouth. He supposed a woman in her situation was wary about who to trust. 'You can trust me. I live just down the road. In this street. The big white house that you can just see from here.' He pointed at it and she glanced in its direction. 'It's my grandfather's house, I live with him. Don't I, Pops?'

Eddie nodded. 'He's a good 'un. Looks after his old grandad, real fine.'

She glanced from Reid to Eddie and back to Reid. He changed tack. 'Look…to be honest, you'd be doing me a favour. I have to go back to work for two more hours and I won't be able to organise someone to be with Pops at such short notice. I know you've already gone above and beyond and I know I don't have any right to ask but if you and Oscar could hang with him until I get back it would be a load off my mind.'

She glanced at Eddie and her face softened a little, her chin lost its defiant jut. *Bingo.*

'He's completely independent,' Reid said, pressing his advantage, although the thought that the dementia might progress until that was no longer true churned in his gut. 'You don't need to do anything with him. He just loves company.' He flicked his gaze to Oscar, smiling at him. 'What you say, little dude? Want to come back to my house and hang out with Eddie for a bit? We have a cat.'

'Oh, yes.' Oscar clapped, bouncing in his chair. 'Mummy, can we, please? Please? *Pleeease?*'

She shot him a withering look. 'Are you *kidding* me?' she murmured, her incredulous gaze calling him out on his blatant manipulation.

Yeah…that had been a bit of a low move. Not quite like offering candy to a baby but not far off. 'Look. The car will probably be fixed by the time I get back from work and you can be on your way.'

Suddenly her shoulders slumped and he knew he'd won. It didn't give him much pleasure, manipulating a woman who probably had few choices in life anyway. But he really wanted to help her if he could and he needed a way in.

She turned her head to face Oscar. 'Of course, darling,'

she said. Her voice was chirpy and Oscar beamed as if he'd just found a million bucks, but as she turned to face him her eyes shot daggers right through his heart.

If looks could kill, he'd be dead for sure.

CHAPTER THREE

'Do you like cricket, young man?'

Oscar's eyes grew to the size of saucers at the massive wall-mounted television screen. It had obviously been on when Eddie had wandered away from the house.

Cartoons and cricket were Oscar's two favourite things in the world. Maybe because one of his earliest memories was the captain of the Australian cricket team visiting during one of his many hospitalisations. Oscar had wanted to play cricket ever since.

'I love cricket,' he said, voice full of reverence.

'Well, come on, then,' Eddie said, pointing to a big, comfy recliner chair. 'Climb up. There's still a couple of hours before they break for lunch.' He eased himself down very gently into a more formal, higher chair.

Back in the familiarity of his surroundings, Eddie seemed perfectly compos mentis. He was pointing to the screen and reciting some stats to Oscar, who was nodding in fascination as if Eddie were some kind of guru.

A big old marmalade cat wandered into the room, tail flicking from side to side. It jumped up on the chair beside Oscar before collapsing regally across his skinny legs.

'That's Ginger,' Eddie said.

Oscar patted the cat as if she were the most precious creature on earth. Ginger, obviously approving, purred like a motor. *God.* How was she ever going to prise Oscar away from this paradise? Cricket on a big-screen television and a marmalade cat?

She looked around her. It *was* paradise. She'd grown up with thin fibro walls and then thin air during her two years living rough on the streets. Reid's house was like a freaking palace by comparison.

She was glad he wasn't here. That he'd left for work as soon as he'd opened the door for them. She hadn't been able to breathe properly since she'd clapped eyes on him so it was nice to re-oxygenate her brain.

To be able to think clearly.

The fact that her car was about to be towed and fixed, which would cost money she didn't have, was uppermost but the surroundings were distracting as well. What would it be like to have grown up in a nice house with grandparents who loved you as much as Eddie clearly loved Reid?

Reid didn't *look* as if he came from a well-to-do suburban background. If anything his badass biker/lumberjack look reminded her of a few guys she'd met while she was living rough.

But he was a doctor?

What the hell kind of doctor? She'd dealt with a lot of doctors these last five years—physicians, specialists, surgeons, intensive-care consultants—and by and large they were a conservative lot.

How had the medical establishment taken to Reid?

As much as Trinity was determined to stay put and not give into the urge to explore the house, the need to go to the toilet got the better of her after an hour and she followed Eddie's directions to the downstairs bathroom.

She passed a huge kitchen and a formal lounge room as well as a bedroom, which looked as if it might be Eddie's if the handrails she spied were any indication. The bathroom was at the end of the hallway and was bigger and whiter and cleaner than the room that Terrible Todd had demanded sex for.

Hell, if his room had been this big and clean she might just have considered it…

There was a huge shower complete with a rose as big as a dinner plate. It sure beat the crappy showers at the service station she and Oscar had used last night.

A hot wave of longing swept over her and Trinity grabbed the vanity as it threatened to overwhelm. This was too much. Just all too much. She should be grateful to have this opportunity to use these beautiful amenities and take a break from her life for a few hours but the pressure growing in her chest wouldn't allow it. Things like this didn't happen to her. She *never* caught a break.

And that panicked her more than anything.

She used the facilities and fled from the bathroom as quickly as her legs would carry her.

An hour later the cricket broke for lunch and Eddie said, 'Who fancies a sandwich?'

'Oh, I'll get them,' Trinity said, jumping to her feet. It was the least she could do. 'You and Oscar stay here and watch all the analysis.'

Eddie's kitchen was the kind she'd always fantasised about having. Large and open and airy, full of light from the massive bay window that jutted out from the sink. Pots of herbs sat on the ledge throwing a splash of green into the mix.

A massive central bench with a stone top dominated the space. It was beautifully smooth and Trinity ran the flat of her palm back and forth over it, hypnotised by its cool sensuality. A bowl of red apples decorated one end.

Underfoot, there were large white tiles, which carried through to the splash-back areas, where an occasional coloured tile broke up the uniformity. She could practically see her face in the sleek white overhead cupboards. Stainless-steel trim helped to break up the clinical feel.

All the appliances were stainless steel too and reeked of money and European innovation.

The fridge was a gleaming four-door with an ice and cold water dispenser on the outside and packed on the inside with an array of beautiful food. Trinity's mouth watered and her stomach growled.

For the third time today she wanted to cry.

This was what Oscar needed. What she couldn't give. A full fridge. Proper nutrition. She did the best she could with what she had and he'd always had a notoriously birdlike appetite, but maybe he'd be bigger and stronger if she could constantly tempt him with this kind of variety?

Trinity shut her eyes, squeezing back the tears. *She would not cry.* 'It's going to get better,' she whispered.

Once Oscar started school.

'Just hold on.'

She opened her eyes, tears now at bay, and grabbed things out of the fridge.

It was closer to three when Reid made it home and Trinity was as antsy as a cat on a hot tin roof. Oscar had already become firm friends with Eddie and Ginger and she was dreading dragging him away from it to spend another couple of nights in the car.

If it was fixed.

She was going to have to talk to Reid's friend about some kind of payment plan for the repair. She hoped like hell he was open to it because she needed Monday's payment to source some accommodation.

Trinity's pulse spiked as she heard the front door open. She'd dozed off in the recliner with her son but she'd obviously been subconsciously tuned into the sound of a key in a lock. Oscar barely looked up from the screen despite being jostled as she practically levitated out of the chair.

She was fuzzy-headed from her nap. *She never napped!* She didn't have the time for such luxuries. Her body, though, was eerily alert as she met him in the hall. On high alert, actually, as his black-leather-clad frame strode towards her and butterflies bloomed in her belly.

The man walked as if he owned the Earth. For a woman who'd spent most of her life trying *not* to be noticed, it was breathtaking. He was big and raw and…*primal* and she couldn't drag her eyes off him.

'Is it fixed?' she blurted as he stopped to dump his keys and backpack on the hallstand.

'And good afternoon to you too,' he said, a wry smile playing on his mouth.

God, even that was primal. Full with a sensual twist that hinted at long, hot, sweaty nights and tangled sheets.

He shrugged out of his jacket and hung it on a wall hook. 'Pops okay?'

Trinity's mouth went dry as her gaze took in his chest. Not because of the way his plain black T-shirt stretched across his chest and shoulders or how snug it sat against a flat abdomen. *No.* Because of the intricate web of ink covering both arms.

Invisible fingers trailed across her belly and the pulse at her temple fibrillated wildly. It wasn't from fear, although God knew it should be. Or even from the kind of revulsion she'd felt when Terrible Todd had caged her in against the storeroom wall with his tat-covered arms.

It was from…fascination. Between the thick waves of his golden hair pushed back carelessly from his forehead to his beard to the tattoos she just knew didn't stop at his arms, she couldn't look away from him.

It had been a long time since she'd felt attracted to a man and even then it hadn't felt like this. Oscar's father had been her first and an ill-conceived choice at that. She'd loved him stupidly, blindly—all the way to the streets. But she'd *never* felt this kind of pull.

This was biology. Chemistry. She knew it in her gut. She knew it a lot lower too…

'He's fine. Still watching cricket with Oscar,' she said, forcing herself to focus on getting out of here, something even more vital now her attraction to Reid was a living, breathing beast. 'Is it ready?' she repeated.

'Not yet.' He brushed past her, heading for the kitchen. 'I'm starving, what about you?' He made a beeline for the fridge.

Trinity ignored the question as her brain grappled with his *not yet*. Where would they stay the night if they didn't have the car and just how long *would* it take to fix? There was no choice now, she was going to have to ring Raylene and see if she could have the couch for the night. Reid had offered to drive them home; maybe he'd drop them at Raylene's?

'What do you mean, not yet?'

He dragged the bread and some sandwich fillers out of the fridge and placed them on the bench. He glanced at her, his hands resting flat on the bench top. 'Gav has to source a starter motor for you from a wrecker's yard. Believe it or not parts that old are hard to find.'

He said it with a twinkle in his eye and dry humour in his voice but it rankled. She pulled her phone out of her back pocket of her three-quarter-length capris. It was a basic model—no fancy apps or data downloads for frivolous things like Facebook and Instagram—just a standard, cheap, pre-paid package but, like her car, something she couldn't do without.

Being contactable and able to make phone calls was essential for someone with a high-needs child. 'If you could give me his number, I'd like to make arrangements about the bill.'

His gaze held hers for long moments before he said, 'I've already covered it.'

Goose bumps pricked at Trinity's neck as her hackles rose. 'I said *no*.' She kept her voice low but even she was impressed with the degree of menace she managed to inject.

He shrugged. 'It's done. Now…' He turned back to the fridge. 'Would you like some wine? There's a nice bottle of Pinot Grigio in here.'

She blinked at his back. Was he freaking kidding?

'No,' she said, testily. 'I don't want a goddamn glass of wine.'

'You're right,' he said, completely undeterred. 'I much prefer beer.' He grabbed two bottles and set them down on the counter with a light *tink*. He twisted both the tops before she could stop him and sent one sailing in her direction with a deft push.

She wasn't much of a beer drinker—not at three in the afternoon, that was for sure—but she caught it automatically.

Keeping her temper in check, she tried again. 'I don't want you paying my bills.' He opened his mouth to object but she waved him quiet. 'I know you feel like you have to thank me somehow but you really don't. *My* bills, *my* responsibility.'

He tipped his head back and took three long swallows of his beer. Her gaze was drawn to the demarcation line between where his beard ended and his throat began. The thick brown and blond bristles of his close-cropped beard hugged the underside of his jaw line before meeting the smooth, bare column of his throat.

Trinity watched it undulate as he swallowed and leaned heavily against the counter as things south of her belly button went a little weak. There was just something so damn masculine about a big, thirsty-looking man drinking beer.

'Look, Trinity,' he said as he wiped the back of his hand across his mouth. 'Let's cut to the chase.' He reached for the loaf of bread and pulled out four slices. 'I'm paying your bill because frankly I don't think you have two brass razoos to rub together and, if I'm not very much mistaken, you need that rusty old car asap because you're homeless.'

He said asap as one word, as she heard American soldiers say it on the television.

'So,' he continued, calmly applying butter, 'how about you—?'

'I am *not* homeless,' Trinity snapped.

He sighed and shook his head as he added sliced ham to the bread. 'I was in the military for fifteen years, Trinity, and I have a very sensitive bullshit detector which at the moment is flickering like crazy. How about you drop the act?'

It wasn't said with any kind of threat or malice but it *was* said with an authority that was plainly not used to being challenged. Her pulse accelerated and, like some errant rookie soldier who'd been caught out saying the wrong thing, she scrambled to qualify her statement. 'I'm just… between domiciles.'

'And how often are you…between domiciles?'

'Only *very* occasionally.'

She'd realised while he'd been gone that Reid being a doctor could mean trouble for her. That it was mandatory for him to report any suspicion of child abuse or neglect. If it hadn't been for Eddie and the car, she'd have picked Oscar up and run like the wind.

'A rare night,' she clarified. 'Here and there.'

He smothered the bread in pickles and mayonnaise and slapped the slices together. He ate half of it in two bites, regarding her the entire time. Trinity didn't like being scrutinised. She'd spent the last five years flying under the radar so Reid's astute gaze made her squirm. Because of the power he could wield over her if he wanted to but mostly because of what it did to her body.

She felt the heat of it *everywhere*. The echo of it in every beat of her heart. It made her nervous and breathless.

Good nervous. *Good* breathless.

Her muscles tensed as he held her to the spot with his eyes. The man had clearly missed his calling. He should have been a cop. If he kept it up she'd probably start admitting to a bunch of unsolved crimes.

Or possibly have an orgasm.

'You should come and live here.'

CHAPTER FOUR

TRINITY BLINKED. IT WAS all she was capable of. She couldn't move or think or talk. Had she had a stroke? Or slipped down the rabbit hole to an alternate reality?

Had he drugged her?

'Wh…what?'

Okay. Good. She *could* talk…or croak anyway.

'Look, it's really simple, Trinity.' He scoffed the rest of the sandwich and wiped the crumbs off his hands by brushing them down the front of his shirt. Her gaze followed helplessly as the shirt moved interestingly against hidden muscles.

'You're homeless and I have a home.'

'But…' She shook her head, trying to wrap her head around such an outlandish proposal. 'You don't even know me.'

'No, I don't. But I do know you came to the aid of an old man today when you could have easily not got involved. And that tells me a lot.'

'I told you I didn't want anything for that.' Stubborn bloody man.

'I know. Which also tells me a lot. Look—' He held up his hands as she opened her mouth to protest and Trinity closed it again. 'I don't know what your situation is exactly but I do understand homelessness. I work with a lot of veterans who are going through the same thing. I think you're doing it tough and I'd like to give you a roof over your head while you get back on your feet. There are eight bedrooms in this house. I couldn't live with myself knowing you're out there in your car when we have plenty of space here.'

Eight bedrooms? Trinity didn't think this could get any more fantasy-like. She was sure she was going to wake up any minute in her crappy Mazda with her back bitching at her. Things like this just did not happen to her. And she'd learned to be suspicious of good fortune.

If something seemed too good to be true, it usually *was* too good to be true.

'Isn't this Eddie's home? Should you just be inviting total strangers to come and live in it without talking to him about it first?'

'Pops will be cool with it, trust me. Just think about it, Trinity. If you won't do it for yourself, you should do it for Oscar.'

A trickle of fear oozed down her spine. What did *that* mean? Was it a threat? Would he report her to child services if she left? Every muscle tensed as her instinct to run took over. How dared he spend five minutes in her world and lord it over her about her son.

Despite her anger, his words struck at the very heart of her. He was offering them something she couldn't. It rankled but could she afford her pride? Pride had walked her out of Todd's door but her options were even crappier now. At least she had a working car yesterday.

She'd spent the last of their money on brand-new school uniforms and books because she hadn't wanted Oscar to look like the poor kid on his first day—she'd been there and kids could be cruel. She hadn't bargained on being turfed out of their accommodation. Or on the car breaking down.

She eyed him as he took another mouthful of his beer. 'I'm not going to sleep with you.'

She said it as much for herself as for him.

He half choked as he struggled to swallow the beer, coughing and spluttering before placing the bottle on the bench. *'What?'*

'The last guy who offered me a roof over my head felt that there should be some kind of *arrangement* attached.'

'I am *not* the last guy.' His voice was low and tight, his knuckles white around the beer bottle. 'I'm not that kind of guy at all. Frankly I find the idea of bribing a homeless, single mother into my bed completely *abhorrent*. I'm sorry that there are douchebags like that out there but *that is not me.'*

His quick, angry admonishment of the Todds of the world was just about the sexiest thing Trinity had ever heard and it did funny things to her pulse.

'There is absolutely *no* agenda here. It's a no-strings-attached deal.'

Trinity couldn't believe it was that easy. 'You must want *something* in return?'

He shrugged, the whiteness of his knuckles dissipating, the tension in his shoulders melting away. 'I can't deny having a presence in the house for Pops when I'm not here would be advantageous.'

Trinity frowned. 'So you want me to look out for him. Or like...be his carer?' She needed to get a job while Oscar was at school; she wouldn't have time to babysit. 'I don't have any qualifications.'

'No, I don't mean anything like that,' he assured her. 'Although if you've raised a kid then you're probably more than qualified to deal with a slightly forgetful, sometimes naughty, definitely cheeky eighty-year-old.'

Trinity laughed then stopped, surprised by the sound in the midst of such a serious conversation. Surprised she could even laugh at all in her predicament. But Reid's description of Eddie was so damn apt.

'I know you're finding this all a little too good to be true and you're probably not used to relying on anyone but sometimes good things *do* happen to good people, Trinity. Maybe it's time you allowed somebody to help you. Aren't you tired of constantly worrying about how you're going to make ends meet?'

Trinity was *so damn tired.* The fact he knew that made her want to burst into tears. But damned if she was going there again. She hadn't survived this long by crying at every hurdle life had thrown her.

'Trust me.' He smiled, wiggling his eyebrows dramatically. 'I'm a doctor.'

His smile wove its way around her ovaries and squeezed. But he had put her dilemma front and centre again. He *was* a doctor. 'What if I say no?'

He gave a half-laugh. 'It's a free world. I'm not going to force you to live all safe and sound in this beautiful house, Trinity.' He smiled the kind of smile that told her she'd be nuts to turn this down.

But that wasn't what she was asking.

'And there won't be any…repercussions?'

'Repercussions?' He frowned.

She decided to put her worst fear out there. She didn't want to be looking over her shoulder all the time. Living life looking forward was hard enough. If he was going to dob her in, she'd appreciate a heads-up.

'You're a doctor,' she said, stripping her voice of any emotion that might betray how desperately worried she was. 'It's your mandatory duty to report incidences of child abuse and neglect to the relevant authorities.'

The light slowly dawned in his eyes. He shook his head slowly, his gaze seeking hers and holding it again. 'You don't need to worry about that. I see *no* evidence of abuse or neglect.'

Trinity blinked back a spurt of unexpected tears at his

quiet conviction. For God's sake—what the hell was with wanting to cry every ten seconds around the man? 'I can't even give him a roof over his head,' she whispered.

'You can now.'

Yes. *Maybe.* Not her roof but a roof nonetheless. If she had the courage to take a risk.

'Say yes, Trinity. Stay here with me and Pops. For as long as you like. Get back on your feet.'

Her brain turned his proposition over and over. On the surface it was a dream come true. She could have a base. A permanent base she could depend on. A chance to forget about her troubles and worries and save some money. Actually make plans for the future. Get back on her feet as he'd said.

But then there was the attraction she felt for Reid. That could complicate the hell out of things. It could potentially screw everything up. If she let it.

If she *indulged* it.

Which was stupid and fanciful. Why would someone like Reid be remotely interested in her?

Oscar chose that moment to wander into the kitchen, carrying an uncomplaining Ginger, who almost dwarfed him, the top half of her body clutched to his chest, the bottom half dangling down.

'Mummy, Ginger purrs so loudly,' he said, beaming at her.

A huge lump lodged in Trinity's throat as Oscar sidled up to her. He leaned his skinny frame against her thigh and rubbed his face on top of Ginger's head.

'Okay,' she said quietly, glancing at Reid. Even just saying the word felt good. As if all the weight had magically disappeared from her shoulders. For now anyway. 'Just for a short while though.'

Christmas was a couple of months away—being in her own place by then seemed like a worthy goal.

He nodded. 'Stay as long as you need.'

* * *

If Reid thought he was going to see a different side to Trinity once she'd agreed to his offer, he was wrong. She might have said yes but it was probably the most reluctant yes on record and she was clearly still not comfortable with the deal.

At dinner she'd tried to talk to him about making a monetary contribution towards their food and board, which he'd dismissed outright, and then she'd tried to make a bargain with him about taking over the cooking from now on so she was at least doing something to contribute. But Reid had shooed her out of the kitchen.

After years of army rations he enjoyed eating homemade meals and found cooking therapeutic. He'd told her she could sit and watch with a glass of wine if she wanted but she'd declined politely, a pleasant smile fixed to her face.

Which had been pretty much par for the course today. She'd been polite and pleasant all day but there was a coolness to it, a reserve, that kept him at a distance.

As far as he was concerned anyway.

It melted away with Oscar. Hell, even with his grandfather she was more at ease. But with him, she was cool and polite.

Not that it surprised him. He didn't know how long Trinity had been doing it tough but long enough to have built a shell of wariness around her. And he knew that time was the only antidote. It was obviously going to take her a while to trust him. She needed time to get to know him. To believe that he meant what he said. No funny business. No strings.

I'm not going to sleep with you.

It had been shocking to hear her say it. To realise that a part of her *actually* believed he had an ulterior motive for inviting her into his home. A sexual one. It'd made him so angry he'd wanted to smash the kitchen bench top in two.

He didn't know who the guy was that had put the hard word on her but it disgusted Reid. He felt insulted on behalf of his entire gender that there were douchebags like that out in the world harassing vulnerable women.

They gave men a bad name.

The thought that he'd take advantage of her situation was sickening. Sure, Trinity had fight and spunk, two attributes he found sexier than a great rack or an awesome booty. But he could see beyond her prickly, standoffish, tough-as-nails exterior to the frightened, vulnerable woman underneath and all he really wanted to do was protect her.

It was what he'd done most of his life and he couldn't switch that off because he no longer wore a set of khakis. There'd been so many women and children he hadn't been able to help, but he *could* protect Trinity and Oscar.

He went in search of her after dinner. She'd told him she was going to put Oscar to bed and he'd assumed she'd come back down and sit with him and Pops for a while—if only out of politeness. But it had been over an hour and she still hadn't showed.

He was worried she was hiding away and he needed her to know that she and Oscar had the entire run of the house. That she didn't have to sit up in her room like some frightened little mouse. That they had several televisions in the house plus a range of DVDs or she could use his computer.

He stopped at the room where he'd dumped Oscar's bag earlier this afternoon but it was empty. In fact it didn't look as if it had been touched. The door was open. There was no rumpled bedspread. No open cupboard doors. No discarded clothes or shoes.

Reid frowned as he moved to the next room along, which he'd given to Trinity because it had an en-suite. If he hadn't been very much mistaken, she'd blinked back tears when she saw it and it had made him happy to throw some luxury her way.

The door was shut. If a closed door wasn't a big old 'keep out' message nothing was. He hesitated for a moment, prevaricating about whether to knock. The last thing he wanted was to encroach on her privacy. And maybe she was asleep.

At eight o'clock at night…

The strip of light at the bottom of the door told him the light was at least on. So maybe she was lying awake staring at four walls worrying about things she didn't have to worry about.

Reid gave himself a mental shake. He was dithering. Reid Hamilton did not dither. He was a surgeon, for crying out loud.

Or used to be anyway.

He knocked gently. Low enough to be heard but hopefully not wake her if she was asleep. There was silence for a moment, then a quiet, 'Come in,' that sounded wary and tight even through the barrier of the door.

He opened it to find a sleeping Oscar tucked up in bed beside his mother, his fine white-blond hair and the pale wedge of his cheekbone a contrast to the crimson pillowcase. A mangy-looking stuffed rabbit tucked in with him.

A surge of pride filled his chest knowing that the kid would be sleeping safe from now on. 'Sorry,' he whispered.

'It's okay,' she said, her voice low, her hand sliding protectively onto her son's back. 'He sleeps like a rock.'

Reid envied the kid that. He slept lightly and dreamed too much.

Trinity was chewing on her bottom lip, regarding him with a solemn gaze. Her hair was wet, or rather it had been. It was half dry now with dozens of dark, fluffy, flyaway strands, which made her look about eighteen and not the thirty he'd originally pegged her as.

Just *how* old was she?

She was wearing some kind of sloppy V-necked T-shirt that dwarfed her shape and fell off her right shoulder. He noted absently there was a hole in her sleeve as his gaze was drawn to the exposed flesh. Her skin was pale, and the hollow between her collarbone and the slope where neck met shoulder was pronounced.

He loved that dip. Hell, he loved all the dips and hollows on a woman's body.

Suddenly it was gone as she yanked the sleeve up. Reid blinked at the action and the direction of his thoughts. *Bloody hell.* What was he thinking? He dragged his gaze back to her face but she wasn't looking at him; her eyes were planted firmly downwards on a book she'd obviously been reading.

Good one, man.

'I…just came to check everything's okay.'

'It is.' Cool and pleasant replaced by stiff and formal.

He glanced at Oscar again. 'You know, you guys don't have to share the same room. There's enough for one each.'

'I know. It's what we're used to. We don't mind.'

Reid nodded. He hoped she'd start to feel comfortable enough to open up to him about her past. To let the apron strings out a little on Oscar.

'Okay. Well… I also wanted you to know that you don't have to hide away up here. Pops and I usually watch some television together each night. We have three TVs and subscribe to a couple of streaming services so there's something for everyone. I also have a stack of DVDs if you'd prefer and you're more than welcome to use the computer if you want to go online for any reason.'

She'd slowly shrunk back into the bed head as he spoke, clearly overwhelmed. Reid rubbed his forehead. 'What I'm trying to say is that you have the run of the house. Help yourself to whatever you want, whenever you want. *Mi casa es su casa.* Okay?'

She nodded. 'Okay.'

But she didn't look convinced.

CHAPTER FIVE

'*MI CASA ES SU CASA.*'

Trinity turned the expression over and over in her head during the course of the weekend. She kept waiting for the other shoe to drop, for the camera crew to pop out from a cupboard and tell her she'd been punked.

Reid's offer had been outstandingly generous and she understood that he wanted her to feel comfortable in his house, but that was going to take a little while. Who knew the luxuries of a fridge full of food and a pillow top mattress would be so difficult to adjust to?

But the street kid in Trinity was never far away. That person had been baptised in the ill will people wrought, not their generosity. She desperately wanted to be able to take a breath and relax but she didn't want to get too used to going to sleep with a full belly and waking up without a sore back in case it all came crashing down.

Two months. That was all she needed. Reid was making it possible for them to have a place of their own by Christmas.

But even if it only was for a few days it was worth it for how happy Oscar was. He hadn't stopped smiling since he'd walked into Reid's house and Trinity swore he actually had some colour back in his cheeks.

For however long it lasted, she was glad that Oscar could

have this bright interlude in his otherwise grey existence. They were used to doing it tough and they would again if this bubble burst tomorrow but, for now, it was a little bit of magic she couldn't deny him.

Or herself.

Like her and Oscar and Eddie heading over the road to the pond the last two mornings to feed the ducks. The rest of the weekend filled up with the cricket. And, right now, it was a spot of soccer.

The afternoon shadows were growing long across the back yard as she sat on the porch swaying gently in Eddie's old white wrought-iron love seat, watching him kick a ball to Oscar.

It was surreal and she had to pinch herself.

The old man was good with Oscar. Infinitely patient and encouraging and Trinity had watched Oscar's confidence in himself grow in just three days. Oscar hadn't had any male role models and, in Eddie, she couldn't have picked a better one for her son.

A foot fall behind her raised the hairs on the back of her neck. Quickened her pulse.

Reid.

Living on the streets had heightened Trinity's senses to danger. But this was different. Her heart didn't beat faster from fear of being threatened or harmed, it was from… *awareness.*

A sexual one. A primal one. An acknowledgement deep in her cells of a *man.*

She hadn't seen a lot of him over the weekend and it'd lulled her into a false sense of security. He'd worked Saturday morning then spent a couple of hours watching cricket with his grandfather and Oscar before disappearing into the room with the computer that Eddie called *the office.*

This morning he'd done a bunch of yard work. With his shirt off. His tattoos did indeed extend further than his arms. In fact his entire back was inked from the wings that stretched across his shoulder blades to the barbed wire in the small of his back.

The real estate between the meaty slabs of his pecs and his collarbones was also decorated but the rest of his torso was ink free. Who needed ink when there were flat, bronzed abs on display? And a tantalising trail of hair arrowing south of his belly button?

Trinity had tried very hard *not* to look at that trail and where it went. She'd mostly succeeded.

After lunch he'd gone next door and done their yard work too, also sans shirt. What the elderly couple who had apparently been Eddie's neighbours for thirty years thought of Reid's big, bare-chested, tattoo-riddled frame she had no idea but, according to Eddie, Reid had been helping them out since he'd moved back in.

A frosty bottle appeared in front of her and she started even though her street-kid senses had tracked every millimetre of his progress towards her. 'Beer?'

Trinity shook her head as Reid—smelling freshly showered, and clad in a T-shirt and denim cut-offs—stepped around her and plonked himself down on the other end of the love seat. She tensed as it rocked and protested under his weight, the steady rhythm disrupted. It didn't feel right to be sitting so close to him. Sure, a whole other person could fit between them but she was excruciatingly aware of the type of chair they were sitting on.

'Come on,' he said, waggling it at her. 'You don't want me to drink alone, do you?'

She quirked an eyebrow. 'That hasn't stopped you the last couple of nights.'

Too late, Trinity realised what she'd said and clapped a hand across her mouth. How many beers he drank and who he drank them with was none of her business.

Reid threw back his head and laughed and her gaze was

drawn to his neck again as fantasies about trailing kisses up it slammed into her.

Mortified—about what she'd said and her neck fixation—she took the beer, the seat falling back into a steady rhythm again as he rocked it back and forth with his feet.

'Oscar's excited about going to school tomorrow.'

'That's an understatement.' Trinity was grateful that schools took four intakes a year these days. Making Oscar wait to the start of next year would have been unbearable.

'It'll be good for him to make some friends his own age.'

Trinity stiffened. 'Yes.' She hoped Reid was talking about the unlikely friendship playing out in front of them between Eddie and Oscar and not making other judgements. He might not have any friends his own age but he was remarkably well adjusted for a kid who'd spent half his life in hospital.

'He never went to any kind of childcare or kindy?'

Trinity's heart thudded inside her ribcage; she was aware of the intensity of his gaze on her profile. But she kept her eyes firmly on Eddie and Oscar. 'I couldn't afford it.'

Once she'd shelled out for accommodation and food and paid bills there had been precious little money left and Trinity had learned to be thrifty. Being able to have Oscar in childcare even a couple of days a week would have allowed her to work more consistently, earn more money but then she'd have lost most of her wage to childcare fees.

Thank God for the public school system.

'You don't meet too many Trinitys.'

She blinked, startled by the change of topic enough to glance his way. 'No.'

'Is there an interesting story behind it?'

Interesting? For some maybe. Trinity would have preferred parents who'd prioritised stability over a creative name. She shrugged and took another sip of her beer. 'My parents had a bit of a thing for *The Matrix.*'

'Ah,' he said, nodding with understanding. He'd clearly seen the movie. 'Well, they chose well. You take after your namesake, putting three guys on the ground.'

Trinity looked away. 'It was only two.'

She suffered more of his scrutiny as his feet kept up the gentle rhythm of the love seat. Eddie was teaching her son how to catch a ball now—something a *father* should be doing—and she clapped and cheered when Oscar caught one on his third attempt.

Oscar smiled at her as if he'd just caught a sunbeam.

'How old are you?' he asked finally as the excitement from the catch died down.

Trinity glanced at him again. She supposed if she were a different woman with a different life she might have batted her eyelids and asked him to guess. But her flirting skills—such as they'd been—were long dead and Reid was not the man to go reviving them on.

'Twenty-four.'

'Really?'

She laughed then, a short, harsh noise. She couldn't help herself. 'Yes. I know I look older than that.'

'No.' He shook his head. 'You *act* older than that.'

Trinity almost rolled her eyes. She was dealing with stuff he wouldn't understand in his eight-bedroom-house world.

'So you were nineteen when you had Oscar?'

'Yes.' But she did not want to get into that with him so she changed the subject. To him. That was what men liked, didn't they? To talk about themselves?

'How old are you?'

She'd been trying to gauge his age since she met him. But it was hard to tell with bearded men—shave it off and it took away ten years. She'd put him at somewhere between thirty and forty.

He laughed. '*Way* older than you.'

Trinity breathed easier as he allowed himself to be sidetracked but also felt her interest being piqued. Maybe he was *over* forty? 'Fifty?' she asked innocently, cocking an eyebrow at him.

He laughed again, a big belly one. 'Very funny. I'm thirty-four.'

So he had ten years on her. Maybe not *way* older but enough for it to be an issue—for some. Not her because there wasn't a thing between them. *No, sirree.* Not even a hope of a thing no matter how sexually attracted she felt. Maybe the age gap would be sufficient to stem the neck fantasies…

'Wow. That *is* old,' she murmured.

He grinned, completely undeterred by her statement, and it took her breath away. Not just because the man appeared to be impervious to insults, but because his smile was flirty and, if she wasn't very much mistaken, her mouth was curving into a smile as well.

She didn't think her smile was flirty but—oh, dear—this was not good. She was *not* to flirt with Reid. Or let his flirtations go to her head. He was being *nice*, for crying out loud. This was how people who could afford decent houses and lived good lives interacted.

Annoyed, she turned her attention back to Oscar. She drank half her beer in three swallows as her brain scrambled to make sense of what had just happened. Maybe she'd gone that long without any kind of *affection* from a man that her body had decided to take over?

Thankfully he didn't say anything for a while and Trinity decided if she ignored him he might go inside or out to play with Oscar and Eddie.

No such luck.

'What are your plans tomorrow when Oscar's at school? You'll be a lady of leisure.'

She snorted. Trinity had a lot of big dreams in her head. She dreamed of a healthy kid and a stable job. A house to rent, enough money to pay bills and put food on the table and a more reliable car. In her biggest fantasy she could actually afford a deposit on a mortgage.

She never dared dream of a life of leisure.

'Get my car back hopefully.'

Oscar's new school was about a half-hour walk from Reid's. Hopefully it'd just be the trip *to* school tomorrow they'd have to walk. They were used to the activity but at this time of year they'd both be a puddle of sweat when they got there. She'd investigated the bus options in the area but it wasn't well serviced by public transport so having her wheels back was paramount.

'Gav's going to drop it back as soon as it's done,' Reid confirmed. 'You can use Pops' car to drop Oscar to school if you like.'

This was the second time Reid had offered her the use of the BMW. Trinity had an excellent driving record but there was no way she'd feel comfortable driving some classic car whose tyres looked as if they cost more than her entire Mazda.

'It's okay, we don't mind walking.'

He looked as if he was going to push but didn't. 'What else have you got planned?'

'I have to look for a job.'

'What kind of job?'

'Bar work,' she said, turning her head to pierce him with a defensive look, lifting her chin. 'Or cleaning jobs.' She worked hard at whatever she did and she refused to be embarrassed by the menial nature of the jobs she'd taken to support her and her son.

She'd made a decision to get her act together when she'd found out she was pregnant with Oscar at sixteen weeks. She hadn't wanted to raise him on the streets with a permanently stoned father and she knew she'd never get ahead by relying on government help alone.

He nodded, unperturbed by the information. 'If you want to use the computer, it's all yours.'

'Thank you.'

Trinity was grateful for the offer. She usually went to the library to use their computers for job searching. Using Reid's meant she wasn't limited to a time slot or aware of the next person hovering in the background ready to leap in when her time was up.

Her name was down with several agencies but she rarely got work through them because she was considered un-reliable. Employers had always been impressed with her diligence and work ethic but having to bring Oscar with her or leave in the middle of a shift or not be able to come in at short notice hadn't made for lengthy stays at any one place of employment.

'What did you want to be?' he asked. 'When you were a kid?'

Trinity gave a half-laugh. *A kid?* God. Had she ever been a kid? She'd always seemed to be the adult in her house. 'I wanted to be Barbie.'

He laughed too and it was deep and sonorous and settled in her marrow. 'I think that job is taken.'

She lifted the beer to her mouth and said, 'Story of my life,' around the opening, her lips turned up in a smile.

'You had Barbie?'

'No.' She smiled at him. *Again.* She really needed to stop doing that.

'This girl I knew had a zillion though. Barbie seemed pretty damn happy with her lot.'

Barbie's life was all pink campervans, glamorous clothes and a steady guy. It had seemed like bliss compared to the wrecking ball of her home life.

'And later?'

It hadn't really mattered what she'd wanted to be later

because, at seventeen, she'd finally walked out on a life of complete and utter dysfunction, swapping it for one even more uncertain and dangerous on the streets but where she'd actually felt loved.

For a while.

Having spent five years in hospitals though, Trinity had entertained the idea of one day being a nurse. She'd even looked into the part-time courses on offer. In a few years, once their lives were on track, maybe she could enrol. Work her way towards a job she knew she'd love and even greater financial stability.

'I've never really been that ambitious,' she dismissed, realising Reid was still waiting for an answer. Her smile was forced now, definitely not flirty. 'Did you always want to be a doctor?'

Subject. Changed.

'Oh, no,' he said with a wide, self-deprecating grin. 'I wanted to be a baddie. Like the ones in the movies.'

The admission surprised a laugh out of Trinity. 'Not the good guy?'

He shook his head. 'The bad guys had cooler gadgets and blew up more stuff.'

Well, he'd succeeded. He looked pretty damn badass to her, with his arm tats taunting her peripheral vision and memories of his other ink taunting her inward eye. He owned the whole bad-boy thing. Tats, beard, bike. The type of guy mothers warned their daughters about.

Well, some mothers. Hers would have probably been all over him.

But she'd seen enough of Dr Reid Hamilton these last few days to know that was just a fashion statement. He'd taken in a single mother with a child—complete strangers—and offered them a chance to get ahead with no strings attached. He was a carer for his grandfather. He mowed his neighbour's lawn, for crying out loud.

There was nothing baddie about him. He was the goodie.
The good guy.

Dr Good Guy.

CHAPTER SIX

'Is THAT WHAT the tats are about?' Trinity asked.

He glanced down, rubbed his left palm over the tats of his right forearm. 'Nah. I got these in the army. It started off as a drunken dare on my first tour to the Middle East then one became two and then I pretty much became obsessed with ink.'

The army? So he'd been a doctor in the military? He'd been to the Middle East. She was bursting with questions over that but where she came from people didn't pry.

'And the long hair? The beard?'

He shoved his hand through his hair, pushing it back off his forehead before stroking his beard. He extended his neck and ran the backs of his fingers up the ridge of his trachea.

'I got out of the military at the beginning of the year. I was sick of buzz cuts and shaving and I needed a sabbatical. When I came home I bought a motorbike and I took off on a trip to ride all the way around Australia. I just… checked out. Which wasn't conducive to shaving or having my hair cut every other week, which suits me just fine.'

Trinity could only imagine how wonderful it would be to have the luxury of *taking off*. Just *checking out* for a while.

'I got a call in August about Pops' fall and came home

to take care of him but the beard…' He stroked it again, a slight smile curving his mouth. 'I decided to keep it.'

His whiskers made a delightfully scratchy sound Trinity felt deep, *deep* inside her. Reid must really love his grandfather to drop everything and come home to care for him. 'How far did you get?' she asked.

''Bout halfway.'

'Oh, that's a shame.'

He shrugged dismissively. 'Pops was more important. He's always been there for me. He took me in when my life started to go off the rails a little in my teenage years. It's the least I could do. I owe him.'

Reid's life had gone off the rails? Curiouser and curiouser. But none of her business. She didn't like it when people snooped into hers so she sure as hell wasn't going to snoop into his. 'He's lucky to have you,' she murmured.

So was she. And Oscar.

'Nah. I'm the lucky one. But one day, after he's gone, I'll be back out on that road as fast as my legs and a two-hundred-horsepower engine can take me.'

For some reason the news surprised her. She'd made assumptions about him being settled in suburbia based on where he lived and what he did even though he looked the exact opposite of suburban guy. She should have known the second he'd swung off his motorbike and taken off his gloves and helmet that he was a rolling stone.

'You don't like Sydney?'

'I *love* Sydney. It was where I was born and raised. It's my home. But I've spent fifteen years of my life with no control over where I went and what I did every day. And that was fine. I was in service to my country. I'm proud of that. But I'm also *done*.'

He tipped his head back and guzzled the rest of his beer.

'I want to go where I want to go and do what I want to do. I want the open road and freedom. I don't want to be tied down to any one place or one way of life any more. I want to stop where I want to stop and leave when I want to leave.'

Trinity didn't know anything about his life or where it had taken him but she'd kill to have what he had right here in suburban Sydney. She supposed that was the difference between *choosing* a transitory life and having one *thrust* upon you.

'I would have thought you'd have cherished the…stability of settling in one place after moving around so much. Of actually…coming home.'

Stability was *everything* to Trinity. She'd lacked it her entire life and she craved it as Oscar's father had craved the pot he'd smoked far too much.

His gaze met and locked with hers as he shook his head slowly. 'I think I was born with a wandering soul.'

Trinity believed him. She could almost see the lone rider in his wild-blue-yonder eyes. 'Well,' she said, turning her attention back to the catching lesson, 'to each their own.'

They watched the game for a few minutes to the steady rock of the chair. 'Listen,' Reid said, twisting his body in a half-turn to face her. 'I wanted to talk to you about something.'

Trinity didn't like the suddenly serious tone of his voice one iota and she stiffened as the possibilities flipped like a Rolodex through her head. Here it came. Her pulse pounded in ominous warning. She knew it was too good to be true. He'd given her a couple of days to get settled and now he was going to pull the rug out from underneath her.

It wasn't as if she hadn't expected something like this but she'd started to let her guard down, actually believe in her good luck. In him.

She was going to be pretty damn angry with him—and herself—if it all went pear-shaped. With Terrible Todd she'd politely told him to remove his hand from her pants and get out of the way or he'd have a sexual harassment suit jammed up his ass quicker than he could blink.

She wasn't sure she could be so polite with Reid.

'Okay…' She gulped down the rest of her beer and forced herself to look at him. If he was going to kick her out or put the hard word on her then he was going to have to look her in the eye.

'I don't want you to take this the wrong way.'

Oh, dear God. 'Just say it.'

'I'd like to offer you a job.'

Trinity blanked out. Her pulse tripped madly as she tried to reconcile the calamity going on inside her head with his words.

I'd like to offer you a job.

Not, *I'd like to come to an arrangement.*

'What?' she asked, slowly letting out the breath that was screaming in her lungs for release.

'I think Pops needs someone with him when I'm not home. You need a job. It's win-win.'

She opened her mouth to protest. Even though she wasn't sure anything would actually come out. He waved it away. 'Just until you find something else and I can arrange something more permanent.'

He shifted in the chair so he was facing her more fully, his expression earnest as the swinging motion went a little haywire. He bent his right leg up, his foot resting on top of his left knee. The frayed edge of his denim cut-offs sat mid-thigh. No tattoos that far south, just golden brown hair, as wild and thick as the hair on his head.

His feet were bare. And *big*.

She pushed back highly inappropriate thoughts about the correlation between foot size and the size of what a guy was packing between his legs.

What was the matter with her? The man had been scrupulously above board with her—hadn't once checked out her legs or ogled her boobs as Terrible Todd had done—and she was thinking about the size of his package.

She scrambled for something useful to say. 'Do you mind me asking…is it Alzheimer's?' She'd been wondering, had assumed it *was*, or something like it, but now she was grateful just to be able to say something—anything—as her brain grappled with his job offer.

And the size of his feet.

'Yes. It was diagnosed when he fractured his hip a couple of months ago.'

'I'm sorry,' Trinity murmured, glancing at Eddie laughing and playing with Oscar. He might not be young but there was still a vitality to the old man.

'It's early stages and he's on a drug trial which has had very promising results so they're hoping we'll halt or at least slow the progress.'

Trinity nodded, turning her thoughts to the next thing. 'He broke his hip?'

'Yes. His neck of femur, actually. It's pretty common in someone his age but it's been pinned. He had some complications with a wound infection, which delayed his recovery, but he's only on twice-weekly physio now and he gets around quite well without an aid as you can see.'

'Is that why he has the higher chair?'

'Yes. While he's in the recovery phase. The therapists at my work do his physio so I normally either take him with me or come back for him. It would be very convenient for me to have someone who can drive him to his appointment and back home again as he hasn't been cleared to drive again yet and, frankly, I'm not sure he should still have his licence but I'll worry about that when we get to it.'

In that moment Trinity felt an affinity with Reid. Caring for an aging grandfather involved the same forward planning as caring for a child and she admired the hell out of him for it. Had there been other family who hadn't stepped up or had Reid volunteered?

'Well?' he asked. 'What do you reckon? I leave here at eight Monday to Saturday and I'm home by two. You'll be able to drop Oscar to school each morning and I'll be home for when you need to pick him up.'

Trinity wasn't sure about this at all. If she was spending all the school hours with Eddie, she wasn't out there actually finding a job that could sustain her after she and Oscar left. But, there was no denying, she felt an obligation towards Reid and Eddie.

'I'll probably be out for about half an hour in the mornings, maybe longer some days, dropping Oscar at school and getting him settled there. What if Eddie…?'

She didn't finish the sentence because the list of things that could happen to an eighty-year-old man suffering from early-stage dementia and prone to broken bones seemed too long to contemplate.

'Pops doesn't need someone with him every minute of the day. He doesn't need a carer or a jailer either. I'll just rest easier knowing someone is around looking out for him. You'd be more like a…companion.'

A companion. It sounded very Victorian.

'You don't have to stay home with him looking at four walls or watching the telly all day either, if you don't want to. Get out of the house with him. Pops loves to go driving. He loves a beach, a museum, a train ride into the city. And he's great company.'

It didn't sound like a hardship. She liked Eddie and Oscar adored him but still Trinity hesitated. She'd learned a long time ago not to rely on anyone and some habits were hard to break. 'Don't they have agencies for this kind of thing?'

'Yes, they do. And I will absolutely set about organising something more permanent. But I think it's going to take a little time because I'll probably also advertise privately. I want to make sure that whoever I employ is compatible with Pops. I don't want to lumber him with someone he can't stand or just anyone an agency might send around.'

Trinity felt a certain pride that he didn't consider her just anyone.

'The going rate for a carer is twenty dollars an hour. Six hours a day, six days a week is seven hundred and twenty dollars a week. Cash, of course.'

The colour drained from Trinity's face and she was grateful she was sitting down. *Say what now?* She'd never earned that much in a week because she hadn't been able to work those kinds of hours. 'But I wouldn't be a carer,' she said, her voice faint to her own ears. 'I'd be a companion.'

'It's a comparable job.' He shrugged, once again waving away her concerns. 'I can afford it and Pops is worth it. Plus,' he said with a look on his face that announced he was about to lay down his trump card, 'it'll also give you another skill set. Some experience at another job other than bar work or cleaning that'd fit in better with Oscar's hours. I'd give you a reference too, of course.'

Trinity's brain buzzed. With that kind of money in two months they could not only be in their own place by Christmas but she could even have a bit of a nest egg built up. Or a buffer anyway. In case something happened—like Oscar ended up back in hospital.

She knew a lot of people would jump at the deal but, there was no way she could take that kind of money from him. Not when he was already doing so much. But maybe he was open to negotiation?

'Trinity?'

She shook her head. 'I can't take that kind of money.'

'You'll have earned it fair and square.'

'No. Those rates don't take into account the fact that Oscar and I are living in your house. Live-in help always get paid less.' She knew that from the times she'd managed to score accommodation with a job.

'That's totally separate to this.'

'No, it isn't.' Not as far as she was concerned. 'If you're going to pay me that much then I insist that you take out money for food and board.'

He sighed and shook his head. 'Trinity.'

He sounded frustrated and a little impatient but she wasn't going to be swayed. Even a couple of hundred dollars extra on top of being able to save her government support would make a huge difference. Enough to pay a bond on an apartment and have the first couple months' rent saved.

'I think two hundred dollars seems fair.'

He snorted. 'Two hundred dollars is slave labour.'

'If I had to pay rent and food out of that seven hundred dollars I'd have *nothing* left over and you know it. Two hundred dollars is more than adequate. Hell, it's a damn good deal.'

He stroked his beard as he regarded her through narrowed eyes. The rasp of his whiskers was utterly sexual. It was completely inappropriate for Trinity to wonder how they'd feel against her nipples. Or the inside of her thighs.

But she did.

In fact her whole body buzzed traitorously with sensations from an *imagined* action. A fantasy. The man was clearly not interested. He was looking at her long and hard and her nipples were two stiffened peaks brazenly trumpeting her arousal and he hadn't dropped his gaze once to check them out even though he *had* to be able to see them.

Hell, they could probably be seen from the moon.

This was highly inappropriate. The man had taken her in and given her *and her son* a place of safety out of kindness and a sense of obligation to her for helping Eddie out at the park.

And, if she took up his offer—she'd be crazy if she didn't—he was about to be her boss.

For God's sake, he probably had a girlfriend. Or a lover. Or a regular booty call. Or however the hell guys with bikes and tats described their relationships with women. Her nipples had no business flirting with him.

She folded her arms.

'Five hundred,' he said, finally.

Trinity swallowed. 'Three hundred.' God, three hundred would be a godsend.

'Four.'

Four hundred dollars? *Cash.* Trinity's head spun. That on top of her government support would be beyond her wildest dreams. Four hundred dollars *every* week.

Maybe her stars really were changing. Maybe she could finally take a breath?

'Done,' she said, straining her vocal cords to keep her voice strong and matter-of-fact.

He held out his hand. Trinity hesitated for a moment before she took it, her nipples still two pebbles inside her bra.

Maybe not touching him at all was a good policy.

'You drive a hard bargain,' he said with a smile as they slowly shook.

Trinity faked a smile and tried not to think about things that were hard.

On her. And the things that could *get* hard, on him.

CHAPTER SEVEN

REID WATCHED CHASE FROST flirt with Trinity through the window of his office that looked out over the large, open therapy room. He'd been flirting with her since she'd arrived with Pops almost an hour ago instead of working out on the weight machines to build up the strength in his thigh. There was a lot of gym equipment they used in therapy specifically to strengthen and tone muscles.

She was sitting on the chairs that lined the wall nearest the door and Chase was sprawled in the chair next to her, his prosthesis on full display. Reid gave a mental eye roll. The above-knee amputee never let the minor matter of a missing leg dent his game with the ladies. If anything he played on it.

Not that Reid blamed him. Hell, he kind of admired him for it. The conflicts in Iraq and Afghanistan had maimed many a good soldier both physically and mentally. Chase, however, aside from the distress of the acute phase, had been philosophical about his injury despite the numerous socket issues he'd had with his prosthesis and problems with phantom limb pains. Reid could hardly judge him for using whatever he could to his advantage.

The man had lost his leg to an IED—he'd paid a high price for his service and if that was what some chicks dug, then more power to him.

He just wished that, today, it hadn't been Trinity in his sights.

She'd been wary at first, keeping that polite distance she kept around him, but she'd relaxed quickly and was actually laughing now.

'The surgeon did a good job, Doc.'

Reid dragged his attention back to Brett, the latest casualty to have returned from the conflict in the Middle East. He'd lost his foot from just above the ankle and, now he was in the recovery phase, had been sent to Allura for outpatient prosthetics and rehab.

'A damn good job,' Reid agreed as he inspected the stump, 'considering how mangled it was.' He'd seen the pictures.

Reid knew, because he'd spent eight years of his life as a combat surgeon, the importance of what was left when the decision was made to amputate. There was nothing that could be done for the lost limb but forming a good stump was paramount for prosthetics and some surgeons were better than others.

He'd been one of the best.

But it also depended on the circumstances and where the patient was. Not all amputations happened in a fully prepped surgical tent. Some happened in the field through necessity and that was guaranteed to have a poorer outcome. Not just for life but for limb as well.

'I don't remember, Doc. Don't remember any of it. I think I was in so much shock I didn't feel the pain.'

'Well, thank God for that,' Reid mused. 'Because getting blown up usually hurts like hell.'

'So Chase tells me.' Brett grinned, remarkably chipper for a young guy who'd suffered a significant injury that would have far-reaching consequences.

He was already talking about competing in the Invictus Games for disabled veterans but Reid suspected it hadn't fully hit him yet. A bit like the pain from his injury. The road to recovery wasn't easy for anyone and Brett was probably going to find that the pain would come back to bite him on the ass when he least suspected it.

Still, that was why Reid was here. Not just for the physical needs of his patients but for the emotional ones as well. Getting on top of any depression, referring on to the right people was essential. Allura was a small, private veterans' hospital but it provided a full service and Reid believed in taking care of military personnel's mental health as well as their stumps and other rehab needs.

It was different from what Reid had spent the previous eight years of his life doing. It was more GP than combat surgeon. In fact, gloves deep in someone's gut, torn apart from shrapnel, or sawing off someone's leg, he'd never seen himself in the rehab sector.

Not in a million years.

But, with his plans to travel around Australia abruptly halted, he'd needed to do something while stuck in suburbia and he hadn't wanted to go back into surgery. Then he'd spotted this job advertised and, even though he wasn't specifically qualified for it, the hospital had been trying to fill the position for months.

They probably would have taken a trained monkey as long as it had a medical degree.

In a lot of ways he was overqualified but, when it was all boiled down, he was actually *perfect* for the job. An ex-military combat surgeon with an exceptional understanding of the injuries that he saw every day. And not just of the mechanics of blast injuries but the mindset of someone who had been in the thick of active combat; all made him *uniquely qualified.*

And it was a good fit for this stage of his life.

'Okay. Head out to Kathy. She'll start the preliminary measurements for your prosthetic.'

Reid followed Brett out, lounging in his doorway, shoulder propped against the frame, ostensibly watching Mario, Allura's head physio, with his grandfather. Mario was leading Pops through his therapy and Reid could tell that his grandfather was getting stronger with each session.

But Trinity laughed *again* at something Chase was saying and Reid's gaze strayed. He hadn't heard her laugh that much in five whole days. And it bugged him. It was none of his damn business but it still bugged him.

Chase had consistently crashed and burned with Kathy and every other female on staff at the rehab clinic. Not because he wasn't charming and good-looking, but because he was a patient *and* a player. One of those guys who had a *fluid* definition of fidelity. So, Trinity was new territory for him.

And, with her smiling at him and actually looking her twenty-four years for a change, he was flirting up a storm.

Smug bastard.

Did she think that because Chase had one leg, he was harmless? He hoped not. According to Chase, he'd got laid more times with one leg than he ever had with two.

Reid probably should warn her about Chase but he knew she could take care of herself. Maybe he should warn Chase about Trinity…

Reid would have given anything to have seen her moves in the park last week. Oscar was still talking about it despite her trying to shush him.

'Okay, Eddie, you're done,' Mario announced, reaching down a hand to help Pops up from the weight machine he'd been working on.

Reid ambled over, walking around the parallel bars where Steve, another physio, was putting John, a homeless Vietnam veteran, through his paces with his first ever prosthetic leg. Trinity had also made her way over, followed closely by Chase.

'Ready to go?' she asked, smiling at Eddie.

'Sure am.'

'You're doing well, Pops,' Reid said.

'Definitely,' Mario reiterated.

'You back on Thursday, Eddie?' Chase asked.

Eddie glanced at Mario, who nodded and said, 'Yep. We'll keep you going twice a week on the weight work. It'll help strengthen all your bones.'

Chase turned flirty eyes on Trinity and smiled at her. 'So that means you'll be back too.'

'Looks like it.'

She returned the smile but it gave Reid some measure of satisfaction that there was nothing flirtatious in the way she looked at Chase. Her demeanour was friendly, not flirty.

Eddie raised his hand and waved at John and at Shaun, who was currently struggling up a short set of wooden steps with his new prosthesis, under the supervision of another physio.

'See you later,' he called. They both acknowledged him before turning back to their tasks.

Chase held out his hand and Eddie shook it. 'Next time, man,' Chase said. Then he turned his gaze on Trinity and put on his best *hey, baby* voice. 'I hope to see you next time too.'

Trinity nodded. 'That would be nice.'

Reid suppressed a smile at her bland response. If Chase was disappointed in *nice* he didn't show it as Reid walked his grandfather and Trinity to the door.

'I'll see you at home this arvo, Pops,' he said before turning to Trinity. 'Thanks again for this. You have no idea how much I appreciate it.'

Her hair had been scraped back into her usual low ponytail at her nape, her fringe feathering her forehead. She wasn't wearing any make-up. She never wore it. Not that he thought she needed it or that women should wear it, he just didn't know any woman who *didn't* apply a little something before leaving the house.

He supposed make-up was a luxury for a woman who didn't have a house to leave.

'It's my job,' she dismissed. 'You pay me to do it.' But there was no mistaking the blush that bloomed across her cheekbones.

Interesting…who needed make-up when flushed cheeks were so damn alluring?

'I know. But it's still appreciated.'

She nodded awkwardly. 'C'mon, Eddie, let's go home,' she said, slipping her hand under his elbow and guiding him out of the clinic.

A low wolf whistle from behind dragged Reid back into the room. He turned to find Chase grinning at him. 'Well, aren't you the lucky one, hiring Eddie Little Miss Sweet Knees as a *companion*.'

'Little Miss Sweet Knees?'

He nodded. 'I think I'm in there.'

'Oh, please,' Kathy chimed in. 'You think you're in with any woman who doesn't throw their drink over you.'

'Kathy—' Chase grabbed his chest and faked a hurt expression '—I'm a one-legged man with a fragile ego. You wound me.'

'Right,' she snorted. 'An IED straight to your ego wouldn't wound you.'

Chase threw his head back and laughed. A lot of people outside these walls might have been horrified by Kathy's seemingly insensitive dig. But this was a hard-core environment. Learning to walk again with a prosthesis was hard-core stuff and sometimes patients had to be goaded and cajoled into doing it.

Physical therapy wasn't for wimps. Their military training helped but there was still a lot of swearing and sometimes even tears. The physical therapy staff were at the coalface—they were trained to know when to push and when to back off and it wasn't uncommon for them to cop some frustrated verbal abuse.

Learning how to give as good as they got was essential.

'I'm thinking I might ask her out when I see her on Thursday,' Chase said, returning his attention to Reid. 'I… won't be stepping on any toes?'

'Since when do you come here on Thursday?'

'Since today.' Chase grinned. 'Well?'

'She doesn't *belong* to me,' Reid grouched. 'She's allowed to see whoever she wants to see.'

Chase's forehead rose at Reid's gruff reply. 'Are you sure about that, man?' he teased. 'You seem kinda pissed off.'

'Your face pisses me off,' Reid deadpanned. Smack talk, the language of the military.

'Aw, Kathy,' Chase said, turning to appeal to the woman who was measuring Brett's stump. 'Help me out here?'

'Don't look at me,' she warned, eyes on her job. 'Your face pisses me off too.'

The whole room cracked up at that.

'You do know she has a kid, right?' Reid said.

'Of course. Ollie.'

'Oscar.'

'He's four.'

Reid shoved his hands on his hips. 'He's five.'

'Right.' Chase grinned. 'Oscar. Who's five.'

'You might have to go somewhere family friendly and take him with you.'

'Aw come on, man. They're living with you—you could babysit for a night, right? You like kids, don't you?'

Reid liked kids just fine but he hardly thought that was the point. 'She might be more amenable to a guy who's willing to include her son right from the get-go, doofus.'

Did he *have* to hand Trinity to Chase on a goddamn freaking platter?

'Or maybe she's just dying to have some adult one-on-one time? You know—' He waggled his eyebrows and Reid wondered if twenty-somethings were getting dumber these days. 'Without her kid hanging around all the time.'

Reid snorted. *Good luck with that.* He'd seen her yesterday morning at breakfast trying to be upbeat about Oscar's first day of school, stoking his excitement, fussing over his uniform and encouraging his chatter even though Reid could see the emotion in her eyes when Oscar's attention was elsewhere.

As if she wanted to snatch him to her side and never let him out in the big bad world.

'Right,' Reid said. 'You should definitely go with that angle.'

He had a feeling that Trinity's heart had been taken five years ago and she was a one-guy woman.

Trinity opened the door and placed her car keys—which also now included a house key—on the hallstand at just before ten, a smile on her face. It was the last day of Oscar's second week and, so far, school had been an outstanding success. All her fears and worries about him not liking it or missing her had been put to bed and he was thriving.

There'd been a special welcome parade for the new parents this morning, which she'd stayed on for. Seeing Oscar up on stage in front of the whole school with the other new kids in his class, singing a welcome song, had filled her heart to bursting.

The sense that things really were going to be all right settled around. The thought of leaving all the difficult times behind them made her giddy and for the first time in a long time she felt as if she could breathe properly.

'Eddie?'

She'd taken some pictures of Oscar up on stage on her phone for Eddie and couldn't wait to show him. She walked into the television room where he'd been when she left. He'd been doing some Sudoku puzzles, which he loved and the hospital had recommended to help keep his brain active.

He wasn't in the living room. 'Eddie?' she called again. Maybe he was out watering the garden?

She checked outside. And in his room. And his en-suite. No Eddie.

'Eddie?'

A note of panic crept into her voice as a trickle of fear slid into her system. She checked the other downstairs bathroom, the office, even the garage. She took the stairs two at a time, calling his name as she looked frantically in all the upstairs rooms. Including Reid's, which she'd kept the hell away from thus far.

'Eddie!' The silence that roared back at her was deafening.

That breath she'd been taking was sucked away.

Where could he have got to? She remembered the thugs at the park and the hot lick of fear chilled to ice in her veins.

She bolted down the stairs, scooped the keys off the hallstand and flew out of the house. She barely looked both ways as she crossed the road, praying like crazy that Eddie had decided to feed the ducks. But there was no Eddie anywhere near the pond. Trinity jogged the length and breadth of the park calling his name, her heart hammering more from fear than exertion.

She didn't find him lying unconscious on the ground either and she couldn't decide if she was relieved or even more petrified. 'Where are you, Eddie?' she muttered.

She ran back across the street, adrenaline and bile settling uneasily like oil on water in her gut. She banged on the doors of the neighbours either side but neither of them had seen Eddie leave. She looked up and down the street, hoping to catch a glimpse of his snowy-white head but there was nothing.

It didn't stop her running up and down it though, calling his name.

God. She'd been watching over him for two weeks—two lousy weeks—and she'd already failed to do the one thing Reid had wanted her to do. Keep an eye on him.

Reid who had offered her so much.

What if Eddie had fallen down somewhere and broken his other hip? What if some other thugs had bailed him up and this time hurt him?

What if he'd had a stroke? Or a heart attack?

The possibilities mounted like boogie men in her mind and by the time she'd got back to the house with still no Eddie she knew she was going to have to call Reid and tell him she'd lost his grandfather.

CHAPTER EIGHT

'REID?' TRINITY WAS jogging along the footpath again, peering down the side streets, her gaze searching for Eddie's big, slightly stooped frame and wild white hair.

'What's wrong?'

His voice was low but alert in her ear and she knew instantly that *he* knew something was up. He'd have to be deaf not to pick up on the panic and distress in her voice.

'I was home later than usual...' she was puffing and panting as she ran to the frantic pound of her heart '...this morning because...' puff, puff '...there was a special welcome parade and—'

'Trinity.' He cut into her rambling. 'What's wrong? Has something happened?'

Trinity stopped jogging, the enormity of the situation pulling her to a dead stop. Her pulse washed like Niagara Falls through her ears and dread filled all the space in her chest she needed to breathe. 'Eddie's gone. I can't find him. He wasn't in the house when I got home.'

There was a long pause and Trinity wished she could see his face. Was he worried, annoyed or flat-out angry? After spending the last two weeks trying to keep some distance between them she suddenly wished he were beside her.

Even if he was angry he was a man who exuded capability as if it was God-given and she could sure as hell do with some of that right now.

'When was the last time you saw him?'

'We left for school at eight-thirty. I'm usually home by just after nine but—'

He cut her off briskly. 'Where are you now? Are you home?'

'I'm searching the side streets.'

'I'm coming now. I'll try a few of his old haunts. Go home.'

She wasn't annoyed by the order—she was pleased he was thinking methodically—but she needed to do *something*. 'I can't just sit at home. Text me some locations I can help search.'

His response was swift. 'No. I need you home in case he turns up there.'

Trinity had been all set to argue her point but she couldn't fault that logic. There was no use them both out combing the streets if Eddie had returned home.

'Okay. Sure.' She turned back for the house. 'Look, Reid… I'm so, *so* sorry.'

'It's fine, Trinity.' The briskness was gone. His voice was soft and compassionate.

'But what if he—?'

'I'll find him.'

Trinity stomped down on all the ways that Eddie could be hurt. The last thing Reid needed was her litany of worst-case scenarios when he probably had a hundred of his own.

'It'll be okay, don't worry,' he assured her. 'He can't have gone too far. Speak soon.'

The phone went dead, his assurances not helping one iota.

An hour later she got the phone call that Eddie was safe and Reid was bringing him home. Trinity groped for the steps behind her, falling back onto the third one as relief flooded her system. She'd been pacing the floor area between the internal staircase and the front door while trying and failing to keep all those thoughts stuffed down.

She'd pictured him dead and maimed in so many different ways.

Now she was dizzy with relief.

Fifteen minutes later she heard the key in the lock and all but ran to greet Eddie as he appeared, launching herself at his big frame, hugging him hard. 'Eddie! You gave me a heart attack.'

The old man caught her and laughed. 'I'm so sorry, my dear,' he said, his eyes twinkling. 'Got a call from a dear friend who was in town. Wanted to meet for a beer in the old stomping ground. I should have let Reid know what I was up to or left you a note. I just forgot…'

Trinity noted Eddie had put on some smart clothes. 'Oh. So you didn't…'

She glanced at a grinning Reid, who shook his head. 'Found him at the local pub a few kilometres away.'

So he'd just…gone out? Drinking. *At nine in the morning.* But he *hadn't* wandered away.

Well. Okay, then. Why shouldn't he? This *was* his life. His house. He'd no doubt been coming and going from it for decades without telling anyone his business. He didn't need her permission or approval. He wasn't a prisoner here and, as Reid had said, she wasn't Eddie's jailer.

Still, he'd scared a decade off her life, and, for someone who already looked more than her twenty-four years, she could do without the addition of grey hair.

'Anything to eat?' Eddie asked, cheerfully. 'Two beers on an empty stomach and I'm as dizzy as a top.'

Trinity blinked. 'Ah…sure. I'll make you a sandwich.'

'Cheese and pickle? That would be lovely,' he said, patting her on the arm before heading in the direction of the living room.

'He can make his own sandwiches,' Reid said, following her into the kitchen.

'I don't mind.'

'Doing things for him won't help keep his brain active.'

'I'm making him one lousy cheese and pickle sandwich,' Trinity chided. She'd have gone out and slain a deer if he'd asked for venison. 'He can make his own tomorrow.'

She dragged the bread, butter and cheese out of the fridge and dumped them on the bench. Her hands shook as reaction to Eddie being safe set in. She grabbed the pickles from the pantry but the adrenaline that had maintained her in a state of high alert chose that moment to drain away in an almost audible *whoosh*.

Eddie was safe. He hadn't had a stroke, broken his hip again or been attacked. Her legs wobbled and the jar fell from suddenly nerveless fingers, smashing on the floor.

She swore under her breath, staring at the pile of glass and the ooze of thick yellow pickles as she knelt to clean it up.

Reid leapt to her aid, grabbing a roll of paper towel off the bench as he crouched beside the mess. 'Be careful, don't cut yourself.'

The adrenaline surge had left her wrung out and irritable. His broad shoulders seemed to loom over her. His thighs, clad in his bike leathers, seemed to loom up at her. And his feet looked huge in his big biker boots.

'Gee thanks,' she muttered as she picked out the larger pieces of glass from the spilled food, placing them on a paper towel he thrust at her. 'I was planning on doing just that.'

Did he think she was stupid?

He ignored her sarcasm and they worked together, her

kneeling, him crouching, his big boots and spread thighs in her direct line of vision.

'I'll get the mop,' she said, once the mess was taken care of.

'No need.' He departed momentarily before crouching down again with a thick wad of wet paper towels. 'A spot-mop'll do. The cleaner will be here tomorrow morning.'

Oh, yes. *The cleaner.* Trinity had never known such luxury. In fact, she'd usually been *the cleaner.*

He went to do the job but she wrested the paper towel off him. He didn't resist too hard, which saved a dumb tug-of-war. She was hyperaware, though, of him watching her as she swiped the stickiness away. Conscious of his nearness. Of the way he filled out his bike leathers and the battered state of his sturdy boots.

'Looks good,' he said, once she'd thoroughly swabbed the area.

Trinity glanced at him. *He was so close.* She didn't think she'd ever been this close—for good reason. She could see the individual golden brown strands of his beard and smell the aftershave he wore so damn well. Her heart rate picked up again but for an entirely different reason than a missing grandfather.

God, what was she doing down here on the floor with him?

She'd already dragged him away from his work and caused him who knew how much stress over his pop and now he was cleaning up another mess of hers.

She needed to apologise and send him back to work.

'Look… I'm *so* sorry for dragging you out of work like that. I just assumed that he'd wandered away and I panicked. I didn't even consider that he might have left with an actual purpose in mind.'

'It's fine,' Reid assured her. 'I assumed the same thing.

And I want you to ring me if you ever have any concerns about Pops. Any time, okay?'

She nodded, the movement of his mouth distracting. She liked the way it sat in amongst his facial hair, the whiskers perfectly groomed to delineate the margins of his lips. She wanted to run her fingers around his mouth and feel the tickle of whiskers against the pads of her finger and the contrasting softness of his lips.

He'd gone very still all of a sudden and her breath hitched as his gaze dropped to *her* mouth.

Oh, Lordy!

'Thank you…for coming.' It was just for something to say but she instantly regretted it when his mouth kicked up at one corner in wicked suggestion. Trinity blushed under the steady heat of his gaze.

'For leaving work,' she clarified quickly. 'For dropping everything. Just…thank you. And thank you *a hundred times* for finding him.'

God, yes. Definitely that. Seeing Eddie again had been such a relief.

He smiled at her and it was so damn sexy she was lost to the pull of his mouth. She'd never kissed a man with a beard. The fact that this man was highly inappropriate didn't seem to matter right now.

'You should get back to work,' she said in an effort to distract herself from the potency of his attraction and the tug of her hormones.

He nodded but didn't move and before she could check the impulse she leaned forward and pressed her lips to his.

That was it. Just a press. A tentative thing. Shy, almost. No opening of lips, no angling of heads to accommodate noses, no aligning of bodies, no sigh as they settled in.

Just her lips on his.

Testing, trying.

His whiskers spiked pleasantly at the outline of her

mouth, his scent teased her nostrils and the husky timbre of his breathing tickled her ears. Time suspended in that moment or two before a kiss became *something else*.

And then common sense rushed in and she pulled back as if she'd been zapped, her tripping pulse stuttering to a momentary halt as shock set in. She stared at Reid, aghast, her hand covering her mouth as he stared too.

'I…' She removed her hand in the hopes she'd say something sensible, something to justify her completely inexcusable actions. She'd *kissed* him, for crying out loud.

'I…'

Nothing. She had nothing. She couldn't think above the bang of her restarted heart fibrillating through her ribcage. But she had to say *something*.

'I'm so…*so* sorry,' she stuttered, her gaze glued to his face with its completely inscrutable expression. 'That was *completely* and *utterly* inappropriate. I don't know—'

'Trinity.'

Her pulse leapt at his interruption but she ignored him. 'What came over me. I was just so…scared—'

'Trinity.'

'That something had happened,' she said, ploughing on, needing to get an apology out before she dissolved in a nervous puddle, 'to Eddie and to see he was okay—'

She cut out as he dropped from a crouch to a kneel bringing him *so much closer*. So close their thighs almost touched and she could feel the warm fan of his breath on her cheek. Her body stiffened and her heart raced as a crazy buzz started up deep inside her pelvis. She eased her torso back, putting some distance between them.

'To…to…to *know* he was okay,' she said, ignoring the dryness of her mouth as she forced herself to continue, 'and to see him come through that door with you—'

'Trinity,' Reid said, interrupting her again, sliding a hand onto the side of her neck before slipping it all the way around to her nape.

'What?'

Her voice, low and husky, was barely audible as his hand urged her closer, her body aligning with his. His lips were just there, the bristles of his beard were just there and she curled her fingers into her palms to stop herself from touching. Her skin sizzled wherever his body made contact with hers.

'Be quiet,' he muttered and brought his mouth down on hers.

There was nothing shy about *this* kiss.

It was open-mouthed from the start. Nothing *pleasant* about the tickle of his whiskers. They scraped erotically against her chin and cheeks as he angled his head to deepen the kiss, prickling in a tidal wave of sensation down her entire body, hardening her nipples and settling right between her legs.

His scent *raged* like a juggernaut through her system. His breathing was the harsh suck of a hurricane in her ears. Her pulse didn't *trip*, it *pounded* like a jackhammer through her head and chest and all her pulse points.

Reid was a full-body experience and she was utterly consumed by the havoc he was wreaking.

And his tongue. God, his tongue. Swiping and thrusting and stroking. Thick and urgent as it explored and demanded hers do the same in return. It tore whimpers from her throat and weakened her knees. If she hadn't already threaded her fingers through his belt loops she'd have slumped to the floor at the first touch of his tongue.

It had been a long time since someone had kissed her. And *never* like this. Brian's kisses paled by comparison. He'd kissed her like the seventeen-year-old he'd been. They'd taught each other, fumbling their way through the joys of sex but too often constrained by lack of privacy.

Doss houses and homeless communities, where people all huddled together for warmth and security under whatever bridge or shelter they could, were not conducive to long, lazy days of sexual exploration.

Bri had kissed like a teenager learning the ropes. Reid kissed like a fully grown man.

Like a master.

Like a grand freaking wizard.

'How's that sandwich coming along?'

Eddie's voice came from somewhere out in the hall but it had a galvanising effect. They sprang apart and were on their feet by the time Eddie poked his head into the kitchen.

'Sorry, Eddie, just dropped the pickles,' Trinity said, her pulse fluttering madly, her face hot as she blindly grabbed two slices of bread out of the packet and started buttering.

'We usually keep more than one jar,' Reid said, heading for the pantry. 'I'll get it.'

'No!' Her knife clattered to the bench.

Reid stopped and Eddie blinked at her vehemence. 'You need to be getting back to work.' She forced herself to look at him but all she could see was his lips, a dark, dusky red from their kisses. 'I can get the damn pickles.'

Their eyes met and held for long moments before his gaze dropped to her mouth too.

'She's right, Reid,' Eddie said, completely oblivious to the highway of crackling electricity arcing between them. 'You really should be at work.'

He dragged his gaze off her and smiled at his grandfather. 'Sure thing, Pops. I'll see you some time after two. No more slipping out for beers without telling Trinity first, okay?'

Eddie chuckled. 'I promise.'

Trinity was aware of Reid switching his attention to her. Aware in the same kind of way she'd been aware of him since the day she'd met him. She didn't need to look at him to feel it. Hell, she could have been totally blind and she'd have felt it.

'See you later, Trinity.'

She wasn't sure whether it was a statement of fact or some kind of illicit promise but she was damned if she was going to clarify it. 'Yep,' she said, refusing to look up from the job at hand.

She sensed his gaze on her, hot and heavy for long moments before he clapped his grandfather on the back and exited the kitchen.

It was only then Trinity dared breathe deeply again.

CHAPTER NINE

REID COULDN'T CONCENTRATE on work once he returned. Trinity had done the right thing ringing him and his grandfather was safe at home but Pops' cheeky pint at the pub with his mates was not what occupied his brain.

It should be. Trying to balance his grandfather's rights to an autonomous, dignified life with the need to keep him safe was going to present all kinds of future challenges if the drug trial wasn't successful and he started to deteriorate. But all he could think about this afternoon was that kiss.

Both of them.

Even her first chaste kiss played on a loop in his head. So innocent compared to the next one but just as sexy.

He couldn't remember ever being kissed by a woman like that. Most women who took the initiative usually went in with all guns blazing. Open mouths. A lot of tongue. Squashing themselves up against him, squirming deliciously, raking their hands into his hair and moaning his name.

Trinity hadn't done any of those things. It had been a closed-mouth, very still, very silent kiss. Yet it was probably one of the sweetest kisses that had ever been laid on his mouth.

It had turned him on more than any kiss he could ever remember.

Frankly he was a fan of all types of kissing but this one

had reminded him a bit of his first. Starting off simple, not daring to move or get too fancy in case he'd screw it up even as his body yearned for more.

Yearning.

He'd seen that in Trinity's eyes just prior to her making her move. As if she couldn't stop herself. As if she couldn't *deny* herself. The knowledge had flared through his system like a lit match and still buzzed through him a couple of hours later.

Reid tried to drag his attention back to the report he was writing for the hospital board on partnering with a robotics lab going into the future but he couldn't stop thinking about Trinity.

About where they went from here.

It was clear she'd been embarrassed at the prospect of being caught kissing him. Although, in all truth, by the time Pops came along *he* was kissing her.

She might have started it but he'd definitely finished it.

Hell, he hadn't been any too pleased at the prospect of being sprung by his grandfather either. He wasn't some fifteen-year-old kid any more and he'd rather not flaunt whatever it was that was happening between him and Trinity when it was something he wasn't exactly proud of. He'd been trying since she'd arrived at his place not to think of her in any kind of sexual way but he couldn't deny he was attracted to her.

He just wished he knew why.

A life in the military hadn't been conducive to forming long-term relationships but a man didn't get to thirty-four without female companionship. He guessed he had a *type* and it wasn't Trinity. Women who were flirty and witty and easy to be around. Who were relaxed and could hold a conversation in a room full of army officers or laugh at a dirty joke. Hell, *tell* a dirty joke. Who were confident in themselves and their bodies and their sex appeal.

Trinity was none of those things.

She was quiet and unassuming. Wary. Contained. Prickly, more often than not. Slow to trust. If anything she hid her sex appeal beneath ill-fitting clothes and a wall of polite indifference that could morph to out-and-out hostility.

He understood why. She was a single mother with a young son who'd been doing it tough for a long time. She didn't have time for the frivolities of life. She was working her fingers to the bone just to survive. Her son was her priority—not herself.

And he admired the hell out of her for that.

But since when had he found it sexually attractive? Because there was something about her that definitely piqued his interest. That didn't just pull at his heart strings but at the ones in his groin too.

Maybe it was her resilience. Her…gumption. It was the word that had popped into his head the first day they'd met and it'd stuck. He'd always admired gumption—in anyone. But Trinity wore it better than anyone he knew.

Who knew that could be so damn sexy?

Maybe it was the fact it had been a long time between drinks for him? He'd had a couple of one-night stands when he'd been on the road. Women he'd met along the way. Fellow travellers.

Maybe it was some weird misplaced, macho, protection thing left over from the military. But Trinity had already demonstrated she didn't need his protection.

Whatever it was, it was a problem because he'd been thinking about kissing her a lot this past couple of weeks. It was that mouth. The fullness, the lushness. For a woman who made nothing of her features, it drew his gaze like moth to flame.

But he hadn't acted on it. The power dynamic between them sucked and he did not want to be *that* guy.

He *wasn't* that guy.

Until today. When he'd thrown his moral high ground right out of the window.

Her kissing him was one thing. But him kissing her? *Taking over?* That was a whole other *thing*. She hadn't even been able to look at him after so he'd no doubt destroyed any kind of fragile trust they'd been building this past couple of weeks. And that wouldn't do. He'd been trying to show her that there were good people out there, that she could trust people.

That she could trust *him*.

So he was going to have to rein himself in because what he wanted here didn't matter. She wasn't the kind of woman that would indulge in a fling and even suggesting something like that to someone in her position was completely abhorrent to him.

He would never put her in that kind of situation.

Trinity and Oscar were with them temporarily. Until she got back on her feet. He was giving her *breathing space*. The last thing she needed was him *breathing down her neck*.

Another guy she couldn't trust.

So kissing Trinity was out. No matter how damn much he wanted to.

Trinity came home from school pickup sans Oscar the following Friday. It was strange to be without him. They'd rarely ever been apart and she was feeling stupidly fragile.

It was so *dumb*. It was what she wanted for him. She just hadn't realised how hard it was going to be.

'Where's the little dude?' Reid asked when she wandered into the kitchen. He was making a giant sandwich.

Of course.

The man was always eating.

Facing him again after their kiss had been awkward to

say the least, even a week later. Facing him in the *kitchen*—the scene of the crime—was especially awkward.

By tacit agreement, neither of them had mentioned the kiss. Trinity figured the less attention that was drawn to it, the quicker it would be to forget. Re-establishing the distance that had been eroded between them had helped too. Keeping herself aloof from him both physically and conversationally had given her back some control.

Now if only she could control what went on in her head when she shut her eyes. A series of very hot dreams about *way* more intimate things than kissing had left her tired and achy in places that hadn't ached in a long time.

She might have actually blushed at the thought as she faced him now but she was battling other emotions. 'He's gone on a play date to Raymond's house.'

Her son had a friend.

The words were foreign and her voice sounded wobbly so she cleared her throat. This was a *good* thing. It was exactly what she'd hoped for when Oscar went to school. That he'd make friends and finally have a normal life.

'Oh. That's *great*,' Reid said. His gorgeous face cracked wide open; he was obviously chuffed at the news, his blue eyes shining.

'Yes.' She nodded, swallowing the massive lump in her throat. It *was* awesome. It was beyond her wildest dreams.

So why then was she about to burst into tears?

The tears she'd been battling all the way home prickled in her nose and burned all the way along her sinuses. They pushed at her tear ducts, threatening imminent appearance. They'd been threatening since Celia, Raymond's mother, had approached and asked if it was okay for Oscar to come over for a few hours.

Trinity had met Celia and Raymond the first day. She'd liked the other woman instantly and they'd chatted outside the classroom most days waiting to pick the kids up in the afternoon. And Oscar had talked about Raymond non-stop.

He'd been barely able to contain his excitement and had wrapped his skinny arms hard around her neck when Trinity had said yes to the play date. Watching him skip away, hand in hand with Raymond, had been the most beautiful thing she'd ever witnessed.

And the hardest.

'She's dropping Oscar home at five on their way to Raymond's swimming lesson.'

'Cool. Do him good to mix with some people his own age for a change.'

Reid munched on his sandwich oblivious to Trinity's inner turmoil. She knew he wasn't criticising her but she wasn't feeling particularly strong at the moment.

Goddamn it. She could count on one hand the number of times she'd cried these last five years and they'd all been at Oscar's hospital bed when things had seemed utterly hopeless.

She hadn't even cried when she'd found out Brian had died. She'd had a premmie baby with a serious heart condition on life support. There hadn't been any spare emotional energy for someone she'd left months beforehand and who hadn't wanted his child anyway.

But she'd been in this house for three weeks and she'd almost cried a dozen bloody times. And now she really *was* going to cry.

But not in front of Reid.

'Will you excuse me?' she said, a smile fixed on her face as she turned and walked out of the room.

She walked to the stairs, her sinuses burning from suppressing the well of emotion. Once she got to them she took them two by two, hurrying to her room, desperate to be tucked away inside when the well overflowed.

She shut the door behind her, her heart racing, silent

tears falling down her cheeks now. Oscar's old, floppy bunny sat in the middle of his pillow and the threatening tears burst like a dam.

She tried to choke them back as she curled up on the bed, bunny clutched to her chest. She tried to tell herself this was stupid and futile and embarrassing. That Oscar was happy. But she'd been so worried about him. About him not making friends or fitting in. About being teased because he was smaller.

And now he had a friend.

And it was wonderful and she was so happy she couldn't stop crying. She tried to muffle her weeping, burying her face in his rabbit, but inhaling the smells of Oscar—the baby powder he still liked to wear after his bath and the orange blossom from the cheap-as-chips shampoo he loved so much—only made it worse.

She didn't hear the knock on the door and, facing away from it, she didn't see it open but she *sensed* Reid's presence the way she always did. 'Trinity.'

It was quiet and tentative, causing another well of emotion in her chest, and she shut her eyes hard against it as she suppressed a rising sob.

'Go away.' There was no way to disguise the sniffles or her voice, cracked and husky with emotion.

'Trinity.'

'God, please, just…go away,' she half cried, half begged. Trinity didn't have much in the world but her dignity and she didn't want Reid to see her like this.

There was a hesitation then a quiet, 'No.'

She sensed him coming closer and swallowed a painful lump. *Bloody hell, Reid!* She sucked in a husky breath, dashing the tears away with her hands as she rolled over to face him.

'I'm fine,' she said, her voice rough and low.

He was standing about a foot away from the bed, a line

creasing his brows together, blue eyes telegraphing their concern and helplessness. He was in usual jeans and T-shirt and stood, hands on hips, looking down at her. Between the broad set of his shoulders and the tattoos on his arms he seemed to take up all the space in the room.

Trinity swung her legs over the side of the bed, levering herself upright. It was bad enough he was witnessing her crying for Australia, she didn't want him looming over her as well.

He cocked an eyebrow. 'You don't look fine. Are you worried about this Raymond kid? Do you think Oscar's not safe?'

'Of course not,' she snapped. 'Do you think I'd let Oscar go and play somewhere I didn't think he'd be *safe*?'

'No. Absolutely not…sorry.' He shoved a hand through his hair. 'But something's obviously upset you. Why else would you be crying?'

She had no idea why, seconds after being annoyed with him, tears swamped her vision and her face was crumpling again. 'Because I'm h…happy,' she choked out, a wave of emotion rolling through her body.

'Oh, God.' He searched her face, looking even more helpless, putting a hand out as if to reach for her then thinking better of it, shoving it on his hip. 'Please…don't cry.'

The statement and the distress in his voice surprised her. Where she'd grown up most men had been impervious to crying women.

'Look… *God*…don't, okay?' He took a step towards her then stopped, raked his hand through his hair again, hesitated another moment then covered the short distance between them and sat next to her on the bed, leaving a space big enough for Oscar to have sat between them.

His denim-clad thighs were big compared to the bared slimness of hers. Her baggy shorts had ridden up to reveal a lot of leg. If she'd been in her right mind she might have cared.

'It's okay,' he repeated, awkwardly sliding a hand around her shoulders, patting her arm absently while scrupulously maintaining their distance.

Trinity was too much of an emotional wreck to pay any heed to her determination to keep a physical distance between them. His arm around her felt *so* good, she actually leaned into him, put her head on his shoulder.

It was a novelty to have someone comforting her. She was so used to wading through the ups and downs of life solo it was a new experience to *not* be alone.

She'd been too afraid in the past that any sign of fragility would be a signal to those in charge that she wasn't coping. Too afraid that deeper questions would be asked. That the prying into her *circumstances* would begin.

It was different with Reid. While she was wary of her physical attraction to him, it was liberating to realise he already *knew* her deepest secret. She could let it all out with him and not worry about the consequences, just soak up how good it felt to lean on a man for a change.

'I don't know why I'm crying,' she said, sniffling loudly as she lifted her head, her gaze fixing on his as well as it could through a tsunami of tears. 'I *never* cry.'

'Yeah.' He inched closer until their thighs were touching and her head was more supported. He urged it back on his shoulder. 'That's probably why.'

His hand was warm, his palm gently rubbing up and down her arm. 'I'm just so h…happy he has a friend,' she said, more tears squeezing out around closed lids. 'I've been so excited for him but I just didn't expect to m…miss him so much.'

She couldn't go on, dissolving into tears again.

He rubbed her arm some more and dropped a kiss on top of her head. It didn't seem strange, it felt *right*.

He held her like that for a long time until her tears stopped and the weeping faded to the odd hiccoughy sobs.

'If it's any consolation,' he murmured, somewhere above her head as she quieted, 'I don't think you're the first mother to find letting their kid go emotionally challenging.'

The word's rumbled through his ribcage. Trinity heard them through the wall of his chest where her ear was half pressed.

'I suppose not,' she said with a wry smile as she glanced at him. 'If only my parents could see me now. Not much of the *Matrix* Trinity about me today, huh?'

'Tough guys have their low moments too. It's how they keep getting up again that has us rooting for them.'

He smiled down at her and kissed her forehead this time and Trinity felt so much better. So damn good and comforted.

For the first time in her life she actually felt she had someone on her side. Someone rooting for her.

'Thank you,' she whispered. And then they were both smiling at each other.

CHAPTER TEN

TRINITY WASN'T SURE who kissed who. All she knew was their mouths fitted together perfectly and it was *just* what the doctor ordered. His warm, male scent swirled around her like fairy dust, his chest was hard and his heart beat a steady thump beneath her palms and she wanted more.

So much more.

He pulled away though and she moaned in protest.

'Trinity…'

The look in his eyes was raw and untamed and her breath hitched. With only one lover to her name, Trinity was no expert in this kind of thing. But she did recognise the potency of desire, could see it in someone else.

'Reid,' she whispered.

She opened to him as he came back for more on a strangled groan, her pulse roaring in her ears, her senses filling with the warm, heady scent of him. The bristles of his beard prickled at her mouth and she whimpered against his lips as the sensation headed south, hitting all her *good* spots.

Her throat. Her nipples. Deep inside her belly. The nerve endings at the base of her spine. Between her legs.

Her body burned for him, slick and achy.

She jammed her hands in his hair, turning to press herself more fully against him, needing to be closer, to feel all of him, to touch all of him. Keeping her lips locked with his, she slid her hands over his shoulders and her leg over his lap, turning until she was straddling him.

He groaned again, breaking away. 'Trinity…'

His voice was a crazy low rumble as they stared at each other, chests heaving, their mouths wet. She was speechless in the presence of her desire. She didn't know how to ask for what she wanted. How to articulate herself in the presence of his intoxicating masculinity. His denim-clad quads rubbed deliciously against the sensitive flesh of her inner thighs, his taste flooded her tongue and his scent filled her nostrils.

They shouldn't be doing this, she knew, yet she was hungry for the physical contact. *Starving.* For this man to lose herself in.

She grabbed at the shoulder muscles beneath her palms and pushed him back. He didn't resist, going down at her insistence, his tattooed arms loose by his sides, his hips pressing warm and firm against the inside of each knee. He didn't say anything for long moments, just searched her gaze, his chest chugging air in and out as their gazes locked and blood throbbed at her temples.

Then he lifted his head and lunged for her mouth. Trinity gasped as their lips made contact, moaning long and loud as she accepted the almost brutal demand of his mouth. She followed his head back down, their mouths fused as his hands slid up the backs of her thighs to her butt. He squeezed and yanked her down to him.

She went willingly, her body collapsing on top of his, aligning perfectly as he urged her thighs apart, splaying wide over the bulge behind his fly, one big hand holding her fast right where it felt best.

Reid could barely think as his senses infused with the taste and smell and the sounds of Trinity *indulging.* Panting and gasping as their heads twisted and turned, their tongues duelling, stoking the passion between them as she rocked and grinded on top of him.

He shoved a hand into her hair at her nape, pressing her mouth closer and harder at the same time he pressed her hips closer and harder. The rub of her pelvis against the taut line of his erection was almost painful but there was something to be said for hurting so good and he wanted every inch of her along every inch of him.

There was no coherence of strategy. Just feeling and moving and instinct. Going with what was good. And damned if her hot, deep kisses didn't *taste* good. And if the little noises at the back of her throat didn't *sound* good. And if the rock of her pelvis over his didn't *feel* good.

Really freaking good.

She gasped, wrenching her mouth from his, throwing her head back, her eyes squeezed shut, her neck bare and exposed and right there. The look of ecstasy on her face was like a shot of testosterone to his already overloaded system and he ground up hard against her as he nuzzled her neck.

'Feels good, huh?' he said, keeping up the grind as he deliberately scraped his whiskers across the pale, delicate skin of her throat.

Her eyes flew open on another gasp, her gaze fixing on his, her tawny eyes wide, turning dark as whiskey. 'I'm coming,' she moaned.

Reid blinked. *She was what now?*

The sudden violent arch of her back and the intense trembling of her arms bracketing his shoulders confirmed it.

'Oh, God…oh, God…*oh, God*!' she gasped, her eyes screwed shut, drumming the flats of her feet against the mattress either side of his hips as she rode him and the powerful wave of her orgasm.

Reid's chest pounded as he held her through it but it was like the bucket of proverbial cold water. She was oblivious to his stillness as she got off on him. She didn't need him to do anything, she was taking what she wanted—what she obviously *needed*—grinding hard against him, gasping and panting and wringing every single second out of her climax.

He wouldn't have denied her a few moments of sexual abandon for the world. For God's sake, the woman was so starved of sex and human *affection* that she'd just come fully clothed from a spot of dry humping.

But it should *not* have been with him.

What the hell had he done? Where the hell had his resolve to keep away from her gone?

Because, regardless of how much he'd wanted her, she was still a poor, highly vulnerable single mother and he was a well-off guy who was offering refuge and paying her to look after his grandfather.

And he'd gone and taken advantage of her situation. Or at least let things get out of control. Not much better than the douchebag who'd demanded sex in turn for accommodation.

Where the hell was his *honour*?

With one last moan and still oblivious to Reid's turmoil, she collapsed on top of him, gasping and shuddering, her fingers curled into the balls of his shoulders.

His hands automatically slid to her back, cradling her as the pound of her heart reverberated through her ribcage. Her weight against him was hardly anything at all but the weight on his conscience was significant.

He lay there, *his* heart also pounding but not from exertion, from uncertainty. He didn't want to mess with her bliss. God knew if anyone deserved a bit of bliss it was her. But he doubted she was going to be too pleased at what had occurred between them when the bliss wore off. Ever since the kiss in the kitchen she'd been all sparks and prickles. Like an electric hedgehog.

If he knew Trinity at all after three weeks in her company, he knew there were bound to be regrets after this little *tête-à-tête*.

She stirred, lifted her head and looked at him, although both actions appeared to take a supreme effort, as did keeping her head upright. A very satisfied, Mona Lisa smile played on her mouth and slugged him straight in the heart.

There was nothing more satisfying, as a man, than putting *that* look on a woman's face.

He watched though as her gaze became clearer. She frowned at him, tentatively touching her finger to the tense line of his mouth. 'What's wrong?'

The pad of her finger was like an erotic brand and Reid fought the urge to suck it into his mouth.

She searched his face some more. 'Oh, God, I'm sorry.' She planted an elbow on his chest, levering herself up some more. 'I just…got off and left you hanging and—' She halted abruptly and slid her hand between their bodies.

'Let me…'

Her hand cupping him, still hard and throbbing despite his mental self-flagellation, had a galvanising effect.

'*Ooo*kay. No.'

He rolled her off him and practically fell from the bed in his haste to put some distance between them, adjusting himself as he went. He stopped just short of the door and turned to face her.

Slowly she rose into a sitting position. Her beautiful full mouth was a deep red from the plunder of *his* mouth. Her too-big T-shirt had slipped off one shoulder. 'I guess we stepped over the line, huh?' she said, her cheeks almost as red as her mouth.

'You could say that.'

She pushed a hand through her hair. 'I'm sorry.'

'No.' He shook his head. 'It was as much my fault.'

The kiss had come out of nowhere, sure, but maybe it had been inevitable the second he'd sat on the bed with her and put his arm around her. He should have known he was vulnerable to her.

To her situation. And her gumption. And her damn mouth.

But that was no excuse to let things get out of hand.

'I was a wreck, Reid. You were just trying to comfort me. Put it down to…extraordinary circumstances.'

'You were *crying*, Trinity. Stop the press.'

'Trust me, for me that *is* extraordinary.'

Reid laughed at her self-deprecation. 'Crying is good for you.' He suspected she needed to do it more often.

'Oh, yeah?'

'Yes, ma'am.' He grinned. 'I learned that in med school.'

She lifted an eyebrow at him. 'You do it a lot, do you?'

'Every night. Twice on Sundays.'

She laughed and Reid's breath hitched. She laughed so little it made the times she did that much more memorable.

At least the atmosphere was a little lighter now.

'We can't do that again,' Reid said. 'Overstep the line. I'm not some creep who opens up his home with some sick ulterior motive. That's not the arrangement here.'

'I know that,' she said quietly.

'I think it's best if we keep things…platonic.' He was a grown-ass man, he could keep this attraction in check, surely?

She nodded. 'I agree.'

'I want you to be able to trust me.'

'I do trust you. I know I've been…wary. And distant. I know I don't trust easily and that's a hard habit to break. Especially when something too good to be true happens. But I *do* know you're a good guy.'

Well, well, despite the awkwardness of the situation it looked as if they'd made some kind of breakthrough. Maybe they should have had almost-sex two weeks ago.

'Does this mean you're going to stop looking at me like I might just shove you and Oscar in the oven at any moment?'

She laughed. 'Sure.'

Considering what had just gone down between them, Reid was relieved by the outcome. 'I like to think we could be friends,' he ventured.

It was a tentative suggestion—not one he was sure she'd go for—but it made sense. Putting Trinity in the friend zone and vice versa, establishing that kind of rock-solid boundary between them, should help keep the attraction at bay.

'I'd like that.'

'Let's start over.' He strode towards her, sticking his hand out to be shaken. 'Welcome, friend.'

She took his hand and shook briefly. 'Thank you.'

A weird tingle flared to life as their palms pressed together. Reid ignored it.

Friends *did not* suffer from weird tingles.

The weeks flew by and it was mid-November before Trinity knew it. Her relationship with Reid had become easier, more relaxed, as he'd hoped for that day she'd totally lost her mind and had the world's fastest orgasm. They'd both put extraordinary effort into it and it didn't feel awkward or fraught between them any more.

It felt as if she'd finally been able to take that breath and relax.

Sure, her attraction was still there. She still dreamed inappropriate dreams about him that woke her in the middle of the night with his name on her lips and an ache between her legs. And she spent an extraordinary amount of time reliving that unorthodox climax he'd given her—or rather, *she'd taken*—despite the fact her cheeks flamed every single time.

But that was a first world problem if ever there was one. She could live with it.

Not that she'd have to for much longer. By her calculations, she'd have enough money put aside in two weeks to start contacting real-estate agencies about an apartment to rent.

They'd be in their own place by Christmas.

'Hey.'

Trinity startled. She'd been so caught up in her thoughts and memories, she hadn't sensed Reid approach and she *always* sensed him approaching.

It was like some really screwed-up super power.

'Hey, Reid.' Eddie grinned as Reid shrugged out of his jacket and threw it around the back of the folding chair that had been set up for him beside his grandfather.

'Hi,' she said. He nodded but she couldn't see his eyes from the sunglasses fixed firmly on his face.

'What's the score?' he asked, turning his attention to the match being played out in the centre.

'Four for twenty-six,' Eddie said. 'Oscar's batting. He's on three.'

Eddie and Reid had accompanied her to every one of Oscar's Saturday school cricket fixtures. Reid didn't show till after work but he hadn't missed a match. Considering the truly terrible calibre of cricket on display *that* was dedication. Untrained five- and six-year-olds had no bat-and-ball skills to speak of. But, they *were* getting better and Eddie and Reid sat and cheered and supported regardless.

And Oscar loved having them amongst the spectators.

'God, it's hot,' Reid said, reaching into the Esky between the two chairs and pulling out a chilled bottle of water.

Neither she nor Eddie bothered to respond. November in Australia might be spring but it was still *painfully hot*. They, along with the other parent supporters dotted around the ground, had staked out a spot under an overhang of some gum trees. But the shady patch was retreating at a rate of knots as the sun blazed directly above them.

It was *stinking* hot.

Trinity had worried about Oscar playing in such conditions, that he didn't have the stamina for it. But he'd taken to it like a duck to water, giving her hope that he truly was over the worst of his ill health.

Suddenly a crack rent the hot, still air and the ball, smacked by Oscar, hurtled along the ground towards the boundary rope. Eddie and Reid whooped and jumped to their feet as a member of the opposing team chased the ball trying to prevent it from becoming a four. Trinity leapt up as well.

'Run,' Eddie yelled at the two stationary boys in the middle who were both staring at it as if they couldn't quite believe what had happened.

It was the first time any of them had hit the ball well and Trinity's heart burst with pride. 'Go, Oscar,' she cheered as the boys put their heads down and ran like the blazes.

They need not have though; the ball reached the boundary and the umpire signalled four runs. Reid cupped his hands around his face and called out, 'Awesome work, Oscar.'

Oscar turned, shot Reid the thumbs up and grinned so big, Trinity thought his face was going to split in two. Her lungs suddenly felt too large for her chest and Trinity was glad she was wearing sunnies too.

Her son had blossomed under the influence of the Hamilton men. *Particularly Reid.* Oscar always stood a foot taller whenever Reid praised him and constantly sought his approval.

'Phew,' Reid said as he sat again, pulling his T-shirt off his abdomen and fanning it. Trinity found her gaze was drawn helplessly to the action, knowing how firm and flat those abs were, and she was pleased for the presence of her sunglasses.

'This heat is ridiculous,' he announced.

Trinity couldn't agree more. She supposed wearing long leather bike pants and big boots made things about a hundred times worse for Reid. At least she was in shorts. Her gaze was drawn to where his fingers fanned his shirt.

Surely *no* shirt would be cooler?

'What say we head to Bondi after this?' he said suddenly, glancing at her. She looked swiftly away, hoping like hell he hadn't caught her ogling his abs.

'Go for a refreshing dip in the ocean? We can get some fish and chips for tea to celebrate that magnificent four. Would Oscar like that?'

Trinity blinked away a hot rush of tears. It seemed once you let the damn things flow you couldn't turn the suckers off. 'Oscar would love it.'

CHAPTER ELEVEN

THE ENDLESS BLUE arc of the sky met the deep blue of the Pacific Ocean at the distant horizon. The brilliant yellow of sun and sand was dazzling to the eye and even at four in the afternoon the soft grains were still warm beneath her feet. The breakers were rolling in and a line of surfers sat on their boards further out.

Red and yellow flags flapped in the stiffening afternoon breeze and surf lifesavers in their yellow shirts and red bathers with *Bondi* emblazoned across the butt patrolled the flagged area.

Trinity never got sick of this sight.

She and Oscar came to Sydney's beaches often. It cost nothing, after all, and building sandcastles and paddling in the shallows where you could easily spot a movie star frolicking in the surf was a fabulous way to forget they were part of the have nots.

They grabbed a section of sand a few metres back from where the waves washed up.

'Can we go in, Mummy?' Oscar said, bouncing on his heels as he stared at the water. He was in a full-length rasher shirt and a pair of boardies that both hung on his skinny frame.

She'd already crammed a hat on his head, lathered his arms and legs in factor fifty and slapped thick, white zinc on his face. 'Yep. Hang ten,' she said. 'Let me just slip, slop, slap too.'

'I can take him while you get ready.'

Trinity glanced up at Reid, who'd peeled down to his boardies. Her mouth dried at the sight of him. As if all the sand on the beach were suddenly in her mouth. She'd seen him without a shirt before but looking all the way up his body like this was something else entirely.

Up his tanned legs encased in pink and purple hibiscus boardies to his flat abs and further to his bronzed shoulders. His tats were in full vibrant colour beneath the spotlight of the sun. The man was tanned, ripped and built.

He was goddamn perfect.

She swore she heard a passing woman sigh at the sight of him.

'Oh…it's okay.' She swallowed. 'Thanks…but we usually just play in the sand and paddle in the shallows.'

He shrugged. 'I can do that. C'mon, little dude.' He held his hand out to Oscar, who took it without hesitation. She opened her mouth to protest but the two of them were already on their way.

'He'll take good care of the little fella,' Eddie assured her.

She nodded but it didn't stop her heartbeat echoing in her head as she tracked their progress. The tall, tattooed man with the pale, skinny kid. Oscar had to walk three paces to Reid's one but his little hand, placed so trustfully in Reid's giant one, caused her heart to squeeze painfully in Trinity's chest.

They stopped at the point where the water pushed high on the beach, foaming to a stop before retreating again. They sat and started piling up wet sand.

'I think they'll be needing these,' Eddie mused as he scooped up a couple of bright plastic buckets and spades he'd found in the shed and trotted off to join them.

Soon Eddie was crouching beside them and Oscar and Reid were on their knees digging in the sand with the spades. A lump the size of Sydney Harbour lodged in her throat at the sight of their three heads together.

Apart from the obvious differences in size and colouring, they could be a family. Father, son and grandfather out for a day at the beach.

This was what Oscar was missing out on. What Trinity couldn't give him.

A family.

Just then Oscar looked back over his shoulder, his hat lopsided on his head, his gaze searching her out, grinning and waving as he located her. He motioned to her to join them and Trinity's chest almost burst with how much she loved him.

She and Oscar *were* a family. And that was enough. She waved and rose to join her son down at the water.

'Look, Mummy, we're making a *super* castle!' Oscar announced as she drew level.

Trinity laughed and said, 'That's super-duper,' as she tried not to notice Reid's head turning in her direction. His eyes were shaded by sunglasses but she could *feel* his gaze on her body.

She suddenly wished she were wearing a bikini or even a one-piece. Something more flattering than her faded, long-sleeved rasher shirt. Sure, it was snug on her body, as were the Lycra bottoms that stopped just above her knee, but there was hardly any skin on show. Even her floppy, practical, Cancer-Council-approved hat felt suddenly daggy.

She might be being sun-sensible but she had about as much sex appeal as the bleached chunk of driftwood they'd passed higher up the beach.

She plonked herself quickly down beside Eddie, the sand cool and wet on the backs of her thighs as she turned her attention to Oscar's creation. *Instead* of the way sand clung to Reid's muscular calves.

'Wow, look at that moat,' she said.

'It was my idea,' Oscar said, puffing out his chest. 'I saw one in a book that Raymond brought to school.'

'How about we fill the buckets up with water and flood it?' Reid suggested.

Oscar's face came alive. 'Oh, yeah!' He grabbed a bucket. 'C'mon, Reid.'

He headed for the water's edge without a backward glance, Reid hot on his heels. Trinity's heart melted as they ran back and forth for what seemed an age, dumping their loads of water into the moat before heading back to the water's edge again.

The mother in her lapped it up. Lapping up the happiness of her son as he played without a care as if he'd never spent one hundred and eighty days in the NICU. The *woman* in her lapped it up too. Lapped up a bare-chested Reid, jogging and bending and twisting and turning, wet boardies clinging to powerful thighs.

And it wasn't just her. Other women checked him out too.

But they didn't just look. They *flirted*. Smiled at him and said, 'Hi,' as they walked past swinging their hips and wiggling their bare butts totally exposed in their teeny-tiny thongs.

It made absolutely no sense to be peeved about it. She was *not* with Reid. Never would be.

But she was peeved anyway.

Finally exhausted, Oscar and Reid collapsed on the sand near the castle, happy and laughing.

'Well,' Eddie announced, pushing to his feet. 'I'm going for a dip.'

Oscar suddenly sprang into a sitting position, staring after Eddie. 'Oh, could I go too, Mummy?'

'No, sweetie,' Trinity said. 'It's too deep and the current can be really strong. When you're older maybe.'

'I can take him,' Reid offered.

'Oh, yeah!' Oscar grinned at Reid before turning pleading eyes on his mother. 'Please, Mummy, can I go with Reid?'

Trinity looked out over the water. She was torn between the blatant begging and the thought of the current tearing Oscar from Reid's arms and sweeping him out to sea. 'Well…'

'Please.'

'I won't let him go. I promise.'

There was that low, gravelly voice again. She glanced at Reid, who'd taken off his sunglasses, the sincerity in his blue eyes as deep as the ocean. She believed him. Not only was he the strongest-looking man she'd ever met but he'd been nothing but protective of Oscar.

He'd asked her to trust him. Told her she could. *Proved* she could. Maybe it was time she showed him a little in return.

'Okay.' She glanced at her son. 'But not too deep,' she warned, raising her voice over Oscar's whooping.

Reid handed her his sunglasses as he stood. 'I won't go out higher than my waist.'

She stood too. 'And you'll hold onto him. Tight.'

'I will.' He held out his hand and Oscar took it.

Trinity grabbed Reid's arm as he stepped away. The skin was warm from the sun and the muscle beneath full and firm. He half turned, glancing at her hand before his gaze landed on her face. 'Thank you.'

He smiled and nodded then walked away with her son towards the ocean.

Reid and Oscar stayed in for close to an hour. He was so excited to be out in the deeper water, splashing around with the rest of their fellow ocean-goers, that Reid was determined to stay as long as Oscar wanted.

His mother needn't have worried about them being separated. For all his bravado, Oscar clung to him like a monkey, his breathing fast and excited as they'd waded in together.

Still, it didn't stop Trinity from pacing up and down the shoreline. She was easy to spot in bathers that would have been perfectly at home at Bondi a hundred years ago. Compared to the other scantily clad women she stuck out like a sore thumb, covered neck to knee, her hair stuffed up inside her big, floppy hat totally obscuring her face and eyes.

Even so, he could *feel* her gaze firmly fixed on him.

Well, *Oscar* anyway.

Reid, on the other hand, could hardly take his eyes off her. She might not have been exposing much skin but it was the first thing she'd worn that actually showed off her body and what she actually had going on under clothes that usually hung.

It was a novelty to be able to see she actually had a waist. And breasts that looked as if they'd fill a man's hand. He'd known they were there. Had felt them pressed to him, mashed up against him that day on her bed, but to see them... Or *glimpse* their outline anyway.

He'd spent an inordinate amount of time while playing with Oscar hoping she might get wet.

'Can we go out to Eddie?'

Pops was out in shoulder-deep water chatting to some other old guy and, while Reid was confident in his own abilities, he'd promised Trinity he wouldn't take Oscar out deep.

'Not this time, dude.'

Oscar took it on the chin as he did everything else. He was a good kid. Well behaved, not prone to sulking if he didn't get his way. Trinity had done an awesome job with him, considering their circumstances.

Not that he was any closer to knowing what her true circumstances actually were. She might have relaxed around him but chatty she was not.

Oscar absently traced the outline of his eagle wings tat with one pruned finger. 'I like your tattoos,' he said.

Reid grinned. Oscar hadn't really mentioned them before—to him anyway—which was unusual. Most kids were agog. 'Thank you. Tattoos sometimes frighten kids but not you, huh?'

He shook his head. 'No. Mummy has a tattoo.'

Reid blinked. *Oh, does she now?* He glanced at her staring at them from the shoreline in her neck-to-knee gear. He really, *really* wished he hadn't known that. He was going to be thinking about it way more than was good for his sanity.

Already questions about where and what rose in his throat. But he was *not* going to pump her kid for information that was none of his damn business.

Oscar shivered and goose bumps broke out on his arms. Reid was pleased for the distraction. 'Cold, little dude?'

'No.'

Reid gave a half-laugh. He was on the cool side himself now but, on closer inspection, Oscar's lips were a nice shade of purple-blue and he was pretty sure Trinity would bundle him straight out if she were here. Because that was what a responsible parent did.

He'd never given a lot of thought to being a parent. A *father*. He'd assumed he would be one day but, at thirty-four, maybe he'd missed that boat?

Oscar's teeth started to chatter.

'Your teeth are chattering.'

'They're j…just exci…excited.'

Reid laughed again. *Excited teeth. Kids!*

'Yeah, I don't think your mum is going to buy that, dude, and she'll have my—' He cut himself off before he said *ass on a platter.* 'I'll be off her Christmas card list.'

Oscar nodded, resigned. 'Yeah. She always worries I might catch a bug and have to go to hospital.'

It was a natural thing for mothers to worry about, even though Reid knew no one caught a bug *just* from being cold. But there was a gravity to Oscar's words that told him it was a legitimate fear of Trinity's.

That Oscar had been in hospital before.

He opened his mouth to press for more then shut it again. He wasn't going to ask about that any more than he was going to ask about Trinity's tattoo. He should just man up and do it himself—the hospital thing, not the tattoo thing—instead of waiting for her to open up to him.

Maybe he would ask her. In a few weeks.

In the meantime, he didn't want to start on the wrong foot by handing over a hypothermic child. He motioned to his grandfather to let him know they were heading back. 'Okay, let's go in.'

Oscar sighed and put his head down on Reid's shoulder. It fitted perfectly. Reid's heart gave a strange little kick and the feeling of restlessness that had dogged him since coming back to stay with Pops stilled. After a moment's hesitation, he placed his chin on top of the snowy-blond head and strode out of the ocean with him.

'Mummy,' Oscar said as Reid placed him down in ankle-deep water and he ran the rest of the way, flinging his arms around Trinity's legs. 'Did you see me?'

'I did, darling,' she said, smiling down at him, obviously uncaring that Oscar was soaking wet.

She was, unfortunately, still depressingly dry. Although now apparently the owner of a tattoo, which only made her more fascinating. Not to mention the fact he could see her nipples were erect through the cling of her rasher shirt.

He dragged his gaze off them, grabbed for his sunglasses, which dangled from her fingertips, and crammed them on his face. Now he could stare at them with impunity.

And he did. Friend zone or not.

No matter how much he castigated himself for acting like a horny teenager, he didn't seem to be able to stop.

'Goodness,' she said. 'You're freezing. Let's get you changed.'

There wasn't any reproach in her voice but, judging by her speed back to their belongings, she wanted Oscar dressed and warmed even though a few minutes in the sun would achieve the same thing.

By the time Reid had reached their little square of sand Oscar's rasher top was off and she was throwing a towel around his shoulders, rubbing his arms briskly.

'Reid,' Oscar said as he drew level. Trinity had turned and was searching through her bag behind her. 'You want to get warm with me?'

Oscar opened the towel, a cheeky grin on his face, exposing his puny little chest before Trinity turned back and pulled it around him and started rubbing again.

But not before Reid had seen what he'd seen. A long, pale scar running straight up the middle of Oscar's chest. An open-heart-surgery scar. And a couple of small round scars between his ribs on both sides. Chest drain insertion sites.

What the hell?

She always worries I might catch a bug and have to go to hospital.

Reid didn't doubt it. The sternotomy scar had confirmed his suspicion that Oscar had been in hospital before. *More than once* if those scars were what he thought they were.

So, Oscar had some kind of heart condition? It explained him being on the small side. Was this a chronic thing with chronic issues or was it something that had been dealt with and was in the past?

He didn't know but he wanted to and she could bet her ass he was *definitely* asking about it. No maybes. No in a few weeks.

Tonight.

A few hours later Trinity sat in the dark, on the love seat, appreciating the stars and the sounds of the night. The trilling of insects, the occasional distant sounds of a car and the muffled murmur of a television. They floated to her on the warm air along with the squeak of the hinges and she sighed contently.

It was moments like this that everything felt surreal. As if she were going to wake up tomorrow and find it was all a dream. She'd never imagined herself sitting idly on an old-fashioned swing, staring out over a beautiful back yard with absolutely nothing to do or worry about.

She hadn't been idle in five years and there'd always been *something* to worry about.

But here she was and she had Reid to thank for it. She was so damn grateful to him it filled up every cell and all the spaces in between. If she lived to be a million years old she'd never be able to repay him for what he'd done for her and Oscar.

Never.

The sound of dishes clanking together drifted to her from next door and the feeling that she should be doing something reared its head. But there wasn't anything. They'd had an early tea of fish and chips, then Oscar had gone for his first ever sleepover at Raymond's house.

Celia had rung as they'd been waiting for their food to be cooked and Oscar was so excited she hadn't been able to say no. Letting out the apron strings was a work in progress and she was taking baby steps every day. This had felt more like a giant leap but Reid had nodded almost imperceptibly and urged her with his eyes to take it and she had.

It was a *big deal* though. For her. There'd been very few nights in five years they'd spent apart. Even during his long hospital stays she'd slept most nights by his crib on lumpy, uncomfortable recliners.

She'd been allocated a small unit at the accommodation block for parents with children who had long-term illnesses but she'd rarely spent a night there. And even when she had succumbed to the nurse's urgings to get a decent sleep for a change, she'd usually ended back at his crib-side a couple of times during the night to express milk or just sit with him.

They'd sure come a long way since those early days. Oscar had gone from lengthy hospital stays to having sleepovers with friends, which was everything Trinity had ever wanted for him so she was going to have to get used to it. Hopefully, when they had their own place, Raymond could come and stay with them.

The sound of the sliding door opening interrupted her reverie. Right on cue, the hair at her nape prickled. 'Hey.'

The low rumble washed over her as the prickle headed south, beading her nipples and scattering goose bumps across her belly. 'Hey.'

'Beer?'

A bottle nudged her upper arm and she took it. 'Thanks.'

She cradled it in her lap, absently running her fingers up and down the frosty surface as he sat on the other end of the love seat, his right leg tucked up under him.

He didn't say anything for a while, just sipped his beer and stared out over the back yard. It was nice to sit in companionable silence, even if her body was excruciatingly aware of him. The bunch of his quad as he idly rocked the chair, the way his lips pressed against the neck of his beer and the movement of his throat as he tipped his head back and drank.

'I noticed Oscar's sternotomy scar on the beach today.'

CHAPTER TWELVE

TRINITY BLINKED AND her heart skipped a beat as she stared at him. Nothing like throwing a hand grenade to ruin the ambience. 'Oh.'

She'd seen it so often she didn't really see it at all any more. Except when he was in hospital battling lung infections and the scar stuck out horrifyingly white as he struggled for breath.

'I assume he had some congenital heart condition?'

Trinity hesitated. 'Yes.' She took a swallow of the beer and fixed her gaze on the distant stars.

'I hope you know you can talk to me, Trinity.'

His voice was soft and sincere. Calm. As if he were talking to a frightened animal that might scarper at any moment. She wasn't frightened though. Not of telling Reid. She was just so used to *not* telling people, actually opening up about it was surprisingly difficult.

Of course, there were plenty of people who knew about Oscar's condition—most of them medical. Also a handful of strangers—parents of sick kids—she'd met over the years whenever Oscar had been an inpatient. The bond formed with someone who was living the same nightmare encouraged those kinds of confidences.

And the school too, of course.

But she didn't tend to talk about it as a general rule.

Especially not to people she didn't know well. She hadn't wanted it to draw attention to Oscar as being different or remarkable. Flying under the radar was what she'd perfected.

A bit of that old tension slid into her bones as she contemplated opening up. She took a deep breath. 'He had Tetralogy of Fallot.'

There was a pause. 'I see.' She could feel his gaze lasering into her profile. 'TOFs are pretty routine cardiac repairs these days. Lots of great paediatric cardiac surgeons out there. Were there complications?'

The tension oozed from Trinity's bones at his matter-of-fact reply. Reid probably knew more about TOF than she did and not having to explain that the condition consisted of four different cardiac defects and what that meant physiologically was a relief. It still didn't stop the rise of hysterical laughter spilling from her throat. TOF repairs were routine enough but Oscar's case had been somewhat complicated.

'You could say that.'

'Yeah. I thought that might be the case. Why don't you start at the beginning?'

Trinity had a choice now. To gloss over the details and move on. Or open up. Reid had taken her and Oscar in, given them a roof and an income and hadn't pried into the circumstances of her life and she was surprised to find she *wanted* to tell him.

Maybe it was because he'd never pushed. Maybe it was his medical knowledge. Maybe it was their fledgling friendship.

Or maybe it was the funny sensation in the centre of her chest today as she'd watched him hold Oscar in the ocean.

Whatever. She *wanted* to tell him.

'Oscar was born at twenty-six weeks.'

Reid whistled. 'Okay. That explains his size.'

'Yes.'

'Was the TOF diagnosed via ultrasound prenatally?'

Trinity shook her head, the rush of guilt she always felt about her lack of prenatal care as keen as ever.

'No. I...didn't know I was pregnant until I was about sixteen weeks and then...' God. Then she hadn't known what to do. 'I was nineteen. I was living on the streets. I didn't really know what to do except I knew I had to get my act together because I did *not* want that kind of life for Oscar.'

'Do you mind me asking why you were on the streets?'

Trinity hesitated. This conversation wasn't about her but she supposed it was only natural that it would go there. She was surprised to find she wanted to tell him about that as well.

'A dysfunctional home life. Parents caught in an inter-generational welfare cycle who spent most of their money on things like booze and cigarettes and the pokies and spent the rest of their time fighting and wrecking whatever hovel we were in at the time. Lots of police call-outs. Then they'd break up and there'd be a whole conga line of new boy-friends or girlfriends before they got back together again. School was a godsend but my parents usually felt their hangover needs were greater than my scholastic ones so I missed more school than I attended.'

Trinity stopped, aware she was talking too fast as she plucked the events of her youth out of her brain from the macabre carousel going around and around. She took another sip of her beer, staring at the stars. It was easier to tell when she wasn't looking at him.

Especially the next bit.

'And then when I was seventeen my mum's latest boy-friend decided he wanted to try a threesome. With her. And me. She was okay with that...but I wasn't.'

Trinity was pleased for the cover of night as her face blazed. That conversation still made her cringe to this day. The way he'd leered at her as if she were the cherry on his pie still made her skin crawl. Reid didn't say anything, for which she was grateful. He just sat and listened, his foot rocking the chair.

'So I walked away. Actually I ran away and never went back. I hooked up with Brian, a guy I knew from having met him in courts and cop stations on and off over the years because of our parents. He was a few years older than me and had had it worse. He'd been in and out of the foster system for years. He was living on the streets but he welcomed me with open arms, showed me the ropes.'

A tendril of the fear that had gripped her in those first few days she'd been alone curled around her gut and Trinity paused for a moment.

Reid must have sensed it because he drew in air between his teeth and said, 'Tough life.'

It wasn't trite *or* judgemental, just a statement of fact.

'It's not for the faint-hearted,' Trinity admitted, finally looking at him. Their gazes locked. 'But it was more harmonious living on the streets with him than it had ever been under my parents' roof. There's a whole homeless community out there and I know it's screwed up but for the first time in my life I felt like people cared about me. That they actually gave a damn.'

He nodded and she felt as if he really understood. 'Is that where you learned to fight?'

Trinity laughed at the unexpected question. 'Yeah. One of the guys we knew was some kind of ex-black-ops dude. I learned enough from him to get by.'

He stroked his beard and the sound became a physical caress down her body. He took a swallow of his beer. 'So... Brian's Oscar's dad?'

'Yes.'

'Is he...around? Involved at all?'

'No. Bri died a couple of months after Oscar was born.'

'I'm sorry.'

His voice had deepened and the resonance of his sincerity was like a physical force. 'Don't be. He was stoned and apparently playing chicken with a train. I loved him but he always did have a bit of a death wish.'

The wince on Reid's face said it all. 'He was a pot-head?'

'Oh, yes.'

It hadn't bothered Trinity that Brian was high seventy-five per cent of the time. Not before she was pregnant. But after—it had mattered a lot.

'Have I shocked you?'

'No. Not at all.' He half turned on the chair to face her. 'I went off the rails a bit in my teens. Divorced parents, shipped between two warring parties, a string of new partners who all wanted to *be my friend*.' He waved his hand in the air dismissively to indicate the usual stuff. 'I was angry…ran away. Fell in with the wrong crowd. Got into some petty crime, was in trouble with the cops a bit. My parents disowned me. It was Pops actually who took me in, turned me around.'

Reid had been into petty crime? It wasn't that hard *looking* at him to imagine him being on the wrong side of the law. He *looked* as if he belonged in an outlaw motorcycle gang. But *knowing* him was a different matter. The big, motorbike-riding, tat-covered, bearded man was the opposite of how he appeared.

'That was very good of Eddie.' Any extended family Trinity owned had all been cut from the same cloth as her parents.

None of them had wanted her either.

'I hadn't had much to do with him at that point. My father and he didn't get along very well but my grandmother had died a few years before and he needed somewhere to put his love and attention as much as I needed love and attention.'

Trinity nodded. 'That sounds like Bri and me.' He'd taken her under his wing as much for himself as for her.

'You were with him?' Reid asked gently. 'When he died?'

'No. We'd already split by then.'

'You'd split?'

She nodded. 'He wanted me to get an abortion. He didn't want to waste any of his precious pot money on a kid. It was him or the baby.'

'Ah. I see.'

'I went there,' she said, dropping her gaze to her beer bottle, picking at the label absently. 'To the clinic. That's where I found out how far along I was. They did an ultrasound. And, of course, at sixteen weeks I couldn't just get a pill and be done with it. But that was okay because I'd seen him on the screen, this little skeletal creature scuttling around, sucking his thumb and... I knew I couldn't do it.'

'They didn't pick up the TOF on that ultrasound?'

'No, it was mainly just for dates. I was supposed to go at nineteen weeks for a proper one but I was couch-surfing and trying to find a job and sort my life out and, frankly, scared out of my wits and I told myself I'd go later for another check-up, towards the end, but...'

'You went into premature labour.'

'Yes.'

'It's okay. They're often not picked up on ultrasound anyway.'

A block of unexpected emotion welled in her chest and lodged in her throat. 'It's not okay. I should have taken better care of myself. Of him. It was...irresponsible.'

'You weren't to know. There was nothing they could have done antenatally anyway.'

'*I* could have done something.'

He shrugged. 'Maybe knowing about it might have helped with forward planning but—'

'No,' she choked out, interrupting him, the beer label half shredded. 'I mean I could have prevented the TOF if I'd known about Oscar earlier.'

He frowned and shook his head very slowly, his gaze fixing on hers. 'Trinity…it's a congenital defect. It happened when Oscar's heart was forming. There's nothing you could have done about that.'

She shook her head. 'It was my fault.'

It was the one phrase she'd never dared speak out loud and now she had. If she'd hoped there'd be some kind of catharsis, some lightening of her burden, she was badly mistaken.

'I fell pregnant in winter,' she said, her voice husky, her heart heavy, her emotions sitting in a giant tangle in her gut. She returned her attention to the label. 'It's cold on the streets in winter. We'd been drinking cask red wine to help keep warm. I mean, I never drank much, nowhere near as much as others. Maybe a couple of glasses every night and I stopped when I found out I was pregnant…immediately. But I've Googled it.'

She shut her eyes. It was a hard thing to admit that a substance she'd put in her body had caused Oscar's condition. That she was responsible for his malformed heart.

'Trinity.'

His voice was low, vibrating with compassion. She sucked in a breath. 'They say drinking alcohol can affect the formation of the growing foetal heart and—'

'*Trinity.*'

She peeped at him through her fringe. He moved closer, the chair rocking a little. Sliding a finger under her chin, he raised it until she was looking him square in the eye. She shivered at the compassion warming his blue gaze.

Or maybe it was his touch.

'They don't know anything definitively.'

Trinity desperately wanted to believe that. 'But—'

'The foetal heart is pretty near formed by six weeks,' he interrupted again. 'TOF is not a common condition. A lot of women don't even know they're pregnant until then. You want to guess how many of them are blissfully drinking unawares during that time? There'd be a helluva lot more TOF if booze was the causal factor, don't you think?'

Trinity hadn't thought of it like that before. Of the bigger picture. Of the many women who'd drunk alcohol while pregnant with absolutely no ill effects on their babies. She'd just read it online and been instantly paralysed by guilt.

'I guess.'

'A risk factor is just that. It doesn't mean that's what caused Oscar's condition. They. Don't. Know.' He whispered the last three words, taking the time to emphasise each one, staring deep into her eyes, as if he was willing her to believe.

For the first time in five years she actually did.

She doubted the guilt over his condition would ever completely disappear. As a struggling single mother, Trinity had found that guilt lay around every corner. But Reid had given her perspective.

She swallowed. 'Okay.'

'Yeah?' He cocked an eyebrow.

Trinity gave a half-smile. 'Yeah.'

'Good.'

He smiled and released her chin. He didn't shift away though and she was hyperaware of her body's reaction to his nearness. Of his finger imprint under her chin, of the dark shadow of his beard and tats, of the way his T-shirt fell against his belly.

The long stretch of his thigh.

Every cell in her body seemed to be undergoing a chemical reaction. Melting down.

'So,' Reid said after a beat or two, turning back to face

the night, 'he was born at twenty-six weeks with a TOF? I'm guessing that complicated things rather a lot.'

Trinity struggled to gather her wits and pick up the threads of what they'd been talking about before they'd become sidetracked by their own life stories.

'Ah...yes.' She took a sip of her beer to cool the heat of her body.

'What did he weigh?'

'Eight hundred and twenty grams.'

'Oh.' He glanced at her. 'Under a kilo.'

'Yes.' The fact she didn't have to tell him that premmie babies under a kilo had much poorer outcomes was a relief. 'Obviously he had tiny lungs, which weren't helped by the severe pulmonary stenosis from his condition. Worst the specialist had seen apparently,' she said, her tone derisive.

'Hell. He really had the odds stacked against him, didn't he?'

'Oh, yes,' she said with a self-deprecating smile. 'This is why I look old and haggard.'

He snorted. 'You don't look old and haggard.'

She blushed at his quick dismissal, his compliment rushing dangerously to her head. '*You* thought I was older than twenty-four,' she accused, keeping her voice light.

'I said you *acted* older.' He grinned at her. 'Different thing entirely.'

Trinity's breath hitched at his grin and the fact that she returned it. Why was he so damn easy to talk to?

'So how old was he when they did the repair?'

'He had a shunt initially as a stopgap measure until he grew big enough to have the surgery, but he was five months, two months corrected age, before he was big enough and well enough to have the full open-heart surgical repair. He was in the NICU for one hundred and eighty days.'

He whistled. 'That sounds incredibly stressful.'

'It was.' Trinity shuddered. How she'd got through it she had no idea. 'There were so many hairy moments. It seems he takes after his father in the dicing-with-death department.'

'So what did you do while he was in the NICU all that time?'

She blinked. 'Nothing. I stayed with him. I *couldn't* leave him.' Her gaze met his; she needed him to understand. 'Plus it was a solution to my housing problem. They have units at the hospital for long-term families. They weren't anything flash but it was like a palace compared to what I was used to. They charged a nominal rent so I was able to save some of my government money for use when he was finally discharged.'

He gave an incredulous half-laugh. 'Did *no one* guess you'd come from the streets?'

'Nope.' She shook her head. 'I became really good at pretence and flying under the radar. I used my parents' address and told them I still lived at home with my mum, who was house bound with crippling agoraphobia. They knew I wasn't with Oscar's dad any more but I was there and engaged in Oscar's care. I was sane and stable. I didn't cause waves or rock any boats. I…became part of the furniture, I guess. They *knew* me. Well, they knew the kind of person I was anyway. That I was a good mother and that Oscar would be in good hands and that's what mattered.'

'But…' he angled himself in the swing to face her again '…you could have talked to social services. They would have hooked you up with all kinds of support. You could have put down for public housing.'

Trinity shook her head. 'The wait list is *years*.'

'But you'd have been fast-tracked if they'd known your situation.'

She was stupidly touched by his earnestness. 'And in the meantime the authorities know I'm not able to provide for my son and they take him off me?' She shook her head. 'If they'd found out I'd been homeless and I had no idea where I was going to live if Oscar was ever well enough to go home, I'd have never seen him again. And I wasn't risking that.'

The one thing Trinity and people like her, who grew up in the kinds of places she had and who'd lived on the streets, had been conditioned to mistrust, was social services. It might have been wrong but it was deep-seated and compelling.

Even the thought of it now was enough to make her blood run cold.

Oscar was her son. She'd sat and watched too often as he'd fought to survive, to breathe, to live. There wasn't any system she wouldn't have fought to keep them together.

CHAPTER THIRTEEN

'So…' HE STARED into her eyes, confusion in his own. 'Where *did* you go? Have you been homeless for five years?'

'No.' Trinity shook her head vehemently. It was important that Reid knew she hadn't been irresponsible with her son's welfare. 'I told you, that's only been a few times.'

'Okay.' He held up his hands in surrender. 'I believe you.'

'Initially I was able to rent a room in a share house. I got a job as a cleaner at a small hotel. The boss allowed me to bring Oscar to work. I strapped him to my chest and went with him from room to room. But then Oscar caught a bug and it knocked him flat. This time he ended up in Paediatric Intensive Care for two weeks. I lost my job. And the accommodation.'

'So. He's had ongoing problems?'

'Multiple readmissions with respiratory infections. Multiple ventilations. Many, many weeks and months in hospital. In fact he's spent more of his life in hospital than out of it.'

'I'm assuming that meant a lot of lost jobs and accommodation.'

'Yes.' Trinity grimaced. 'We got by though. I always found work again and another place to live. But…it was stressful. Nowhere near as stressful as seeing your kid hooked up to monitors and machines, struggling to breathe though.'

He nodded and she could see in his eyes that he knew what it was like to witness someone in respiratory distress.

'You wouldn't know it now,' he said. 'I mean, he's a little pale and a bit on the skinny side but he seems healthy. He's bright and alert and has oodles of energy.'

Trinity smiled. 'It's been six months since his last admission at the beginning of winter. The specialists told me he should improve as he grew and his lungs got bigger and I'm starting to hope that he really *is* over the worst of it. Knock on wood.'

She looked around for some wood but in the wrought-iron love seat there was nothing. She wasn't superstitious but she'd learned not to tempt any kind of fate where Oscar's health was concerned. Reid smiled and dipped his head towards her for Trinity to knock.

She stared at the long glossy hair for a few moments. A patch of dull gleamed where it caught the muted starlight. The urge to tunnel her fingers into it, to sift through it, almost overrode her need to pander to superstition. Not trusting herself, she gave a quick knock, her knuckles protesting as they met unyielding skin and bone.

'Ow.' She gave a half-laugh as she withdrew her hand, rubbing the bony knobs absently. 'I think it's made of rock, not wood.'

He lifted his head and grinned at her. 'Are you accusing me of being hard-headed, Ms Walker?'

Trinity's breath hitched at the lightness in his gaze, at the tease. Almost as if he was…flirting. The knowledge whispered against her nipples and trembled through her thighs.

'Well,' she said, smiling at him, trying to keep it friendly and not flirty, which was what they'd agreed to, 'your head did almost break my knuckles.'

He threw his head back and laughed, big and full and

strong, and her heart fluttered a wild tango as the deep, rich sound resonated through every cell of her being. Her gaze fell helplessly to the bare stretch of his neck, to the line where his beard ended and his throat began. To the thick thud of the pulse bounding just within touching distance.

Licking distance.

The laughter cut out and he lowered his chin until his eyes met hers again. 'I've been called worse. Including *soft*-headed.'

Trinity smiled at his self-deprecation. 'Well, I don't know about that but definitely soft-hearted.'

His low dismissive snort oozed all over her, her breath stuttering to a halt as his gaze strayed, zeroing in on her mouth. He stared at it—hard. As if he was mapping its contours, deciding just how he was going to kiss it.

Her pulse fluttered madly at her pulse points.

There wasn't much distance separating them, he could lean in and his lips would be on hers in a heartbeat and for a crazy moment she thought he was actually going to do it. He made a slight, almost imperceptible, move towards her. Less than a move, really, more a disruption of the air currents.

But then it was gone, in the blink of an eye, leaving nothing but her madly pounding heart.

'Okay,' he muttered, swivelling his eyes forward again, shaking his head. 'I think I should *definitely* leave now.'

It wasn't a question. It was a statement. A purely rhetorical one that required none of her input. He drained his drink. 'Thank you,' he said, not looking at her, staring out into the night instead. 'For telling me about your stuff. I know it's not something you usually talk about and I appreciate that you shared it with me. I'm really sorry that you've had to go through all you've had to go through. I'm sorry that life is so unfair to so many while it's abundantly good to others.'

Before she had a chance to answer, the love seat was swinging crazily and he was gone, passing in front of her like a shadow. Trinity blinked as the door slid and clicked shut behind her.

Soft-hearted indeed.

Five hours later, Trinity was still wide awake staring at the ceiling. She'd like to pretend that it was because Oscar wasn't snuggled in bed with her or that she was fretting about how he was getting on at Raymond's, but that would be a lie.

She was lying awake thinking about *that* moment with Reid. The one where he'd almost kissed her. If that was what it had been. If it hadn't been a trick of the dark. If her fevered body hadn't just…imagined it.

But it was circling around and around in her head, refusing to leave.

He'd looked at her mouth as if he'd wanted to devour it. As if he'd wanted to *own* it. And the way he'd lectured himself about needing to go inside? As if he was trying to convince *himself. Compel* himself.

Because why?

Because he might be too tempted to kiss her if he stayed?

For so long now she'd been denying that Reid was really attracted to her. Telling herself that the great dry-humping incident had been mostly one-sided and he'd just reacted as any red-blooded man would. That it was only her who thought about kissing him way more than was good for her. Who dreamed erotic dreams. Who woke with her body on fire and an ache between her legs.

It seemed ludicrous that he could reciprocate such desires. He was a well-to-do, successful, self-assured guy. He had a home, a job, he had family and every kind of creature comfort. He wasn't hard up for *anything*.

She'd bet he wasn't hard up for women either. Just because she'd never seen a woman and he spent all his time either at work or home with Eddie, Oscar and her, didn't mean there wasn't one.

Why would he lust after some chick who came with a sickly kid and more baggage than an airport who he'd plucked off the street?

Trinity's fist curled into the sheet and she rolled on her side, a frustrated growl gurgling in the back of her throat. She stuffed her hands between her legs, pressing hard to ease the ache that was slowly becoming a roar.

She couldn't deny how much she wanted him. How this feeling had grown from an initial flare of attraction to a full-blown obsession. Was it possible that he could actually want her too?

The man did funny things to her heart, things she *didn't understand* and didn't want to examine too closely. But what he did to her body she *did* understand.

Desire and passion had been dormant in her for so long but they were *roaring* to life with a potency that was blinding. Trinity tried to convince herself it was because it had been an age since she'd felt them but deep down she knew it was because of the man who'd roused them.

She rolled onto her back, her body burning as she stared at the ceiling. If she had any kind of courage she'd slip into bed with him and find out once and for all whether that look in his eyes tonight had been real or imagined.

Why not? Oscar wasn't home and Eddie, all the way downstairs, would never hear them. Her heart beat so frantically at the illicit thought, it practically exploded out of her chest.

But…she couldn't. *She was no seductress.* She lacked the guts. *And* the finesse.

Something bumped in the hallway and her heart stopped with one loud definitive bang. Her breath cut off with a strangled gargle high in her throat. Her limbs froze.

Reid?

Her eyes darted to the door. Was he coming *to her*? Had he been lying awake too, burning with desire, wishing he'd kissed her?

Was *he* coming to seduce *her*?

Trinity shut her eyes and wished like hell he was. It was selfish and indulgent and very possibly *crazy* but she didn't care.

Her ears strained for the slightest noise. Anything that indicated it *might* be him. But there were no footsteps. She couldn't hear her name being called. Her door didn't open.

Nothing.

Then she heard it again, followed by a loud meow outside her door. Her breath burst from starving lungs, her heart kicked in, belting along like a runaway train, her limbs jerked back into use as she rolled off the bed and opened the door for Ginger, who had taken to joining them in the middle of the night, much to Oscar's delight.

The cat strutted in and Trinity's gaze followed the high, proud flick of its tail as it leapt onto the bed. She looked down the end of the hallway where Reid's door stood open. He never slept with it shut because he wanted to be able to hear his grandfather if he called out in the middle of the night.

But now it just sat there open. Taunting her. Nothing but night shadows on the other side, beckoning her to the dark side. She willed him to appear in the doorway but of course he didn't.

He wasn't coming for her.

Of course he wasn't coming for her.

If she wanted to have a night of passion with Reid then she was going to have to make the first move because he was too honourable to do so himself. He'd told her he would never take advantage of the situation and she'd learned enough about him these past weeks to know that he wouldn't break that promise, no matter how much he might have wanted to kiss her earlier.

Trinity stared at the door, her heart racing, torn between the needs of her body and the dictates of her head. It had been five years—*longer*—since she'd been with a man. Given herself up to sexual pleasure. Well, apart from a spot of dry humping with Reid.

She flushed at the memory even as her body tingled from top to toe. One thing she knew for sure: she was never going to be able to sleep like this and she didn't want to lie in bed tossing and turning all night, aware of the ache between her legs and him just down the hallway.

Not even a session of self-love to take the edge off appealed. Her body burned for one person only. Her fingers just weren't going to cut it.

She sighed. Lying horizontal in a bed was not going to take her mind off what her body craved. If anything it was going to keep reminding her of what she couldn't have. She needed a distraction. So, she was going to take her book— a hard-core science-fiction tome—go downstairs, make a cup of tea and read it in the living room until she fell asleep.

Problem solved.

The moon had risen in the hours Trinity had lain in bed and milky moonlight flooded into the kitchen through the large bay window. It spilled over the central bench and the floor, turning the already white kitchen candescent. She stood at the sink, glass of water in hand as she waited for the jug to boil, staring out of the window, soaking up the moonbeams.

It was so beautiful she had a mad urge to strip off her clothes and run around in it.

Yeah, just what Reid needed. *Not.* A crazy, pagan woman

running around his back yard in the nuddy. She really had to do something about her horniness or she'd be howling at the moon next.

Another thump behind her dragged her gaze from the window. Damn cat.

Except it wasn't the cat.

It was Reid. In nothing but boxer shorts. The sexy kind that clung to *everything*. As if her hormone-crazed brain needed any more stimulus.

He was standing beyond the line of moonlight but she could still make out the dark outline of his tats and his beard. Not to mention his shoulders, hips and quads.

The contours of his boxers too.

Trinity clenched the sink behind her. And her legs together as everything inside her dropped about a foot. Her pulse tripped as if she'd taken a little something other than the desperation of five years of celibacy.

Like cocaine.

'Reid?' Her voice was almost a squeak and she cleared it.

'Oh…sorry.' The apology rumbled out. 'I couldn't sleep.'

'Me either,' she said, her voice several octaves lower now, more husky than squeaky.

His eyes were hooded in shadow but she could *feel* his gaze eating her up. She was in her tatty old T-shirt that was too big for her and had a hole in the sleeve. It was about as sexy as a sack.

'I was just coming to get a drink.'

The way he said it left Trinity in no doubt that he hadn't been heading to the kitchen for a cup of tea. More like beer.

'You want one?' he asked as he strode out of the shadows into the full blaze of moonlight. It bathed his body to perfection, delineating every dip, line and contour. Every tattoo. Every muscle group.

Trinity pushed through a temporary circuit failure in her brain. 'No… I'm just making tea.'

He didn't head for the fridge but for the high cupboards, reaching up effortlessly for something and placing it on the central bench.

A bottle of Jack. The big guns.

He opened the dishwasher that had finished its cycle hours ago and pulled out a glass that sparkled with diamond clarity in the alabaster light and *tinked* as it was placed on the bench top. He unscrewed, poured a slug into the glass, then threw his head back and downed it in one hit.

He didn't even wince.

'You sure you don't want one?'

Trinity shook her head, crossing to the bench where the boiled jug was waiting to be poured. She slid the glass of water onto the counter top and tipped hot water into the waiting mug, teabag already in situ.

'You going to read?' he asked, tipping his chin at her book that also sat on the bench top.

'Yes.'

A muscle worked in his jaw as he glanced from her to the book then back to her. His knuckles whitened where they gripped the edge of the bench and he looked as if he was about to say something else but he didn't, just poured himself another drink.

She crossed to the fridge as he downed that one too. She grabbed the milk and poured some into her cup, conscious of his gaze on her. It cranked every muscle in her body to attention.

'Reading helps put me to sleep when my mind is going round and round,' she said, needing to fill up the brooding silence in case she took leave of her senses and got grabby.

'Worried about Oscar?'

'A little.' Although God knew that was *not* what was keeping her awake.

'Reading doesn't help me sleep,' he said, his voice gruff.

'You've tried?'

'Army psychologist recommended it for post-nightmare management.'

Trinity slid her mug on the bench. She took a step closer. 'You have nightmares?' She supposed he must have seen some terrible things while in the military.

'Not a lot,' he dismissed, his tone terse, clearly not wanting to elaborate.

Trinity backed off. 'And the Scotch helps?'

'Usually.' He poured himself a third.

'Not tonight?'

'Apparently.' He swirled the liquid in the glass, watching it intently.

'So…' She turned sideways, her hip resting against the counter. 'Were nightmares keeping you up tonight?'

A short sharp laugh escaped his lips. 'Not nightmares.' He shook his head, still staring into his drink. 'Dreams.'

He glanced at her then, his gaze lasering into hers. 'You know the type?'

The timbre of his breathing roughened, becoming a tangible force. Caressing right between her legs. The caress became an ache, which morphed into a screaming demand.

The man had also been having sex dreams. She swallowed. 'Yes,' she said, her voice not much more than a husky whisper.

'God, Trinity,' he muttered, throwing the last drink down and hauling her close. 'I'm drowning here.'

Reid was insensible with need as his mouth took hers. He'd come to the kitchen for a drink or two to obliterate the nagging desire that constantly pulled at him, to stop himself from knocking on her door, to *do the right thing*.

Only to find temptation waiting for him in the moonlight in a baggy T-shirt, her hair long and loose.

She moaned against his mouth as his hands grabbed the backs of her thighs and hauled her up, settling her on the bench with her legs wide apart. Moving on autopilot, he stepped between them, his body knowing exactly where it needed to be. His crotch aligned perfectly with the heat at the juncture of her thighs as her ankles locked tight around his back telling him he was exactly where she needed him too.

God, yes, this. This was what he'd been craving.

Trinity.

His hands slid up her thighs under the loose T-shirt, around to her ass then up her back, rucking the shirt up as he went, exposing more and more of her to his view. His nostrils filled with the scent of her, her soap and shampoo and the earthier scent of her arousal. His ears reverberated with the pounding of his pulse and the frantic nonsensical noises coming from the back of her throat.

His hands moved around to cup her bare breasts and she cried out, breaking off their kiss, her head falling back as he brushed his thumbs over her nipples. He took her hands from his waist and laid them palm down on the counter top, sliding them back behind her, forcing her torso into a slight recline, presenting her breasts to him.

'Don't move,' he whispered, staring at them. Not too big, not too small, the rosy tips almost alabaster in the moon's glow.

He ducked to nuzzle one, swirling his tongue around it, knowing the whiskers of his beard would also be prickling against the sensitive flesh. She gasped and he repeated the process on the other side before sucking it deep into the hot cavern of his mouth.

She moaned and arched her back and it went straight to Reid's groin. *'Reid.'*

He taunted it, stretching it with his teeth and tongue as far as it would go before it slipped from his mouth. 'They're perfect,' he muttered. 'You're perfect,' before seeking the other one.

Reid couldn't get enough. Of her nipples. Or the way she arched into his mouth, her hair almost brushing against the bench top every time, or the increasingly desperate noises Trinity made at the back of her throat.

Knowing that he was getting her so damn hot was intoxicating.

He was so lost in the pleasure of it he didn't realised she'd manoeuvred herself more upright until her fingers breached the band of his underwear. They slid onto the taut flesh of his erection, wrapping around him, squeezing and sliding up and down.

He groaned, his mouth leaving her nipples to press his forehead against hers. *'God, yes.'*

He shut his eyes as pleasure rolled through him from his thighs to his buttocks. To the sling of muscles deep inside his pelvis to his abdominals. It moved in one long, luxurious undulation that weakened his knees as well as his resistance. The urge to find release between her thighs, slake his unruly desire for her, ran hot and insistent through his veins.

And then an almighty smash stopped them in their tracks.

His brain still fogged, Reid glanced over to find Ginger, sitting on the bench where Trinity's glass of water had been seconds before.

'Miaow.'

His heart thundered in his chest as he glanced at Trinity like a siren in the moonlight, her shirt rucked up, her chest rising and falling fast, beard burn marking her breasts and throat, her eyes glazed…

What the *hell* was he doing? What about being platonic? And friendship?

What about not crossing that line?

'God…' He shoved a hand through his hair, sucking

in air, trying to regulate his breathing. 'We shouldn't be doing this.'

He yanked her shirt down, stuffed his erection back in his pants and took a step back. Then another, holding his hands up and away from his body. And hers. Not worried about broken glass. Just their predicament.

She stared at him, her tongue darting out to wet her lips. 'Right.' Although she didn't sound convinced.

'We agreed to be platonic.'

'Yes.' She nodded. 'But.'

The but didn't need anything added to it. He knew what it meant. *But look at us anyway,* not *being platonic.*

God, he was too keyed up for this. Too horny. Too close to the edge.

'Do you think we can talk about it in the morning?'

Maybe in the morning he wouldn't feel so much like pushing her down on the cold stone bench top and burying his head between her legs until she screamed his name. He was one yank of his underwear from penetration and he needed some distance.

'Okay.' She glanced at the smashed glass.

'I'll take care of it,' he assured her hastily.

She looked at him for long moments, the confusion on her face rather unhelpfully spotlighted by the moon, before finally swinging her legs around the other side of the bench, away from the broken glass, and sliding off. He watched her until she disappeared into the shadows.

If he'd thought her leaving would make him feel better, he was sadly mistaken.

CHAPTER FOURTEEN

THEY DIDN'T TALK about it the next morning, or the next day or the next, or the next. And now it was Thursday and Trinity was sitting waiting for Eddie's physio appointment to finish, being ignored by Reid, who did not have a patient but was squirrelled away in his office anyway. She could see him through the window that faced the central rehab area.

Trinity had tried to talk to Reid about it on Sunday but he'd dismissed her attempts irritably and had pretty much been irritable ever since.

With her anyway.

He was obviously regretting his slip in judgement big time. Because he'd stepped over the line he'd told her he wasn't going to step again and Reid was a man of his word. But that could have easily been addressed on Sunday.

So it had to be more.

Like maybe he just didn't fancy her. Sure, he was *attracted* to her but was it because of *her* or because she was a woman and he was a man and they were in close proximity?

A person didn't have to like another person to have sex with them, after all. Her parents were a classic example of that.

She'd thought his talk about dreams had referred to her but maybe he'd been dreaming about someone else and she'd just been a convenient body to slake his thirst and then the glass had smashed and he'd suddenly realised *who* he was with.

The thought hurt. More than it should have. But she should have known that a guy like Reid couldn't possibly be into a woman like her.

'Hey, Trinity. Now aren't you a sight for sore eyes.'

She glanced up from her magazine to find Chase beaming down at her. His smile was a balm to her ravaged ego and she beamed right back.

At least someone was into her.

'Hey,' she said as he lowered himself into the hard plastic chair beside her, his high-tech prosthetic leg almost completely bared in his workout shorts. 'You're here for your session?'

'Nah, I only came to flirt with you. But don't tell Reid. He can be a grumpy bastard when he wants to be.'

Trinity laughed. *Wasn't that the truth?* She caught a movement in her peripheral vision and glanced over. Reid was standing in his doorway, looking at her and Chase, his lips pursed, his brow furrowed, disapproval pouring off him in waves.

He didn't look like any kind of doctor in his jeans and dark T-shirt, his arm tats on full display. Not even the stethoscope slung casually around his neck helped. He just looked like a…lumberjack with a stethoscope.

Which was seriously freaking hot. *Damn him.*

'Shouldn't you be hitting the machines?' Reid said, folding his arms.

'All in good time.' Chase winked at her and Trinity stifled another laugh.

Reid stiffened. 'We have three people arriving in half an hour. If you don't get on now you'll miss out.'

He turned and stalked back into his room. Chase whistled. 'Who put a bug up his ass?'

'I have no idea.'

Except she did. And it couldn't go on. She made a mental note to contact some local real-estate agents this week. Might as well get the ball rolling.

'Well—' Chase stood '—I'd better get on before he gives me a yellow card.'

He smiled at Trinity, not looking remotely concerned about any consequences Reid might dish out. She glanced in the direction of Reid's office, catching him looking at her, before he returned his attention to his computer.

Well, screw him.

He couldn't reject her and then be annoyed that some other guy was interested. She left the magazine on the chair beside her and wandered over to Chase, who was starting his warm up.

She could feel the burn of Reid's gaze in the centre of her back as she sat on the floor beside Chase and chatted. In fact she relished it. It was utterly childish but it felt damn good.

Chase wasn't fooled though. 'So I'm guessing you're over here with me to make Reid jealous. Am I right?'

Trinity blinked at his directness. But Chase didn't seem perturbed by the prospect. 'Jealous? No.' *Absolutely not.* 'To piss him off, yes.'

Chase laughed a wicked laugh. 'That works for me.'

Trinity was in the kitchen making a banana cake when Reid came home. She tensed as she glanced at the clock— ten past two. His footsteps diverted to the living room and she heard the rumble of two male voices for a couple of minutes.

Then he appeared in the kitchen.

He hesitated for a moment when he spotted her at the bench before nodding and crossing to the fridge. He pulled out a beer, twisted the top and tossed it into the sink from where he stood.

It landed with a clink.

He tipped his head back and took several long swallows. It took all Trinity's willpower to keep her eyes on the job at hand and not feast her gaze on his neck.

'You do know Chase flirts with every woman with a pulse, right?'

The sentence came from out of the blue. She'd been in a good mood since returning from Allura. But Reid seemed hell-bent on ruining that too.

'Gee thanks,' she said, her voice dripping with sarcasm as a spike of temper infected her bloodstream. 'You sure know how to make a girl feel *real* special.'

'Oh, for—' He bit off whatever expletive he'd been about to utter. 'I just meant you should be careful. The guy wouldn't know monogamy if it bit him on the ass.'

'Who says I'm after monogamy?'

He blinked, clearly taken aback. *Good.* A slightly crazed sensation pushed at the inside of her skull as an urge to let fly took hold. She'd learned not to argue over the years. Not to rock the boat. To grind her teeth and quietly submit.

But, he was really starting to annoy her now.

'I would have thought being a single mum and having to think about Oscar—'

'*Don't* bring Oscar into this.'

'I'm just saying,' Reid pushed, obviously not going to let it drop. 'He's not daddy material.'

'I'm not going to marry the man,' Trinity said, letting the spoon fall to the bench with a loud clatter as she crossed to the pantry and opened the doors.

She searched the shelves for vanilla. She knew it was in here because Reid used it to make French toast on the weekends.

God, she'd never be able to eat French toast again without thinking of him in this kitchen, beating eggs and flipping bread fried to a perfect golden brown.

Her anger cranked up another notch.

She glanced over her shoulder. Reid was glowering at her and it frustrated her even more.

'Maybe I just want a quick tumble,' she said, her cheeks burning, her pulse throbbing wildly at her temples. 'A few hours of *goddamn* pleasure. You ever thought of that?'

She turned back to stare blindly at the shelves.

Where was the bloody vanilla?

'Seeing as how *you* don't fancy me,' she said, not bothering to turn this time because his rejection of her still stung, 'why shouldn't I look somewhere else?'

'Don't *fancy* you?' His voice was deep and dark, brimming with annoyance.

Before she could blink his hands were on her shoulders and she was spun around and pushed hard against the pantry door. His face loomed up close, white-hot flame burning in the blue eyes that raked her face. His breathing was husky, his chest heaving.

'I can't get you out of my head,' he muttered, each word puffing his breath in her face, disturbing her fringe. 'If you had any idea how much I wanted to rip your underwear off *with my teeth* the other night you'd run screaming from this house.'

Trinity's heart rate skyrocketed as his grip on her upper arms tightened and his lips slammed onto hers.

It was a kiss that took. That ruled. That owned.

Possessive. Demanding. His tongue thrusting into her mouth, taking the kiss deeper. The graze of his beard marked her face, prickling *everywhere*.

She felt it *everywhere*.

She was a slave to the sensation. A slave to the onslaught.

His thigh jammed between her legs, high and hard, grinding against the apex of her thighs. She moaned as her aching flesh revelled in the delicious torture, rubbing herself shamelessly against him.

But as quickly as it had started, it was over. His mouth was gone. The kiss was done. His hands still gripped her arms though, his thigh still jammed between her legs.

They stared at each other for long moments, nothing but ragged breathing between them. His mouth was wet and swollen, the white-hot flame in his gaze burning brighter. He grabbed her hand and shoved it on the hard bulge pressing against the zipper of his bike leathers.

'This is *not*,' he whispered, 'about me not fancying you.'

He let her go abruptly and stormed out of the room.

Trinity's legs wobbled for a beat or two before they lost the ability to keep her upright and she slid down the pantry door to the floor, her fingers pressed to her mouth, her mind wiped of coherent thought.

As dramatic as the kiss had been, it seemed to have cleared the air between them a little. At least they both knew where they stood. He *did* fancy her. And she fancied him. They were attracted to one another.

But that was as far as it was going to go.

He hadn't articulated that part exactly but the things he *hadn't* said were just as potent as what he had.

Strangely enough, despite her level of sexual frustration, Trinity was okay with that. Knowing Reid fancied her had done wonders for her ego even if she struggled to wrap her head around the why of it.

Knowing he wasn't going to act on it was something she could live with.

Reid was trying hard to do the right thing. The guy had a strong sense of ethics, which wasn't something she'd seen in a lot of men. Frankly, it was admirable as hell.

And what was one more thing she couldn't have?

It didn't mean she didn't want to get out of Reid's house as soon as possible though. She had enough money saved to start looking for somewhere to live and moving out was probably best all round.

Denial was easier when temptation wasn't staring you in the face day in, day out.

But, as Trinity soon discovered, it wasn't going to be as easy as she'd thought. It seemed late November through December was a busy time of year. Everyone wanted to be in new rentals by Christmas and real-estate agents had nothing on their books—nothing she could reasonably afford anyway that was within a ten-kilometre radius of the hospital because that was non-negotiable.

She'd seen Oscar deteriorate too quickly to be blasé about their address.

About a dozen realtors today had told her that she probably wouldn't get anything now until the new year. She was on a wait list with them but she didn't hold out much hope.

'Damn it,' she swore at the phone as she hung up from yet another *Sorry, try us in January* response.

'Problem?'

Trinity looked over her shoulder, her pulse doing its usual tap dance at Reid's voice. He was in the office doorway, taking up all the space as he shrugged out of his jacket, his T-shirt pulling taut across his abs.

'Apparently trying to get a place to rent in December is like trying to find the pot of gold at the end of the rainbow.' She turned back to the desk and scrubbed another realtor off the list. 'I've been getting no room at the inn for two whole days now.'

'I…didn't realise you were planning on leaving so soon.'

She heard the frown in his voice and sensed him approaching. He sat on the chair positioned beside the desk so she couldn't not look at him. 'I have enough saved up, thanks to you, and I'd hoped to be in our own place by Christmas. Our *first* Christmas in a place that's just ours. Oscar's never had that.'

He nodded. 'That's fair enough. But you know you're more than welcome to stay on here. Pops and I do a pretty mean Christmas. He loves buying the biggest tree and stuffing presents under it. He's like a big kid. And we ignore the fact it's forty degrees outside and have the full turkey and pudding with all the trimmings. Pops would love to have you both here.'

Pops? What about him?

'I would too.'

His smile was genuine and Trinity had to admit it sounded like nirvana. The only Christmas lunch they'd had in the last five years that hadn't been in hospital had been at a soup kitchen. 'Yes, but I'm reliably informed it'll probably be January before more rentals become available.'

'So?' He shrugged and it stretched out the confines of his T-shirt. 'Stay till January.'

It seemed so simple. So straightforward. But they'd impinged on Reid's hospitality long enough. And then there was the elephant in the room. 'It sounds great but…it's probably for the best if we move as soon as possible, don't you think?'

The gaze that met hers was frank. It was the first time either had made reference to their attraction and he didn't bother to pretend he didn't know what she was talking about.

'I'm sure we can both survive each other's company until the new year,' he said with a dry twist in his tone. 'And think how much better off your financial position would be by then.'

Trinity had to admit he made a good point. About her finances. She wasn't entirely sure about the other. The urge to straddle him right now, feel the soft leather of his bike pants against her inner thighs, feel him driving into her, was so strong she returned her attention to the computer.

'Look, I assume you're on some kind of wait list with some agencies?'

'Yes.'

'Well, if something comes up then take it. Pops and I will help you move. If not, stay here with us. It's absolutely fine. No pressure either way, okay?'

If anybody had told her the first time she'd clapped eyes on Reid that this big, bearded, tattooed lumberjack of a guy was good and kind and decent, she wouldn't have believed it. But he'd proved her wrong at every turn.

She glanced at him. 'Okay. Thank you.'

He gave a brief nod of acknowledgement then hauled himself out of the chair and out of reach.

The first of December arrived. It was hot and sticky, a storm was brewing but Eddie, Reid and Oscar paid that no heed as they went out and bought the biggest Christmas tree they could find.

They'd picked him up from school and taken him to a farm on the outskirts of the city where they sold fresh trees. It was a male bonding experience, Reid had insisted in a big gruff lumberjack voice, which had made Oscar laugh and Trinity go a little weak below her belly button.

The fact Reid looked as if he spent all day chopping down trees with a giant axe only added to the weakness.

The guys walked through the door at six in the evening with the biggest tree Trinity had ever seen in her life. It stood a foot higher than Reid—at least.

'I picked it, Mummy,' Oscar announced, his chest puffing out as Trinity wondered how in hell they were going to get it through the door.

They managed and it fitted perfectly in the living room with its raked ceiling.

'Can we decorate it now?'

Oscar hopped from foot to foot, utterly beside himself

with excitement. 'Sure thing, little dude,' Reid said and they fist-bumped. 'You'll need to give me a hand with the lights first though. They have to go on before everything else.'

'I'll get the music,' Eddie volunteered.

Bing Crosby crooned from the sound system as the tree took shape from plain green foliage to a sparkly, tinselled, beribboned, glorious mishmash.

Oscar had been given the responsibility of decorating all the lower branches to where he could reach and Trinity and Reid had decorated the top branches. The tree was, consequently, a little unbalanced. Trinity had tried to subtly encourage Oscar to spread things out and stop him from using *all* the ornaments.

It wasn't, after all, *their* tree.

But Eddie had said, 'Nonsense,' and knelt down to help Oscar pile on some more.

Trinity was sure window decorators all around the world were probably dropping into dead faints but she'd never seen anything more messily beautiful than this tree.

'And now, young sir,' Eddie said, pulling a star out of a battered box. It looked crazed with age and fragile. 'My wife and I bought this on our honeymoon at the Christmas markets in Vienna over fifty years ago. Would you like to do the honour?'

Oscar stared at the huge golden ornament with wonder. 'Yes, please,' he said on a reverent whisper.

'Here, little dude.' Reid picked him up and hoisted Oscar onto his shoulders, his skinny little legs either side of Reid's neck. He took the star from Eddie then handed it up to Oscar.

'Be very careful,' Trinity murmured, her heart in her mouth as she watched in trepidation the fragile family heirloom change hands.

'There you go,' Reid said as he stood close to the tree and tipped forward slightly. 'Put it on top, there.'

Trinity's chest just about exploded at the picture before

her. Oscar, his face serious, his tongue sticking out of the side of his mouth in concentration. Reid, one hand on Oscar's back, the other on a thigh, holding him firmly, his confidence that her son was capable of the honour sitting Oscar a little taller.

They looked good together. Like father and son. Her heart squeezed painfully. This was the kind of life Oscar deserved. Bing Crosby singing carols. Heirlooms.

Family.

'Merry Christmas, Mummy,' Oscar said.

Trinity blinked out of her reverie to find Oscar and Reid facing her. His hands hung on around Reid's neck now, one little finger absently stroking the scratchiness of Reid's beard.

'Merry Christmas, Oscar,' she said, her heart filled to bursting.

'Thank you,' she mouthed to Reid.

He smiled and set Oscar down.

CHAPTER FIFTEEN

TWO WEEKS LATER, with no word from an agency, Trinity had resigned herself to waiting until the new year to find a place to live. But that was moot right now as she sat in Oscar's school hall with Reid and Eddie, watching Oscar's class perform 'Jingle Bells' at the Christmas concert.

School would be over in a few days but for now the students were singing their little hearts out. The hall had been decorated in tinsel and fairy lights and all the classes would be performing tonight.

Trinity was hyperaware of Reid sitting next to her. They were sitting on plastic chairs jammed close together so they were shoulder to shoulder, thigh to thigh. They might not have been had he not been so big and broad, but he was and they were. The heat of his leg through the thin fabric of her Christmas dress was *very* distracting.

Yes. A dress. She'd seen it in the local op shop window and had decided, for the first time in a long time, to splurge on something for *her*. It had been brand new, the label still attached, but had only cost ten dollars. It was red with shoestring straps, a sweetheart neckline, fitted bodice and an A-line skirt that swished around her thighs. It came to just below her knee, and encircling the hem was a cherry and holly leaves motif.

It had been love at first sight.

She'd even gone to a hair salon known for its budget prices and had a good couple of inches chopped off as well as some layers cut in around her face. The woman had even used the hair straightener to add some curls.

Between the dress and the hair she'd spent fifty dollars but she felt like a freaking princess.

A guilty twinge about spending money on herself had spoilt things a little but she had quite a nest egg now and she knew the other parents would be dressing up tonight. She didn't want to wear something ill-fitting and old. She didn't want to look poor.

She didn't want to *embarrass* Oscar either.

Or that was what she'd told herself. The fact that Reid had done a double take and stared at her when she'd come down the stairs had been a bonus.

'Doesn't Mummy look pretty, Reid?' Oscar had said.

And he'd looked at her glossed-up mouth as he had that day he'd kissed her in the pantry and said, 'She does indeed, little dude.'

Butterflies fluttered in her belly just thinking about it now.

The song came to an end and the applause was instantaneous. Oscar grinned at her from the stage, wiping a hand across his runny nose. Other parents might have been embarrassed by the action but it caused a much more visceral reaction in Trinity.

Ever since it had started a few days ago, she'd been on edge about it. Waiting for the roller coaster to begin. For the fever to start, for the lethargy to set in. Poised to whisk him off to hospital at the first sign of his condition worsening.

She'd checked on him half a dozen times the last few nights. Oscar had decided last week that he *did* want his own room. Because Raymond had one. But with the development of this sniffle she wished he were still in with her.

He'd been fine though—so far. No temps or malaise. No

croaky voice or cough or wheeze. No telling her he didn't feel well. Just a clear runny nose that hadn't seemed to bother him in the least.

Normally he would have crashed into a heap by now. But he'd been bright-eyed and bushy-tailed. Energetic and bubbly, excited about Christmas and having some play dates with Raymond over the holidays.

Trinity had begun to hope that he was over the worst of his prematurity and his lungs were now big enough and strong enough to cope with a sniffle or two.

That truly would be a Christmas miracle.

Two hours later they were home after the concert and Reid was banging a nail into the front door to hang the wreath Oscar had made at school. It looked cheap and childish amongst the posh neighbourhood wreaths but Reid treated it as if it had been bought from Harrods.

'That,' Reid proclaimed, standing back to admire Oscar's creation, 'is the most awesome wreath I have seen. Best in the street, don't you reckon, Pops?'

Eddie nodded. 'The best ever.'

Oscar stood a foot taller and Trinity wanted to cry. These two guys were so *good* for him. Something, somewhere had been smiling on her the day she'd run off those thugs.

'Okay.' She clapped her hands. 'Time for bed.'

Trinity expected resistance. She didn't think Oscar would—*could*—go to sleep after all the excitement. He'd been on such a high all day. But he went happily and was out like a light as soon as his head hit the pillow. She smiled, snapping off his lamp and kissing his forehead.

A prickle of anxiety needled her at its warmth but she gave herself a shake. It was warm. *Not* hot. Not *feverish*.

He was fine.

And the fact she had a doctor in the house was even more reassuring.

She paused at his door for one last look before leaving

it slightly ajar and went downstairs. She made three cups of coffee, one each for Reid and Eddie, who were watching *Carols by Candlelight* on the television, and one for her, which she took outside to her favourite spot—the love seat.

Trinity swung idly, a smile on her lips, her thoughts full of the concert and Oscar's delight at being involved. It was as tranquil as ever out here. The night filled with the promise of Christmas. That intangible change in the atmosphere that infected everything and everyone as the big day approached.

She hummed 'Jingle Bells' to herself and smiled some more.

She didn't know how long she sat outside. A long time. The night was gorgeous and it seemed fitting to be out here thanking her lucky stars for the position she was in right now. Plus, she didn't want to take her dress off just yet. It was so nice to feel *female* for a night, she was loath to bring it to an end.

There was also a vague churn of restlessness inside her. The heat in Reid's gaze tonight had been unsettling, stirring up things she'd been trying to suppress. There was no way her body was in a state to sleep just yet.

At some stage the television noises cut out and a minute later the back door was sliding open.

'I thought I'd find you out here.' His low voice carried to her easily on the night.

Goose bumps swept from her nape all the way down her spine. The churn kicked up a notch. The swing rocked as he sat beside her, closer than he usually did. It was still a respectable distance away but her body was so in tune to him.

The churn went into overdrive.

He was still in the trousers and dress shirt he'd worn to the concert, his hair slicked back with some kind of product rather than just pushed messily back off his forehead. She'd never seen him so formal. But even all dressed up, wearing the same kind of clothes as the other men at the concert tonight, there was still something...*untamed* about him.

Maybe it was the beard. Maybe it was the tats beneath that very respectable shirt. Maybe it was those lumberjack shoulders testing the limits of the seams.

Whatever it was, she hadn't been the only one who'd noticed. He'd turned heads.

'That was a great night,' he said, taking over the motion of the swing with his foot.

She glanced at him and smiled. 'Yes,' she murmured before turning back to contemplate the night again. They sat in companionable silence for a few moments.

'You look beautiful tonight.'

Trinity blinked, startled at his husky compliment. Her pulse quickened. No one had ever called her beautiful. Not even Bri. He'd told her she was cute and had used words like *mighty fine*. But never beautiful. It seemed like a much deeper compliment. More measured. More meaningful.

The kind of compliment a *man* would give.

'Oh...thank you.' She swallowed, suddenly conscious of the lip gloss she'd slicked on and the curls in her hair. 'You don't scrub up too badly yourself.'

She'd kept her voice light, his low chuckle feathering down her arms.

'That's a great outfit you're wearing.'

Trinity glanced down at herself. 'It's just a dress.'

'*That* is not just a dress.' His eyes raked over her, taking in her hair and her cleavage and the fall of the fabric over her legs. Everything tingled in their wake. 'That's like... a walking advert for Christmas. Red looks good on you.'

His compliments were going to her head. And other parts of her body. Warmth stole into her cheeks. Heat flared between her legs.

'You should wear more clothes like that.'

This conversation was dicing pretty close to the wind

as far as their attraction went but Trinity didn't seem to be able to help herself around him.

And he'd started it.

'Like what? Dresses?'

'No, I mean things that aren't two sizes too big for you or hang like a sack.'

'I don't deliberately buy them like that,' she said waspishly. 'I've had most of my clothes a long time and I've lost weight in the last five years. I haven't been able to afford to buy new ones so I've just…made do.'

'How much weight?'

The question was fired back at her, a wrinkle drawing his brows together. Obviously it had come from Reid the doctor.

'A couple of dress sizes.'

He nodded, thoughtful for a moment. 'You don't splash out on yourself much, do you?'

Trinity fingered the dress. 'This is it.'

'Well, you should never take it off,' he said, a grin on his face and in his voice as he dragged his eyes off her. 'It's your turn now to say how a respectable doctor should be wearing more of these kinds of clothes.' He pulled at his shirt with a disdainful curl to his lips.

'Fishing for compliments?' she teased. Her breath hitching at how easy he was to tease.

'Maybe.'

Trinity shook her head. The urge to stroke the front of his shirt, to feel the fabric and the muscles beneath, was surprisingly strong. 'I like what you wear.'

He turned his head to look at her, clearly surprised at her admission. 'Do you, now?'

It was on the tip of Trinity's tongue to say, *Especially when you're mowing*, but she dragged her gaze away, returning her attention to the stars, not willing to give too much away.

They lapsed into silence again. Nothing but the squeak of the swing between them.

'Did you see that kid tonight in the back row pick his nose during "Silent Night"?'

Trinity pressed her lips together to stop the threatening laughter. 'Yes.'

He didn't bother to suppress it. He laughed into the night, deep and throaty, and she joined him. She'd felt a shudder of silent laughter ripple through Reid's shoulders at the time and had bit her own cheek to stop from doing likewise but neither of them felt similarly constrained now.

In fact Trinity laughed so hard she almost had tears running down her face.

When their laughter slowly faded they were half turned towards each other and Reid said, 'Oscar was brilliant though.'

She nodded. 'Yes. He was.' Without any thought she reached her hand across and squeezed his arm. The muscle tensed beneath her touch and she quickly withdrew.

'Thank you,' she said, ignoring the hammer of her heartbeat to say what had to be said. 'Just...*thank you*...from the bottom of my heart. For you and Eddie coming tonight and for hanging the wreath.' She shook her head, overwhelmed by Reid's generosity. 'I'm just so—'

The swift, hot press of his mouth cut her off. It stole her breath and robbed her brain of any thought other than *yes*.

And *more*.

He kept it brief though, withdrawing as quickly as he had lunged, causing her to almost pitch forward at the abrupt disconnect. She blinked at him, her mouth tingling, her lungs burning as if she'd just run a hundred metres in under ten seconds.

'Sorry.' He grimaced. 'I've wanted to do that ever since you walked down the stairs tonight wearing that lip gloss.'

Trinity blinked. 'Oh.' She drew in a shaky breath. 'So… we're disregarding the line tonight?'

'Goddamn it,' he muttered, *thunking* his head back against the seat cushion, his gaze fixed on the stars. 'I hate that line. I swear trying to do the right thing is *killing* me.'

The crazy low rumble of his voice scraped along her nerve endings. She couldn't believe what he was saying.

'It doesn't matter what I do or what I tell myself, I can't stop thinking about you and then I go to bed and, *God…*' He groaned and rolled his head along the cushion to face her. 'I dream about you. These…erotic dreams that wake me in the middle of the night and I'm so hard for you and then you wear this dress tonight and I swear I'm going to go to hell for kissing you just now but—'

It was Trinity's turn to kiss him, to cut him off, to feel the prick of his beard and taste the coffee on his breath.

He wanted her. He dreamed about her. He couldn't stop thinking about her. If he was going to hell then she was going along for the ride.

She didn't know what that meant for them long term; she didn't care. She needed this tonight. They both did.

Without any coherent thought she was turning, twisting, sliding a leg over his lap, sending the love seat into a rocking frenzy as she grabbed his shoulders and straddled him.

He groaned and muttered, *'Trinity,'* against her mouth as her dress flared out over his lap and his hands found the smooth bare skin of her ass.

Trinity ploughed her fingers into his hair as he squeezed her cheeks and everything inside her clenched tight. She was so hot, so wet, so needy.

So ready.

Her underwear met the zip of his trousers and the bulge beneath and she moaned—*loud*—her head falling back, the kiss abandoned to the pleasure of rubbing her aching flesh in just the right spot.

'Okay,' he said, his lips at her neck, his beard scratching *so damn good* at the sensitive hollows. 'I think we need to move this inside because I'm about to relieve you of this dress and the neighbours might get a show they hadn't bargained for.'

There was a smile in his voice as he ground against her and Trinity gasped at how good it felt.

'I thought you said I should never take it off.'

'I lied.'

Then he picked her up, still straddling him, and strode into the house.

CHAPTER SIXTEEN

FIVE MINUTES LATER Trinity found Reid in his bedroom, lamplight bathing him in a soft glow. She'd checked on Oscar and now here she was. He was barefoot and had undone the buttons of his shirt and the top button of his trousers but had taken neither of them off.

How could a partially dressed man be just as sexy as a completely naked one?

She glimpsed the tats that ran under the ridge of his collarbones and was looking forward to exploring them all.

Later…

'Take off your dress.'

His bold command was as visceral as if he'd stroked his hand along her belly. He hadn't moved. He hadn't come nearer or tried to touch her but it *felt* like it.

Quickly, hands trembling behind her, she unzipped. The shoestring straps fell off her shoulders and in one shrug the dress had pooled around her feet. She wasn't wearing a bra. All that stood between her and naked was faded pink underwear.

'My God…' he muttered under his breath, the air hissing out of his lungs as his gaze fell to her bare breasts.

'Take off your shirt.'

Her request was tremulous with desire, far less steady than his had been. But he stopped her breath as she watched him strip out of it. She feasted her eyes on the acres of tanned and tatted flesh before her just as he was feasting his eyes on her.

She admired the musculature *and* the art, her heart belting along as his gaze roamed over every inch of her body.

Her nipples puckered tight as he stared at them as if they were his own personal toys.

Trinity didn't know who was supposed to make the first move now. She didn't care either. She only cared about his skin on hers. His mouth on hers. The bulge behind his zipper filling her up.

Enough looking. She needed touching.

She needed it *now*.

She stumbled towards him as if on autopilot. They met somewhere in the middle, at the foot of his bed, her calf brushing the edge of the mattress. She twined her arms around his neck, rising up on tiptoe, her breasts brushing his chest as she sought his mouth, whimpering when she found it, moaning when their lips clashed and clung and opened.

She kissed him deep and hard and wet. She kissed him fast. She kissed him thorough. She kissed him all the ways she knew and all the ways she'd never known. Pressing herself to him, forgetting to breathe, forgetting to think.

'Slow down,' he whispered, against her lips. 'We've got all night.'

But she didn't want to wait all night. She didn't want to wait another *second*. She wanted him inside her. She *needed* him inside her.

Her knee slid onto the bed and she half pulled, half dragged him down to the mattress with her, groping for his fly, desperate to hold him in her hand again, to guide him to where she needed him most.

His lips buzzed her neck, his beard prickling, beading her nipples to unbearable tightness as her hand found the zipper and yanked. Her pulse was like a freight train in her head as she reached inside, her hand finding exactly what she needed.

He was full and thick and Trinity gripped him—hard—stroking up and down the length of him. He was like forged steel wrapped in rose petals and he groaned, deep and low, his forehead jammed to her temple as she kept up the pace.

But she was too damn restricted to do what she really wanted to do. Too many clothes. 'Off,' she said, panting in his ear as she used her spare hand to push at the waistband of his trousers where they covered his ass. 'Take your pants off.'

He didn't argue, just rolled on his back and wriggled out of the offending articles. Trinity watched, her gaze glued to the jut of his erection—thick and perfect. And then he was back, looming over her on all fours, his hair wild, his tattoos framing him perfectly. He slid an arm under her body and scooped her up the bed until they were fully on the mattress, yanking her underwear off and stripping them down her legs in one easy move.

He sat back on his haunches admiring what he saw. She wasn't embarrassed by such a thorough inspection; she was beyond that, his heated gaze only cranking her fever higher. He looked at her as if he wanted to devour every inch of her and couldn't decide where to start.

She knew where *she* wanted to start. His erection sprang from the nest of hair between his legs, proud and potent. She levered herself up on her elbows, reached for the hard jut of him, but he caught her hand, kissed it, shook his head. 'Patience,' he murmured.

Trinity fell back against the mattress, her hair flying as frustration burned through her veins like sulphur. Her breasts jiggled with the movement and Reid's gaze zeroed in on them. A light that was almost feral, totally befitting his lumberjack masculinity, flared in his eyes and he was on her, his head dipping to claim one nipple as his hand slid onto the other.

'Oh… God…' She moaned, arched her back, ploughed her hand into his hair as he settled his body against the mattress, his tongue repeatedly flicking back and forth over the hard nub.

She felt a corresponding twinge in the hard nub between her legs as if his tongue were down there, flicking back and forth. Down where she needed him to be. Where it roared and ached.

Where she wanted the hard, thick length of him to fill and stretch and burn. To rock and pound. To drive her into the bed until she clamped tight around him. To remind her she was a *woman*.

In the most base way possible.

She needed that.

'Reid,' she muttered, dragging all the discombobulated parts of herself together, pulling at his hair, dragging him off. 'I need you *inside* me.'

His mouth was wet from the havoc he'd been creating. 'All in good time,' he muttered, his head dipping again to reclaim a nipple begging for the hot suck of his mouth and the delicious burn of his beard.

Trinity forced herself to calm, to breathe, to slow down. To let him have it his way, to let him explore. But her pulse would not be slowed, nor would the tremble in her hands or the deeper tremble in her body.

It was seismic. And not willing to be ignored.

Screw it. *The time was now.*

She yanked on his hair. *Hard.* He didn't even wince; there was too much lumberjack about him for that. If anything a flare of something lit his eyes as if maybe he'd enjoyed it.

A corresponding flare lit deep in her body.

'Now.' Her gaze locked with his, her breath ragged. 'I swear to God, Reid, I need you in me now.'

He didn't say anything for long moments, his gaze searching hers. Then he reached over her to his bedside table, yanking out the drawer, and pulled out a foil packet.

Tearing it quickly with his teeth, he had himself sheathed in five seconds flat before he loomed over her, supporting himself on his forearms as he settled between her legs. She opened for him, her heart hammering, her breath chugging in and out.

She wanted it *so* bad.

He flexed his hips and she cried out at the fullness of that first thick nudge. 'Are you okay?' he asked, easing back the pressure.

He was big, she knew that from what she'd already seen of him and how he'd filled her hand, and she was out of practice but women *were* designed to stretch.

'God, yes,' she said, clamping her hand tight on his ass, shamelessly rotating her hips.

He slid all the way in then. Slow and steady and sure. A long low groan spilling from his throat as he eased in to the hilt. 'God,' he said, his voice a husky rumble, his forehead resting on hers. 'You feel good.'

Trinity let out a shaky breath, shifting against the mattress to better accommodate him. 'You feel *incredible*.'

He grunted something unintelligible as he withdrew—slowly, slowly—his forehead still planted on hers, then eased back in again just as slowly.

She tightened her hand on his ass. 'Faster.'

'No,' he said as he withdrew and entered again, so slow she could feel every wet inch of herself pulsing around every hard inch of him.

He did it a few more times, stoking the embers deep inside her pelvis, slowly breathing them to life. But they were out of kilter with the frenzy in her nerves and the fever in her blood. She didn't want embers, she wanted *flames*. 'Damn it, Reid, faster.'

'So bossy,' he chuckled as his hips delivered more torturously slow thrusts.

'Please,' she whispered, clamping down around him and pushing him out as he withdrew, expelling him faster.

She gasped and he groaned at the action, his forehead falling into the crook of her neck as he hunched into it more, adding an extra punch to entry right at the end as he reached her limit.

She moaned at the quick spasmodic jab. The coarse rasp of his beard at her throat intensified the sensation, streaking like a bolt of lightning between her legs.

But it still wasn't enough. *'Please.'*

He dragged his head off her neck, the liquid blue heat of his gaze locking with hers as he held himself buried deep inside her. The pressure was so intense she could barely breathe.

'You deserve a man to love you right, Trinity. To take it slow. To worship you. Let me do that.'

Crazy tears pricked at the backs of her eyes. Even in something so base and elemental as sex, Reid was looking out for her. It was sweet and kind. So at odds with his lumberjack physicality but so typical of the gentle man she'd come to know.

But she didn't want that. Not right *now*.

She didn't want slow and steady. She wanted it hard. She wanted it dirty. She wanted it to hurt *so damn good*. She wanted to feel the ache for days to come. She wanted to leave this bed having had her world thoroughly rocked.

To have a memory she could bring out in the future if things got tough again.

And she knew he could give that to her. She had no doubt

he could be a considerate and generous lover but she wanted the lumberjack she knew he was holding back. She could feel it in the tremble of his biceps and the hard clench of his glute beneath her hand.

'I'm not some fragile chick who needs kid gloves,' she said, her cheeks flushed, her pulse hammering at her temples and throbbing deep inside her where she gripped him. *'I'm tough.'*

He chuckled. 'You don't think I know that?'

'Then why are you treating me like I'm going to break?' she demanded. 'I don't want you to *worship* me, damn it. I want you to *possess* me.'

He stared at her for long moments. His gaze searching, assessing. She saw the moment his mind was made up, the sudden clarity followed by his swift withdrawal from her body.

She opened her mouth to protest but in the blink of an eye he'd flipped her over, wrapped his hand in her hair, dragged her right hip up and used his thigh to push her right knee into a bend, completely exposing her to his view.

Trinity's heart rate careened crazily in her chest as his erection prodded her slick entrance again but there was nothing slow and steady about this penetration; it was fast and quick, ripping a cry from her throat and a grunt of satisfaction from him.

He tugged on her hair, forcing her head off the bed and her back into an arch, sparks of electricity showering from her scalp all the way down her spine. 'Like that?' he whispered in her ear, his beard prickling at her neck and shoulder.

She panted. *'Yes.* God, yes. More.'

'Good,' he grunted and gave her more.

Hard and fast and relentless.

He held her like that, one hand wrapped in her hair, keeping her head up and her back arched as his mouth ravaged the muscle that sloped from her neck to her shoulder and his hips hammered into her from behind. It was hard and intense and perfect and all she was capable of was moaning and writhing until the hand he had on her hip slid around to her front and ploughed through the slickness between her legs, finding the hard knot of nerves.

'Come for me,' he demanded in her ear, low and ragged.

And she did. The pressure that had been building blew out in one hot flare and she came. Loud and long. Bucking against him as he mercilessly drove into her over and over again.

'*Trinity.*'

He groaned into her neck as the piston of his hips suddenly stopped. One second. Two. And then he bellowed his own release, muffling it in her shoulder as his hips bucked again and he rocked them towards the light together.

They lay unmoving for a long time in the aftermath, their bodies still intimately connected. Reid had collapsed against her, his weight pressing her to the bed, his mouth pressed to her nape, sweat slicking them together.

And she revelled in it.

Trinity had known she'd shatter. Hell, she'd *craved* it. But in a physical sense only. She hadn't been prepared to be broken into a thousand pieces *emotionally*. She hadn't been prepared for the gates of her heart to break open too and for love to flow in.

She hadn't been prepared for love at all.

But, as they lay in a sweaty heap, she knew it had happened anyway, could feel the burden of it sink to the pit of her belly.

She was in love with Reid Hamilton. It wasn't lust or gratitude or friendship. It was the deep and totally gut-wrenching abyss of unrequited love.

She'd wanted him to remind her she was a woman. She

just hadn't expected that taking Reid into her body would make her *his* woman.

And he could *never, ever* know.

CHAPTER SEVENTEEN

REID SHIVERED AND his groin tightened as Trinity traced the feathers of his eagle wings with her index fingers. She was firmly snuggled into his side, her hand reaching across to his opposite arm. The tattoo was on his back but the wings stretched all the way around to brush the tops of his biceps.

It was two in the morning and they'd already had sex three times. The second two not as hurried as the first. She *had* let him love her slow and easy the next time. And the third time, he'd headed down her body and shown her there were many, *many* ways to make a woman call out to God.

They were sated—for now—as they lay in each other's arms. His hand was stroking from her ass to her hip and back again as they drifted in the aftermath. He'd always enjoyed the post-coital haze, floating in his own bone-deep satisfaction, knowing whoever he was with was floating in hers.

But this was different. There was no exit strategy forming in his head as per usual. Lying here with Trinity was... grounding. And not in a bad way. Ever since she and Oscar had moved in he'd felt...settled. Not something he'd experienced since before his parents got divorced.

He'd forgotten how good it felt.

'You like them?' he murmured, prying heavy eyelids open as her exploring fingers brushed down his biceps.

She wrinkled her nose slightly as her gaze followed the

path of her finger. 'I'm not a big fan of tattoos, I have to admit, but they suit the whole lumberjack thing you've got going on.'

That surprised a laugh out of Reid. *'Lumberjack?'*

'Yes.' She smiled as she levered herself up on one elbow, looking down at him. 'The whole big, macho, bearded biker thing. All you need is a flannel shirt and a big old axe and you'd be the real deal.'

Reid shook his head, amused at the thought. A lock of hair had fallen forward over her shoulder and he pushed it back. 'Any particular reason why you're not into them?'

She sighed. 'Those couple of years on the streets...tats were usually a signal that you were someone who shouldn't be messed with. That was their point, I guess. I learned to be wary.'

Reid had known a lot of badass guys in the military who had been fully aware of how intimidating their tats could be and had revelled in it. He just appreciated the art.

'And yet you have one,' he murmured, his fingers tracing the ladybird tattoo on her right hip he'd thoroughly checked out on his way down earlier.

'Brian talked me into it. The place we went to was a real dive. I'm surprised I didn't get hepatitis. If I can ever afford the luxury of having it lasered off, I will.'

There was a grimness to her voice. 'Well, I like it,' he teased, to lighten the mood, his fingers stroking the offending piece of artwork.

'It takes me back to a dark time in my life every time I see it.' She shuddered. 'I hate being reminded of it all the time.'

Reid couldn't fault her reasons. Hell, he understood them. All of his tattoos had been acquired during his tours of duty in the Middle East. A lot of bad memories there.

But good ones also.

'Sometimes,' he said, picking up the same, persistent

lock of hair he'd pushed back earlier, toying with it, 'those reminders can be good.'

She regarded him for long moments. 'Is that what yours do?' Her fingers had shifted to his mouth now, tracing around the line where his beard rimmed his lips. 'Remind you of your time in the military?'

'Yeah.'

'And that's…good?' She frowned. 'I wouldn't have thought you'd want to be reminded of it.'

He shut his eyes as her fingers fluttered like moth wings over his lips. 'There are some bad memories,' he murmured, his eyes drifting open, fixing on hers. 'Things that still give me nightmares from time to time. Soldiers we lost. People I couldn't help. The *children* in the villages… But more than anything it reminds me that we did good over there. Every time people talk about the disaster of it, I know we did *good* as well. I need that.'

She nodded slowly and it felt as if she understood. Then she lowered her mouth and kissed him, sweet and slow and full of something deep and earnest he couldn't quite put his finger on. A kiss that seemed to say sorry and thank you and…goodbye?

She pulled away, her tawny gaze heated, her mouth wet from his and he wanted to crush her to him so there wouldn't be a goodbye.

'You don't ever think of going back?' she asked, her voice husky.

'No.' His hand slid to her ass and he squeezed. 'I'm feeling remarkably good about being home, actually.'

'Oh, yeah?' She smiled. 'That doesn't sound very rolling stone of you.'

He shrugged. 'What can I say? You're a good influence. I think I'm feeling more settled in my old age.'

'Really?' There was an odd little hitch to her voice, but then his fingers *were* trailing down the slope of her buttocks.

'I might celebrate with a new tattoo, actually.'

She slid her knee forward over his thighs and his fingers slid into the slick heat between her legs. 'Oh?' she said, her eyes fluttering closed as he explored.

'A big axe.' He grinned, his gaze roaming her face, enjoying her bliss. 'Embedded right in the centre of my chest.'

Her eyes opened and he tapped the area near his heart as his thumb grazed the hard little nub between her legs. She leaned in, kissed the spot, then slid her leg all the way over his hips and straddled him.

Trinity woke with a start, disorientated, a few hours later. Something had disturbed her but she didn't know what.

'Mummy!'

Oscar. Crying. Distressed.

'Oscar?'

She was lying with Reid spooned behind her and she had to push his arm out of the way to leap from the bed.

'What's wrong?' Reid asked, his voice sleepy and confused.

But she wasn't thinking about Reid. 'I'm coming,' she called out, her heart beating rapidly as the all-too-familiar sense of dread flooded her system. Conscious of being naked, she groped for her discarded dress and threw it over her head, zipping it up as she hurried out of the door.

Her heart rate almost doubled when Oscar wasn't in his room. *'Oscar!'*

'I'm here, Mummy,' came a plaintive little voice from the direction of her bedroom.

She flew next door to find Oscar standing beside her bed. *'Oscar!'*

'Where were you, Mummy?' he asked as she swept him up in her arms and hugged him to her fiercely.

'What's wrong,' she said, disregarding his question as unimportant right at this moment.

'I don't feel very well.'

Trinity squeezed her eyes shut at his typical understatement. His forehead was burning up and the rest of his body burned beneath the thin cotton of his pyjamas.

She could hear and feel the rattle of his breathing through his chest and the faint end note of a wheeze.

She sat with him on the bed. 'Is it hard to breathe?'

'A little bit,' he confirmed, lying slack in her arms as a weak, moist cough emphasised his condition.

Reid suddenly appeared in the doorway, pretty much as he'd been when she'd first gone to his room. Trousers, top button undone, shirt flapping open. 'Is he okay?' he asked, flipping on the light and advancing into the room.

Trinity shut her eyes against the sudden insult to her pupils. 'No.' She shook her head. 'He's not. I'm going to have to take him to the hospital.'

He crouched before them, placing a hand on Oscar's back. 'He doesn't sound very good and he's definitely got a temp. Does he have any recession?'

She wished she didn't know what Reid was talking about but unfortunately she was all too familiar with medical terminology. Trinity didn't have to look to know that the intercostal spaces between Oscar's ribs would be prominent. That his accessory muscles of respiration would be sucking in, working overtime. They'd need to take his shirt off to confirm but she didn't want to faff around.

'I would bet my life on it.'

'I can get my stethoscope and have a listen?'

Trinity shook her head. It wasn't that she didn't trust his doctoring skills, it just seemed pointless and time wasting when action was what she needed. 'I know how this goes, Reid. He can go from a sniffle to being ventilated in a matter of hours. I just want to get him to hospital.'

'Okay.'

She was grateful he didn't try to override her or tell

her to calm down, that she was panicking for no reason as she'd heard too often in the past from people—some of them medical—who just didn't understand.

His faith in her ability to know her own son and his condition, his faith in her motherly instincts, almost undid her. If she hadn't loved him before now, she would have in this moment. But she *could not* indulge in flights of fancy about the two of them *or* the threatening tears.

She was going to need to be extra tough for the days ahead.

He stood. 'I'll drive.'

Trinity blinked at the offer and for one brief moment allowed herself the fantasy of having Reid—the man she loved—by her side throughout the ordeal she knew was about to unfold. Someone to lean on.

But…

It could be a long haul and it wasn't practical for Reid, who had a job and his grandfather to worry about. She'd been living a fantasy here with him and she needed to get back to the real world.

'You can't. There's Eddie,' she said, standing as well.

He shrugged. 'He sleeps like a rock and doesn't usually wake till after six. It's just after two. I'll leave a note but I can stay with you guys for a bit and be back here by then.'

Trinity hated how much she wanted that. How the prospect of him staying with her filled her with yearning. 'But if he—'

'It's fine, Trinity,' he cut in gently, his hand squeezing her forearm. 'Let's just get the little dude to the hospital, okay?'

Trinity swallowed the lump in her throat and nodded.

They were walking into the hospital twenty minutes later, a lethargic Oscar bundled in Trinity's arms. She instantly felt better—safer—the cartoon murals decorating the walls and the staff wearing brightly coloured scrubs as familiar to her as her own breathing.

The triage nurse knew them on sight. 'Oh, dear, what have we got here, Master Oscar?' she said, her smile bright but her eyes knowing as they flicked from mother to son. 'Thought your frequent flyer days were done.'

'So did I.' Trinity grimaced.

'We might pop him straight into the resus cube,' she said, not bothering with the usual triage procedure. Her voice was casually calm but Trinity could read between the lines.

Oscar had crashed in this emergency department too many times for anyone to take any risks.

Trinity nodded, grateful for the assurance, but it didn't stop the worry and fear gnawing at her. Or the despair. After six months of being well she'd desperately hoped that they'd turned a corner with his health so this episode was gutting.

'He's in good hands,' Reid murmured as they followed the nurse.

She nodded, not trusting her voice as an entire catalogue of emotions swamped her. *She* was in good hands with *him*. The warmth of his palm in the small of her back was infinitely assuring and she had to fight the urge to lean against him.

Trinity laid Oscar on the gurney in the resus cube. He didn't protest, just looked at her with resigned, knowing eyes that broke her heart even more than his frightened eyes did. There were kids crying all around them, being combative, clinging to their mothers and protesting interventions. Not Oscar.

In the centre of the activity that had sprung up around him, he lay quiet and accepting. Which was worrying on a whole other level. Trinity fretted that he was becoming exhausted, which could escalate things rapidly.

Reid, standing behind her, squeezed Trinity's shoulder

as they undid Oscar's pyjama shirt to stick ECG dots to his chest. His intercostal recession was pronounced, as was his sternal and tracheal recession, the garish white line of his sternotomy scar horrifyingly mobile with each suck of his chest.

There was oxygen then and chest X-rays, intravenous therapy and medications. A whole battery of blood tests. Oscar barely flinched when they stabbed him to insert the IV, and sticking a suction catheter down his nose to get a naso-pharyngeal sample raised only a feeble cry.

Doctors came and went. The blood tests were okay. The chest X-ray wasn't too bad. He was holding his own. So many faces she knew. Reassurances given that she trusted, that meant something. But the rapid beeping noise from the monitor formed a terrible backbeat to her concern. She knew a lot of his tachycardia was due to his temperature but it always frightened her to see it belting along at one hundred and sixty beats per minute.

As if surely his heart was going to explode under the pressure or just…stop.

The helplessness was the worst as she stood by the gurney, his little hand furled in hers, alternating between anxiety and hope. Knowing that these doctors and nurses had him, that they were experienced, that they were good at this, that they were fighting for him was immensely reassuring. Then thoughts of how bad this could get crept up on her and she was plunged into despair.

But every time it happened, when the hopelessness seemed overwhelming, Reid's hand would slide onto her shoulder, as if he knew she *needed* it at that precise moment, and it kept her going.

CHAPTER EIGHTEEN

THEY WERE SETTLED in the high dependency unit within two hours. The loud hiss of the high-flow nasal cannula delivering warmed, moist oxygen formed a truly garish white noise in the isolation room, but it was soothing to Trinity's frazzled nerves. As was the now slower, more steady blip of the monitor. Oscar's temp was coming down and his vital signs were less scary.

He was asleep, looking very small and very pale in the big bed, ECG wires, IV tubing and oxygen tubing all crisscrossing his body. He didn't have a shirt on and it was heartening to see that his recession had markedly improved.

The ICU doctor had just been. She was hoping that the high-flow oxygen would be enough to get Oscar over the hump. So was Trinity. Normally, though, his condition would continue to deteriorate and medical interventions would escalate.

But, as always, it was going to be an hour-by-hour thing.

Despite the lack of promises, Trinity felt infinitely better than she had when Oscar's cry had dragged her out of sexually sated slumber.

Was that only a few hours ago?

'I might head off for a bit,' Reid announced as the doctor left. The sun was poking yellow fingers through the partially open blinds. 'I'll clear my day and get back here when I can.'

Trinity frowned. 'It's okay, Reid.' She shook her head. He couldn't just *clear his day*. He had his patients to see. His grandfather to take care of. His own responsibilities.

'You don't have to.'

He smiled. 'I want to.'

'Is this because...?' Trinity was conscious of the nurse in the room. 'You don't have to feel obligated to me because of...what happened earlier.'

Heat rose in her cheeks. She shouldn't be embarrassed considering what she'd done to his body. But there'd been such an abrupt ending to their...tryst, she wasn't sure where they stood.

'Trinity.' His voice was low as his hands smoothed up her arms and he held her gently by the shoulders. 'I want to.'

And then he pulled her in for a hug. She resisted for about two seconds before melting into him, grateful for his broad chest and solid warmth. Grateful that he'd been with her and she hadn't felt so alone. Grateful for his silent support and understanding.

'Thank you,' she said, her voice muffled in his pecs. 'For being here.'

'I'll always be here for you, Trinity.'

Trinity looked at him. She didn't know what that meant. Or the meaning of his deep, searching gaze. And she didn't want to speculate in case her heart took over and came to the wrong conclusion.

She glanced away from the intensity of his eyes to her son. 'He seems to be doing better now, right?' She sought Reid's gaze again, needing him to be Dr Hamilton now, to hear his medical opinion.

'Yes.' He nodded. 'He does. But how are *you* doing?' he asked softly.

How she was doing seemed so frivolous compared to

the battle Oscar was facing and Trinity wanted to dismiss it out of hand as she always did in these situations, but his gaze was still so damn intense, demanding she think about herself for a moment.

'I'll…be okay,' she said even if the adrenaline that had been keeping her going the last few hours had left her shaky and strung out.

'You have to take care of *you*, Trinity. You're no good to Oscar if you're exhausted.'

How many times had she heard that from well-meaning doctors and nurses these past five years? Too many times to count. But to hear it from Reid, the man she loved, who was here to support *her*… To even *have* a support person for a change, to know that someone other than paid strangers *cared*, touched her deeply.

Tears pricked the backs of her eyes and she blinked them away. 'I know,' she said. Because she *did* know, but she also knew that it was a pointless discussion. Her biological drive would always put the welfare of her child first.

The look he gave her told her he knew it too. 'Okay. I'll be back later. Text me if…' His gaze flicked briefly to Oscar then back to her. 'Keep me up to date.'

Trinity nodded, knowing he'd been about to say, *If Oscar deteriorates* and appreciating that he hadn't. And then, much to her surprise, he dropped a light kiss on her mouth before he turned away and left the room.

As if they were in some kind of a *relationship*, not on the tail end of what had been, essentially, a roll in the hay.

In a daze, Trinity sat by Oscar's bed, her lips tingling from Reid's kiss. The colourful squiggles of the monitor blurred before her eyes as she tried to stop herself from hoping a relationship with Reid was possible.

It was ten at night when Reid strode past the nurses at the central work station, giving them a smile as he headed for

Oscar's room. This was his second time back since he'd left this morning.

The first thing he'd done once he'd let himself in the house was ring work and organise cover for the next few days. There were some appointments that had needed re-jigging but it had all been sorted.

Trinity had looked so stricken last night. So worried and anxious. He'd been as concerned for her as he had been for Oscar and it was important to him to be there for Trinity. He doubted she'd ever had support during any of Oscar's hospitalisations and he was determined she wasn't going to go through this episode alone.

She—*and Oscar*—had come to mean a whole lot more to him than some kind of charity case. He *liked* her. Hell, after last night, he hoped she *liked* him too. In the kind of way that involved seeing more of each other.

Still…that wasn't important right now. Oscar getting better was all that mattered.

Reid had brought his grandfather to see Oscar for three hours in the middle of the day. Oscar had pretty much slept all the way through the visit but it had seemed to cheer Trinity up. She'd looked dog-tired with big dark circles under her eyes but Oscar had been holding his own. He was still on the high flow and while they hadn't been able to wean any of the oxygen, it hadn't been increased either.

The results had come in on his naso-pharyngeal aspirate. It was RSV, a common respiratory virus that most people could easily shake but could be devastating to kids like Oscar still suffering the effects of premature lungs. Unfortunately it couldn't be treated with antibiotics, just time and supportive respiratory therapy.

The news hadn't been comforting to Trinity. Apparently Oscar had had it several times before and had been ventilated each time.

Reid could hear the noise of Oscar's high-flow oxygen

even before he reached the room. A nurse, sitting at the computer in the room, glanced up at him as he stopped in the open doorway. He glanced at Trinity. Oscar's nearest hand was folded in hers but her head was on the bed and she was sound asleep, her long, low ponytail falling down her back.

The nurse slipped off her stool and headed towards him with a smile.

'How is he?' Reid asked, keeping his voice low, as she drew level.

'We've managed to wean the oxygen a titch,' she murmured.

Relief flooded Reid at the news. Used to operating in high-stress environments, he hadn't realised how worried he'd been. Oscar's reliance on such high levels of oxygen was concerning. Being able to wean it was a positive step forward.

'How's she?'

'I've tried to get her to go and have a proper sleep,' the nurse said with a sigh. 'There are some great pull-out couches in the parents' lounge but she won't leave him.'

Reid nodded. He didn't doubt it for a moment. 'Okay, thanks.'

The nurse left and he advanced into the room, standing close to the bed, looking down at Trinity. Her face was turned towards Oscar and spotlighted in a pool of light from overhead. The black circles had increased to smudges and the wedge of her cheek looked gaunt and pale.

She looked absolutely exhausted. His belly clenched at the sight and his heart turned over. A rush of love swamped his chest.

Yes...*love*.

God, he'd been fooling himself.

This hadn't been about protection or charity. She'd had

an impact on him from that very first day they'd met but he'd ignored it. And she'd been under his skin ever since.

He didn't just *like* her. He *loved* her.

In a couple of months she—and Oscar—had come to mean *everything* to him.

Reid put a hand on the mattress to support legs suddenly not that steady. He should have known when the usual disquiet over staying in one place died down that something was up. But he'd been too busy trying to put her into the friend zone. Too busy mitigating his feelings because of the power imbalance in their relationship. Too busy trying *not to have* feelings for her to really listen to what his body had been telling him.

What his *heart* had been telling him.

He was in love with her.

Pure and simple. Although, not, if she didn't feel the same way.

He knew she was attracted to him. But that wasn't love. And he didn't want to settle for anything less with her. He'd been aware of his feelings for ten seconds but already he knew he wanted the whole shebang. A relationship. A chance to be a father to Oscar. A chance to make them a family.

But whatever he felt at the moment was moot. He couldn't tell her *now*. It all had to go on ice until Oscar was well again and Trinity had space in her head for something other than Oscar's illness.

And, more than that, *right now*, she needed to go and have a proper sleep so she woke up refreshed and not with a kink in her neck.

He crouched beside her chair, one hand sliding on top of her thigh. 'Trinity,' he murmured, pressing a kiss to her cheek.

She stirred, lifted her head, looked quickly at Oscar and

the monitor to assure herself he was okay then at him, her brows beetled together. 'Reid?'

'Hey, sleepyhead,' he teased, keeping his voice low.

'I'm sorry.' She wiped a hand across her eyes. 'I must have drifted off.'

'Of course you did. You're exhausted, Trinity.' Neither of them had got much sleep the night before after all...

'What are you doing back here?' she said, ignoring his observation. 'You should be with Eddie.'

'He's pushing out Z's. Just like you.'

'I'm fine.' She shook her head as if clearing a fog. 'It was just a catnap.'

'Trinity.' Reid squeezed her leg gently and she glanced down at it. At his hand on her leg. She stared at it for long moments and he thought he heard her breath hitch before she locked her gaze with his. 'You. Are. *Exhausted.* Go to the parents' lounge and have a proper sleep.' She started to protest but he cut her off. 'I will stay right here with Oscar. I promise I will not leave this seat.'

She shook her head. 'But if he wakes up he's going to expect to see me. He'll want *me.*'

'I know.' Reid nodded. 'And if he wakes, I will get them to get you straight away.'

The indecision on her face was nearly his undoing. She was clearly torn between a mother's need to be with her child and the needs of her fatigued body. He wanted to drag her into his arms, tell her that he loved her and that everything was going to be okay. That he was here for Oscar as well as her.

But it wasn't the right time for that.

'You don't have to do this all by yourself any more, Trinity,' he whispered. 'I'm here for you. *I'm here.* Let me do this. Please?'

A tear rolled down her face. 'You'll get them to fetch me if he wakes?'

Reid slid a palm onto her cheek, smearing the tear in its track, his heart bursting with love. *This was big.* She was trusting him with Oscar. 'I promise.'

Then he leaned in and kissed her again. As he had this morning. As he hoped he'd be able to do a lot more.

She seemed less startled this time, which was heartening but probably spoke more about her exhaustion than anything else. He stood and stepped back so she could ease out of the chair, sitting in her place as soon as she'd vacated it, sliding his hand over the top of Oscar's as soon as she withdrew hers.

The weight of her trust was a precious gift and he wouldn't let her down.

Trinity couldn't believe how quickly Oscar improved. Five days later he was off all oxygen and they were on a normal hospital ward. He'd hovered on the verge of needing further assistance for two days, but then he'd turned a corner and started to pick up and had recovered so quickly. They were even talking about discharge for him tomorrow.

His respiratory specialist was very happy. And she was over the moon. Being dragged back into the abyss of hospitalisation again had been scary and disheartening, but seeing how much stronger his lungs were now gave Trinity great hope for the future.

Of course he was ultra-clingy now, which was normal for him after being so sick. Trinity didn't mind, nor did she blame him. Not even at ten o'clock when he was squirming restlessly in his sleep on her lap in the small recliner *beside* his bed instead of *in* his roomy hospital bed.

The curtain she'd pulled around their bed space earlier so Oscar wouldn't keep getting distracted by the goings-on flicked back a little. She glanced up to find Reid grinning at her.

'Hey,' he said, voice low.

She smiled back. She couldn't help it. Her heart did a funny little giddy-up. He'd visited twice every day. Once with Eddie and then later at night, just him. 'Hey.'

Strictly speaking, now they were out of HDU, it was after visiting hours but being a doctor—and a hottie—got him certain privileges with the nurses. And Trinity looked forward to his night visits with all the stupidity of a love-sick teenager.

Ever since he'd told her she didn't have to do it by her-self any more, she'd been spinning hopeless fantasies about their future.

'Is he asleep?' he asked, navigating between the end of the bed and the curtain until he reached the hard plastic chair beside the recliner.

'Yes.' She glanced at Oscar's face, relaxed in slumber. 'Mostly.'

He chuckled as he pulled the seat around, so it was fac-ing the recliner, his thighs wedged either side of the arm, the denim of his jeans pulling taut across his quads.

'You want me to switch with you so you can go and have a shower?'

The last few nights, Trinity had used Reid's visits to have a shower, entrusting Oscar to Reid's care. 'I actually had a shower earlier this afternoon when Oscar was asleep.'

The look of surprise on Reid's face was comical. 'He *must* be better,' Reid teased.

Trinity took it good-naturedly. 'Yes. Thank goodness.'

It was also good to not be her usual bedraggled mess. Reid always turned up fresh and clean and smelling won-derful whereas she was all rumpled and smelled like hos-pital food and disinfectant.

But not tonight. She was in jeans and a long-sleeved T-shirt—the least baggy one she owned—and she was wearing one of those fancy spray deodorants that some-one had left behind in the parent showers.

She smelled like vanilla and pop rocks.

They chatted about Oscar and their respective days and the weather and Christmas and a bunch of other things.

'There was a message on the answering machine for you,' Reid said, after they'd run out of their usual topics. 'From a Wendy someone…wanting you to ring her back.'

Trinity frowned. Wendy?

'Wendy Argos, maybe?' Reid said, his brow scrunched as he tried to remember the name.

'Oh. Argent.' Trinity nodded. 'She's a real-estate agent. It must be about one of the apartments I had my name down for.'

With everything else on her plate Trinity hadn't given a thought to her housing situation all week. She'd resigned herself to Christmas with Reid and Eddie a few weeks ago and, if she was honest, she'd been looking forward to it.

It didn't seem to bring Reid any joy either if his, 'Oh,' was anything to go by.

'It's a good thing,' she told him. And herself. Because it was.

He opened his mouth to say something but shut it again and said, 'Yes. Of course.'

But he didn't sound very convinced.

'Well, we can't…stay with you for ever, Reid,' she said even as the idea fluttered seductively like a sugar-coated butterfly just out of her reach.

He looked at her for long moments, his gaze searching and assessing. 'Why not?' he asked finally, leaning forward on his elbows, his gaze earnest. He'd kept his voice low but the frustration in it was barely disguised.

Trinity blinked. 'Because…'

Because they came from different worlds. Because he had itchy feet and she needed roots. Because she couldn't live with him and pretend not to love him.

'Don't go,' he said. 'Stay.'

'Reid?' Trinity's heart all but stopped in her chest. It wasn't fair of him to dangle something so seductive in front of her. 'What are you talking about?'

'I'm talking about being in love with you.'

Trinity stared at him. He was *in love* with her? But...? Her pulse quickened. 'You love me?'

'Yes.'

She shook her head, dazed by the admission. He looked serious but she dared not even hope he was telling the truth. 'I...don't understand. Why?'

Why would he love someone like her?

He leaned forward in the chair and grabbed the hand that wasn't wrapped around Oscar. 'Because of your pluck and your gumption and how fiercely you love Oscar. And how you are with Eddie and how much Ginger adores you. And how nice you are to everyone despite how bad things have been for you and... *God.*' He shoved a hand through his hair. 'Because of your mouth.'

Trinity couldn't believe what she was hearing. 'My... mouth?'

'Yes.' He gave a half-laugh and kissed the hand he'd enclosed in both of his. 'I stood here that first night looking down at you when you'd fallen asleep at Oscar's bedside and I just...knew. I'd been telling myself it was just *like* I felt and that I had to forget what we'd done in bed and be your friend, especially *now*, but then I realised you'd been under my skin since that first day. When you rescued Pops. And how you would have started that damn car through pride alone if it had been remotely possible. And it just flooded in and it keeps flooding in and I can't bear the thought of you and Oscar being anywhere else but with me and Pops.'

'Reid...' She searched his face, his gorgeous lumberjack face. He looked one hundred per cent serious. Her heart banged in her chest—slow and loud. Her blood poured thick and sluggish through her veins. 'I thought you wanted to move on. Not settle down.'

He buried his face in his hands again, kissing her fingers once, twice, three times. 'I did. And then I fell in love with you and I realise *nothing* else matters.'

Trinity shook her head, too overwhelmed to believe it. 'I…don't know what to say.'

'God, *Trinity*… I love you too would be *really* nice about now.'

Trinity smiled as she let everything go inside her and let her love flood in too. '*Of course* I love you. I realised that night in bed with you. I realised I hadn't just let you into my body but into my heart. I'm pretty sure it would have made me miserable in the weeks to come but I've been kinda—'

She glanced at a stirring Oscar. 'Preoccupied.'

He dropped his forehead to their clasped hands and dragged in some deep breaths. 'Thank God,' he finally said, glancing up at her, a broad grin lighting his whole face.

'So you'll stay. You and Oscar?'

Trinity wanted to cherish the moment. Her son was getting better, Reid loved her and he wanted them to stay. But…she needed to be sure. She needed Reid to be sure. Because she wasn't the only person in this equation.

'Are you sure, Reid? Are you sure this isn't some misplaced sense of honour or duty or some weird ex-army need to protect me? I love you and nothing would make me happier than to be with you but only if you *love* me.'

He shook his head emphatically. 'This is not about honour or protection, Trinity. I know what that feels like. This is something I've *never* felt before. I *am* in love with you.'

Sincerity shone in his eyes and his voice rang with conviction. She believed him. But still she pressed. 'I have a child. I can't just enter into relationships lightly. My parents did that. *Your* parents did that. And it screws kids up. If you take me on, you gotta take on Oscar.'

'You think I don't know you guys come as a team? You think I don't love Oscar as much as I love you?' His tone was full of reproach. 'Because I do, Trinity. And besides, you take me on you gotta take on Eddie. And that might get really rough.'

Trinity knew how much Reid was already dreading that time.

'We both come with dependants,' he said, kissing her hand again. 'It just...' he shrugged '...makes us a bigger, happier family.'

A bigger, happier family. The one thing Trinity had always craved.

'That sounds wonderful,' she whispered, her vision blurring with tears, her heart singing in her chest.

He leaned forward then, careful not to disturb Oscar as he kissed the tears from her cheek then pressed his lips to hers. Trinity sighed against his mouth, lapping up the gentle kiss full of love and compassion and all the years to come.

'Why are you kissing Reid, Mummy?'

Startled, they broke apart to find Oscar staring at them. Trinity, her mind blank, her cheeks heating, groped around for *something* to say. God, how did she explain to a five-year-old what was happening with her and Reid?

And how much was too much information?

'Because she loves me,' Reid said simply, smiling at Oscar then at her.

Trinity blushed some more. 'Yeah.' She smiled. 'Because I love him.'

Oscar reached out and patted Reid's beard. 'I love you too, Reid.'

And Trinity's heart overflowed.

* * * * *

*And if you enjoyed this story, check out
these other great reads from Amy Andrews*

*SWEPT AWAY BY THE SEDUCTIVE STRANGER
IT HAPPENED ONE NIGHT SHIFT
200 HARLEY STREET: THE TORTURED HERO
GOLD COAST ANGELS: HOW TO
RESIST TEMPTATION*

All available now!

REUNITED
WITH HER
SURGEON PRINCE

BY
MARION LENNOX

MILLS
BOON®

All rights reserved including the right of reproduction in whole
or in part in any form. This edition is published by arrangement with
Harlequin Books S.A.

This is a work of fiction. Names, characters, places, locations and
incidents are purely fictional and bear no relationship to any real
life individuals, living or dead, or to any actual places, business
establishments, locations, events or incidents. Any resemblance is
entirely coincidental.

This book is sold subject to the condition that it shall not, by way of
trade or otherwise, be lent, resold, hired out or otherwise circulated
without the prior consent of the publisher in any form of binding or
cover other than that in which it is published and without a similar
condition including this condition being imposed on the subsequent
purchaser.

® and TM are trademarks owned and used by the trademark owner
and/or its licensee. Trademarks marked with ® are registered with the
United Kingdom Patent Office and/or the Office for Harmonisation in
the Internal Market and in other countries.

Published in Great Britain 2017
By Mills & Boon, an imprint of HarperCollins*Publishers*
1 London Bridge Street, London, SE1 9GF

© 2017 Marion Lennox

ISBN: 978-0-263-92670-5

Our policy is to use papers that are natural, renewable and recyclable
products and made from wood grown in sustainable forests. The logging
and manufacturing processes conform to the legal environmental
regulations of the country of origin.

Printed and bound in Spain
by CPI, Barcelona

Dear Reader,

What *is* it with royalty? The combination of tradition,
power and wealth is a heady mix that I suspect would
be difficult to handle in real life, but as a writer I
love playing with 'what ifs?'. What if an entire royal
family was wiped out in one hit? That's a theme that's
been explored before—an unimaginable tragedy,
but to a fiction writer the idea's gold. What if the
unexpected heir to the throne is a doctor, dedicated
to his calling, who wants nothing to do with royalty?
And what if, years ago, that doctor had a secret son
who's suddenly the new Crown Prince?

The situation had me wiggling my toes in the sand
in delight as I took my dog for her daily beach walk.
I love a good 'what if?', and if it combines the
pageantry of a royal coronation, a feel-good romance
and a secret baby thrown in for good measure,
hooray! The dog and I needed to walk our legs off
in order for me to sort out all the complications, but
we loved how it all turned out. At least I did. Sadly,
Bonnie was too busy chasing seagulls to care.

Marion

Books by Marion Lennox

Mills & Boon Medical Romance

Wildfire Island Docs

Saving Maddie's Baby
A Child to Open Their Hearts

Meant-to-Be Family
From Christmas to Forever?
Falling for Her Wounded Hero

Mills & Boon Cherish

His Cinderella Heiress
Stepping into the Prince's World

Visit the Author Profile page
at millsandboon.co.uk for more titles.

CHAPTER ONE

THE BRAND-NEW Crown Prince of Falkenstein managed three hours of nightmare-filled sleep. He rose at dawn, desperate for coffee and a walk to clear his head. Instead, he found the Secretary of State waiting. The massive palace dining table was covered with newspapers, and their front pages all screamed versions of the same.

Entire Royal Family Killed in Plane Tragedy!

'This is what you get for breaking rules,' Josef said in greeting, and Marc wanted to thump him. At such a time, to be thinking of rules...

He headed for the huge silver coffee pot before deigning to answer. Being Crown Prince had to count for something. Half a cup of coffee in, his head was clear enough to respond. 'How did breaking the rules cause this?'

'Heirs in succession to the throne should never travel in the same plane,' Josef told him. 'Your uncle and his wife, your cousin, his sons and their assorted mistresses. All in the one small plane, on one indulgent holiday—and at vast expense when so much needs to be done at home. No consideration for rules. It's all part of the same. Your grandfather was a warlord. Your uncle was a playboy. Your cousin was a wastrel, and his sons were already mixing with women of the worst kind.' Josef heaved a sigh and laid the newspaper aside. 'Now it's up to you, boy, to fix the mess.'

'I have messes of my own to fix.'

'Not as big as this one. Your Highness—'

'Don't call me that.'

'It's who you are,' Josef said simply. 'You're Marc Pierre Henri de Falken, Crown Prince of Falkenstein. After your coronation you'll be His Majesty.' He hesitated but then forged on. 'And, might I say, this tragedy is appalling, but for the country it may well be a force for good.'

'I'm no prince,' Marc exploded. 'I'm a surgeon and I need to stay a surgeon. If you look at the mess our country's health system is in…'

'That's why you have no choice but to take the throne.' There'd been hours now to take in the news, and the country's chief administrator obviously saw the path ahead as being without obstacles. 'You've been doing your best with rundown hospitals, fighting for funds from a royal family who doesn't care. Now the reins are yours. Think of the bigger picture. The schools. The courts. Our welfare system. If you refuse the throne then it goes to Ranald de Bougier, and heaven help us if that happens. He'll propel us back to war.'

'But I don't want it.'

Marc took his coffee and stood at the vast bay window of the King's private dining room. Though it was the informal part of the palace, even this part was intimidating.

Marc's father had been the ignored younger son of the King. He'd been a pacifist who had hated his father's warlike tendencies. He'd studied medicine, he'd struggled to build the country's health system and he'd been appalled when the King propelled the country into a meaningless border conflict.

Marc had only been in this palace once, as an awed

seven-year-old, brought to be introduced to a family his parents had little to do with. There'd been continual fights about health funding and then an epic fight when war broke out. Marc had never been back. Until now.

Marc raked his long surgeon's fingers through his dark hair and stared into the future with horror.

He glanced through to the family's 'informal' sitting room. It was an opulent display of gilt, brocades and price-less furniture.

He wanted nothing to do with it.

The huge mirror above the dining room's massive fireplace showed Marc as he was, a thirty-five-year-old surgeon, a man who was weary from operating until midnight and who'd been brought to the palace straight from Theatre. After four hours of horrified discussion, he'd fallen asleep in his clothes. He was wearing faded jeans and a plain white T-shirt. He hadn't had time to shave.

A king? *Ha!*

'I can't,' he said simply. 'I love my work.'

'You have no choice,' Josef told him, and Marc thought of the mess the country's healthcare system was in, of the theatres without equipment, of the rundown hospitals, of the endless waiting lists.

If he turned his back on the throne, he could do more of what he was doing now. He could save lives, one patient at a time. If he accepted the throne…how many more could he save?

Josef was right. He had no choice, but he felt ill. He dug his hands into his pockets and kicked the heirloom rug at his feet.

'We need to move on,' Josef was saying, gently now, obviously knowing his argument had been won. 'You need to face the press. We need to get you shaved, dressed in something…' he eyed Marc's clothes with distaste '…more fitting. And we need to have a statement ready. The country's in uproar. We need reassurance of continuity. Even at this time we need the implication that this tragedy might make things better.'

'Why? Surely there's no need to talk of the future yet?'

'There is a need,' Josef told him. 'The country's desperate for a lifeline. You know there's no one fit to form government. Marc, we need steadiness and the promise of a better future. Moving on, we need to find you a wife. Get you a son. I believe you'll make a great king, and your sons after you.'

And that made Marc think of something else. Something that had played on his mind many times these past ten years. Something else that made him unfit to be royal.

He hesitated but it had to be said.

'There may be another…issue.'

'Yes?' Josef looked as if nothing could surprise him, but Marc knew this would.

'I have a son.'

He was right. To say Josef looked stunned would be an understatement.

Marc refilled his coffee mug and realised this was the first time ever that he'd said those words.

I have a son. The words seemed unreal in this situation that was already unreal. Having a son was part of another world. And yet, when it was said out loud it assumed a reality that shocked him as well as Josef.

He watched the colour drain from the old man's face. His grandfather's and then his uncle's reign had been marred by scandal after scandal, Marc knew, and now he was asking Josef to cope with more. He was under no illusions as to the old man's role in the royal household. Somehow Josef had kept the royal family intact, holding the country together. He'd served his country with honour. He didn't deserve to have to cope with this.

'A son…' Josef whispered. 'Where? When?'

'You knew I was married, briefly?'

'I…yes.' The old man was struggling to regroup, sifting long-forgotten information about a Marc he barely knew, a doctor on the outer fringes of the royal family. 'I had heard that,' he said. 'It was just after you qualified as a doctor, wasn't it? In Australia. A momentary aberration. You came home when war broke out. The divorce was almost immediate?'

'It was,' Marc said heavily. 'The marriage was…a mistake. I didn't know Ellie was pregnant when we separated, and the child was born well after I returned. A son.'

'It was never said.'

'There was no need. Neither of us was in a position to keep a child. I was flying back into a war zone. Ellie was a second-year medical student and she wished to continue. The baby was adopted at birth.'

'Formally adopted?'

'Yes.'

'Do you know the adoptive parents?'

'No. I had nothing to do with the adoption.'

He watched Josef think through the ramifications while he considered a third coffee. Josef's background was legal, Marc knew, and he'd spent a lifetime getting the royal family out of trouble. Scotching scandals was his principal skill. Marc could almost see the cogs whirring.

'There should be no concern,' he said at last. 'This was a child conceived in an impulsive marriage when you were little more than a child yourself. If he's been formally adopted, there can be no claim on inheritance. That can be explained to him if there's ever contact. But then…' he hesitated '…there may be more immediate repercussions. As the unexpected heir to the throne, you'll face media scrutiny of the worst kind. The country hardly knows you, so the media frenzy will be extraordinary. They'll dig out this old marriage. Where's your ex-wife now?'

'I presume she's still in Australia. I haven't spoken to her in years.'

'Tell me about her.'

He was too tired for this. He was too tired for everything. To be dredging up memories of Ellie…

But, strangely, it was easy. She should have been a distant memory. Instead she was a vivid reality, a warm, vibrant woman, curvy, laughing…

Except when he'd last seen her, ten years ago, standing in the airport lounge. She'd been wan with what he'd learned later was morning sickness, but she'd been resolute in the direction they had to take.

'We've been stupid, Marc, but you know what we need to do.'

He did. The senseless war was bringing his country to its knees. He was a qualified doctor—just—but his place was at home. Ellie was only two years into her medical course. Even after he'd learned of the pregnancy, they'd both known there was no room in their lives for a child.

'Ellie's a doctor too,' he told Josef but he didn't even know that for sure. Their separation had been absolute. She'd reluctantly allowed him to provide funds to keep studying—because of the pregnancy—but the amount she'd decided was 'over the top' had been returned and he hadn't heard from her since.

'Our marriage was a mistake by both of us,' she'd told him. 'I have no intention of profiting by it.'

And he'd had no choice but to agree. He'd been desperate to be with her for the birth but the conflict at home had escalated. The need for doctors had been dire, and by the time her—their?—baby was born, getting out of the country had been impossible.

Her email telling him of the birth had been business-like, informing him only of the bare fact that she'd given birth to a boy. The feeling he'd had then was indescribable.

Pain. Helplessness. Anger at a situation which made it impossible for him to claim his son.

And when he'd finally found a way to phone, her response had been curt.

'Leave it, Marc. He'll have a good home, I promise. You're needed where you are and so am I. Our marriage was a fantasy, and we need to put it behind us. Good luck, Marc, and goodbye.'

Their son was no longer their son, yet the anger and helplessness had stayed. And guilt. Disconnecting from that phone call had seemed the hardest thing he'd ever done, and there'd been many times since when mother and child had been in his dreams.

'She's intelligent enough to be discreet?' Josef asked, dragging him back to the present.

'Of course.' It was a snap, inappropriately terse.

'Has she married again? Has she told her new husband?'

'I have no idea. She made it clear she wanted no further contact.'

'And the divorce? It was amicable?'

He thought of Ellie's face that last time. They'd both known the impossibility of their situation. There'd been no argument, just bleak acceptance. 'Yes.'

'That's a help.' Josef wasn't seeing Marc's emotion. He was thinking ahead, anticipating trouble. 'But you don't know where the boy is?'

'Ellie never shared adoption details.' He hadn't asked. In the midst of the chaos of war, he hadn't had the energy to ask questions, and it had seemed unfair—even cruel— to question Ellie's judgement.

'Then that's how it must remain,' Josef decreed. 'For the child's sake, it's imperative his adoption records remain confidential. There's no problem with inheritance but the media would love it.'

'I can't guarantee—'

'We need to guarantee,' Josef said flatly. 'If the media finds him, can you imagine the headlines? We need to contact this woman before the media does. Press the need for silence. Pay her if necessary.'

'She won't accept payment.'

He remembered that last conversation almost word for word.

You have a disaster to deal with. How many people dead, Marc? What's the adoption of one child compared to that? Marc, you've helped enough. I don't want to continue contact. It's over.

'We'll do what's necessary and do it fast,' Josef was saying. 'If she's remarried and hasn't told her husband, then it could become messy. I'll brief one of our best lawyers. We'll research her background while he's on the way to Australia. He'll meet her face to face, tell her exactly what's involved, tell her she has to keep her mouth shut. Most countries allow contact between adoptive parents and birth mothers. If she has that contact then she needs to be silent about where he is. Did she name you as the father?'

'No.' That was down to him too. She'd asked him in that first curt email:

Do you want your name on his birth certificate?

The choice he'd made was wrong.

In his defence, he'd been stressed to the point of breaking. The war had been going badly. He'd been overworked past exhaustion, doing work far beyond his range of expertise, but there'd been no choice. For every patient he'd treated there'd been three more waiting. He'd also been gutted by the thought of Ellie having the baby alone. He couldn't bear the thought of what he'd lost. He'd made an instant decision then that he still regretted.

Leave it blank,' he'd told her. *'I can't be there for him. I have no right to be his father. The adoptive father should have all the rights.'*

It still hurt but Josef's face cleared. 'There you are, then,' he said. 'Even if the media finds out, it can be implied he wasn't yours. What better reason to end the marriage?'

'That's not fair to Ellie.'

'We'll pay her enough to compensate.'

As if that would work.

He turned and faced out of the window again, across the manicured palace gardens to the mountains in the distance. Somewhere, on the other side of the world, Ellie was making a life for herself, without him and without their son. It was a decision they'd made together.

Ellie was tough. She'd had to be, with her background. She called life as she saw it.

And now? A legal expert would come blustering in from her past, offering her bribes. Even asking her to swear a child wasn't his.

He thought of the Ellie he'd known. She was feisty, opinionated...moral. She also had a temper.

'No,' he told Josef. 'It could turn the situation into a disaster.'

'There's no other way,' Josef told him.

'There is,' he said heavily and he saw his path clear. This part, at least. 'If this is as important as you say, then let me do it. I must be able to fly under the radar for a few days. I'll face the media this morning and then I have a week's grace until the funeral. Say I'm stricken with grief, incommunicado. If I board a plane this morning no one will notice—the media surely won't expect me to be leaving the country. I'll go to Australia and talk to Ellie myself. I'll make sure the child's privacy is protected and there are no cracks the media can chisel open. And then...'

He put down his coffee cup. It was fine china with the royal coat of arms emblazoned on the front, and he found himself thinking almost longingly of the paper cups he grabbed after all-night Theatre shifts. That part of his life was over and he had to accept it. 'Then I'll come home,' he said heavily. 'I'll bury my family and I'll accept the throne.'

CHAPTER TWO

LIFE AS BORRAWONG'S only doctor was sometimes boring, but just as often it was chaotic. If one person went down with the flu, the whole town usually followed. Kids never seemed to fall out of trees on their own. Ellie had a great team at the hospital, though. Usually she could cope.

But not with this.

Two carloads of kids had been drag racing on a minor road with a rail crossing without boom gates. Maybe the drifting fog had hidden the crossing's flashing lights and the sight of the oncoming train until it was too late. Or maybe alcohol had made them decide to race the train. Whatever the reason, the results had been disastrous.

The train had just left the station so it had been travelling slowly, but not slowly enough. It had ploughed into one car, pushing it into the car beside it.

If the train had been up to speed, every occupant of the cars would have been killed. Instead, Ellie had seven kids in various stages of injury, distress and hysteria. Parents, grandparents, aunts, uncles, cousins—practically the whole town—were crammed into the waiting room or spilling into the car park outside.

Air ambulances were on their way from Sydney but the fog was widespread and there were delays. The doctor from the neighbouring town was caught up with an unexpected traumatic birth.

She was the only doctor.

Right now, she was focusing on intubating seventeen-year-old May-Belle Harris. May-Belle was the town's champion netballer, blonde, beautiful, confident. At least she had been. Her facial injuries would take months of reconstruction—if Ellie could get her to live past the next few minutes.

Ellie's team was fighting behind her, nurses and paramedics coping with trauma far beyond their training. But while she fought for May-Belle's life, she had to block them out.

'You can make it,' she told May-Belle as she finally got the tube secure. At least she now had a safe air supply. The girl was deeply anaesthetised. She should have an anaesthetist to watch over her before she could be transferred to Sydney for specialist reconstructive surgery. Instead of which, she had Joe.

'Can you take over?' Ellie asked the seventy-year-old hospital orderly. 'Watch that tube like a hawk and watch those monitors. Any change at all, yell. Loud.'

'Louder than these?' Joe said with a wry grimace. There were six others kids waiting for attention, plus the injuries and bruises of the train crew who'd been thrown about on impact. Some of these kids—the least injured—were… well, loud would be an understatement. One of the girls was having noisy hysterics and the very junior nurse allocated to her couldn't quieten her.

With years of experience, Ellie knew she could quieten her in a minute but she didn't have a minute.

'Grab me by the hair and pull me over here if you need me,' Ellie told Joe. Block everything out and focus on that breathing.

Moving on…

A boy with bubbling breathing also needed urgent attention. There had to be a punctured lung.

A girl with a shattered elbow needed her too. She risked losing her hand if Ellie didn't re-establish a secure blood supply soon. The lung had to be a priority but that elbow was at an appalling angle. If the blood supply cut...

And what if there were internal injuries?

Focus, she told herself. *Do what comes next.*

He was heading for Borrawong's Bush Nursing Hospital.

Marc hadn't been surprised when Josef's discreet investigators had told him Ellie was back working here. This was where her mother had lived, the town Ellie was raised in.

The last time he'd seen her she'd been heading home to care for her mum.

Borrawong was a tiny town miles from anywhere. A wheat train ran through at need, hauling the grain from the giant silos that seemed to make up the bulk of the town. The train felt like the town's only link with civilisation.

He'd never been there. 'As long as Mum stays well, I'm never going back,' Ellie had told him. She was jubilant at having escaped her small-town upbringing, her childhood spent as her mother's carer. Until those last days when their combined worlds had seemed to implode, she'd put Borrawong far behind her.

But now Josef's investigator had given Marc the lowdown on Borrawong as well. 'Population six hundred. Bush nursing hospital, currently staffed with one doctor and four nurses, servicing an extended farming district.'

To be the only doctor in such a remote community, to have returned to Borrawong... What was Ellie doing?

Had her mother died? Why had he never asked?

Because he had no right to know?

He landed in Sydney, then drove for five hours, heading across vast fog-shrouded fields obviously used for cropping. It was mid-afternoon when he arrived, and midwinter. The time difference made him feel weird. The main street of Borrawong—such as it was—seemed deserted. The general store had a sign: 'Closed' pinned to the door. The town seemed deserted.

Then he turned off the main street towards the hospital—and this was where everybody was.

The tiny brick hospital was surrounded by a sea of cars. There were people milling by the entrance. People were hugging each other, sobbing. Two groups were involved in a yelling match, screaming abuse.

What the...?

He pulled up in the far reaches of the car park and made his way through the mass of people. By the time he reached the hospital entrance, he had the gist. A train had crashed into two carloads of kids.

How many casualties?

The reception area was packed. Here, though, people were quieter. This would be mum and dad territory, the place where the closest relatives waited for news.

He made his way towards the desk and a burly farming type guy blocked his path.

'Can't go any further, mate,' the man told him. 'Doc Ellie says no one goes past this point.'

Ellie. So she was here. Coping with this alone?

'I'm a doctor,' he told him.

The man's shoulders sagged. 'You're kidding me, right? Mate, you're welcome.' He turned back to his huddled wife. 'See, Claire, I told you help'd come.'

He was the help?

There was no one at the reception desk, but double doors led to the room beyond.

A child was sitting across the doors. He was small, maybe nine or ten years old.

He was in a wheelchair but he didn't look like a patient.

He was seated as if he was a guard. He had his back to the doors and he held a pair of crutches across his chest. Anyone wanting to get past clearly had to negotiate the crutches, and the kid was holding them as if he knew how to use them.

Right now he seemed the only person with any official role.

'I'm here to see Dr Carson,' Marc told him. The kid's expression was mulish, belligerent. The crutches were raised to chest height, held widthways across the doors. 'I understand there's been an accident,' Marc said hurriedly. 'I might be able to help.'

'No one goes in,' the kid told him. 'Unless you're Doc Brandon from Cowrang, or from the air ambulance. But you're not.'

'I'm a doctor.'

'You're not a relative? They all want to go in.'

'I'm not family. I'm a doctor,' he repeated. 'And I might be able to help.'

'A real doctor?'

'Yes. I'm a surgeon.'

'You have a funny accent.'

'I'm a surgeon with a funny accent, yes, but I do know how to treat people after car accidents. I knew Dr Carson back when we were both training. When she was at university. Believe me, if she needs help then she'll be pleased to see me.'

Pleased? That was stretching it, he thought grimly, but right now didn't seem the time for niceties.

The crutches were still raised. The kid was taking a couple of moments to think about it. He eyed him up and down, assessing, and for a moment Marc took the time to assess back.

And then...

Then he almost forgot to breathe.

The kid was small and skinny, freckled, with dark hair

that spiked into an odd little cowlick. He was dressed in jogging pants and an oversized red and black football jumper. One foot was encased in a worn and filthy trainer. The other foot was hidden by a cast, starting at the thigh.

He could be anyone's kid.

His hair was jet-black, his brows were thick and black as well, and his eyes…they were almost black too.

And those freckles! He'd seen those freckles before, and the boy's chin jutted upward in a way Marc remembered.

He looked like Ellie. But Ellie had glossy auburn hair that curled into a riot. Ellie had green eyes.

The kid had Marc's hair and Marc's eyes.

Surely not.

And then, from the other side of the door, someone screamed. It was a scream Marc recognised from years of working as a trauma surgeon. It spoke of unbearable pain. It spoke of a medical team without the resources to prevent such pain.

Shock or not, now wasn't the time to be looking at a kid with dark eyes and asking questions.

'You need to let me in,' he told the boy, urgently now, as he pulled himself together. 'Ask Dr Carson if she needs help.'

'You really are a proper doctor?' The boy's voice was incredulous.

'I am.'

'Then go on in.' There was suddenly no hesitation. He peeped a grin at Marc and there was that jolt again. He knew that grin! 'But you're either in or out,' he warned. 'If another doctor ever walks into this town Mum says we'll set up roadblocks to stop them leaving. That's me. I'm the roadblock. No one gets past these crutches.'

'Ellie!'

Chris was Ellie's best trained nurse. While Ellie was

treating the kid with a suspected pneumothorax she'd put Chris in charge of the girl with the smashed elbow. Lisa Harley had smashed a few other things as well, but it was her elbow that was Ellie's greatest concern. The fracture was compound. She'd found a pulse on the other side of the break but it was faint. The blood supply was compromised.

But the kid with the pneumothorax had taken priority.

'I've lost the pulse,' Chris called urgently. 'And I'm worrying about her blood pressure. Ellie...'

She couldn't go. She had to release pressure in the chest of the kid under her hands. One lung had collapsed—she was sure of it. Any more pressure and she'd lose him.

A life or a hand...

'Five minutes,' she called back to Chris. Could she close this in time? No matter. She had to focus on what she was doing.

The door swung open.

It was too soon to expect the air ambulance from Sydney. It was too soon to expect the doctor from the neighbouring town, but Felix wouldn't have let anyone in unless they could help. Unless they were a doctor.

So she looked up with hope—and then felt herself freeze.

Marc.

He was older. There was a trace of silver in his jet-black hair. He looked taller, broader...more distinguished.

But he was still Marc.

Marc, here!

Her world seemed to wobble. If she'd had time she would have found a chair and sat down hard.

The boy she was treating needed all her attention. A smashed rib piercing the lung meant air was going in and not getting out. The pressure would be building. The second lung could collapse at any minute. She needed to insert a tube to drain the air compressing the lung and she needed to do it fast.

Marc was here.

'Where can I help?' he asked and somehow she forced her world back into focus. No matter why he was here; the one thing she knew was that he was a skilled doctor. A surgeon. Every complication that had suddenly hit her world had to give way to imperative.

'Chris needs help,' she told him, gesturing towards the nurse. 'Lisa Harley, seventeen, smashed elbow—I'm sure it's comminuted. There must be fragments of bone cutting the circulation. Feeble pulse in her fingers until a moment ago, but now nothing. Chris says blood pressure's dropping too, but I haven't had time to figure out why. I've given her morphine, ten milligrams. She probably also has alcohol on board.'

Marc's attention switched instantly to Lisa, lying wanly on the trolley. The morphine had kicked in but the kid looked pallid.

'I'm on it,' Marc said, in his perfect English with that French-plus-something-exotic accent that had made Ellie's toes curl all those years ago. He crossed to Lisa and touched her fingers. He'd be feeling for the pulse, Ellie knew. Even though it was Marc, she could only feel relief.

'You're right,' he said calmly, smiling down at Lisa in a way that would be medicine all by itself. 'Hi, Lisa. I'm Dr Falken. We need to get your arm sorted, but it's your lucky day. I treat hurt elbows all the time.' He checked her blood pressure and frowned. 'We might also check your tummy and see if there's anything else going on.' He flicked a glance back to Ellie. 'Lisa's priority one?'

'I'm coping with a pneumothorax but I have it under control,' she told him. She hoped. 'We also have a severe facial injury but I've intubated and she seems stable. Nothing else seems life-threatening. Chris, can you assist Marc? Everyone, this is Dr Marc Falken. He's…he's an old friend from university and he's good. Give him all the assistance he needs. Marc, sorry, but you're on your own.'

There was no time for shock or questions. There was only time to work.

With Chris's help he did a fast X-ray. The elbow was a jigsaw of shattered bone fragments.

It wasn't the greatest of her problems, though. Lisa's blood pressure continued to drop. Chris helped him set up an ultrasound and that confirmed his fears.

Ruptured spleen. She'd have internal bleeding. This was life or death.

Ellie had far more than she could cope with already. This was his call.

He'd like a full theatre of trained staff. He had Chris.

But, even though Chris looked as if she could be anyone's mum, the nurse was cool, efficient and exactly what he needed.

'I can give an anaesthetic,' she told him. 'I've done it before when Ellie's been in trouble. We can take Lisa into Theatre and go for it if that's what you want.'

He'd worked on battlefields with less help than this. 'That's what I want.'

From the next cubicle, Ellie must have heard. She was focusing on the kid with the punctured lung but she must have the whole room under broader surveillance.

'You can't just straighten for the time being?' she called.

Marc moved so he could talk without being overheard. The last thing Lisa needed to hear was a fearful diagnosis. 'There are bone fragments everywhere,' Marc told her. 'I can re-establish blood supply but if something moves it'll block again. It's not safe to transfer her without surgery. But priority's the ruptured spleen. I'll need to go in to check for sure but her blood pressure's dropping fast and the symptoms fit.'

She swore. 'You can do it?'

'I can.' His gaze swept the room, seeing the mass of trouble she was facing. 'You have enough on your hands.' More than enough.

'I can't help,' she said.

'I know.'

'Then do it. Chris, give him all the help he needs.'

And Chris was already wheeling Lisa's trolley through the doors marked Theatre.

He had no choice but to follow.

The cavalry arrived two hours later. Helicopters with skilled paramedics. The doctor from the neighbouring town. Everyone and everything she needed was suddenly there, and Ellie was able to step back and catch her breath.

The door to Theatre was still closed. There hadn't been time to investigate. She'd had to trust that Marc knew what he was doing.

Now, though, as paramedics fired questions at her, as each of these kids got the attention they needed, she was able to think of what—and who—was behind those doors.

'I have a kid with a shattered elbow and possible ruptured spleen,' she told the senior paramedic. 'A visiting surgeon was on hand. He's in Theatre now.'

'Here?' the guy said incredulously, and Ellie thought again of the mixed emotions his arrival meant for her.

Marc was behind those doors. Her old life was a life of secrets. A life that now had to be faced.

She took a deep breath and opened the door to Theatre.

Chris was at the head of the table. She smiled and gave Ellie a swift thumbs-up, then went back to monitor-gazing.

Chris was magnificent, Ellie thought, not for the first time. Ellie had needed to talk her charge nurse through an anaesthetic more times than she could count and she'd coped magnificently every time. She should be a doctor herself. She practically was.

But her attention wasn't on Chris.

Masked and gowned, Marc could be any surgeon in any theatre anywhere in the world. He was totally focused on the job at hand.

'Nearly closed,' he growled and his voice was a shock all by itself.

She'd never thought she'd hear it again.

'What's happening?' she asked.

'We've stabilised the elbow, removing bone fragments that could shift. The circulation should hold until she receives specialist orthopaedic attention. The worst risk was the spleen. It was a mess. There was no choice but removal. Sorry, Ellie, to leave you with everything else. I had Chris slip out and tell Joe to call if there was any priority you couldn't cope with, but then we went for it.'

'He's done the whole thing,' Chris breathed. 'He's removed the spleen but he's done so much more. He's stopped the internal bleeding completely. Blood pressure's already rising. And the elbow! Look at the X-rays, Ellie. To get the circulation back. He's saved her life and he's saved her arm. Oh, Ellie, I can't tell you...'

'Thanks to Chris,' Marc growled, still focused. 'You have a gem of a nurse, Ellie.'

'Don't I know it,' she said a trifle unsteadily.

This was surgery way beyond her field of expertise. Maybe she could have diagnosed and removed the spleen but the pneumothorax had been just as urgent. She would have lost one of the two kids, and how appalling a choice would that have been? But the elbow... She glanced at the X-ray, saw the mess, and knew without a doubt that Lisa would be facing amputation if Marc hadn't been here.

Marc's battlefield training had come to the fore. She never could have done this alone.

A bullet had been dodged. Or multiple bullets. She wanted to sit down. Badly.

It wasn't going to happen.

'I'm just applying an external fixator and then I'm done,' Marc told her. 'Ten minutes? I gather the air ambulance is here. I'd like Lisa transferred to Sydney as soon as possible. The elbow will need attention from a specialist. I'm not an orthopod.'

'You could have fooled me,' Chris muttered, and Ellie looked at Marc and thought, *What good fairy brought you here today?*

And then she thought of the repercussions of him being here and she stopped thinking of good fairies.

She didn't have time to go there. She had to face the relatives.

But there was no longer any urgency. She had room for thought.

Marc was here.

Good fairies? She didn't think so.

The first chopper took the most seriously injured, including Lisa, but the boy with the pneumothorax left by road. Air travel wasn't recommended when lungs were compromised. The road ambulance also took the driver of one of the cars and his girlfriend. The pair had suffered lacerations; the girl had a minor fracture. They could have stayed, but feelings were running high in the town and a driver with only minor injuries could well turn into a scapegoat.

The second chopper, a big one, had places to spare and the battered train crew chose to leave on it. They, too, could have been cared for here, but their homes, their families, were in Sydney. Borrawong Hospital was suddenly almost deserted.

But Marc was still inside and, as Ellie watched the second chopper disappear, that fact seemed more terrifying than a room full of casualties.

'You can get through this.' She said it to herself, but she was suddenly thinking of all the times she'd said it before. During the trauma of being the kid of a defiant, erratic single mum with cystic fibrosis. The roller coaster of a childhood living with her mother's illness. The relief of her mother's first lung transplant and then the despair when it had failed.

And then the moment the doors had closed at Sydney Airport and Marc was gone for ever. The moment she'd looked at the lines on the pregnancy testing kit. The moment she'd seen her baby's ultrasound.

The day she'd made the decision to keep her baby, to stay here, to cope alone.

But it was no use thinking of that now.

The sun was sinking behind the town's wheat silos, casting shadows that almost reached the hospital. Somewhere a dog was barking. This was Borrawong's nightlife. Marc was about to see Borrawong at its best.

Why was he here?

'You can get through this,' she said again but heaven only knew the effort it cost her to turn and re-enter the hospital.

Felix was still in the waiting room. He'd pushed his wheelchair behind the reception desk and was engrossed in a computer game but he looked up as she entered and grinned.

'Got rid of them all?'

'We have. Felix, you were wonderful.'

'I know,' he said, his grin broadening. 'I kept 'em all out. Except the doctor with the funny accent. He's still in there now, helping clean up. Joe says if we have a doctor who cleans we should lock the doors and keep him. He said he's your friend?'

'I…yes. He's someone I knew a long time ago. When I was at university.'

And Felix's face changed.

Uh oh.

Felix was smart. He was also right at the age where he was asking questions, and the questions had been getting harder.

'So you met my dad when you were at uni. Why won't you tell me his name? The kids at school reckon he must have been married to someone else. Or he was a scumbag. Otherwise you'd tell me. Why can't I meet him?'

And now Felix had met a strange doctor three hours ago while he'd been bored and had time to think—a guy who'd appeared from the past, a man his mum had never talked about.

A man with hair and eyes exactly the same as his.

'Is he my father?' Felix demanded and Ellie closed her eyes.

And when she opened them Marc was in the doorway.

He'd ditched his theatre gear. He was wearing casual chinos and a white open-necked shirt.

His dark hair, wavy just like her son's, was rumpled. He'd raked it, she thought. He always raked his hair.

Felix looked like him. Felix was Marc in miniature— except for the freckles. And the wheelchair.

But there was no use denying it. Felix's face was bristling with suspicion, but also with something else. Hope, perhaps? He wanted a father.

How wrong had it been not to tell Marc what she'd done?

She glanced at Marc again. His face was impassive. Shuttered.

She thought of the first time she'd met him. She'd been nineteen, a second-year university student, working her butt off to put herself through medicine. Marc had been twenty-four, just completed training, headed to Australia for a gap year before he started surgical training.

He'd intended working his way around Australia's coastline, but in his first week in Sydney there'd been an international conference on vascular surgery. He'd cadged an invitation because, gap year or not, he was interested.

She'd been there as a waitress. On the edges. Soaking up knowledge any way she could. She'd been working the crowd, carrying drinks.

An eminent vascular surgeon had been holding forth to a small group of similarly esteemed professionals, talking of the latest cardiovascular techniques. She'd paused to listen, intrigued by the discussion of a technique she'd never heard of.

And then one of the group had caught her eye, maybe suspecting she was eavesdropping. *Uh oh.* If she lost this job it'd be a disaster. She'd spun away fast—and crashed into Marc.

Her tray had been loaded with red and white wine and orange juice. The whole lot had spilled down his front. Glasses smashed on the floor. The attention of the whole room had suddenly been on her, and she'd stood, appalled, expecting to be sacked.

But Marc had moved with a decisiveness that had taken her breath away. He'd stopped people moving onto the broken glass, and he'd talked to her boss before she could say a word.

'I'm so sorry,' he'd said in his lovely broken English. 'So stupid. I was caught by something Professor Kramer was discussing, and it seemed important to catch it. So I turned suddenly and I hit your waitress hard. *Mam'selle*, are you hurt? A thousand apologies. Sir, may I make recompense? The cost of the glasses? The wine? Something extra for your work? And, *mam'selle*, I will pay the cost of your cleaning...'

He'd charmed her right back into her job—and that night, when she'd finished work, he'd been waiting for her at the staff entrance.

'I messed with your night,' he said simply. 'The least I can do is take you to supper.'

'It was my fault.'

'The fault is immaterial. It was my body you crashed into. Therefore my body will propel you to supper.'

He'd been irresistible. His looks, his accent, his smile… His kindness.

She'd fallen in love right there and then and, amazingly, he'd seemed to feel the same.

And now he was here.

'Ellie?' he said gently, but there was no smile.

He was waiting for an answer.

Felix was waiting for an answer.

She looked from one to the other. Her son. Her ex-husband. The man she'd loved with all her heart.

Once. Not now.

Is he my father?

There was nowhere to go.

'Felix, this is Marc Falken,' she managed and was amazed at the way her voice sounded. It was almost steady. 'He's from Falkenstein, near Austria, in Europe. Marc's a doctor. He and I met at university and for a few short months we were married. But then there was a war in Marc's country, a disaster that lasted for years. He was needed. I'd imagine he's still needed. But, for whatever reason, he's here now, and yes, Felix, Marc is your father.'

CHAPTER THREE

AFTER THAT, THE NIGHT seemed to pass out of her control. Felix was excited and full of questions. Marc seemed calm, courteous and kind.

She could stay silent—and she did.

Between Marc and Felix, they sorted that Marc would have dinner with them. The hospital cook was making bulk fish and chips, so they ended up at the kitchen table in El- lie's hospital apartment with a mound of fish and chips in front of them.

Ellie simply went along with it. She didn't have the strength for anything else.

She ate her fish and chips in silence and was vaguely grateful for them—how long since she'd eaten?

There was a bottle of wine in the fridge. She offered it to Marc but he refused. 'Jet lag,' he told her and she nod- ded and reflected that that was how she herself was feeling. She was pretty much ready to fall over now.

And Marc? He must be shocked to the core, but he was being kind.

For Felix was hammering him with questions. One part of Ellie was numb, but there was still a part of her that was taking in Marc's responses.

'Are you really a surgeon?'

'Yes.'

'Do you work in a big hospital?'

'I travel a lot, Felix. I'm in charge of the country's health system. I do operate when I'm needed, but a lot of my time's spent checking our remote hospitals are up to standard.'

'What's remote? Like the Outback here?'

'We don't have deserts,' he told him. 'But we do have mountains. Lots of mountains and many of our tiny hospitals are cut off in bad weather. Like your mum's hospital here, they're a long way from anywhere and it's my job to see they're not cut off completely.'

'But you still operate.'

'I love my job so yes, I operate, whenever I can. I have an apartment in one of the city hospitals and I operate there when I'm needed.'

'Like this afternoon.'

'Like this afternoon.'

And then the questions got personal.

'Are you married?'

'No.' He glanced at Ellie and Ellie concentrated fiercely on her pile of chips.

'Why not?'

'I guess I've been too busy.'

'You weren't too busy to marry my mum.'

'I wasn't,' he said gravely. 'But your mum and I were both students then, so we had more time. We hadn't realised just how many responsibilities we faced. There was a war in my country and I had to go home. Your grandmother was ill and your mum was needed here. There wasn't time for us to stay married.'

And finally Felix fixed his eyes on his father and asked the question she'd been dreading. 'There was time to make me,' he said flatly. 'Didn't you want me?'

If ever she wanted to turn into a puddle of nothing, it was now. What had she been thinking, not telling Marc what she intended?

It had been for all the right reasons, she told herself, but her silent reasoning sounded hysterical. It sounded wrong.

And Marc? He'd respond with anger, she thought, and he had every right. He could slam her decision of nine years ago. He could drive a wedge between her and her son, give Felix a reason to turn to her with bewilderment and betrayal.

Marc glanced at her, for just a moment. Their eyes locked.

She saw anger, but underneath there was mostly confusion. And concern.

All that she could see at a glance. Why?

Because she knew this man. She'd married him. Three glorious months…

'Felix, this takes some understanding,' Marc said, and whatever betrayal he was feeling seemed to have been set aside.

But she hadn't betrayed Marc, she told herself. She'd told him the truth.

Sort of.

'Your mum and I were very young when we met,' Marc continued. 'We were not much more than kids. We fell in love and we got married. It was all very fast and very romantic. But sometimes you do things that you hope might work out, even if they probably won't. Have you ever done that?'

'Like riding Sam Thomas's brother's bike down the hill at top speed,' Felix said. Marc was talking to him as an adult and he was responding in kind. 'It was too big for me and I couldn't make the brakes work but there was a grassy paddock at the bottom so I sort of hoped it'd be okay.'

'It wasn't, huh?'

'No,' Felix said but he peeped a cautious smile at Marc, obviously looking for a reaction. 'I broke my leg. Getting married was like that? Getting on a bike with no brakes?'

'I guess so,' Marc said and Ellie saw a faint smile in response. 'Only in this case we didn't break our legs. A war started in my country. A big one. There were many, many people killed and more hurt. And your grandma was ill here. So your mum and I had to part.'

'You didn't write to me.'

'No,' Marc said softly and Ellie thought, *Here it comes.* But it didn't.

'I didn't write,' Marc continued. 'And I'm very, very sorry.'

And, just like that, he'd let her off the hook. Of all the things he could have said, the anger, the blame…

He could be telling Felix it was his mother's fault, his mother's deception. Instead of which, he was simply apologising.

'When I left I didn't know your mother was pregnant,' Marc said. 'And when she told me, I was in the middle of a war zone, helping people survive. But I should have come back for you and I'm very sorry I didn't.'

All the questions Felix had been firing at her had been becoming increasingly belligerent. Increasingly angry.

She'd known that she'd have to face that anger some time. Now, Marc had taken it all on himself. He'd let her off the hook.

She'd been staring into her water glass sightlessly, numbly. Now she looked up and met his gaze.

Not quite. She wasn't off the hook. There were still questions she had to answer. Accusations to face.

But not from her son. For that, at least, she was so grateful she could weep.

'So, the wheelchair,' Marc said, and she thought, *He hasn't asked it until now.* That was a gift in itself. For most people it was the obvious focus, and now he asked. 'What's the matter with your leg?' And it was a simple follow-up on the preceding conversation. 'That was the bike, huh? Bad break?'

Felix hated the questions. The sympathy. The constant probing from a small community. 'How are the feet? Does it hurt? Oh, you poor little boy...'

Felix routinely reacted either by pretending he hadn't heard or by an angry brush-off. Now, though, for some reason he faced the question head-on.

'I was born with club feet,' he told Marc. 'Talipes equinovarus. You know about it?'

'I do,' Marc told him. 'Rotten luck. Both feet?'

'Yeah, but the left's worse than the right. I had to have operations and wear braces for years and now the right one's almost normal. But my left leg won't stay in position and it's been shorter than the right one. Then I broke it and the surgeon in Sydney said let's go for it and see if we can get a really good cure for the foot as well as for my leg. So it was a big operation and I'm in a wheelchair for another two weeks and then braces again for a bit. But Mum reckons it should be the last thing. Won't it, Mum?'

'We hope so.' Ellie was having trouble getting her voice to work. Somehow she had to make things normal.

As if they could ever be normal again.

She had to try, but she had a moment's grace. It was well past Felix's bedtime. 'You have school in the morning,' she managed. 'Bed.'

'You weren't at school today?' Marc asked.

'The doctor who did my leg had a clinic at Wollongong,' Felix told him. 'Mum and I drove down early and got the first appointment. We only just got back when the accident happened.'

'Which is why you need to go to bed now,' Ellie said, struggling to sound firm.

'But you'll stay?' Felix looked anxiously at Marc. 'You'll be here when I get home from school tomorrow?'

'I'm booked into the motel.'

'So you will be here.'

Marc met her gaze and held it. Questions were asked in that look. Questions she had no hope of answering.

But obviously Marc was more in charge of the situation than she was. He knew what he was here for, even if she didn't.

'Yes, Felix, I will.'

'Cool,' Felix told him. 'I might bring my mate to meet you. He's always ragging me about not having a dad. You want to meet him?'

'Of course.'

'Cool,' Felix said again and yawned.

'You did a great job today, by the way,' Marc told him and Ellie found herself flushing. *You compliment my kid, you compliment me.* It shouldn't happen like that but it did. And then Marc added, 'Both of you.'

'You didn't do too badly yourself,' Ellie muttered. She could feel herself blushing but there wasn't a thing she could do about it. 'Are you heading back to the motel now?'

'In a while,' Marc told her. 'You and I need to talk.'

'Felix and I usually read. His leg often aches and reading helps him sleep.'

'Would you mind if I read to my son tonight?'

And what was she to say to that?

My son.

Her world had changed.

Felix was obviously exhausted, too tired to ask any more questions but, under instructions, Marc sat on his bed and read. This wasn't a storybook, though. What he and Ellie were obviously halfway through was a manual on the inner workings of the Baby Austin—a British car built between nineteen-twenty-two and nineteen-thirty-nine.

The back axles of spiral bevel type with ratios between 4.4.1 and 4.6.1 5.6:1. A short torque tube runs

*forward from the differential housing to a bearing
and bracket on the rear axle cross member...*

It was enough to put anyone to sleep, Marc thought, but as he read Felix snuggled down in his bedclothes and his eyes turned dreamy.

'One day I'm going to find one and do her up,' he whispered. 'Do you know anything about cars?'

'A bit. I don't know much about short torque tubes.'

'But you could find out about them with me,' Felix whispered. 'Wouldn't that be cool?'

And then his eyes closed and he was asleep.

For a few moments Marc didn't move. He sat looking down at the sleeping child.

He had a son.

A kid who coped with club feet with courage. A kid who guarded doors with crutches. A kid who wanted to introduce his dad to his mate and who needed help with something called short torque tubes.

A son to be proud of.

The feeling was almost overwhelming.

He'd known of Felix's existence for years but it had always seemed theoretical rather than real. He hadn't been with Ellie when she'd found out she was pregnant. He hadn't been here for the birth.

He hadn't questioned her decision to put the baby up for adoption.

Maybe he should feel anger that she'd kept this from him for so long but all he managed was sadness. It had been an appalling time. His country had had to come first, but what a price he'd paid. He'd missed out on nine years of Felix's life.

Walking away from Ellie had been the hardest thing he'd ever had to do in his life. He'd felt it had broken something inside that could never be repaired. And when she'd told him she was pregnant, and he couldn't go to her...

The nights he'd lain awake on his hard bunk and thought of her; the fantasies he'd had of his dream life, where they could be a family...

But the dreams had been just that. Fantasies. He hadn't been able to go to her. He'd been in no position to be a husband or a father.

He'd lost his family. He'd lost Ellie.

He thought of her now, out in the sparse little sitting room she called home. She'd changed after work, into faded jeans and an old windcheater. She looked tired. Worn.

He'd thought he'd had to cope with trauma. How much more had she had to deal with?

Felix was deeply asleep. He touched his son's face, tracing the cheekbones. His son who looked like him. But who also looked like Ellie.

Back in the kitchen, Ellie was waiting for him. She'd cleared the dishes and was standing with her back to the sink, hands behind her back. She looked...trapped.

'Marc, I'm sorry,' she managed. 'I should have told you that I kept him.'

'Why didn't you?' He wasn't sure where to go with this. There were accusations everywhere.

'You didn't want him.' But she shook her head. 'No. That's unfair to you. At the time, neither of us wanted him. We were kids. The pregnancy was a mistake, Marc, as was our marriage. We should have known that it was never going to work. Our backgrounds were so different it was impossible.'

'If it hadn't been for the war...'

'And if it hadn't been for my mum's illness...' She shrugged. 'But even without, there were responsibilities. You never told me how important your role was at home. And maybe I didn't tell you how much my mum needed me.'

'So when did you decide to keep him?'

She tilted her chin, like a kid facing the headmaster. Defiant.

'I came back here after you left,' she told him. 'As I told you I had to. Mum's lung transplant had failed. She loved the freedom the transplant gave her, the illusion of health, but she didn't take care. She refused to follow the doctors' instructions and maybe I can understand why. For the first time in her life she felt healthy and she made the most of it. Until she crashed. Then, you knew I had to put my studies on hold to care for her. When I found I was pregnant, life became even more impossible.'

He remembered. He'd received the email after a day coping with massive trauma wounds, when he was so exhausted the words had blurred.

Ellie was pregnant.

What could he do? Where he was, he couldn't even phone her.

But the email had been blessedly practical. She couldn't support a baby and care for her mother. She still—eventually—wanted to study medicine. There were so many good parents out there desperate for a baby, she told him, so the logical answer was surely adoption. Did he agree?

He'd felt gutted but there seemed no choice but to accept her decision. The war looked as if it would drag on for years. Ellie would have to cope on her own, so what right did he have to interfere?

'So I was back here and pregnant,' she told him. 'Mum was totally dependent. I had your funds which kept us, but there was no way I could go back to university. University, our marriage, they seemed like a dream that had happened to someone else. Mum seemed to be dying and the pregnancy hardly mattered. When I thought about the pregnancy at all, it was just a blanket decision that adoption was the only answer.

'Then, when I was thirty weeks pregnant, Mum was so bad she had to be hospitalised. And one of the nurses asked if I was looking after myself—if I'd had my check-ups, my scans. It was the first time anyone had asked, and it sort of shook me. So the nurse got bossy. She sent me for scans and the radiographer told me to take a few deep breaths and relax. And I lay there and listened to my baby's heartbeat, and suddenly it was real. I was having a baby.'

'Our baby,' he said softly.

There was a long silence. *Our baby.* How loaded were those two words?

'I think that was in the mix too,' she whispered at last. 'Yours and mine. What we had…it was good, Marc.'

'It was.'

'But I was still planning on adoption,' she told him. 'I remember lying there thinking, *He's real. He was conceived out of love. He has to go to a wonderful home.* And then the radiographer's wand reached his feet.'

'Which were clubbed.'

'I could see them,' she whispered. 'I could see how badly they were clubbed. And of course I'd done two years of medicine. I knew what he'd be facing, but I also knew there was the chance of more.'

Marc did too. Of course he did. Club feet were sometimes associated with other problems. He thought them through and they weren't pretty. Trisomy 18 syndrome. Distal arthrogryposis. Myotonic dystrophy. The chance of each of those was small, but real.

'I know it's only twenty per cent of cases,' she told him. 'Club feet are usually the only presenting condition, but that was enough. I lay there and watched his image and thought, *Who do I trust to look after my baby?* Because suddenly he was *my* baby. And there was no need to answer, because by the time I walked out of that room no one was going to have the chance.'

He understood. He hated probing more, but he had to have answers. 'So you decided to keep him—but you also decided not to tell me?'

'How could I? I'd been following the situation in Falkenstein. I'd seen the war shattering your country. I'd even seen you on the news, working in a field hospital, talking to reporters of the struggles you were having after so many months, with the international community losing interest, with winter coming, with so many homeless. I knew you felt guilty about me anyway, so why hang more guilt on you? You'd agreed to adoption so why not just let you think he was adopted? What's the difference, Marc, between someone unknown taking care of our son and me?'

'For a start I would have funded you.'

'I didn't need funding. You sent me two years' income and paid the rest of my university fees. You insisted I keep that. What more could I ask?'

'That I care for my son!' The shock, the frustration, the rage that he'd kept at bay all day suddenly vented itself in those six fierce words. He slammed his fist on the table so hard that the salt and pepper shakers toppled and rolled to the floor.

Neither of them noticed.

His rage was so great he could scarcely contain it, but it wasn't rage at Ellie. It was rage at himself.

He hadn't enquired. He hadn't followed up.

What sort of low-life left a woman with a baby and didn't find out how she was—for nine years?

'Marc, you did ask,' Ellie whispered, and her response shocked him. It was as if she guessed what he was thinking. 'You rang after Felix was born.'

He remembered the call.

He'd spent the night operating in a field hospital after

yet another bomb blast had shattered lives. He'd come back to his quarters to find the email, telling him that he had a son. He'd driven for hours to the nearest place there was reception, trying to put a call through. When he'd finally reached her, Ellie had sounded tired, spent, but okay.

'He's a beautiful little boy, Marc. You can be proud. He'll have a good home, I promise. Yes, I'm okay and amazingly Mum's okay too. She's had another transplant and this one looks like it's taken. My plan is to go back to university and Mum's promised to help. No, there's nothing you can do. Would you like me to send you a photograph of your—? Of the baby?'

And, idiot that he was, he'd said no. He'd wanted no picture of his son. How many times had he regretted it? But after having said it—that he didn't want the hurt of seeing what could have been—how could he turn back?

The events of the last few days—the royal tragedy, his ascension to the throne, things that had seemed overwhelming—were suddenly nothing.

He'd walked out on his wife, she'd borne him a son and she'd kept him. She was here now, and his son was right through the door, dreaming of splash-lubricated crankshafts and magneto ignition…*and a father who might share his life.*

Ellie was looking at him as if she was scared. What, that he'd hit her? Sure, he was angry. He had every right to be, but he wasn't angry at Ellie.

He'd been a doctor for years. How many times had he seen the grief of a lost baby? How could he not have guessed that a decision taken when Ellie had first learned she was pregnant couldn't be carried through when she'd held her son in her arms?

Once she'd known her baby had formation issues she could never have given him away. She'd have fought for him to the death.

But that was the Ellie he'd known then. The Ellie he looked at now seemed as if the fight had been knocked out of her.

'Marc, why are you here?' she whispered and he struggled to swallow self-loathing and answer.

'Why did you call him Felix?' he asked tangentially.

'It means lucky. Blessed. When I first saw him, I swore that's what he'd be.'

'If he has you for a mum, that's a given.'

But she shook her head. 'Marc, don't. I don't need compliments. What was between us was over nine years ago. I haven't heard from you since our divorce. I assumed you'd have a wife and kids by now and be ruling the health system of Falkenstein. I've searched for you on the Internet from time to time,' she confessed. 'You seem to have been doing really well. I'm sorry about your dad, by the way. Heart attack?'

She'd been keeping tabs on him while he'd blocked her out completely. That made him feel even worse.

What did he know about her?

Involuntarily, he checked her ring finger. There was nothing there.

He thought of the ring that had once lain there—his great-grandmother's, a ring of beauty and antiquity. Ellie had returned it after the divorce but he'd sent it straight back.

'I want you to keep it, Ellie. You're a woman of honour and I'm sure my great-grandmother would be proud if you kept wearing it. Move it to another finger and wear it with pride.'

Why would she still be wearing it?

No reason at all.

What had she asked? His father. A heart attack. 'Yes. It was sudden. He was still working full-time.' He hesitated. 'Your mum?'

'She died five years ago. The first transplant lasted three years, the second one four. It was a good four years, though. She loved Felix and helped me care for him.'

'And you managed to get through university.'

'Somehow. We eked out your money. I had a room in Sydney where we all stayed. Mum looked after Felix as best she could. When she couldn't, I'd bring them both back here. I made a deal with the town—if they helped me with Felix and Mum, I'd come back and be the local doctor.'

'But you wanted to specialise.'

'Family practice is a specialty.'

'But it's not what you wanted.'

'So I've learned we can't always have what we want.' She looked directly at him. 'What do you want, Marc?'

And how much would he have given to be able to say he didn't want anything? That this was a spur-of-the-moment visit, popping in to visit his ex-wife who he hoped could still be a friend.

Ha.

'I needed to see you,' he tried.

She looked at him directly and shrugged. 'No. We're over that long since. Didn't we figure need was another name for lust?'

'What was between us wasn't just lust.'

'No. It was a juvenile love affair. But I'm asking again, Marc. Why are you here? I thought it must be that you learned about me keeping Felix, but by your reaction it seems it's not. So, you happened to be visiting Australia and decided to see how much your ex-wife has aged? What?'

There was no easy way to say this. *Just say it, Marc.*

'I came because the entire Falkenstein royal family died in a plane crash. Three days ago I was fourth in line for the throne. Now the crown is mine.'

Her face creased in shock. 'That's appalling. Why wasn't it on the news? Or maybe it was. I've been so busy.' And then her face softened. 'They're your family. Marc, I'm so sorry.'

'I don't need sympathy,' he said roughly. 'There's never been any love lost between us. I've always kept as far from the palace as possible. But now…'

'Now?' She took a moment to take in the full implications of what he'd said. 'You're…you're the new King?'

'Yes.'

Her face changed again, becoming wary. 'And that means…what? Why are you here?'

There was no way to soften what needed to be said.

'I travelled all this way, fast, to ask you to keep Felix's adoption records quiet,' he told her. 'There's already intense media interest in an obscure doctor who's suddenly their monarch. Enough people know of our short marriage that it can't be hidden. I hoped, however, that the birth would go unnoticed, or at least you could hide the adoption details.'

'Why?'

'Because adoption is accepted as legal abdication,' he said heavily. 'According to our constitution, if Felix had been formally adopted at birth he'd have no rights to succession but the media interest could still be upsetting. Now…'

Marc paused, overwhelmed by what he had to tell her.

Ellie rose and opened the sideboard. She poured two whiskies. Large ones.

'I don't drink this except in emergencies,' she told him. 'I suspect I need it now. Maybe we both do. So tell me.'

He took the glass and drained it, and then he looked at Ellie.

He could still see the girl he'd loved behind those tired eyes. He could still see the laughter, the fun… But he could also see the care and the responsibility.

When their world had crashed, she'd looked at things dispassionately.

'You're needed where you are and so am I. Our mar-

riage was a fantasy and we need to put it behind us. Good luck, Marc, and goodbye.'

He watched her shoulders brace yet again, and he hated it.

'Ellie, I'm now the Crown Prince of Falkenstein and Felix is my son. It takes a year to formalise a divorce in Australia so Felix was born while we were still legally married. This may mess with all our lives in ways I can't imagine but, once I'm crowned, Felix will take my current title. Your son—*our* son—will be the new Crown Prince of Falkenstein.'

CHAPTER FOUR

SILENCE. IT STRETCHED on and on, deep and threatening. The shock seemed endless.

Marc thought of his stupefaction when he'd first learned of this, and he thought it must be the same or even greater for Ellie.

One of the reasons he'd loved her was her courage. How much courage did she need to face this?

'I don't think I like this,' she whispered at last. And then she looked up and met his gaze head-on. 'That's an understatement. It terrifies me.'

'I remember when you first found out I was a prince.'

'That terrified me too.'

'Enough to end our marriage.'

'Is that fair?' she snapped. 'We were in a bubble and suddenly everything burst. The war in your country, finding out you were a prince, Mum's illness… Why didn't you even tell me you were a prince?'

'Because I didn't feel like one. I never did.' He'd tried to explain it then, but she'd been too angry, too confused. And he understood. Their short marriage had seemed idyllic, but suddenly there were images of war. The international spotlight shining on a country that had almost escaped the notice of the world in general had been bad enough, but superimposed on that was the news that Ellie's mother was fighting for her life.

In the face of her mother's illness she'd turned to him for support, and he'd had to point to the headlines and tell her he had to go home.

And tell her why. That he was indeed a prince. That his father was trying to hold the country's health service together. That the need was desperate.

He looked at her now and saw the same look of betrayal that he'd seen then. She'd understood why he'd needed to return to his country. What she hadn't forgiven was that he hadn't told her he was royal.

'The title of Prince remains for two generations,' he told her now. 'So yes, I'm a prince. My father used his title only because it gave him authority as head of the country's health system, but as a kid it only gave me grief. I dropped it.'

'But you can't lose it altogether.'

'I can't,' he told her. 'Not officially. And now neither can Felix. Because he's third generation, he's not had a title up until now, but Ellie, I'm sorry, that's changed. He's the new Crown Prince.'

'He's a little boy,' she said, sounding desperate. 'He's a country kid who's just coming out of a childhood marred by operation after operation for feet that don't work.' She closed her eyes and he saw a wash of anguish. 'You can't take him, Marc. I won't let you.'

'Is that why you think I'm here? To take my son? I won't take him from you.'

But, even as he said it, the words slammed home a truth impossible to ignore. *My son.* He had a son.

A kid with courage and humour and intelligence. A son to be proud of.

Like Ellie... She'd been a wife to be proud of.

'So where does that leave us?' she demanded. 'Am I

to hide him? Is that what you want? What, Marc? What demands does your country make of you—of us—now?'

'That's not fair.'

'It is fair,' she flashed. 'An accident of birth made you Prince of a country I'd never heard of and then a stupid war that achieved nothing killed our marriage. And now the death of a man you say you had nothing to do with has catapulted you into a role I don't understand. Do you even want it?'

And there was the Ellie he knew. He remembered that about her, that she always saw behind the façade. He'd come to Australia fresh out of medical school, determined to have fun, sow a few wild oats before he settled down to the grim struggle he knew was facing him. But as soon as he'd met Ellie he'd forgotten the wild oats. She seemed to see inside his soul.

He'd had more fun with her than he'd ever dreamed of, but it had been gentle fun, dictated by her need to study. It had been working through her texts with her. It had been swimming at Bondi, ducking each other in the waves, slapping on not enough sunscreen. It had been massaging each other with after-sun lotion, slowly, languorously.

It had been waking in each other's arms.

Now, looking across the table at her, he remembered every moment, and the rush of sudden desire almost blindsided him. *Ellie. His wife.*

'Don't,' she said and he knew she'd seen it too. 'Don't even think about going there. Get back to what matters. You've inherited the throne. You don't want it? Why can't you abdicate?'

'Because my grandfather propelled us into a war that almost destroyed my country.' Somehow he hauled himself back to the issue at hand. He'd had enough time on the long flight out here to accept the inevitable. 'Because another cousin will inherit if I don't accept, and Ranald's a battle-hungry fool. There's always been conflict on our eastern border and Ranald would see himself as a general, ordering our people to fight.'

'But now Felix stands between Ranald and the throne?'

'I can abdicate for myself but not for Felix. If I abdicate, Ranald will be Prince Regent. He would have a say in how Felix is raised. He'd be in control.'

'I get to say how Felix is raised.'

There were more things that had to be said. 'Ellie, succession's vital for the stability of the country and the region. In the circumstances, Ranald could apply to an international court for Felix's custody. He might even win.'

There was an angry gasp. She was thinking fast. He could see it.

And she saw the next chasm.

'If Ranald could apply for custody and win, that means you could demand it too.'

'I suspect so.' He couldn't deny it.

'But you don't want him. You never wanted him!'

This was beyond impossible. Did he want his son? He thought again of Ellie's long-ago message telling him of Felix's birth. The pain had been unbearable—was still unbearable. Ellie and his baby were all he'd ever wanted and he'd had to turn his back.

But there was no turning his back on this situation. Did the stability of the country demand he tear his son from his mother? He needed to talk to the lawyers back at home, figure out the implications.

He needed to find a nice, peaceful operating theatre and do something tricky, like repairing that elbow this afternoon. Strangely, that had settled him. It had taken all his concentration but by the time he'd walked out of Theatre the shock of seeing Ellie—and Felix—had somehow been put into perspective.

So now what? He could hardly demand that a gall bladder repair appear on cue. Ellie was looking at him for answers, and she needed them now.

Ellie. The woman who'd been his wife.

What had he done to her?

'I won't take Felix,' he told her and, despite the complications, despite the massive uproar he foresaw when Felix's existence was discovered, he knew that this was his line in the sand. 'Felix is your son and his upbringing is your business. But…'

'But?'

He took a deep breath. 'This will take some getting your head around,' he told her. 'But Felix stands to inherit the throne and until he's of an age where he can decide for himself, there's nothing we can do about it.'

'Which means…'

'Which means we tell him. Which means we introduce him to his country.'

'He's not leaving here.'

'Not permanently. But at first… Ellie, how do you feel about bringing him to Falkenstein for the coronation? Let the people see him. Let the media talk openly about what happened between us. Introduce Felix to his people with all honour.'

'His people…' She seemed dazed.

'The more I think about it, the more it seems the only way. Otherwise you'll have the media filling in gaps with speculation. The coronation's at the end of next month. You'd need to come a few weeks beforehand so Felix can get his head around what's expected of him. Then we can ask for media cooperation to leave Felix be until he reaches maturity. We could arrange for a photo shoot once a year— maybe you could bring him over to the palace for your summer holidays. But he'll mostly be here, out of the spotlight.'

'But not now.' It was practically a wail. 'He can't travel. His leg… The risk of thrombosis…'

'We can pay for the whole of first class if we need—or hire our own jet. That'll give him more than enough room to move around and negate the risk of a clot.'

'You're kidding.'

'Felix is a prince,' he said gently. 'You need to get used to it.'

'But I'd have to come with him.'

'You would,' he agreed gravely. 'It'd be overwhelming for a nine-year-old to face without his mother.'

'I can't.'

'Because?' He was watching her face, watching anguish. 'Ellie, you couldn't come with me before because of your mother, and because you needed to finish your medical training. I'm not asking you to return as my wife. I'm asking you to come for a few weeks. What's stopping you?'

'I couldn't come then for all sorts of reasons,' she snapped, anguish veering towards anger. 'You were flying back into a war zone. I was a student. I had no skills to help. What was I supposed to do, sit back and play doctor's wife while you played the hero?'

'Ellie…'

'It was all sorts of impossible,' she flashed. 'And it's impossible now. I'm a country doctor. This is where I'm needed. I can't just leave for what…six weeks?'

'There must be some way…'

'Even if there was I wouldn't take it. You broke my heart once. You think I'd let you do it again?'

And that was a conversation-changer.

'This isn't about us,' he managed.

'No,' she flashed. 'And it's not going to be. There's nothing between us and there's nothing between you and your son. As far as you were concerned, for the last nine years we haven't existed.'

'That's not true.'

'It has to be true. I'm the only doctor in this place. I'm needed here, and Felix needs to be here too. His leg—'

'There are specialists in Falkenstein.'

'I'm not listening. I'm not going. Bring on your lawyers, Marc, because I'll fight you every inch of the way.'

'Ellie, see reason.'

'I am seeing reason.' Her green eyes were flashing fire and suddenly the years fell away. This was the Ellie he knew.

He remembered the first time he'd met her. She'd been in a waitress uniform, a silly, frilly apron and a cap that was slightly skewed with her auburn hair escaping from the regulation knot. She'd been surrounded by a sea of wine and broken glass. He'd caught her shoulders to stop her falling.

He'd been wearing a dinner jacket and a crisp white shirt. His shirt had suddenly looked like a kindergarten finger painting. She'd gazed at him in horror, but then, just for a moment, their gazes had locked.

'Whoops,' she'd said and it had been all he could do not to laugh. Amazingly, her eyes had twinkled back.

Then she'd swung into penitent mode, and gratitude that he'd accepted the blame, but her first reaction had been laughter. It had been that twinkle, that defiance in seeing the funny side in what should, for her, have been a catastrophe, that made him wait for her that night.

The defiance was here now. But not the humour.

'Go away, Marc. This is scaring me to death.'

'The Ellie I knew had courage.'

'I'm not the Ellie you knew.'

'Ellie, the royal thing…' How to make her see? 'It's just like Felix's club feet. It's non-negotiable. It's something we have to deal with.'

'You deal with it. Leave us alone.'

He raked his hair.

But there were other things now that were messing with his head. He'd almost forgotten how much this woman had meant to him. He'd almost forgotten how much he wanted her.

They were feelings he couldn't possibly admit to now. He gazed across to her in baffled silence. Where to go from here?

Maybe it would have been best to send a lawyer, he thought. A lawyer could spell things out without emotion. Emotions were doing his head in. He needed help.

But so did Ellie, far more than him. He looked at her tired face and he tried to look dispassionately. Tried to see the big picture.

'Ellie, why are you working here on your own?' he said tangentially. 'Why are you looking as if you haven't had enough sleep for weeks?'

'Maybe I haven't.'

'So the practice is too big for one doctor?'

'I— Yes, it is.'

'Then why...?'

'Because Felix costs me a fortune.' She might not have said it if she hadn't been pushed close to the edge, he thought. He remembered her flat refusal to accept financial aid once their marriage had ended and he realised this admission, for Ellie, was huge. 'His specialist...the operations... This isn't a rich district and people often can't afford to pay but I promised...'

And anger surged again.

'Then that stops now,' he said flatly. 'I owe you for ten years of child maintenance for a start. I can afford to pay for locums, starting now. You will accept help, Ellie.'

'You can't buy me.'

'I'm not buying. I'm paying what I owe. Ellie...'

But she'd had enough. She ran her fingers through her

hair in a gesture of pure exhaustion and it was all he could do not to reach out and take her hand in his. To reassure her.

But he'd frightened her to death and reassurance wasn't possible.

'Go away, Marc,' she managed.

'You know I can't do that.'

'Then go… I don't know…wherever you're staying. I need space. I need to think.'

'We can sort this out.'

'Maybe, but I need to get my head clear,' she snapped. 'You've had time to come to terms with this. I haven't.' She took a deep breath. 'Tomorrow, I have clinic…'

'Could I help?'

'You've helped enough.' She rose and opened the door into the night. 'I finish clinic at midday. I usually eat lunch here but if you buy me sandwiches we can talk during lunch.'

'I could—'

'That's all, Marc,' she said flatly, drearily. 'Please. Let me be.'

And he looked at her for a long moment, but there was nothing for him to do except leave.

There were sheep in the paddock beside the motel, snuffling and bleating under his window.

It wasn't the sheep keeping him awake.

He felt as if he'd been picked up and placed into a parallel universe.

A universe where he had a son.

He'd always known Felix existed but there'd been a job opening as a father nine years ago, and he'd missed it.

'I couldn't have come,' he said out loud into the dark. 'Even if I'd known Ellie was doing the parenting…'

Ellie.

Why was the image of Ellie's face, Ellie's shock, Ellie's weariness, superimposed on every other thought?

His phone buzzed. Josef.

The explanation of what had happened left the old man stunned.

'You have a legitimate heir? Do you realise what uproar this will cause? You need to bring him home. Is your ex-wife reasonable? Does she agree?'

'I don't know,' he said heavily. 'To be honest, I don't know anything about her. Give me time.'

'You have two days. Has she remarried?'

'No.'

'So why did you divorce? Would it be possible to re-marry?' Josef sounded so stunned he was clutching at straws. 'No matter. You do need to marry but that can be sorted later and you obviously can't remarry if she's unsuitable. What's important now is to get the child here any way you can but, whatever you do, keep your ex-wife onside. The last thing you need is a tell-all exposé in the press.'

'I'll do my best.'

'Promise her anything within reason. The last thing we need is more scandal. Give her anything she wants.'

He disconnected and lay there, staring into the dark.

Give her anything she wants?

I'll do my best.

Ellie had received a lot less than his best in the past. What made him think she'd accept any more now?

And in her hospital apartment Ellie lay and looked sightlessly into the same dark.

Marc was here.

She'd thought she was over him. How could the sight of him sitting at her kitchen table do her head in?

Marc belonged to a crazy time in her life. For a short few months she'd forgotten the responsibilities life had thrust on her almost as soon as she was able to walk. An invalid mother who'd refused to take care of herself. A father who'd walked out on them. A town who'd helped her train and expected medical care in return.

She buried her head in the pillows but it didn't help. She climbed out of bed and went and stared out of the window into the dark.

Marc was just down the road, in the local motel. Marc, the most gorgeous man she'd ever set eyes on. The man who'd turned her world upside down.

Who'd just turned it upside down again.

Be practical. She forced herself to put aside the image of her ex-husband—tricky that—and focus on what he was asking of her.

Could she go to Falkenstein?

'It might be exciting,' she muttered. 'Maybe I'd get to stay in a palace.'

'Felix would stay in the palace.' She was arguing with herself. 'They'd probably put me in an attic. But an attic in Falkenstein might be more exciting than here.'

'Oh, for heaven's sake…' She threw the window open so the night air could cool her heated face. The night was full of the vision of Marc. Her head felt as if it might explode.

To take Felix to Falkenstein, or to let him go without her. To lose control.

The alternative, to spend weeks near Marc…

The in-house phone rang, the connection between her apartment and the hospital, and she almost fell on it with relief. Anything to stop herself thinking of Marc.

The nurse was apologetic. 'Ellie? Sorry to wake you but Mrs Ferguson's restless. Permission to up the diazepam?'

An intercom in Felix's room connected to the nurses' station meant she could come and go to the hospital without worrying. 'Yes! I'll come.'

'There's no need,' the nurse said, startled. 'If you can

just give me a phone order… She's not uncomfortable, just doing her usual moaning, but she's getting loud.'

That wasn't so unusual. Eighty years old and in hospital because she'd broken her foot while trying to kick her son's dog, Myra Ferguson moaned at the world.

But Ellie had the choice. She could stay here staring into the dark or she could go and hear how appalling the world was treating Myra and how inconsiderate her son was to own a dog.

There wasn't a choice. The dark involved thinking of Marc.

Myra's moans were nothing in comparison.

CHAPTER FIVE

SOMETIMES ELLIE'S CLINICS ran over time. Often. Sometimes she finished her morning clinic to find her afternoon patients already queueing.

But not this morning. She ushered out her last patient and her receptionist was beaming.

'All done, and not a single house call. And your gorgeous doctor friend is waiting in the car park. You should see the car he's driving! It's a bright red sports car, and he has the sun roof down. He's about to whisk you off to an assignation.'

'Sandwiches and soda in the park,' she said dryly. 'I'll be back in thirty minutes.'

'I've cleared an hour if you need it,' Marilyn said serenely. 'Oh, Ellie, he's beautiful. And the rumours are that he's Felix's father.'

This town! Word would have flown throughout the district before breakfast.

'You want to put a bit of lippy on?' Marilyn said happily. 'And unfasten that top button.'

'Oh, for heaven's sake…'

But she did just happen to glance in the mirror before she left. A woman had some pride.

What had happened to her in the past ten years?

He watched her walk towards him and he worried.

She was wearing faded black pants, a white shirt and a soft grey cardigan. Plain black shoes, old. Her auburn hair was caught into a sensible knot.

She wore no make-up, no jewellery.

She looked as if she'd turned into a workhorse. His beautiful, vibrant Ellie...

He'd done this to her. He'd turned her into a single parent.

Maybe he should be angry that she'd kept things from him, and part of him was, but the overwhelming feeling he had was guilt.

And grief.

'Do you have sandwiches or will I grab some from the hospital kitchen?' she called, and he thought, great, he'd eaten her fish and chips and now she was offering to bring hospital sandwiches. What would he give to be able to say he had a picnic basket loaded with lobster, caviar, the finest selection of breads from a French *boulangerie*, champagne on ice...?

'I have pies,' he told her. 'Courtesy of the general store. And fruit and soda.' How exotic was that? What was the use in being King? he thought ruefully. He should have called for the army to fly in truffles before dawn.

But it seemed they were acceptable. 'Pies?' Her face lit and he thought, *Wow*. What a small thing to give her pleasure.

And why did that make him feel so good?

'Mrs Thomas makes the best pies,' she told him as she reached him. 'You can't think how tired I get of hospital food, but there's seldom enough time for me to cook or even shop. There's a park down by the creek and the creek has water at this time of year. I have my phone. We might get lucky and it'll stay silent long enough for us to eat.'

'I need time to talk.'

'I know,' she told him and slid into his car. 'So talk.'

But he couldn't for a bit. The pleasure on her face had unsettled him. Disarmed him even.

He followed her directions down to what she'd optimistically referred to as a park—a stand of gum trees on a bend in a creek bed. They set themselves up on the lone park bench. He handed Ellie a pie and she attacked it as if there was no tomorrow.

'You were hungry?' he asked, startled, and she smiled between mouthfuls.

'I'm experienced,' she told him. 'My beeper goes and my food gets forgotten. I learned early to feed rather than graze.'

'Just how busy are you?'

'Twenty-four-seven.' She paused and looked down at the remains of her pie with respect. 'But I do get fed. The hospital cook has been known to show up when I'm inundated with house calls. I'll come out of someone's front door and she'll be standing there with a plate of lasagne and arms akimbo, glaring at me and daring me not to eat before I go to the next job. They look after me,' she said simply. 'It's why I'm here. This town is desperate for a doctor and they'll do what they must to keep me. Including looking after Felix. I've never had to worry about childcare. As a single mum, I have it easy.'

'You don't look like you have it easy.'

'We're not here to talk about me. We need to talk about Felix.'

'Ellie...'

'We'll come,' she said simply. 'I'll accept your help finding locums. I understand this is Felix's life. I can't refuse. But I won't leave him there, Marc. He comes home with me after the coronation. He can spend a couple of weeks every year with you, as long as I have your written assurance, overseen by international lawyers, that he returns to

Australia after each two weeks away. When he's eighteen, he can make up his own mind what to do.'

So he'd got what he wanted. Sort of.

'You'll come with him?'

'For the first visit, yes, but for the rest, as long as you make sure he's safely escorted and cared for, my place is here.'

'He'll need to come a bit before. There'll be a media frenzy. We need to prepare you both.'

'We?'

'The royal minders. They'll also be preparing me for my role but that's not…'

'My business? No.' Her mouth set. 'He'll need to stay at the palace?'

'Yes.'

'I can stay with him?'

'I hope you will.'

'I can't imagine me in a palace.'

'I can't imagine me in a palace,' he told her and she looked swiftly up at him.

'You don't want this?'

'What do you think?'

She stared up at him for a long moment. 'I guess… I don't know anything at all about you, Marc. Or make that Your Highness. I know nothing at all.'

'You knew enough to marry me.'

'I was nineteen years old. A lovestruck teenager.'

'And you've regretted it ever since?'

Why had he asked? What difference did it make? Was it vanity—or something else?

When the thought of marriage had come up it had seemed impossible, fraught with problems, a fairy tale. But the day after Ellie's exams, he'd woken with her beside him. He'd lain in the filtered dawn light and thought of the last weeks, during which he should have been travelling, enjoying the freedom he'd craved. Instead of which, he'd stayed in Ellie's bedsit, helping her cram, or walking her to and from her endless waitressing jobs, or thinking of what to make for dinner—and actually cooking! He'd swotted up on student medicine—the things he'd had to learn for exams but had promptly forgotten the moment he'd passed. He'd pushed her, bullied her, hugged her, worried with her…

And that morning she'd woken in his arms and he'd kissed her and said, 'Ellie, I know marriage is impossible but dammit, let's do it anyway. Let's face the impossible afterwards.' She'd kissed him and said a drowsy, deliriously happy yes. And four weeks later, despite the sonorous drone of the marriage celebrant intoning the age-old vows in a council chamber, those vows had seemed like life itself.

For as long as you both shall live…

Maybe that was why he'd never thought of marrying again.

And you've regretted it ever since? His question hung in the air between them.

'I have Felix,' she said and bit into her remaining pie with a decisive crunch. 'How can I regret that?'

That was enough to shut him up. It wasn't about him. It was about a son he'd never known.

'What about you?' she said as she demolished the last crust and looked consideringly at the apple he'd provided. 'I'm not asking if you regret our marriage. That's a given— apart from Felix it was an appalling mistake. But wife? Kids? Why not?'

'No time.'

'Like me.'

'And you've been working too hard so you can pay for Felix's medical costs. And your mother's too, I'll bet. Ellie, why the hell didn't you tell me?' It was an explosion and a couple of ducks that had been edging nearer, eyeing crusts, took to the air in flight.

'It wasn't your business.'

'Of course it was my business.'

She'd picked up the apple. Now she laid it back down on the bench and stood and faced him. 'I lied to you,' she told him. 'Oh, I didn't tell outright lies but I let you believe Felix had been adopted. That was deceit. And at first I did it to protect you. I was reading about the situation in Falkenstein and I knew the pressure you were under. I knew how impossible it would be for you to drop everything and come. But afterwards, when the war ended...'

'Yes?' He was still angry, still frustrated. She was standing before him, a shadow of the vibrant girl he'd married. She was weary, careworn, worried. Her hair could do with a cut. Her clothes were...serviceable.

Half his frustration was that he wanted to pick her up and change things. Give her time to sleep. Send her to a decent hairdresser. Buy her some attractive clothes.

Care for her...

'I was afraid you'd still care,' she said and it brought him up short. 'I was afraid...the feelings we had...they were so strong they threw our lives out of control. My mum needed me. The town needed me and Felix needed me. When I was with you I forgot everything and it scared me witless. I couldn't go there again. I couldn't risk it. I thought, if I told you, you'd come. You were honourable, you'd want a say in how Felix was raised, but most of all you'd be in my life. I couldn't afford to feel like that.' She took a deep breath. 'And, Marc, I still can't.'

And he understood.

Anger faded as he faced her fear head-on. He thought of the times he'd wanted to contact her, to find out how her life was going. He thought of the times he'd come close and then pulled away.

He had no life to offer a bride. Even now. The goldfish bowl of royalty, the appalling media attention he was about to attract, the resentment the people had for a royal family who'd brought them nothing but trouble—combined, it was the stuff of nightmares.

He thought fleetingly of Josef's assertion…

'We need to find you a wife. Get you a son…'

What a joke! There was so much to do to put the country back on a stable footing, how could he possibly have time to woo and wed a suitable bride?

Fraught as things were, Felix at least answered this problem. He now had a son.

He didn't need a wife. He could stay in control. Sort of.

Ellie was looking straight at him, her gaze defiant. What she'd said had been a confession of sorts, he thought. A confirmation that what had been between them was a wildfire, impossible to control.

But, like a wildfire, even though the flames were long gone, embers glowed underground for years, awaiting their chance to flare again.

'I get it,' he said roughly. 'I don't have to like it, but I understand. But you'll let me help now. You'll come back here after the coronation, but from now on the financial responsibility for Felix is mine. He's to receive the best medical care available and you—Ellie, you're officially mother to the Crown Prince and as such you'll receive an allowance.'

'I don't want your money.'

'It's not my money. It's a state allowance for the Crown Prince and his mother, and it's not negotiable. I *will* care for you.' There was that anger again. The wildfire analogy flashed back—an ember smouldering deep underground.

He caught himself. He gathered the remains of the picnic and carried it to the trash can. When he returned, Ellie was still standing, watching him. Her face was expressionless but he knew this woman.

Was he seeing fear?

'Ellie…' He reached out and touched her face, but she slapped his hand away as if he were a viper.

'Don't touch me.'

'I didn't mean—'

'Neither of us meant anything. What happened between us was stupid on so many levels.'

'We loved each other.'

'Did either of us know what love is? I loved my mum and she needed me. You loved your country and you were needed at home. Now I love Felix. That's the love we need to focus on. What was between us was crazy, a stupid denial of responsibilities.'

He watched her face and still saw fear, but also the wash of raw emotion she couldn't conceal. His presence was reawakening something she had no control over and he understood. He felt the same.

Ten years ago he'd fallen for this woman in a way he could never understand, and somewhere under the fear, despite the years of separation, that incomprehensible feeling still lingered.

But it had to be ignored. For one crazy moment he thought about what it would be like to be a medieval royal prince. He could summon his knights, point to Ellie and say *I'll have that one*. His knights would carry her to his bed. His women would bathe her and dress her as she deserved to be dressed. All honour would be bestowed on her and she'd be his Queen.

Yeah. Like that was going to happen. The time for impulse, for passion was over. For behind Ellie's fear there was anger. Ellie's life was here. He was messing with it enough. He couldn't risk pushing it further.

'I won't touch you,' he told her.

But was that enough? She was staring at him as if baffled. 'What?'

'I have no idea,' she snapped. 'I don't have a clue what I'm feeling, much less why. All I know is that you lay a hand on me and all deals are off. I'll fight you every inch of the way for Felix, and maybe you'll win because you have the resources to fight, but I'll try anyway. And you won't make friends with Felix that way. If you want to be his dad, you respect my boundaries.'

'Of course.'

But even then she was looking at him as if he was some kind of puzzle she couldn't work out.

Her phone buzzed. She glanced at it and he saw relief.

'I need to go. Rebecca Taylor's parents have just brought her in and Chris thinks it's appendicitis. If Chris thinks it's appendix, it's ninety nine per cent sure to be appendix.'

And wasn't that just what he needed? Medicine. Something he understood. 'Would you like me to help?'

'No!'

'You can't operate on your own.'

'Chris will help if necessary but I'll try and settle things, and evacuate her to the city.'

'I'm a surgeon. You know as well as I do that sometimes an appendix can turn into an emergency. Let me check.'

Her expression changed, from defensive to understanding and sympathy.

'You want to work.'

There was no response but the truth. 'Yes.'

'Marc...' He saw compassion in her eyes. 'They're asking you to give up medicine?'

'I have no choice.'

'Again?'

'What's that supposed to mean?'

She shook her head. 'You had no choice when you walked away from us. If that hurt you as much as it hurt me...' She paused, catching herself. 'No matter. That's history. But for you to walk away from your medicine as well as everything else…'

'I can handle it.'

'I'm sure you can,' she whispered. 'But oh, Marc, it'll hurt.' She considered for a moment and then came to a decision. 'Okay. Yesterday we worked on emergency principles. In a life or death situation a doctor can't be sued. An overseas doctor can step in at need. Today's probably not an emergency, but if you work as my official assistant— under supervision—there shouldn't be a problem.'

Ellie's assistant… It sounded good to him.

'There's nothing I'd like better.'

'Then don't smile at me like that,' she snapped, suddenly angry. 'Because when you do—'

'When I do—what?'

'When you do, I feel like I have no business to feel what I feel,' she managed and her voice wobbled. 'Marc, I have no intention of ever feeling like I did ten years ago, but we *can* work together. Let's see to this appendix and then move on.'

Rebecca Taylor was thirteen years old and terrified. She was retching when Marc and Ellie walked into the ward. When the retching eased she cringed back into herself, folding into the foetal position.

'Hey,' Ellie said, stooping and brushing her hair from the girl's face, removing the bowl, putting her face at the level of Rebecca's. She had obviously been retching for a while; she was producing nothing. 'Becky, hugs. This is horrid. We're here to get it sorted, to get this pain to stop. Do you mind if Dr Falken takes a look at you? He's a surgeon. He's also my friend, and he's good.'

The words gave Marc a jolt. *He's also my friend, and he's good.* It was a normal thing for one doctor to say of a colleague. Why did it sound different coming from Ellie? Why did it sound…more?

He glanced at Becky's parents and saw their shoulders ease. The way Ellie had introduced him was a reassurance all on its own.

And, through her pain, Becky's attention was caught. 'He's the doc from yesterday? The one they're all talking about?' Despite her distress she looked across at Marc. 'He's…he's cute.'

'He is, isn't he?' Ellie said smoothly. 'And he's a very good doctor. He's a surgeon, which I'm not, and we think you may have appendicitis, which is something surgeons are good at. I'll stay with you, but is it okay if Dr Falken examines you?'

The fear surged back. 'Mum?'

Becky's mum took her daughter's hand. 'You can do this, Becky,' she whispered. 'Relax and let Dr Falken fix the problem.'

'Let's see your tummy,' Marc told her. 'Becky, I need you to tell me if my hands are cold. I'm known for warm hands but sometimes my central heating lets me down. Chris has told you she thinks it's appendicitis? You know you don't need your appendix. You would if you were a rabbit and ate grass but I can't see you as a grass-eating type of girl. If you let me check your tummy, and I find that Chris is right, it's simply a matter of popping you to sleep, nicking the appendix out and popping it into a jar so you can gross out your friends. Then you get a couple of weeks off school while your mum and dad spoil you rotten. Would that be okay?'

He had Becky mesmerised. She gave him a weak smile and managed to roll so her tummy was available for inspection. 'You heard that, Mum?' she whispered. 'Would that mean a new video game? Of my choice?'

'I guess,' her mum said with a wavering smile at her husband. 'If that's what the doctor says.'

'That's what both doctors say,' Ellie told them. 'Thanks, Becky. Okay, Dr Falken, rub those hands until they're warm and let's get on with it.'

Marc gently probed Becky's abdomen. She let him press and then cried out in pain as he released the pressure.

Rebound.

Ellie had thought she was doing Marc a favour by asking him to help, but now the favour was reversed. Rebound was a sign that the appendix had burst. She could send Becky to Sydney but the longer they waited the more the infected matter would spread.

So once again Marc was in the operating theatre. This time Ellie gave the anaesthetic while Chris assisted.

Becky was a healthy thirteen-year-old. Anaesthetising and intubating was relatively straightforward. Ellie had time to watch.

There was no doubting this man was good. His fingers were nimble, sure, skilled as he removed the mess of an appendix. There was no hesitation. If she'd had to operate she'd have struggled. Someone more skilled might well have had to go in after her.

Oh, to have someone like this working beside her.

And that made her think. *To work beside Marc every day...*

That had been a dream from a long time ago. Some time during their honeymoon—a few days spent on the beach at Bondi—they'd planned a future where they set up a hospital together, where they worked side by side, where they were partners in every sense of the word.

But then the world had stepped in, as it had stepped in again now.

What Marc was doing was brilliant. He'd removed the gangrenous appendix and was cleaning the cavity with scrupulous care. He couldn't have been more careful if he'd been operating on the King himself.

The King himself... That was what *he* was.

His role must be vital, Ellie conceded, but part of her was thinking, *What a waste.* To lose the skill those fingers possessed...

'All done,' Marc pronounced. While Ellie had been mostly silent, lost in her own thoughts, he and Chris had been chatting like long-term workmates. Now he took the prepared sutures from Chris and grinned. Procedure done, he had time to relax. 'Want to watch my needlework?' he demanded. 'My mama taught me. If you're going to be a doctor then you learn the basics, she told me, and she had me stitching samplers when boys my age were out playing football. I thought it was sissy.'

'There's nothing sissy about you now,' Chris said soundly and glanced at Ellie. 'I can see why Ellie fell for you.'

'For my needlework? Maybe,' he said and his smile died. 'Not so much for my partner potential.' He went back to concentrating on giving Becky a hairline closure that would hardly mar her bikini line.

And Ellie thought... Ellie thought...

She thought about this town. She thought about her nice, controlled life.

And she thought it was time she got back to not thinking about Marc at all.

With Becky regaining consciousness, with IV and antibiotic lines set up, with Chris and Becky's parents in attendance, there was nothing more for Marc to do. Ellie, on the other hand, had a queue for a now very late afternoon clinic.

She was stressed, she was tired—she'd hardly slept the night before—and she needed to get away from Marc. His presence had her so confused she couldn't think.

'Can I help here too?' he asked.

'Thanks, but I can cope.' She hesitated, knowing she'd sounded brusque. 'But maybe you'd like to collect Felix after school? If you like I can phone his teacher and have him expect you. You can spend a couple of hours telling him about his new future.'

'Thank you,' he said gravely. 'I'd like that.' And then, 'Ellie, I need to go back to Falkenstein tomorrow. Can we have dinner tonight?'

'I do evening surgery on Tuesday.' She glanced at her watch, and he saw her hand suddenly tremble. 'Marc, I'm sorry but I need to go.'

And what was he to say to that?

She was heading back to her medicine.

As mother to the Crown Prince she'd be entitled to a life of luxury. There'd be no need for her to do a thing for the rest of her life except support her son.

He'd tell her that, but he knew already how she'd take it. She'd look at him and return to the medicine she loved.

How jealous was he?

He wouldn't see her again for a month. She was moving out of his life again.

It did his head in.

He'd vowed to take this woman to him, *for as long as we both shall live*. The divorce papers should have negated that, but somehow they hadn't. More than anything in the world he wanted to gather her in his arms and claim her. It felt as if she belonged.

'Goodbye then, Ellie,' he managed and she looked at him calmly, gravely.

'The next few weeks will be hard for you.'

She understood? Of course she did. This woman knew how desperately he'd wanted to be a doctor. And now, instead of the medicine that was a part of him, he was facing the overwhelming responsibilities of head of state. 'They'll be fine,' he managed, even though he knew they'd be hard to the point of unbearable.

'We'll be thinking of you. Me and Felix. Best of luck in learning to be King.'

'I—' He stopped and smiled ruefully. 'Thank you.'

'It can't be harder than first-year internship.' She tried a smile in return. 'The first time you faced a rowdy drunk needing stitches was trial by fire. What could be worse than that? As doctors we've all been there. All else pales.'

'Ellie…' He could hardly get his voice to work.

'You'll do brilliantly,' she said, and then to his astonishment she stepped forward and kissed him. It was a feather touch, a mere brushing of lips on lips, and she pulled away fast before he could respond.

'Best of luck,' she said and she smiled at him. 'You'll make a great king, Your Majesty. See you in Falkenstein.'

CHAPTER SIX

ELLIE HAD BEEN on a plane four times in her life. They'd been short flights to Sydney to attend conferences, sitting in the cheap seats. This flight was different. To say she was nervous would be an understatement.

But Felix wasn't nervous at all. Newly out of his wheelchair, he gloried in this new adventure. He spent hours with his nose glued to the window, explaining to Ellie that Siberia was underneath and he was sure he'd just seen a polar bear. He made friends with everyone. He slept for eight hours in his gorgeous first class bed, his braced leg straight out and safe, and as the plane landed in Falkenstein he was quivering with excitement.

Ellie was quivering too, but it wasn't with excitement.

'Ladies and gentlemen, we're privileged to be carrying members of Falkenstein's royal family on this flight. If you could all please stay seated until they disembark…'

The announcement took her breath away.

Members of the royal family. *Members, plural.*

Felix was still on crutches, but he was clean and brushed and as prince-like as she was able to get him. He might almost qualify as a baby prince.

Ellie was wearing her customary black trousers, white shirt and black jacket. She'd twisted her curls into a knot, as severe as she could make it. *Royal family? Ha!*

'This is nothing to do with me,' she told herself. 'I'll stay in the background.' She took a deep breath, put her hands firmly on Felix's shoulders and led him out of the plane. And in that instant she knew staying in the background would be impossible.

A red carpet lined the steps. A crowd of dignitaries and media was waiting below.

And Marc was there.

The first time she'd seen Marc he'd been wearing a simple suit, shirt and tie. His dark hair had been in need of a cut. He'd just finished med school and that was what he'd looked like. She'd thought he looked gorgeous. But now...

It wasn't fair, Ellie thought, as she blinked in the sunlight, trying to get her head around this new Marc. If she'd seen him like this the first time she'd met him she'd have run a mile.

Because this man was beyond gorgeous.

She knew he'd been part of Falkenstein's army, working as a medic, so she should have expected the uniform, but this was no ordinary uniform. Tassels, gilt, medals...

Oh, for heaven's sake... She wanted to get back into the plane, now.

But Felix had no such reservations. Over the past weeks he'd spent time on the phone to his new-found father. He'd decided he approved, and Marc in uniform clearly met with more of the same.

'Wow! Papa!'

Marc waved and grinned and formality went out of the window. He ran lightly up the plane steps, reached Felix and scooped him off his feet to hug him. Crutches clattered aside, unneeded.

The assembled media went nuts. A hundred-odd cameras were pointed in their direction.

She almost abandoned Felix to his fate. Almost. But this was her baby. She wasn't about to hand him over and run.

Marc was setting him down, holding his shoulders with pride—as if he'd been Felix's father all his life.

Which she supposed he had been, biologically speaking, but still...

And then he smiled at her and she forgot to think of Felix. Who could think of anything past that smile?

'Hey,' he said and his smile was a caress all by itself. 'Ellie. Welcome to Falkenstein. How was the flight?'

'It was awesome,' Felix answered for her. 'I saw a bear and I watched two movies. I had a whole bed and I have a bag full of free stuff. Toothpaste. Earplugs. You want to see?'

'Absolutely,' Marc said, still smiling at Ellie. His smile was a question, though. 'But first, Ellie, I'm sorry but the press got wind of your arrival. Which explains the media, the limousines down there, and my uniform. This is the anticipated arrival of the heir to the throne.'

'You could have warned me,' she muttered. 'I look...'

'You look great.'

'Says the guy with the gold tassels.'

'They come with the job description.'

'I'm a prince now,' Felix interjected importantly. 'Can I have tassels? And medals?'

'Yes to the tassels but you need to earn your medals,' Marc told him. 'Starting now. We need to look royal and wave to the cameras. Ellie...'

'I'll go back inside,' Ellie muttered. 'You two get all the pictures you want. I'm an outsider.'

'You're not,' Marc said gently. 'You're the mother of the heir to the throne of Falkenstein and you'll be accorded all honour. As is your right. Felix, you do need to earn your medals, but your mother should have them pinned to her right now.' And, before she knew what he was about, he took her hand and tugged her around to face the media below. Felix stood before them with Marc's hand on his shoulder. Mother and father and son.

One royal prince in his regimentals. One child who'd one day inherit the throne.

One scared doctor in a suit that needed replacing, with shadows under her eyes from lack of sleep, with all the worry of the world in her heart.

But Marc's arm came around her waist and he smiled at the cameras and there was nothing for it. Ellie smiled too.

She was so far out of her comfort zone she felt as if she might be about to fall off.

The only thing securing her was Marc's arm and that felt dangerous too.

Prince Marc, Crown Prince of Falkenstein. Dr Falken. Her ex-lover and ex-husband.

None of the descriptions seemed to fit. All she knew was that, for now, he was holding her and she needed that hold to steady her.

How had she ever got herself into this mess?

They drove in a limousine to the castle. A sober-faced, dark-suited bodyguard sat beside a uniformed driver. Two dark cars drove front and rear, and armed outriders rode motorbikes beside them.

'Is this necessary?' Ellie managed.

'Royalty comes with a price,' Marc told her. 'Constant security is part of it. But don't worry. For the next few weeks all you need to do is take a holiday. Enjoy yourself.'

'Like that's possible in a million years,' she muttered and then Felix bounced in with information about the flight. He and Marc proceeded to chat about Siberia and bears and an alien movie while Ellie pressed her nose against the window and wondered what she'd got herself into.

The country seemed beautiful. Falkenstein was a tiny

kingdom, bordered by massive mountain ranges. The villages they were passing through were full of weathered stone cottages, beautiful churches, quaint shops.

'We have modern centres,' Marc told her, interrupting his conversation with Felix to cut across her thoughts. 'But this approach to the castle is tourist country. We play to it.'

'And why wouldn't you?' she murmured. Then the cavalcade rounded a bend and the palace was just…there.

As if it were hanging in the clouds, it was a fairy tale high on the cliffs, its white stone glistening in the afternoon sun, all turrets and spires and multi-coloured pennants waving gaily in the breeze.

It was vast. It was beautiful.

It took her breath away.

'Wow,' Felix breathed and Ellie thought she couldn't have said better herself. 'Do people really live here?'

'I live here,' Marc said ruefully.

'And do you have servants and butlers and…stuff?'

'Yes, we do.'

'Awesome,' Felix breathed. 'Wait till I tell the guys back home. Do you have horses and swords and dungeons?'

'I believe we do.'

'Wow. Mum, isn't this awesome?'

'Awesome indeed,' Ellie managed and glanced across at Marc.

He was the Crown Prince, complete with tassels and medals and epaulettes and whatever else those decorations on his dress uniform were.

He was smiling with what might even be understanding, but she wasn't in the mood for understanding. No one could possibly know what she was feeling right now.

The only word she could think of was panic.

'If you look down to your left, you'll see a modern red-roofed building beside the river,' Marc told her, and she looked, even though the castle kept drawing her gaze, terrifying the life out of her.

A building with a red roof. Okay, she had it. It seemed to be set in some sort of park leading down to the river.

'That's our local hospital,' Marc told her. 'It's where I've been based for the last six years. Maybe you'd like to see it while you're here.'

'You still have a key?'

He smiled but it was suddenly strained. 'I can go there wherever I want, but I go now as ruling sovereign.'

'Bodyguards included.'

'Bodyguards included.'

'That must suck.'

'It does indeed suck,' he said gravely. 'I miss my job more than I can say. But what I'm doing is more important.'

'Playing dress-up?'

His smile disappeared altogether. He looked down at his beautiful uniform and then he met her gaze head-on.

'If you knew how much I'd rather be in scrubs right now…'

She did know. And with that knowledge part of her panic fell away.

She'd been feeling trapped, but how much more so must Marc feel? She knew how passionate he was about his medicine, yet now he was forced to live in a sugar-frosted fantasy of a palace while the world he loved operated just below him.

'I'm sorry,' she whispered.

His gaze held hers. 'You understand.'

'I guess I do.'

'Thank you,' he said simply. And then his smile returned and her heart twisted as it had no right to twist. *Oh, Marc…*

But her heart had better get itself under control, she told herself harshly.

Marc might be trapped for ever but she wasn't. Four weeks, tops.

It was nine that night before Ellie finally had time to herself.

The day had been crazy, a jumbled mix of introductions, formality and pomp.

She was now in a suite designated for the mother of the heir to the throne. Her bedroom looked the size of a small football field and the attached living room took her breath away. Her meagre luggage had been unpacked by a maid who was more impressively dressed than she was. A woman had arrived and done a quick measure and promised a few outfits 'to make you more comfortable in your surroundings, ma'am.' She was so out of her depth she didn't argue.

Felix was asleep on the other side of the door in an adjoining room. His apartment was similarly impressive. It was set up as a nursery, but not for babies. It was a space most nine-year-olds could only dream of.

There was a nurse sleeping in yet another room, a twinkly lady in her sixties. 'He doesn't need a nurse,' Ellie had stammered when Marc had introduced them and Marc had put a finger to his lips to shush her.

'Hilda was my good, kind nurse when I was a baby. She understands boys and, what's more important, she understands what Felix needs to know. She also has a grandson of about Felix's age. She'll introduce them tomorrow and see if they hit it off. Pierre's English is sketchy but he's bright and fun and Felix might feel better with a friend. Hilda might help you both feel more at home. Now, I'm sorry, Ellie, but I have things I need to attend to. I'll see you later tonight.'

That had been five hours ago. Hilda had taken them on

a mind-boggling tour of the palace. She'd answered Felix's thousands of questions. She'd given Felix his dinner and clucked because Ellie wasn't hungry, but finally she'd let Ellie be.

In Ellie's cavernous apartment the silence was deafening.

She peeked through to Felix's room for about the twentieth time. He was in a similar bed, a bed considerably rumpled from having been bounced on. He was fast asleep.

She should be too, but she stood at the great bay window and gazed across the palace gardens to the moonlit mountains beyond and wondered where she'd found herself.

There was a soft knock, as though the person thought she might be asleep.

She was far from asleep, but heaven only knew how much courage it took to open the door.

Marc.

He'd lost the uniform. *Thank heaven for small mercies*, she thought numbly. The uniform alone had been enough to scare her. Now he was dressed in faded jeans and a black T-shirt which stretched tightly across the six-pack of a chest she remembered only too well.

His face was darkened with a five o'clock shadow. It was nine o'clock, she reminded herself, though it didn't feel anything like that. What time was it back in Australia? Who knew?

But she had other things to think about. Marc was here, smiling in concern.

'Hey,' he said softly. 'You should be asleep.'

'I think my body thinks it's seven in the morning.'

'Hilda says you haven't eaten.'

'My body said it was five in the morning when dinner was on offer.'

'So breakfast now?' he asked and looked towards the great bell rope hanging by the mantel.

'Don't you dare,' she said, startled. 'Wake the whole palace because I feel like a toasted cheese sandwich?'

'Is that what you'd like?' His face creased into another smile and it was almost her undoing. Once upon a time she'd fallen in love with that smile.

Whoa. She was not going there again. She was a sensible woman, here to do what had to be done before returning to her sensible life.

If only he wouldn't smile.

'I don't feel like it enough to pull the rope,' she managed. 'Next thing I know there'll be a booming announcement—all staff to the scullery—and I'll be seated at your grand thirty-seater dining table with four footmen and a butler and one cheese sandwich on a silver platter...'

'It is a bit like that,' he said and his smile softened. 'But not quite. The bell pull looks amazing but all it does is light the palace switchboard.'

'Manned by someone who could make booming announcements?'

'I suppose so, but...'

'And the palace cook who's probably just gone to bed would be pulled out to cook again?'

'That's what he's paid for,' he said and then his smile changed again. Suddenly there was a twinkle of mischief lurking within. 'But you know what? I make a mean cheese toastie and I know where the kitchens are.'

'Kitchens?'

'Kitchen,' he said hastily, seeing her look.

She skewered him with a glare. 'How many kitchens?'

'Well, three,' he told her. 'Number one's for everyday use, two's for banquets, three's for State Occasions.'

'So making myself a cheese toastie wouldn't qualify as a State Occasion?'

'It should,' he told her, his smile disappearing. He touched her lightly on the cheek, only a trace, hardly a caress, but it seemed like one to Ellie.

Why? This man was a ghost from her past, nothing more. *Get a grip*, she told herself.

'It should be a State Occasion,' he was saying. 'What you've done for the last ten years, on your own...'

'Is nothing compared with what you've achieved,' she managed. She'd done some intense research over the last weeks and she pretty much had a handle on what his life had been like. 'For your work during the war you're regarded as some sort of superhero. Since then I gather you've been helping run the health system, as well as working behind the scenes, actively politicking so Falkenstein stays peaceful.'

'That's why I need to stay where I am right now,' he told her and his voice turned grim. 'That's why I'm trapped.'

'It's an impressive trap.' Unconsciously her gaze went back to the bell pull and his smile returned.

'It is. To be honest I've pulled that about twice. But come my coronation, with the crown on my head, I imagine I'll be pulling the bell rope like anything. Meanwhile, may I escort you to the smallest of our kitchens and cook you a toastie?'

And what woman could resist a toastie?

What woman could resist that smile?

Not her, she thought helplessly. She was exhausted in every sense of the word. She should close the door on Marc, sink onto the amazing bed and close her eyes on the world.

But a cheese toastie was calling.

And Marc. Prince of the Blood. Her husband.

No, she thought frantically. Not her husband. Just Marc. The father of her son. A man who should be—must be— her friend.

So, it was entirely reasonable to make overtures of

friendship. That was what mature couples did in the face of a need for co-parenting.

She could even feel virtuous as he led her out of her room and started the trek through the vast network of portrait-lined galleries and down the back stairs that led eventually to the palace kitchens.

She was doing this for Felix's sake, she told herself. And she was doing this because she was hungry.

She wasn't doing this because Marc made her toes curl at all.

CHAPTER SEVEN

THE 'EVERYDAY' KITCHEN was still grand to the point of intimidating, but Marc was accustomed to cooking for himself. Army messes, campfires, hospital kitchens—he'd learned to ignore his surroundings and get on with it. His French chef might well be miffed that Marc was taking liberties with his frying pan, but for now Marc's focus was on Ellie.

Who sat, pale-faced, worried, watching him as he searched the bank of refrigerators. With increasing frustration.

'Are you sure you wouldn't like a caviar sandwich instead?' he demanded as he found a shelf stocked with smoked salmon and pâté. *Make a note*, he told himself. *Basic Cheddar for toasties needs to be added to the royal shopping list.* He did, however, finally find cheese.

'Pont l'Évêque?' Ellie said faintly, and he grinned.

'Only the best, m'lady. That's all there seems to be.'

'That's all you normally eat?'

'Up until four weeks ago my normal fare's been what's left at the back of the fridge in my apartment. Which isn't pretty. Often it's cheese I've forgotten to wrap. With the furry bits chopped off it makes an awesome sandwich, but obviously tonight we need to slum it.'

'You really had no connection to the royal family?'

'Only as my job dictated. My uncle allowed me to take over the role of Director of Health after my father died. I've battled with his funding ministers but my uncle never concerned himself directly.'

'So government positions…?'

'Have been assigned purely by whim and favouritism,' he told her, abandoning his search for tomatoes. White asparagus, tick. Tiny designer potatoes? Something that might be kale? Who cooked sandwiches with kale? No tomatoes. *Hmm.* 'My uncle liked the idea that I was family,' he conceded as he searched. 'He seemed to think it gave him more control, but he never bothered to take an interest anyway.'

'Will you?'

He paused. For a long moment he stayed, staring into the fridge as if an answer might magically appear, but then he shrugged and straightened. 'This'll be a toastie with a difference. Hold your hat.'

'Will you?' she asked again.

'Take an interest?' He shrugged. 'I will, but where do I start? Immediately after the coronation I need to sack half the administrators of this country. They've been lining their own pockets for years. It's going to be—'

'Hell?' she finished for him.

'You said it.'

'And your medicine?'

He'd been unwrapping cheese and was about to slice it. Now he closed his eyes as if in pain. 'I can't think,' he said savagely. 'All that training… Never to operate again…'

And he sliced down hard.

Which was a mistake. He stared down in disbelief at the slash on the side of his forefinger.

'Wow,' Ellie said, reaching for the dishcloth. 'Nicely done, Dr Falken. Hold it up. High.' She wrapped the finger tight and propelled it upward and he was left feeling like a king-sized fool.

One large carving knife. One very soft cheese. *What an idiot.*

'Where's the first aid kit?' Ellie demanded, still holding his hand up.

'It's fine. I can…'

'Bleed all over my toastie? I don't think so. I need disinfectant, a couple of Steri-Strips and a bit of gauze. And don't tell me to pull the bell rope. I can deal with this.'

'I can do it myself.'

'Yeah?' A crimson stain was seeping from under the dishcloth. 'Shut up, Marc, and tell me where I can find what I need.'

'There should be a cupboard in the main kitchen with a red cross on it. But—'

'Then don't move. Keep your hand up. Sit and don't faint.'

'I don't faint,' he said, revolted, and she grinned.

'And as a surgeon you don't slice your own finger with a carving knife. It's a whole new world we're living in, Your Highness. Sit down and let me play doctor.'

And for the first time in what seemed like weeks, she felt okay.

Okay? That was a strange word. She was walking through cavernous kitchens looking for a cupboard with a red cross on the front. Marc was in the next room hugging his sliced finger.

Marc was the future King of Falkenstein and she was in a place that did her head in. But, right now, her world had suddenly got domestic.

Marc had a cut finger and she could fix it.

She thought suddenly of how their lives could have been. Rewind the clock. Cancel the war in Falkenstein. Cancel her mother's illness. She and Marc could have stayed married, had their baby, maybe settled down in some nice country practice together. Patched each other's scrapes, supported each other, maybe had a few fights along the way.

Celebrated birthdays, Christmas, wedding anniversaries. Stuff normal couples did.

Ten years later she finally got to put a bandage on a sore finger. *Woo-hoo!*

But for now, suddenly, she was simply grateful for what she could get. Was that stupid? Yes, it was, but it felt okay.

She found the right cupboard and was truly impressed. This wasn't a standard kitchen first aid kit. She needed to move oxygen canisters and a CPR kit out of the way before she could reach what looked like a box of dressings.

There was a dressing for everything. Plus suture material, antiseptic washes and equipment for giving local anaesthetics. This place seemed equipped for everything from childbirth to snakebite.

She fished out an almost embarrassingly large amount of kit and headed back to Marc.

'You want to lie down?' she asked him. 'I have enough dressings to cover you from the toes up.'

'One finger,' he growled. 'I can do it.'

'Like you sliced the cheese? I don't think so.'

'I'm the surgeon.'

'I have a very poor opinion of doctors who have other careers on the side,' she said primly. 'Your carving skills... Being King has obviously messed with your head.'

'Slicing cheese as expensive as Pont l'Évêque messes with my head.'

'Then that's another career you should avoid. You know, it's so soft you could have used a spoon? Hush, Marc, and let me see.'

He cast her a strange look and subsided.

Silence. He sat motionless while she washed his finger,

assessed it and decided stitches weren't needed. It'd pull together okay with Steri-Strips. But she needed to get the finger totally dry and apply the Steri-Strips carefully, pulling the sides of the slice together firmly but not rounding the entire finger. It'd swell a bit over the next few hours and if she encased the entire finger, at best it could throb, at worst she'd cut off circulation.

She focused and Marc sat and watched her head bent over his hand—and it felt okay.

To have Ellie treating him.

To have Ellie touching him.

After ten years there should be nothing, he told himself. Or, there again, if there'd been real sexual attraction then there should have been a zing of sheer magnetic pull.

But this reaction was different. Strange.

He was watching the top of her auburn curls. Her attention was absolute. If he cocked his head to the side he could see the tip of her tongue, just emerging, a sign of pure concentration.

He wanted to touch those curls, not for any proprietorial reason, not because he wanted to tug her to him and declare she was still his wife but because he wanted to assure himself she was real.

Their marriage had been so brief, a moment out of time that had seemed almost fantasy. When he'd left her, he'd come home to chaos, war and destruction on an unbelievable level. He'd had to put his head down and work as he'd never worked before and never wished to work again. But at night, lying on the various camp beds in which he'd found himself, he'd often conjured up a vision of Ellie.

Of a life he couldn't have. Of a fantasy.

She'd been that fantasy for almost ten years, his quiet place, a memory that helped him stay steady in times of trouble. Yet here she was, no memory but a woman with premature threads of silver in her hair. A woman with worry lines, put there by a life as demanding as the one he'd faced.

Reality and fantasy were fusing and he didn't know where to take it.

Nowhere at all, he told himself harshly. Ellie's life was back in Australia. Keep your thoughts—and your hands— to yourself, and play the patient.

With the Steri-Strips in place, she was applying gauze dressing. Finally she stepped back, satisfied. 'It should heal fast if you look after it,' she told him. 'It's a sharp knife so the cut's not ragged. Keep it dry and try and keep that dressing intact for a couple of days.'

'Yes, ma'am.'

She cast him an odd look—maybe she was finding this situation as disconcerting as he was—and started clearing up.

'I can do that.'

'Not in my surgery,' she told him. 'And I'm making the toasties now. I might have known a king couldn't cook to save himself.'

'I'm not a king yet.'

'You're surely acting like the coronation's already happened. Pont l'Évêque? I ask you! Maybe I should ask for a frying pan and a fridge in my room so I can cook things normal people eat.'

She was back to being bossy. He remembered Ellie's bossiness. He'd liked it.

With the bench wiped and her hands well washed, she set to inspecting the fridges. There wasn't a lot that met with her approval.

She found bread and butter. She checked the Pont l'Évêque for blood. She set the frying pan on to heat and then glared at the basic supplies.

'You want more than cheese?' he asked.

'We might need to make do.'

'What about using the caviar?'

'Caviar?' She stared at him blankly and then turned to the appropriate fridge. A container of caviar sat on the top shelf, huge and unopened.

'I've never had caviar,' she managed.

'It's good.'

'You have it all the time?'

'Hey, I've been self-funded until now. Caviar hasn't been in my budget. But I have tried it. It might go okay with cheese.'

'You're kidding me, right?'

'A Pont l'Évêque and caviar toastie? Let's try it.'

'Marc…'

But he was grinning. 'You remember those chocolate whisky microwave puddings we invented? We never got around to patenting the recipe. Let's try this as a second invention. Hey, at this rate we could write a cookbook.'

And she flashed a look up at him that was almost fearful.

He could guess why. Memories were everywhere.

Those puddings had been an experiment, made while she was studying and he was in carer mode. The night before her last exam she'd studied to the point where the pages were blurring. He'd made his puddings, lathered them with cream and then fed hers to her, spoon by spoon.

She'd protested and giggled and fed his back to him.

And then they'd made love. The next morning she'd blitzed the exam.

The memory was suddenly so real it almost made him gasp. Ellie was concentrating fiercely on the fridge, then turned back to the table with the tub of caviar, but he knew the same memories were with her. 'Right,' she said in a strained voice and picked up the knife to cut the cheese.

He put his hand over hers. 'Ellie…'

'What?' The look she flashed him was fearful.

'Put the memories aside while you chop the cheese,' he

told her. He looked ruefully at his bandaged finger. 'I'm speaking from experience here.'

She looked up. Her gaze met his and held.

He smiled, but for a minute she didn't smile back. She just looked at him, long and hard. As if trying to get him in focus.

And then she sighed and concentrated as ordered on the cheese.

'Right,' she said. 'Chop cheese with care. Ladle caviar without spilling. Fry toasties without burning. I can do this.'

'Of course you can,' he said softly. 'You can do anything.'

They should definitely patent this recipe.

Toasted to perfection, the crusty, golden toasties oozed creamy goodness mixed with golden balls of tang. The sensation was amazing.

While she'd supervised toasting, Marc had foraged in yet another refrigerator and produced a champagne whose label made her jaw drop.

'We can't,' she gasped.

'We have no choice,' he told her. 'My uncle and his family considered this the cheap stuff. In time I'll restock, but for now we're forced to slum it.'

So slum it she did, eating her astounding toastie, savouring the way the caviar burst in her mouth, feeling her tongue tingle with the truly wonderful champagne.

But she was being careful. One glass of bubbles and one glass only.

For this was a night out of frame, she told herself.

For a short few months all those years ago, she'd thought this man could be her soulmate. It was a stupid hope but her heart—and her body—had taken over her sense. She was older now and a whole lot wiser, but this man still made her feel on the verge of something dangerous.

She had herself under control for now—but one glass of champagne was definitely enough.

So she sipped cautiously and she nibbled her toastie and Marc watched her, sort of like the Cheshire Cat watched Alice.

'You're enjoying it,' he said, satisfied.

'You'd better believe it.'

'We can make more. We can open another bottle if we like.'

'You might need to get used to champagne and caviar. I need to go home to Cheddar cheese and soda water.'

'Not on the royal allowance you'll receive,' he said firmly. 'Ellie, whatever course you choose to take, you'll never need to struggle financially again.'

She cast him a fearful look and went back to concentrating on her toastie. There was so much behind that statement. As if she was somehow bound.

Maybe she was. Because of Felix.

No. Two weeks a year here, max, and only then when Felix needed her, she told herself. Her reality was sense. Her little hospital in Borrawong.

But jet lag was making her feel strange, or maybe it was the champagne, or even the crunch from the toastie. The caviar. The setting…

Not the man smiling at her from across the table. Never that.

She finished the last of her toastie and rose. Her champagne was only half drunk. She looked down at it with regret. It was a crime to leave it, and yet the way she was feeling there was no way she was game to take another sip.

'Chicken,' Marc teased and she cast a look at him that clearly displayed her apprehension. Right from the start this man had seemed to be able to read her mind. Once upon a time that had seemed so sexy, so right, so perfect that it set her body on fire.

Now it seemed a threat. This whole situation was a threat.

'Ellie, I won't hurt you,' he told her. 'There's no need to look like that. I understand the terms of this contract. I won't push you further than you wish to go.'

'Why would you want to push me?' She said it almost angrily. She was so far out of her depth.

'I wouldn't. I promise.'

She took a deep breath, trying to move on. 'Marc, what am I going to do for the next few weeks? Hilda's told us the plans for Felix. Introduction to swords and crowns and rings. Meet a friend. Pageantry and fun. It all seems de-signed to make him want to come back next year. That's okay with me—I understand. But he champs at the bit if I watch. He's learned to be independent and his gammy leg has made that need almost fierce. If he has a friend he'll be better without me.'

'Then take a holiday,' he suggested. 'The palace has three swimming pools. We can organise a chauffeur to take you anywhere you wish. The village has magnificent tour-ist shopping. I wish I could take you myself but…'

'But you'd be mobbed. And you have other things to do.'

'I do,' he said reluctantly. 'But, Ellie, you need a vaca-tion. Indulge yourself.'

'I don't know how.'

'Learn.'

'I don't think I want to. Marc, isn't there something I can do?'

He hesitated, frowning. She watched his face and there was that recognition again. He knew her. He understood.

It was a jab of knowledge that hurt. It was as if that brief, dry ceremony ten years ago had created a conduit between them, a current of understanding so deep that di-vorce couldn't break it.

Or maybe it hadn't been the ceremony. Maybe that cur-rent had always been there. She thought of the first time she'd seen him, when she'd straightened from the carnage of broken glass and wine and found those dark eyes twinkling at her. That recognition that life could never be the same again.

She was trying to corral her tumbling thoughts, but Marc was still watching her. Did he know what she was thinking now?

She needed an off-switch.

She needed to stay as far away from him as she could for the next four weeks.

'If you'd like a little work...' he said and that helped her steady. Work. That sounded good. She understood the parameters of medicine.

'I guess...the language would be a problem,' he was saying and she thought, *Okay, here goes*. She had to tell him some time.

What would he think? Pathetic? That she'd been clinging to shades of him all this time?

Just say it.

'I don't have a problem with the language,' she told him. 'At least, I don't think I do.'

'What do you mean?'

'I speak your language fluently,' she told him, slipping effortlessly into the lilting Falkenstein dialect that resembled a mix of French, Italian and German, making it relatively simple for Falkenstein's populace to make itself understood all over Europe.

He'd been holding his glass of champagne.

It was all he could do not to drop it.

She sounded as if she'd been born and bred in the streets of Falkenstein.

What the...?

'You taught me some,' she said diffidently, still in his language. 'Just a smattering, but it was enough to get me interested. I got hooked. I bought lessons online and put headphones on as something to do when I needed to relax. And then...' She became even more diffident. 'When Felix was born I started teaching him. I used to sing Falkenstein lullabies to him. How embarrassing is that?'

'Why?' He was staring at her in amazement.

'Who knows?' She tried to talk as if it didn't matter, but she knew she was failing. 'I guess I do know why. I've always felt if you adopt a child from another country you should at least try to let him learn of his background. I thought one day Felix might want to meet you. I know you have brilliant English but who knew? By the time Felix was old enough to travel you might have forgotten.' She grew more tentative. 'Or...or he might wish speak to his half-brothers or sisters. It might...it might make things easier.'

He sounded winded. 'You did this...for me?'

She jutted her chin, almost defiant. 'I'd lied to you about Felix's adoption,' she said. 'You had your reasons for needing to leave us and I understood. This seemed the least I could do. It's no big deal.'

'No big deal! How fluent is Felix?'

'Ask him for yourself. It's a wonder he hasn't already told you, but he's been excited about the surprise and you speak such good English. But he's good.' She smiled, thinking of the indulgence of talking to Felix in a language no one at home understood. It had been like their own secret code.

Now it was a bond to this guy who stood before her.

'So the future Crown Prince of Falkenstein speaks our language,' Marc said, stunned. 'And you didn't tell me.'

'You never asked.'

'I never asked all sorts of things. I never asked how you were. I didn't know your mother died. I simply walked away.'

'Hey, Marc—we had a relationship that lasted exactly five months.'

'Which included marriage.'

'The marriage wasn't real. We closed our eyes to every problem and jumped. It was a fantasy bubble. It burst and that was that.'

'Leaving you holding the baby.'

'Will you cut it out? You talk as if he were a burden. Felix has never been a burden.' She thought of her beautiful boy, sleeping now in his grand apartment. Her boy who looked like his father. 'He's my one true thing,' she whispered. 'My gift. My Felix.'

'I wish I'd shared that.' And it was too much. The tension between them was escalating to the point where they had to touch or run—and running was unthinkable.

Marc reached out and took her hands and held her before him. He didn't say anything. He didn't need to.

She stared down at their linked hands. She was way out of her depth here. She had no idea where her emotions were taking her. She only knew that tugging away was impossible.

'I hate that I haven't had a chance to love Felix,' he said, softly now.

'I know you do, and I'm sorry.'

Silence. There was something building between them. Something so huge.

'Ellie, I did love you,' Marc said at last, as if the words had been forced out.

She turned her gaze to his face. She expected to see confusion. Instead there was wonder.

Admiration?

Intention.

'Marc, no.'

But she knew already what would happen.

She should pull away. She should head straight back to her over-the-top apartment, step through the door and lock it behind her.

'If you really mean no, then I won't touch you,' Marc said and it needed only that. Ever the gentleman. And suddenly she was close to screaming.

What she needed right now was a Neanderthal man, a guy with a club who took all the decisions out of her hands.

Or not?

Neanderthal man might expect a clubbing right back from Dr Ellie Carson. She was no shrinking violet, ready to be carried off at the whim of any man. But then, this wasn't Dr Carson. This was just Ellie, holding hands with Marc.

Or maybe that wasn't the truth either.

Maybe she was still Ellie Falken, the nineteen-year-old who'd met and married this guy out of hand. Who'd fallen in lust at first sight.

Who'd stayed in lust with him all that time?

Only because he hasn't been in your life, she told herself. Her head was screaming advice, trying to make her hormones see sense.

You divorced for a reason, and even if you hadn't divorced, all sorts of other reasons would have reared their heads over time. You've made this man into some sort of fantasy. You're a doctor. You've spent your life working hard, raising Felix, doing the practical things you've needed to do to survive. Be practical now.

But her hormones weren't listening. Her hormones were tilting her chin. Her hormones were raising her feet onto tiptoe but there was no need. Somehow Marc had her by the waist.

Somehow Marc's mouth was claiming hers.

And her body remembered.

The instant surge of heat. The feel of him. The taste, the strength, the sheer animal magnetism. It had blown her away ten years ago and here it was again, fusing their bodies, destroying her defences in an instant. She felt herself whimper as her barriers came down in a cloud of lust. She felt her hands slide up to his face, her fingers glorying in the shape of him, the size of him, the knowledge that this perfect, gorgeous, wonderful man wanted her.

Her.

Had she no sense? She did have sense, she thought dazedly, but right now her sense was a pool of jelly lying uselessly at her feet. Maybe she'd gather it around her again, but not now, not yet. Not while this mouth claimed hers. Not while his arms held her against him, while her breasts were crushed against his chest, while her mouth tasted him, savoured him, owned him.

There was no future for her here. She had enough sense to know it, but surely there was no harm in kissing.

And it wasn't as if she had a choice. He was kissing and she was kissing back, and if World War Three erupted around them right now she wouldn't notice. All she wanted was this man.

He could take her, she thought wildly. Right here. Her hands were tugging him closer. She wanted him more than life itself.

Ten long years. Her body remembered and screamed that this was what she'd been missing for all these years and she'd blocked it out, but it had never properly disappeared.

This man. Her husband.

'Ellie…' Somehow he tugged back, just a little. He was holding her face now, cupping her chin, looking down at her with an expression she'd never seen before.

'Marc…'

'You are my wife.'

She wasn't. The sensible part of her shouted it. She'd never been a wife to this man, the Crown Prince of Falkenstein. She'd been wife to just-qualified Dr Marc Falken, a friend, a colleague, a guy who'd been a little bit older but almost equal.

But now wasn't the time to say it. Not now, not when her body was making demands she had no hope of denying.

'Enough of the complications,' she managed. 'Just kiss me.'

He wanted her as he'd never wanted anything or anyone in his life before. She felt like his.

She was his.

He'd had relationships over the last ten years—of course he had. He was a divorcee but most women didn't hold that against him. One failed marriage didn't mean a life of celibacy.

And yet that one sweet time had messed things for him. No one felt the same as Ellie. No one moved him as Ellie did.

He'd told himself what he'd had with Ellie had been his first real passion. That if it had been allowed to run its course, with luck it would have mellowed into the day-to-day fondness and friction he assumed most marriages became. It was simply that he'd been wrenched away before that initial passion had dried up, meaning it had messed with his head for years.

So there was no reason why that passion should flare as it did now. There was no reason his body should respond as if this was his place, his right. As if Ellie was part of him and he was part of her.

How could a marriage vow do this? It couldn't.

Fate, duty, lawyers had separated them for sensible reasons. So why was his heart feeling as if it might burst in his chest with the joy of holding her?

Ellie…

His love. His wife.

But, even as he thought it, the door opened behind them. And Ellie pulled back as if she'd been struck.

The look of bliss, the look he'd remembered and loved, was suddenly replaced by distress.

Which was matched by the men at the door, two security guards with horror written clearly on their faces as they recognised what—and who—they were interrupting. 'Your Highness... So sorry... The motion sensors— Uh...the camera angle was blocked by the fridge door, so we were asked to check. If we'd known... A million apologies. A million...' And they backed out as if they expected the firing squad to follow.

Leaving Ellie staring at Marc as if he was part of the same firing squad.

'Love, Ellie, don't...'

'I'm not your love.' It was a fierce whisper.

'No.' He took a deep breath. 'But you could be.'

'Not any more. You walked away.'

The security guards were forgotten. What was between them was too overwhelming to admit thoughts of anything else.

All he wanted to do was step forward and take her into his arms again, but the fear on her face stopped him dead.

'I did walk out on you,' he said, somehow managing to make his voice calm, maybe even reasonable. 'Ellie, I didn't have a choice. And you didn't follow.'

One accusation was now two.

'You knew I couldn't.'

'I know that. We had no choice.'

'But if we'd really loved each other...' Her voice cracked. 'I know. The whole thing was impossible but it still felt... mad. Wrong. That you were suddenly in the midst of war on one side of the world and I was coping with my mother's illness and a fraught pregnancy on the other. But we were married, Marc. Married! It was a mockery and it hurt like you wouldn't believe. Do you think I'd want to put myself through that again? Leave me be, Marc Falken. Your

Majesty. Whoever you are. I don't care who you are. All I know is that you're not my husband. You never were and you never can be.'

'We could—'

'We couldn't,' she said flatly. 'Marriage is for ever and we can't do for ever. It's not our fault, but we can't. Leave it, Marc. Thank you for the toastie. I'm going to bed.'

There didn't seem to be anything left to say.

She walked to the door and then turned. 'Marc?'

'Mmm?' He was feeling kicked. Winded. Blasted by the surge of raw emotion that had washed through his body, leaving him gutted at the end of it.

'We're here for four weeks. I need a job. You implied I might be able to work.'

'You need a holiday. There are swimming pools, a gym, a library loaded with English books as well as books in our language…'

'Holidays do my head in,' she said shortly. 'I need to stay busy. That hospital—could I do something? Even hospital visiting or helping in rehab, something to take my head out of where it's at.'

And he got it. He knew what she was saying because he felt the same.

The tension was tangible. Inescapable. The only thing to do was escape.

Into medicine? Wasn't that what he longed to do also?

'I'll make enquiries,' he told her. 'If possible, I'll take you over the hospital tomorrow afternoon.'

'Thank you, but I don't need an escort.'

'Give me that honour, please.'

'Marc…'

'Yes?'

'What's between us is too complicated for words,' she whispered. 'Please, don't make it any harder.'

CHAPTER EIGHT

How was a person supposed to sleep in a cloud of feather comforters, silk sheets and velvet hangings? In a room where windows opened to a view to the mountains beyond, where peacocks roamed in the foreground, where generations of royals led their pampered existence—and she was now one of them?

But not really.

She was the wrong actress for this set. She slept fitfully and woke feeling just as discombobulated.

Felix, however, had none of her qualms. The moment he woke he limped through to join her.

'Isn't this awesome? I can bounce and bounce on my bed and Hilda says I'm a prince so if I want to bounce then it's okay.' He climbed on her bed and prepared to demonstrate.

She edged sideways fast. 'Felix, crutches, floor.'

'I'm the boss of the world. I should be able to take my crutches anywhere.'

'You're not the boss of your mum or your mum's bed.'

'No, but I'm important.'

'For four weeks, Felix, and then we go home.'

His face fell. 'I don't think I want to.'

'Can I come in?'

Marc.

Felix whooped. 'Of course! Hooray! Mum, it's Papa.'

Great. The memory of the night before was all around her. Ellie wanted to pull up the covers and disappear, but Felix was grinning a welcome and shifting on the bed. 'Come in. This is a pyjama party.'

Except Ellie wasn't wearing pyjamas. Her nightgown was awful and her hair was a bird's nest and she felt…as if she didn't belong here.

'Is it okay with you, Ellie?' Marc was still at the door, waiting for her to speak. 'I'm not in pyjamas.'

He wasn't. He was in jeans and a T-shirt and he looked almost normal. Except there was nothing normal about this man.

Talk about sex on legs!

Um…maybe that was a really dangerous thing to think.

'I didn't want to wake you,' he told her, coming further into the room. 'But Hilda said Felix had bounced in here.'

'Bounced being the operative word.'

'You sound bitter.'

'Really?' She glowered at her son. 'Why would that be? Surely I like being hit on the nose with crutches at the crack of dawn.'

Marc chuckled and her heart did that crazy lurch again. *Oh, for heaven's sake…*

But Marc, at least, was moving on. 'Felix, have you ever ridden a horse?'

'No.' Felix was suddenly glowering. 'I can't even ride a bike now. My legs…'

'Have been all over the place,' Marc said, matter-of-factly. 'With one leg shorter than the other, it must have been hard. But your mum sent me your medical history and the doctors' notes on your last operation. Your legs should be fine with some physical therapy.'

'But I'm still on crutches.'

'Crutches won't stop you learning to ride.' He hesitated. 'Felix, for the coronation it's usual for the King to ride. Your leg will still be in a brace, but if you could learn to keep your seat…' He grinned. 'I know you'd rather ride in a Baby Austin, but royal tradition doesn't stretch that far. It would be excellent if you rode with me. What do you think?'

'R…ride?' Felix stammered. 'Cool!'

Marc grinned. 'Brave kid. But there's not much to it. We'll give you lessons. We'll find you a quiet horse and you and your mum can ride together.'

'I don't ride.' It was a desperate snap and in fact it was a lie. Her grandfather had taught her as a child but the thought of riding beside her son—and Marc—in a coronation parade was overwhelming.

'You should learn too,' Marc told her. 'I'll teach you.'

'It's not that I can't ride. It's that I don't—and I don't need you to teach me!'

'Mum!' Felix stared in astonishment. 'You should be polite.'

She chewed her lip and glared at Marc, but he only smiled at her. He knew what he was doing. That twinkle…

This man was so dangerous.

'It's okay, Ellie. I'm not dragging you into the royal family.' The twinkle deepened. 'The opposite, in fact. I've talked to the director of the hospital and organised to take you for a tour. Felix, if you're happy doing your riding lesson without me, our chief groom, Louis, has taught more kids to ride than you've had hot dinners. The brace on your leg will protect it and the mare we have in mind won't let a brace worry her.' His smile widened. 'Louis doesn't speak English but your mum says that won't be a problem for you.'

'I didn't realise it was your language Mum taught me until yesterday,' Felix said, indignant. 'She never told me why we were learning.'

'That's my fault,' he said, suddenly grave. 'Your mum

did it as a surprise for me, and it's wonderful. So, would you like to ride a horse?'

'If he's careful,' Ellie said, feeling desperate. 'If he falls…'

'We'll take care. Ellie, you know I'd never suggest it if it could do harm.'

'You think teaching him he's boss of the world won't do harm? He even says he's now allowed to bounce on his bed.'

And Marc laughed again, that lovely deep chuckle that made her heart twist and twist again.

'What kid doesn't bounce on his bed?' he demanded.

And Ellie thought of the narrow bed Felix slept in at home—and the deep sag in the middle. She had to smile back.

That was a mistake. Her smile faded and so did Marc's.

Oh, help.

She could so easily fall.

She'd fallen so hard, so fast, last time, but she hadn't considered the consequences.

Ten years on, she was no longer a green girl, falling into lust with a handsome prince. She gave herself a good mental shake, and seemingly so did he.

'I have a meeting now,' he told her, glancing at his watch, suddenly businesslike. 'But if you can be ready at ten we'll go to the hospital together.'

'I can go by myself. There's no need…'

'There is a need,' he said, suddenly fierce. 'This job takes up ninety per cent of my time. Allow me to choose what I do with the rest.'

'You want to go to the hospital?'

'I'm a surgeon. What do you think? If I can't take my wife…'

'I'm not your wife.'

'No.' He sighed. 'You're not. And I'm no longer a surgeon. But grant me this indulgence, Ellie. I'll take you to the hospital and introduce you to the world I've left behind.'

'Marc…'

'Ten,' he said harshly. 'Yes?'

'Yes,' she said because there was nothing else to say. Because she was suddenly seeing a pain as great as any she'd seen as a doctor, and it was a pain she could do nothing about.

The hospital was a short walk down from the fortified cliffs that formed the first part of the palace wall. The path crossed the river and then meandered through the cobbled streets of the old part of the town. The day was beautiful. Ellie was itching for a walk—but a limousine was waiting in the palace courtyard. A royal flag was mounted on the car's bonnet. A uniformed chauffeur was holding the door wide and four outriders were mounted on huge black motorbikes.

Marc was dressed in a suit now and his face was set. He'd met her inside but hardly spoken.

The chauffeur ushered them into the car and closed the door behind them. A glass panel between driver and passengers gave them privacy. The big car purred out from the palace grounds, their motorbike escort riding in perfect symmetry.

People paused as they passed. The younger generation stared. Older people bowed or curtsied.

'Get this,' Ellie breathed. 'It's like something out of a fairy tale.'

'Or a nightmare,' Marc muttered and then they were at the hospital and there was a reception committee lined up to receive them. The hospital director. The head of medicine. The head of surgery. The charge nurse.

Marc had had responsibility for the healthcare system of the country, Ellie knew, but he'd also worked here as a surgeon. These people would have considered him a colleague. Now they were reacting to him with deference, even a little fear.

She could sense his tension and she knew he hated it.

For the director was showing them through the hospital as if Marc hadn't seen it before. They were ushered from ward to ward, the director giving an efficient overview. Every ward was beautifully ordered. Even the patients looked neat. Patients and nursing staff were looking on with deference but also, Ellie sensed, with concealed impatience. This formal visit was an interruption in their day. They had things to do.

The last place they were ushered was Emergency. Here, too, the place was clinically clean, cubicles pristine and ready to receive anyone needing assistance. But there seemed little need. Nurses in each occupied cubicle tended patients whose care looked well under control but only half the cubicles were full. The young doctor in charge—*very* young—greeted them with what seemed strained formality.

The director was talking hard at Marc, boasting of efficiency, but the place didn't seem normal. What emergency department in the world ever looked like this? And Marc was frowning at the director, eyeing the ward with disbelief.

On impulse she edged to the door leading to the ambulance bay.

There were five ambulances lined up outside.

'Do you have patients waiting to be admitted?' she asked.

'Everything is under control,' the young doctor said, with a nervous glance at the director.

'Really?' But Marc must have been sensing exactly what Ellie was feeling—maybe more so, because he'd worked here before. Until now he seemed to have been holding himself in rigid control. Now that control seemed to snap. He stalked over to Ellie so he, too, could see the waiting ambulances, then turned back to the director. 'I didn't come here expecting to see a pretty hospital,' he snapped. 'What is this? You've directed the ambulances not to unload until we're gone?' He turned to the young doctor, ignoring the director. 'Why?' And the force of his question demanded the truth.

'Because royalty's not supposed to see this place when it's under stress,' the young doctor said, sounding desperate. 'You know that, sir… Your Highness. We don't have enough doctors—you know that too. I'm the only one on duty this morning. Yes, we have patients lined up and as soon as you leave it'll be hell. But for now we're ready for inspection, as requested.' And the look he cast at the director was one of pure defiance.

'Stefan?' Marc growled, staring at the director and the director spread his hands.

'We were given a directive from the palace,' he said simply. 'We were to expect a royal visit with overseas dignitaries. The rule is never to lose face.'

'And lose lives instead?' Marc's face was like thunder. He glanced at Ellie and then shrugged. 'Sorry, Ellie, I guess you're the overseas dignitary but the tour stops now.' He tugged off his jacket and tie and tossed them onto the admissions desk. 'Right. Let's get them in.'

The director stared at him as if he were from another planet. 'Sir… Your Highness, it's not fitting…'

'Of course it's fitting,' Marc growled. 'Those are my people out there. Ellie, I'll have someone escort you back to the palace.'

'Are you kidding?' For the first time since she'd arrived Ellie felt a surge of belonging. Ambulances filled with need were her stock-in-trade. 'If I'm allowed to work here…' She turned to the director. 'I have current Australian medical registration. Will your insurance cover me if I start work now?'

The man looked like a goldfish, mouth open, eyes boggling. His royal tour had just been turned on its head.

'Of course it will,' Marc snapped. 'One phone call… Stefan, go make it. Dr Eleanor Carson, Australian Medical Practitioner, has just joined your staff, starting now.'

The administrators disappeared. The emergency room filled and Ellie put her head down and went for it.

She blessed the fact that she spoke the language. She had minor hiccups—the language tapes she'd worked on hadn't foreseen convoluted explanations such as: *I tripped over the kid's skateboard and stuck my arm with a tray of satay skewers…* Or: *I have a bit of pain in my gut and the wife fusses—but it's her bloody fish bake that did it…*

But she had enough vocabulary to get by, and the nurses were great. They were ready to speak slowly or translate into English.

And Marc was just across the room.

He was handling the serious stuff. A woman arrested just as they brought her in—what had they been thinking to leave someone with severe chest pain waiting in an ambulance? The young doctor—a couple of years out of med school at most, Ellie thought—deferred to Marc with obvious relief. Together they managed to get a heartbeat. Then Marc barked the demand to call in a cardiac specialist.

But the young doctor was hesitant. 'He's not on call except for emergencies,' he quavered and Marc stared at him in incredulity.

'What exactly do you think qualifies as an emergency? Ring him now!'

Ellie looked through at the woman's husband, wringing his hands through the glass door leading to the waiting room. He was covered with dust from what looked like mining or some other equally filthy task and she also wondered what qualified as an emergency if not a cardiac arrest.

And why were they so short-staffed?

But now wasn't the time to discuss staffing issues. She had the dad with the arm pierced with skewers to cope with and Marc was moving on to a toddler with a burned hand.

They had their triage worked out. Somehow they'd become a team, figuring what the young doctor was capable of, filling the gaps, working around him, with him, for him.

Who knew what Marc had scheduled for the rest of the day? For now it didn't matter.

At one stage Josef appeared, looking frantic, but another ambulance had just rolled up and Marc waved him away with a snap.

'Nothing's more important than this. Reschedule. Oh, and let Felix know where his mother is. Hilda will make sure he's okay.'

Josef looked at Marc's grim face and disappeared without a word.

They worked on. The place settled into the normal chaos of an emergency ward, with the three doctors working together, doing what they did best.

It felt okay.

Who needed a holiday? Ellie thought as the morning became afternoon. This felt great.

But why did this feel so different than at home?

And she glanced at the young doctor, Luc. He was discussing ongoing care with Marc, deferring to Marc as the senior doctor. Now he looked competent, intelligent, decisive, but he'd looked strained to the point of breaking when they'd walked in. She could only imagine the orders that had come from above. *Royal visit—clear the area and make it look pristine and under control.* He didn't look old enough or assured enough to defy such an order. What was such a young doctor doing in charge of a department as busy as this?

And to be alone, as she was alone at home…

The afternoon Marc had arrived she'd been faced with a carload of injured teens and she'd been terrified. She'd had too much work and every decision had been hers. She watched Luc now, discussing the current case with Marc, and she realised loneliness had many guises.

She was going home to more of the same.

What was she doing, thinking she was lonely when she had a community to envelop her? She could remarry. A couple of the local farmers had made it clear they were interested.

Why had she never been interested in them?

'Will I be okay?' The elderly lady she'd been treating quavered her question and Ellie's attention jerked back to where it should be. The woman had fallen and jarred her hip, but the X-ray had shown no break.

'You'll be more than okay,' she told the woman in her own language. 'But you've been lucky. You need handrails on those steps straight away.'

'I'm on a list,' the woman told her. She nodded towards Marc, who was treating a young girl who'd burned herself trying to wax her own legs. The girl had arrived feeling frightened and embarrassed, and then she was stunned to silence when her treating doctor turned out to be the new King. But Marc now had her laughing. He was telling her a silly story about his first ever attempt to shave. True or not, it had the girl relaxed. Smiling. Adoring.

The woman Ellie was treating had exactly the same worshipful look on her face, and suddenly Ellie realised she did too.

Oh, for heaven's sake...

'They say he'll change things,' the woman told her. 'They say hospital waiting lists will go down and schools will get more money. But there's so much work for him to do. I can't understand why he's here.'

'I guess he's needed here now,' Ellie told her.

'He's needed everywhere.'

'Then let's play our part and get that scrape cleaned so your daughter can take you home,' Ellie said, with a last glance across at Marc. He had so much on his plate. So much responsibility, but his sole intent now seemed to be making one teenager smile.

He was needed everywhere and he knew it. And so did she.

Marc worked through until three. He spoke again to the director—who just happened to keep checking in—and at change of shift two doctors appeared instead of one.

'It'll blow my budget,' the director fussed but Marc shrugged.

'Wear the loss until after the coronation. The budget of the entire country is about to be rewritten.'

And that could be the rest of my life right there, he thought grimly, envisaging the budget calculations, foreseeing hour upon hour of endless negotiations with so many needs.

The country's funding had been skewed for years towards indulging royal whims. Marc himself had fought for medical funding. He could grant that now, but there was desperate need in education, housing, welfare, infrastructure… So many things. But for now he'd worked for five hours beside Ellie and it felt good.

He needed to return to the palace. Ellie needed to return to Felix. They both wanted a walk.

He said as much and his security people stared at him as if he'd grown two heads.

Walking home was what people did every day, yet it turned out to be an undertaking so extraordinary Marc almost gave up.

But he was the new King. Surely the title had to be good

for something. 'Deal with it,' he growled and led Ellie out into the sunshine.

His outriders were still there, patiently waiting. Here was a cost saving he could make, he thought, and he attempted to wave them away. But his chief of security was having kittens, so a compromise was reached. He and Ellie walked but they had bodyguards walking before and after.

Five minutes after they left the hospital a helicopter appeared and hovered overhead.

And Ellie got the giggles. 'I feel like an ocean liner with tug boats,' she told him. 'So much for our peaceful stroll. What do you think a chopper could do if I attacked you with the secret knife inside my left shoe? Drop a bomb?'

'They're not worried about you.'

'Then what are they worried about?'

'The royal family's made themselves amazingly unpopular.'

'But you're going to fix that, right?' she said and she suddenly tucked her arm into his. It was a gesture of friendship, nothing more, he told himself, but it felt...great. 'You started today. The patients you treated loved you.'

'Only one I treated was able to talk!'

'Yeah, well, she loved you. Swapping shaving stories—I can't think of any better way to win adoration.'

He chuckled and the mood, blackened with the fuss made by security, lightened immeasurably. They were approaching the ancient bridge over the river. The castle was beyond, a fairy tale of turrets and shimmering stonework. The sun was shining and the river was shimmering and calm.

He had a sudden urge to highjack one of the boats beneath them and leave. Go where the river took him.

'You need to figure out a way to keep your medicine,' Ellie told him and his mind jerked from fantasy back to reality.

'You think I can do this every day? Have you any idea how many appointments were set aside because—?'

'Because you saved lives? Which is what you want to do.'

'You know more than anyone we can't always do what we want.'

'No,' she said softly, and her hand suddenly slipped into his. Naturally, as if it had the right to be there. 'But how often do you have to give in?'

'Is that you asking? The Ellie who wanted to be a neurologist? The Ellie who's now a country doctor, working in a place she vowed never to return to?'

Silence. He hadn't meant to sound angry. He hadn't meant to sound frustrated. But both of those things were obvious. The afternoon was still. Sound carried and the bodyguards glanced in astonishment before regaining their impassive demeanour.

'There must be some way.' Ellie didn't seem to have heard his anger. Her hand was still tucked in his, as if he hadn't just tried to hurt her. 'Marc, you can't spend the rest of your life sitting in your oval office being King. You're not that sort of guy.'

'It's not oval.'

'I bet it's big.'

'It is big.'

'And scary?'

'And scary,' he admitted.

'And I've seen the films of the Queen. Do you have red boxes too?'

'Gold boxes.'

'Oh, of course. Gold.' She nodded. 'Important, huh?'

'Very important.'

'All of it?'

'I'm not supposed to discuss…'

'Of course you're not. So you're not discussing. Just nodding. All of it important?'

He said nothing. They were approaching the far end of the bridge but their steps slowed. There were things to be sorted before they entered the intimidating walls of the palace.

'So a secretary could maybe sort the boxes and mark the important stuff?' Ellie tried cautiously. 'That could give you time.'

'Who could I trust to tell me what's important? That's what my uncle did—left the decisions to minions. As long as the royal family got what they wanted, they were happy.'

'You're not that sort of King.' She hesitated. 'But, Marc, you've given up so much already.'

'Our marriage, you mean? Our son?'

And there it was, out in the open.

They stopped. The security guys edged closer. Marc waved them back, out of earshot.

'Very imperious,' Ellie commented and Marc glowered.

'No, I meant it as a compliment,' Ellie told him. 'Is that what Felix will be doing for the next few weeks? Going to Imperious School?'

'Ellie...'

'You did give up Felix for your country,' she said softly. 'You did give up our marriage.'

'If I remember correctly, you did the same. You made the decision to care for your mother and to put our son up for adoption.'

'There didn't seem a choice,' she whispered. 'But, Marc, if we'd really tried...'

'How could we have tried any harder?'

'Maybe by honouring the vows we made? Maybe by at least staying in contact. I don't know. It all seemed impossible at the time, just as your decision to take on the throne to the exclusion of everything else seems the only option now. But surely—'

'Surely nothing. There is no choice.'

'So you'll sit in your grand office and play with gold boxes and live happily ever after.'

'Don't belittle what I'm trying to do.'

'I can't. Nor can I judge. I made decisions too, Marc. All I know is that my decision ten years ago, to abandon you—' she caught herself '—to abandon our son was the wrong one. Thankfully, I could reverse it. But your decision now to walk away from medicine…'

But his attention was no longer on his choice. It was on her words. 'Your decision to walk away from me was wrong? What are you saying…?'

'We were kids,' she managed. 'What's done can't be undone. But it made us…it made me unhappy, and seeing you today, seeing you do what you do best, but knowing you need to walk away again…it's breaking my heart. Marc, I know you need to take the throne but to walk away from your medicine seems equally impossible. You're needed.'

'I can organise funds for more doctors. As ruler I can make things better.'

'Of course, but maybe you can do that in the afternoons and in the morning you can take out the odd appendix.'

'With my security guards at the ready.'

'They'd be just as bored watching you work through boxes, and this way they can flirt with the nurses. Surely you can do a few sessions a week. And hey, it'll keep your hand in. If the peasants revolt then you can go back to work.'

'My job is to stop the peasants revolting.'

'Which is much more likely if your people see you care. What you did today…'

'Ellie, you can't tell me how to run my life. What about

yours? Are you planning to bury yourself in Borrawong for the rest of your life?'

Silence. They should keep going, Marc thought grimly. Officials would be waiting. Boxes would be waiting.

The rest of his life was waiting.

He turned again to the river. House martins were swooping under the parapets, in and out of the shadows. A dragonfly flittered past. Two birds dived with precision, carrying their unfortunate victim triumphantly towards land.

He felt like the dragonfly. Caught.

And then he thought, *The birds worked as a team.*

A team...

'Ellie?'

'Mmm?'

'Stay with me.'

Silence.

'What...?' she managed at last. 'What do you mean?'

He hardly knew himself. He hadn't meant to say it but it was out there, demanding a continuation.

He didn't turn to look at her. He couldn't. But what needed to be said had to be said.

'You still feel like my wife.'

Her breath hissed in so sharply it hurt. 'That's...that's nonsense. We've been divorced for nine years.'

'Then why does it still feel as if we're married?'

'It doesn't.'

'Liar. Last night—'

'Was only a kiss. It didn't mean—'

'It was more than a kiss.' He hesitated. This wasn't the time or place to say it, but his thoughts were so huge, so urgent they had to find words. The bodyguards had backed off a little. They almost had privacy.

'Ellie, when we separated we broke each other's hearts,' he said, feeling his way through each word. 'You've said as much. I've never remarried and that's been for a reason. I've always felt married. Seeing you again…nothing's changed. It still feels like you're my wife. If you feel the same…why not remarry? Bring Felix up together. Share our lives again.'

She turned and stared at him in incredulity. 'What are you saying?'

'You heard,' he said evenly. 'Ellie, it makes sense. To share our lives…'

'Again. That's what I thought you said. Are you kidding? We never shared our lives.' Her voice was almost a yell. She'd forgotten the bodyguards; she was too shocked, too angry to consider. 'We were together for mere months, for not much longer than one long vacation. My life was Borrawong, my community, my mum. Your life was your country. We met and forgot everything we should have remembered. You weren't even truthful about who you were. So sharing our lives again? You're saying now that we could pick up pieces that didn't exist in the first place?'

This was impossible. How much would he give to be able to step forward now, take her into his arms, tell her how much she was loved? That he'd never stopped loving her. That walking away from her had killed something in him that he'd thought was gone for ever.

But she was looking at him as if he was crazy, and maybe he was. What had she said? *One long vacation…* Maybe that was all their marriage had been, yet what havoc it had wrought in their lives! And here he was again, suggesting an even greater upheaval.

What right did he have? None, he thought grimly, but he thought again of the advantages and knew he needed to press on.

'Ellie, it could be sensible. Setting aside the attraction we feel for each other…'

'Yeah, let's set that aside. It scares me stupid.'

'Okay.' He held up his hands as if in surrender. 'But I

would like some say in Felix's upbringing. I would like to share him. And yes, that's all about me, but for you... Ellie, you could have fun. Felix could be brought up here, knowing the palace, knowing his people and you could do what you like. Work as a doctor if you wish. Relax and do nothing if you wish that more.'

'Lie beside one of your over-the-top pools and sip drinks with little umbrellas.' She was still staring at him as if he had two heads. Or as if he frightened her, which was far, far worse.

He was struggling to hold it together, to sound practical rather than emotional. To take that look of fear away. 'That's what the women of this family have done from time immemorial.'

'Gee, thanks. I don't think so.'

'Ellie, ten years ago I came home because there was no choice,' he tried. 'You stayed with your mother because there was no choice. But you have a choice now.'

'But you still don't,' she said flatly.

And he didn't. 'The throne is non-negotiable,' he agreed. He paused, fighting his own anger and frustration. Fighting to make this proposition sound logical. 'I know it's a huge ask, but it might just work. I could offer you my support and protection, things you should have had for the last ten years. I can help with Felix. Felix would have a father as well as a mother and you know he'd enjoy that. What do we have to lose? And it'd make it so much easier...'

'For you.'

'Yes.' What else could he say but the truth? 'But for you too. And for Felix as well.'

'Leave us out of it. What are you proposing—that I marry you again so you'll have more time for your boxes?'

'I didn't mean that.'

'So what did you mean?'

'I mean I've never considered us not married.'

She shook her head in disbelief. 'You're kidding. Nine years...'

'I'm not saying I've been faithful.' He was fighting to explain something he barely understood himself. 'But all these years... Ellie, our divorce was supposed to nullify our vows but it didn't work. Not for me. I've never imagined marrying someone else. I knew I never could.'

'Because the country would call? Because imperatives would win and marriage would be put aside again?'

'You sound bitter.'

'Why would I be bitter? Haven't I had long enough to get over it?' She shrugged. 'Of course I have, but for me, like you, it's left scars. We married in passion, but that passion wasn't enough to hold us together. So it broke my heart. And, yes, I was only nineteen and having a broken heart is what all nineteen-year-olds are expected to experience, but it hurt so much I learned never to go down that path again. You say you haven't been chaste. You haven't held our marriage vows sacred after divorce. Well, neither have I, but the men I've dated have been sensible.'

'Sensible?'

'What's wrong with sensible? Sensible's safe. Sensible doesn't leave me whimpering under the covers at three in the morning.'

'Ellie...'

'And don't you feel sorry for me. I didn't whimper for long,' she snapped. 'I'm over it. I'm over you. Marc, I know you'll make this country a better place because that's your role. But for me to stay here and play part-time wife when you have a few moments to spare... Marc, that might just break my heart all over again.'

She met his gaze with defiance.

But he saw through it. She still looked tired. Worried.

And afraid. He wished she could have rested instead of working this morning. If she was his wife he could insist…

Insist? Who was he kidding? She was strong, feisty, determined, a country doctor from Australia. He had no right to demand she give that up.

He couldn't demand. He couldn't even ask.

'Leave it,' she was saying, and she sounded infinitely tired. 'Just leave it, Marc. Coming here was a mistake. It was hard for both of us but let's not make things worse. I'll stay as I promised, but as soon as the coronation's over I'll take Felix home.' She hesitated, closing her eyes for a minute. When she spoke again it seemed she was struggling to find the right words.

'Marc, you walked away from me nine years ago. I don't blame you, because I walked away from you as well. But, no matter whose fault it was, no matter how stupid we were for marrying in the first place, after nine years I've pulled myself together. Felix has been a big part of that, the part I didn't walk away from. I can't walk away from him and I won't, but neither will I let myself lose control again.'

Then she took a deep breath and faced him head-on.

'Enough. Forget the marrying bit. It's forgotten. Over. But, Marc…you know what else I didn't walk away from? My medicine. I'm a doctor. Even today, discombobulated as I am, medicine settles me and I know it does you too. It's what we trained for; it's what we are. But here you are, walking away again.'

'I have no choice!'

'Exactly. You know, if I was stupid enough to agree to marry you again, to be part of this goldfish bowl, who's to say someone won't come to me in the future and say it's not safe, it's not proper, the people don't want me to be both Queen and doctor. What if they say I have responsibilities to the palace and I need to give up medicine? Like they're saying to you.'

'It won't happen.' But he felt ill. Her words were battering, and he couldn't defend himself because everything she said was true.

'Marc, all those years ago you suggested I might follow you out here, play the little wife, only you said don't come until the war's over because it'll be dangerous. You had important work to do and you couldn't be worrying about me while you did it. But you never once asked me to share your burden. And I had Mum and my responsibilities and I didn't ask you to share my burden either. So I stayed independent. But you know what? I've loathed bringing my son up not knowing his father. And I loathe the fact that I still love you!'

'You still…?'

But she held up her hands, as if to fend him off. 'Don't go there,' she said wearily. 'Because my loving you now feels like some sort of internal blackmail and I won't listen. I need to go home. Marc, if you need a consort, find someone sensible. Find someone who'll enjoy this life, who'll keep your bed warm when you have time to join her. Who won't be hurt when you leave her. You need to be sensible.'

'But if you love me…isn't that cowardice?'

And she lost it. 'Back off!' she yelled and then, as Marc's bodyguard took a synchronised, instinctive step forward, she grimaced and lowered her voice. 'Thinking we were in love wasn't enough to save our marriage nine years ago and, with the stress you're under, how can it be any different now? Forget this conversation, Your Highness. From now on our dealings need to be strictly official, starting now. This conversation is finished because, from this moment on, I'm being sensible for both of us.'

CHAPTER NINE

ELLIE DIDN'T SEE Marc for the rest of the day. 'His Highness is needed for state matters. He sends his apologies,' Josef told her that night and she felt vindicated.

She also felt sick. She was right but there was no joy down that road.

Marc wanted her, but he wanted her on his terms, or terms decreed by this appalling job, and how could she reconcile the two?

'When do you think we'll see him again?' Felix demanded as she tucked him in that night. She thought of all the years she'd tucked Felix in alone and she felt her chest clench in pain.

She should never have agreed to come. It hurt so much. To see him. To work with him today. To see him hurt and to understand there was nothing she could do about it. To refuse to remarry and know it was the right decision.

It made something inside her feel a little bit dead. But she'd asked for their dealings to be official from now on, and she had to stick to that.

'Being the King is a very big job,' she told Felix. 'He's trying to do the best he can, and that takes time.'

'Louis says I'll make a great king one day too. He says I can sit on a horse like a champion.'

'Did you enjoy it?'

'It was ace. Pierre came too. He's Hilda's grandson and he likes all the stuff I like. Louis let him ride a big black horse. Today I had to ride a little fat pony called Grizelda but that's only because I'm not very good yet. And because they're worried I might fall off onto my leg. But I want to ride one of the big ones.'

'You do what Louis tells you,' she said, startled.

'Yeah, but Pierre's horse is awesome. Mum, when *will* we get to see Papa? I thought he might have time to read to me tonight.'

'He'll come when he has time.'

He glowered. 'Like he didn't come to Australia for nine years?'

'Felix, that was my fault. I knew he was busy so I told him we didn't need him.'

'So tell him we need him now.'

'Do we need him?'

'Yes,' Felix said sleepily. 'He's my papa.'

'He's the King.'

'He should be able to be both,' Felix said fretfully.

'He's doing important stuff.'

'What's more important than us?' Felix demanded, but then sleep began to get the better of him and a difficult conversation was closed.

He slept.

Ellie returned to her own apartment. There was a state dinner happening downstairs. Josef had asked her if she wished to attend but she'd looked at him incredulously.

She settled down with a book but the pages blurred before her.

What's more important than us?

It was a line she could have used years ago, she thought. Standing in the airport, waving goodbye to her husband.

What's more important than us?

Everything.

* * *

The dinner was vital, ponderous, boring. Because he'd spent so much of today at the hospital, the royal boxes were waiting for him as soon as his guests left but, by the look of his guests, that wouldn't happen any time soon.

His ministers were here, a group appointed by his uncle. Marc was the youngest man in the room and the conversation after the third or fourth drink was stultifying.

He'd sent Josef to invite Ellie—as mother of the future King, his ministers had wished to meet her—but he was pleased she hadn't come. She would have been bored witless.

Except he wanted her to be here. She would have met these pompous dignitaries and maybe she'd have dared a smile at him. Ponderous men in black suits, with portly abdomens and ruddy complexions. Overweight matrons, dripping jewels, full of their own importance. Heart attacks waiting to happen. Strokes. They could have bet on who did and didn't have type two diabetes.

Practically all of them?

The gentleman beside him was indulging in a tirade about money being needed for a new race track. It seemed the track was no longer suitable for international events, and the members' room was a disgrace!

Ellie would have seen the ridiculous side of this night.

But she didn't want any part of it, and he didn't blame her.

He glanced at his watch. Eleven-thirty.

Even if they left now it was too late to go to her, even if she hadn't stipulated their contact from now on should be only official. Besides, he had today's boxes and tomorrow's boxes and tomorrow's Very Important Meetings to think about, plus all the meetings he'd missed today.

He looked again at the self-important dignitaries around his table and he knew the meetings were important. This country needed sweeping changes. Race courses were not a priority, but there were so many priorities they were doing his head in.

Ellie had suggested he share the burden, but how could he do that? Who could he trust?

No one, he thought grimly, looking at each of his ministers in turn. Each of these men had been lining their own pockets for years.

His thoughts went back to Ellie and stayed there.

He'd trust her with his life but that was a joke.

She didn't want his life, and why should she?

'Gentlemen, a toast to our new King.' One of the men was on his feet, wavering a little on legs that were distinctly unsteady. 'May he continue to keep this country as comfortable as it's always been.'

In your dreams, Marc thought, eyeing the minister with dislike.

There was, though, a tiny voice in the back of his mind saying, *What if?* What if he let things go on as they were? What if he let these people do what they pleased, as they'd done for years? Maybe then he could have time for medicine.

And time for Ellie.

He knew he couldn't. There was no one he could trust but himself, and he had to face it.

Upstairs, Ellie and Felix were sleeping. As soon as the coronation was done they'd return to Australia and he'd be alone.

So what was new?

Oh, for heaven's sake. He was getting maudlin, and he hadn't even touched the port.

To hell with this. He rose, ostensibly to answer the toast.

'Thank you, and thank you for attending tonight,' he told them. 'Stay on as long as you wish but I'm afraid I have pressing matters needing my attention.'

He turned and left. When he reached the foot of the grand staircase he hesitated.

Upstairs was Ellie.

Official contact only.

The boxes were waiting.

Duty won.

The days turned into weeks faster than Ellie could imagine.

It was a holiday with a difference. Leisure didn't suit her. Being busy did.

She woke early each morning, pulled on her running shoes and headed off around the castle wall before Felix woke. It was a decent half hour hike, making her satisfactorily puffed, satisfactorily tired, and it helped her sleep at night. She and Felix then had breakfast together. Marc was well into his day's meetings by the time they ate, but she wouldn't think of that.

After breakfast Felix headed off with Pierre to listen to whatever tutor had been allocated to the boys that day. Ellie went to the hospital. Under guard. She was deemed part of the royal family and therefore someone requiring protection.

In the emergency ward, though, she could forget about being royal. The staff there seemed to forget too. They were simply too busy to notice. Every time she turned around there was another patient to see. That was the way she liked it, although the obvious need was troubling.

'His Royal Highness promised more staff,' the young doctor she'd worked with on the first day told her. 'But it'll take years. The university courses have been starved of funds. What doctors we do have soon leave because the pay and conditions are so bad. But now, with Prince Marc... he gives the country a sense of hope.'

'It might be useful if he could spend a few hours a

day hands-on,' Ellie retorted, but the young doctor shook his head.

'It wouldn't be seemly. He did it once. We can't ask him to do it again.'

Felix saw him in the evenings—they both did. Often he had dinners, meetings, interminable work, but after that first night he'd made a new rule.

'The hours between five and seven are mine to spend with my son,' he'd told Josef, and he had ignored all of Josef's protests.

And Ellie was included, for those two precious hours. She should back off, she thought. This was the time for Marc to form a long-term relationship with his son and that relationship had to be separate from her.

So she shouldn't stick around as Marc listened with every sign of enjoyment to everything Felix had done that day.

'I'm doing so well on the pony that I'm sure I could ride that ginormous black stallion you ride. But Louis says it's a mount fit for a king, and I'll be a king some day, but not yet...'

Then there was, 'I know all our borders now, and who'll be at the coronation, and who I have to meet, and Pierre helps, and sometimes it's interesting...'

And all about his regime of exercise to get strength back in his leg. 'I hate using crutches. I'm sure I could manage without...'

To all this Marc listened with interest and sympathy and wry smiles. And then they'd head down to the palace lawns and maybe swim in the massive solar-heated pool—or watch Felix swim. And if Marc just happened to tug himself out of the pool and sit beside Ellie while Felix kept swimming it seemed entirely natural. It could even fit with her decree of *official only*. They were supervising while their kid messed around in the water.

Marc asked about her day and she tried not to see the hunger in his eyes as he listened to her account of what had happened in the ER.

Then he told her about his day, a clipped version that she knew was edited to make it seem manageable. And Ellie listened and tried not to care. She tried not to feel as if she was getting to know the man rather than the boy she'd married. She tried not to feel the sweet siren call of those moments where she could almost pretend they were family.

She tried not to fall deeper and deeper in love...

Finally Josef would come to find him and Felix and Ellie were left to entertain themselves for the evening.

'Why can't you stay longer with us?' Felix demanded the week before the coronation was due to take place, and Marc sighed.

'There's too much to do, Felix.'

'So what are you doing tonight?'

'I'm entertaining three royal princes from over the border for dinner and then I'm helping Josef plan the seating for the state banquet before the coronation. Only the most important people are invited and, believe it or not, important people are fussy about who they get to sit beside.'

'That's silly. Make them come out and have hamburgers by the pool.'

'I wish.' His smile was rueful. 'Believe it or not, important people often like fuss.'

'Well, I don't,' Felix said fretfully. 'Just stick everyone's names in a hat and pull them out.

'Tempting, but it might cause problems.'

'Will you sit beside Mum?'

Marc glanced at her, raising a quizzical eyebrow.

'I've asked your mother. She won't come.'

'Isn't she important enough?' Felix demanded.

'She's the most important of all, but I can't make her.'

'It's not suitable,' Ellie managed, trying—and failing—

to drag her gaze from Marc's. *Please don't look at me like this*, she thought desperately. *Please...*

'But you're going to the coronation,' Felix demanded, suddenly anxious. 'I'm not going by myself.'

'I'll come to the coronation,' Ellie muttered and then thought that sounded incredibly ungracious. 'I mean, it's a generous invitation and of course I accept.' She plucked a blade of grass, though the way these gardens were manicured, each blade was probably numbered for security reasons.

Years ago that was a thought she might have shared with Marc and made him laugh. But not now.

She wasn't game to make him laugh now. She wasn't game to get any closer.

'The coronation can't take place without you,' Marc was telling Felix, with a last look at Ellie before focusing again on his son. 'You both need to be there.'

'And I have to ride the fat old horse.' He looked mutinous. 'Louis says.'

'Felix, you'll be in the royal procession. A fat old horse is better than no horse.'

'But I want to ride a big black one like yours. And I want Mum to ride one too.'

'I'll be sitting in the cathedral, keeping your seat warm.' Ellie told him. 'Felix, we've gone through this. You're royal but I'm not. I stay in the background.'

'And we have to go home straight after the coronation?' Felix still looked mutinous.

'We must. We live in Australia.'

'What if I want to live here? With Papa?'

Ellie sighed, suddenly so tired she couldn't find the energy to answer. She rose and tucked a towel around her bathing suit. This place was unreal, she thought, this garden, this swimming pool, this palace, this...man.

This was Marc's world. Her world was Borrawong.

Never the twain shall meet, she thought, but right now Borrawong seemed very far away.

And here came Josef again, to remind Marc that his life was waiting inside the palace. The life they couldn't share.

'There's always a place for you here,' Marc said. He was speaking to Felix but she knew the words were intended for her too. 'Any time you want to come… We'll pay for locums, as we're paying now. Any time you need time out from Borrawong…'

'Why would we need time out from Borrawong?' she demanded. 'That's where our life is. Felix, when you're an adult you can decide where you want to live but, for the time being, your home is with me. Felix, let's just enjoy the next few days. We'll watch your papa be crowned King and then we'll go home.'

He came at midnight. The faint tap on her door was of someone unsure if she was asleep or not, so she still had the choice.

Except somehow she knew he'd sense she was awake. Somehow she knew he needed to talk, that this wasn't a social call.

And somehow she knew she didn't have a choice.

She was wearing her faded nightgown, pink with grey and white spots. She'd scrubbed her face. Her curls were tangling every which way around her face.

She'd gone to bed at ten but failed to sleep and that was what she looked like, but calling out to wait until she was respectable wasn't going to work.

Besides, Marc was… Marc had been her husband. He'd seen her in a nightgown before.

He'd seen her in a lot less.

And that was enough of thinking like that, she told herself as she stumped across the room. She'd do annoyance, she told herself. She'd tell him to go away. Make an official appointment. Anything that had to be said should be said in the far safer light of day.

On that thought, she hauled open the door. And blinked. Marc.

No. This wasn't Marc. This was His Royal Highness, the Crown Prince of Falkenstein.

The dinner he'd just attended had been a royal occasion. It would have been disrespectful of him to attend wearing anything less than monarchical splendour. His dark suit. The slashes of gold. The royal insignia. Even his face seemed darker, more regal.

The new King of Falkenstein.

It was all she could do not to slam the door and whimper.

But he was already inside, setting her gently aside so he could close the door behind him.

'I don't… I don't…'

'It's okay,' he told her, hauling off his beautiful jacket and tossing it casually on the back of a chair. As if it wasn't worth a month's salary or more. 'I'm not here to claim husbandly privileges. But we need to talk. Ellie, please stop looking at me like that.'

'I feel like Cinders in her kitchen when the Prince came calling,' she muttered. 'And don't tell me they lived happily ever after because I don't believe it. Sure, he'd have carted her off to his castle but then he'd have headed off to his gold boxes or his royal meetings or his whatever it is all you kings do and she'd be left feeling stupid, sitting around all day in her glass slippers.'

'I've already said if you stay we could organise you to work in the hospital.'

'Why would I stay?'

'Because we loved one another once. Because the pull's getting stronger and we need to give us more time. You must feel it too.'

'Is that what you came to say? Then don't. If the pull's getting stronger, all the more reason for me to leave.'

'Ellie, what's between us…'

'Needs to be forgotten.' She wanted to be a pink puddle, oozing downward in her spots, disappearing between the ancient floorboards. But what was between them had to be faced.

He was watching her with those eyes she'd fallen in love with. With eyes that had seen into her heart—and maybe still did. It was so hard to say it, but she thought this was an honourable man. He deserved the truth.

'That night in the kitchen…' she managed. 'We kissed. And I knew…' At the look on his face she held her hands up, defensive. 'But, regardless of how we feel, it means nothing. Or nothing for the future.'

She looked down, focusing weirdly on Marc's hands. They were good hands, she thought inconsequentially. Surgeon's hands.

'Ellie, all I ask for is another few weeks,' he said. 'You don't need to make a decision about our future now, but you could work here for a while, think about us.'

'How would that make it better?' Her voice sounded as if it came from a long way away but she couldn't help it. It was as if part of her was dissociated from herself.

The Ellie of ten years ago would have reached up, taken his darling face in her hands and kissed that beautiful mouth. She would have melted into his body. She would have surrendered.

But this wasn't the Ellie of ten years ago. This was an Ellie who'd lived with choices, who'd seen the heartbreak that surrendering could cause.

Marc had walked away. He'd had no choice, as she'd had no choice, but the pain…

And that other choice that had lain before her—to give up her baby. If she'd gone down that road…

She shuddered. 'I loved you once,' she whispered, trying to sort it in her own mind. 'And it's true, I love you still. But Marc, I gave you up for your country and that allegiance still holds. If Felix and I stayed here we'd fit in around the edges, wouldn't we? You're giving up your medicine, which is part of you. You're giving it up for noble reasons, but it's still a part of you that's being ripped out. Felix and I can't be yet another part that can be ripped out whenever it's required. You can't ask that of us.'

'I'm not.'

'You are,' she said steadily. 'And yes, maybe it'd be a noble calling, to be your wife again.' She paused and blinked as the repercussions of that path crashed home. 'For heaven's sake, I'd be the Queen.' And that was enough to make her even more sure. 'Marc, no amount of time could make me accept that role. To stay here and take whatever slivers of time you have left, to know that Felix and I always come second, it would break something in me that was shattered ten years ago and has still only partly healed. Let me go home, Marc, to the medicine I love, to the people who need me.'

'I need you.'

'You don't.' Then she shook her head. 'No, that's unfair. It's that you can't need me. You know you can't let yourself need me or need Felix because your country needs you more. We tried once, Marc, and we failed. Let's leave it at that.'

So that was that. No arguments. Nothing. He knew she was right. She could see it in the blank stoicism on his face.

How much did this hurt? How much would it always hurt?

His body was ramrod-stiff. He was holding himself as a soldier, but she saw loss, longing—love? All the things that made her want to reach for him, hold him, cradle him against her. He was a prince, a soldier, a surgeon, but he was so much more.

It took all the will in the world not to reach out and hug him. To agree to whatever he wanted.

'Attend the ball with me,' Marc said, suddenly urgent, and she flashed a scared look at him.

'Why?'

'Because it's the only time.' He took a deep breath. 'That's what I came here to ask. Ellie, everything you're saying is true, but do this one last thing for me. The palace will put pressure on me to marry again and that's unthinkable. I already feel married. In your short time here, you've made an impression on the people. Your work at the hospital has been reported in the media. You'll be going home to Australia to continue with your medicine and the media will respect that. They'll see that you're doing your duty. But, for this last time, we're separating because we have no choice and I'd like to make that a public statement. Come with me, dance with me, be my wife one last time.'

'I can't…' she said weakly and then, even more weakly, 'I don't have a thing to wear.'

And his weary face creased into a smile. It was a resigned smile and, though it didn't light his eyes, it was a smile just the same.

'We can fix that,' he told her. 'Come to the ball and be a princess. Being royal is something I need to live with for the rest of my life but, for one night, Ellie, share my crown.'

'For one night.'

'Yes,' he said steadily. 'And then you can watch the coronation and go home.'

'Marc…'

'This one thing, Ellie. It's all I'm asking.'

And what was a woman to say to that? How could she deny him?

'One night,' she told him. 'Like Cinderella, until midnight. But that's it. Royal's what you are, not me. I'll see you crowned and then I'm going home.'

His valet was waiting for him. Marc had never in his life thought he'd have any use for a valet. In truth, the day he'd moved into the palace he'd told Josef that Ernst should be retired.

Ernst had served his grandfather and his uncle. He was creaky with age. He could no longer manage to pull on the hessian boots Marc's grandfather had worn and Marc now needed to wear for ceremonial occasions. Indeed, there was little he could do.

But on that first night, when the dignitaries had assembled for that interminable dinner, Ernst had adjusted the insignia on Marc's chest, tweaked his clothes until he was up to snuff—and then gone through all the names Marc would meet that night. He'd started tentatively but, once encouraged, he'd spelt out, simply but with brutal frankness, a character assessment of each and what Marc should look out for.

And Marc knew the unspoken truth that such a service hadn't been provided for his uncle or his grandfather. That Ernst, as well as most of the kingdom, was imbued with a sense of hope.

So Ernst stayed, his stooped yet dignified figure waiting now to assist Marc to remove his uniform and take it away to places unseen to polish and clean and press.

Marc was accustomed to the old man's presence now; in fact he almost found it a comfort. Ernst seemed to know when to speak and when not to speak.

Tonight he looked at Marc's face and stayed silent. He gathered Marc's uniform, gave a small formal bow and would have left. Marc stopped him.

'Ernst?'

'Yes, sir?'

'Could you tell—? Hell, I don't know *who* you tell, but could you tell someone that Dr Carson will be requiring a ball gown?'

The old man's face lit up. 'We can have a dressmaker here first thing in the morning—or after Dr Carson gets back from the hospital. This is good news, sir.'

'She's only staying until the coronation. I'd like her to stay afterwards, but it's impossible.'

'Yes, sir.' Ernst's face was once again inscrutable. He paused as if considering. 'If I could ask, sir…why?'

'She's a doctor. She has her own life.' And then he thought, *Why not say it like it is?* 'I had to leave her ten years ago because of the war,' he confessed. 'How can I promise never to leave her again? There are demands on my time everywhere.'

Ernst hesitated. 'Your uncle, your grandfather, they never allowed their royal duties to interfere with what they thought was important.'

'And look where that got the country.'

'Yes, sir,' Ernst said softly, and he opened the door and turned to leave. 'But you, sir, will be a very different monarch to those who came before you. It will be up to you to decide what's important, and what isn't.'

He left. Marc headed to the great canopied affair that served as the royal bed. He lay and stared up at the ornate room, lit by the moonlight still flooding in the windows.

This bed was huge. *Dumb.*

He was destined to sleep in it for ever.

And Ellie? She was sleeping in a bed just as big, but hers was temporary. In the morning she'd have breakfast with Felix and then head to the hospital.

He'd have meeting after interminable meeting, all of which were important.

He thought of Ernst's words. *It will be up to you to decide what's important.*

Ha.

Ellie knew what was important, he thought. She'd made the decision to raise Felix herself. She'd fought to make it through medicine, to do the work she loved.

Lucky Ellie.

Desirable Ellie. Beautiful Ellie. Ellie, the woman he wanted to hold, *for as long as we both shall live.*

They'd made that vow.

So keep it!

And drag Ellie into this goldfish bowl? Assure her there'd be no more crises? Assure her his country would always come second after his marriage?

He swore, threw back the covers and headed for the window. Here he could see the distant moonlit mountains. His country. Full of his people. People he'd helped until now with his hands, with his medicine, but people he needed to help now with so much more.

He ached to be at the hospital. His fingers ached to be doing the job he was trained for.

And along the vast palace hall was Ellie. And his son. His family. He ached to be there too.

To have and to hold. That was what he'd promised. But to hold in this place, knowing there were no guarantees? That life could rip them apart again?

How could he ask Ellie to share a life he loathed?

CHAPTER TEN

THE PROBLEM WITH coronations was that they involved parties. Not just for the royal family and those in close proximity, but for the entire country.

And with parties came trouble.

Some of the hardest times in a hospital emergency department were Christmas afternoon, with its gut traumas from overeating and its appalling injuries from trying out new 'toys', and New Year's Eve when it seemed the whole world set out to get drunk.

The coronation of the King of Falkenstein was like a combination of both these events—only bigger.

Two days had been deemed public holidays—the day before the coronation and the day of the coronation itself. The theory was that the country could party hard the day before, then watch the coronation, take a wee nap and get on with life.

The day before the coronation Ellie headed to the hospital as usual. She had the ball that night, but it had her so nervous she was glad she had work to block it out.

Felix was busy—he was having a last practice on his horse with Pierre. 'You should see my uniform,' he breathed to Ellie at breakfast. 'They've even made the trouser leg wider so it can hide my brace. If only I had a bigger horse, I'd look bee*yoo*tiful.'

'You'll look beautiful anyway,' Ellie told him as she left. She watched with a mixture of pride and worry as he scooted off with Pierre to learn to be a prince.

The hospital was the only place where worry could take a back seat to need.

The morning was quiet but the workload soon built. She usually finished by two, but by then there was already a rush. A warm summer's day, too much alcohol, too many kids doing stupid things...

A teenager arrived with a slashed arm from a broken beer bottle just as she was about to go off duty. He was drunk and belligerent and there was no one else to control him.

She sent a message to Hilda and Felix and set about quieting the kid down so she could stitch him.

And tried not to think of Marc.

What would he be doing now? Practising his dance steps? Polishing his speech?

'There's no need to be bitter,' she told herself, and somehow she'd said it out loud.

'I'm not bitter,' the kid she was treating declared. 'I'm pissed.'

'And lucky,' she retorted. 'A fraction to the left and you'd have sliced a vein.'

'I'd have bled for my King and country,' the kid boasted.

Yeah, right.

And then, of course, the appalling happened, as it did so often in the emergency departments of hospitals around the world. A family party. Accelerant used to boost the barbecue. The container left open and too close to the fire. The inevitable.

Eight children and fifteen adults with burns from the flash explosion.

The hospital was running on a skeleton staff anyway— something about extra pay rates for the public holiday. An emergency call went out for doctors to come in. Two responded, which meant they were staffed with four doctors, including Ellie.

Major burns.

'Maybe we could ring M… His Highness,' she said tentatively as she realised the enormity of the need, but the director wouldn't hear of it.

'Disturb His Majesty on this of all days? He's at parliament right now, taking the official oaths. Tomorrow is the crowning but today is just as important. To drag him away…his priority must be his country.'

'At least let him decide,' Ellie muttered but the director shook his head.

'His Majesty is no longer a doctor. He's our King and all the people here would agree that he's needed as our leader.'

And so he was, Ellie thought. She was splitting her time between two patients, a girl of three and a boy of six. The blast had been low and spread upward. The kids had been playing close so they both had vicious burns to their legs. The rest of their bodies were blessedly unmarked but it'd take all her skill and more to prevent amputation.

She had both kids in an induced coma and that worried her too. She needed a specialist anaesthetist.

She wanted Marc. She wanted his skill, but she also realised that she wanted his authority—to call in specialists, to kick butt to get things done.

He was being sworn in by parliament so that long-term he could fix this mess, she told herself.

And as she worked on through the long afternoon and evening something settled inside her. This was an emergency and yes, it would be great if he was here, hands-on, but how many emergencies were being played out around the country right now? How many hospitals were understaffed? How many children like the little girl whose leg she was dressing needed skilled doctors? The only way they could be provided was if someone—Marc—accepted that he couldn't be here now.

But *she* was here. She worked on, oblivious to outside needs. Hilda would be caring for Felix. He had Pierre, he was used to medical imperatives, he'd be okay.

And Marc? She'd promised to attend the ball, but if Marc didn't understand medical need no one would.

At nine at night Ellie finally emerged from the wards to speak to the relatives of the kids she'd been working on. Aunts, uncles, grandparents were all burdened with unspeakable anxiety.

'She should be okay,' Ellie told the little girl's family. 'It'll be a long road to recovery but we've relieved the pressure. There'll be scarring, she'll need specialist attention, but we're confident she'll recover. Her parents are sleeping in chairs by her bed, so maybe you could go home and do the same? The family will need you in the long road ahead.'

'We won't go home,' the grandmother told her. 'This is our son, our daughter, our granddaughter. This is where our hearts are. This is where we stay.'

'You're tired…'

'We can be tired when we're no longer needed. Thank you, Doctor,' the woman said simply. 'You go and rest. It's you who must be tired.'

She was tired but she'd been this tired before. She talked to the little boy's family, then walked out through the throng of gathered relatives and thought that two children were alive, their scars hopefully minimised, because of her presence today. She thought, *it felt okay*.

She thought of Marc, who'd spent his day in ceremonial clothing, ticking off box after box of his long list of coronation duties, and she thought he'd be so much more tired than she was.

This is where our hearts are.

The grandmother's words came back to her, and her heart twisted.

Her bodyguards were waiting. A chauffeur was holding a car door wide.

She slipped into the luxurious interior and closed her eyes.

The ball would have started.

All she wanted was to hug Felix and then sleep. But, tucked away at the back of her heart, was another desire. To go to Marc as she'd done for those few short months all those years ago. To be held by him, comforted by him, find solace and joy in his body. In his love.

Yeah, that's not going to happen, she thought bleakly, but she thought again of Marc and what he'd faced today.

This is where our hearts are.

When the car pulled up at the palace, Hilda met her and gave her a hug and she took it gratefully.

'We hear you've done amazing work,' Hilda said simply. 'Our people are grateful. His Highness knows what you've been doing—he was briefed a couple of hours ago. He expresses his gratitude and says if you don't wish to attend the ball he understands. Felix is asleep. I can run you a bath, give you some supper and you can sleep.'

And that was a siren song. A bath, supper and then sleep.

But those words kept echoing.

This is where our hearts are.

We can be tired when we're no longer needed.

Did Marc need her? He didn't, she thought. He couldn't. They'd made that mutual decision years ago.

But for now...

For now, even though her day had been tough, she knew without being told that Marc's had been worse, trapped in bureaucracy, in ceremonial imperatives.

We can be tired when we're no longer needed.

He couldn't need her for ever. She was going home, but

for now, for tonight, maybe her presence might help. It was an indulgent thought, probably stupid, but he'd wanted her to attend the ball. It had seemed important.

He'd organised her a gown.

So, as doctors did the world over, she fought for and found a second wind. She braced and smiled at Hilda and moved onto the next thing.

'A bath would put me to sleep,' she told her. 'A shower and a sandwich—and then my ball gown, please. I have a Cinderella moment I need to attend to.'

Ten o'clock and already the night had been interminable.

He'd spent an hour every afternoon for almost two weeks with a dancing master. It had chafed him to absolute fury, but Josef had deemed it imperative.

'The dances at ceremonial balls are set pieces. Every Royal in Europe is trained from birth. Not to dance would be deemed an insult, to dance badly a bigger one.'

So politics demanded he danced. Politics demanded he looked like something out of the archaic portraits lining his ancestral hall.

Politics demanded he danced with one 'imperative' after another while he knew Ellie was coping with far more important things. Like saving lives.

Except this was important. Cooperation with neighbouring countries was crucial to stability. He needed to gain the trust of the dignitaries here tonight and one of the ways to do that was to show he respected their world.

Thus he danced when all he wanted was to be with Ellie.

He'd sent word to find out how things were panning out. 'The crisis is over,' Josef had told him half an hour ago. 'The specialists you had flown in have arrived. There are now enough medical staff on the ground to handle the work and we seem to have got off without fatalities.' He'd given a small smile, which was huge for Josef. 'If we're not careful we'll have your Ellie acclaimed as a national heroine. She stands to be as popular as you are.'

'Except she's going home.'

Josef's smile had died. 'As you say.'

'She won't come now.'

Josef had glanced at his watch and agreed. 'Our people tell me she's been overwhelmed by work from this morning. I believe we must excuse her. At least there's no imperative. For your wife not to attend would be an insult but at least she's not your wife.'

And how lucky was that? Marc thought grimly, and went to do his duty.

He danced. He felt ill about Ellie.

And then, as he danced with the Queen Mother of a neighbouring country, there was a stir at the door and he glanced across. It was Ellie.

She looked absurdly nervous. Absurdly self-conscious.

She looked stunning.

Who had designed her gown? Maybe Ellie had decreed its style herself, he thought, for in this ballroom full of glitz and tizz, of diamonds and gold, of chandeliers, of pure unmitigated opulence, Ellie stood apart.

Wearing anything but a beautiful ball gown in this magnificent place would have been yet another of those thousand chasms that could be construed as a royal insult. But this was built with elegance as well as simplicity. It had a scooped sweetheart neckline, tiny sleeves, a figure-hugging bodice and a skirt that flared in soft folds, sweeping all the way to the floor.

The gown had no embellishments. Its beauty was in the cloth itself, Marc thought, shot silk or some such. It was sapphire showered with the merest shadows of silver, making it shimmer as she moved.

She'd caught her hair in a simple knot so her auburn curls were escaping. Simple and yet beautiful.

She was wearing a single pearl at her throat, and his own throat seemed to constrict as he realised it was the pearl he'd given her for the only one of her birthdays they'd been together.

She looked stunning. Ethereal. Breathtaking. But she was standing in the doorway looking scared to death.

Marc turned to the woman he'd been dancing with. 'Will you excuse me, madam? I need to go to my wife.'

'Your ex-wife, surely?' But there was a smile playing at the corners of the Queen Mother's lips.

'Is there such a thing?' Marc murmured. 'For me, I'm not sure.' And he bowed and turned and strode through the dancers to Ellie. The couples parted before him. He reached Ellie and he couldn't think of a thing to say.

'Hey.' How inane was that?

'Hey, yourself.' She looked at him with relief. 'Thank you for coming to rescue me.'

'Thank you for coming.' He smiled down at her, thinking she was more beautiful than anyone in the room. Her face was pale and her eyes were too large in her face. She wore minimal make-up—she must have dressed in a hurry— and he recognised her shadows. She'd spent too long in the emergency room, fighting to save lives. But, oh, she was lovely.

'My people tell me you've done some stunning work,' he told her, his eyes not leaving hers.

'We were lucky. No fatalities. But, Marc, there might have been. More doctors...'

'There will be more doctors,' he swore. 'I appointed a new Minister for Health yesterday, an excellent woman. She knows what you've been doing and she intends to personally thank you before you leave. But, Ellie...' he held out his hand '...for tonight can we forget about today and forget about tomorrow? For now... I seem to remember you can dance.'

He thought of that first time they'd gone out for a pub dinner all those years ago. A pianist had started up— honky-tonk, jazz, fun. And Ellie had laughed with delight and grabbed his hand and dragged him out to the dance floor. 'Let's jive.'

'This isn't the music I'm used to,' she muttered now. There was a thirty-piece orchestra centre stage, playing a classical waltz.

'So you're not up to it?' His eyes gleamed a challenge and the ready laughter sprang back into hers.

'Are you kidding? Bring it on.'

Forget the jive. The waltz was much better.

She hadn't waltzed, not properly, since she was eight years old and her grandma died. But that memory was deeply embedded. Ellie's mother had been ill, flighty, reckless. There'd been many nights when her mother had simply disappeared. But she remembered her grandmother being there, turning up their sound system, putting on the songs she'd learned to dance to.

Dancing with her Grandma, Ellie had felt special, safe, loved.

That was how she felt now—only so much more.

Safe? That was a weird description, she thought. The eyes of everyone in the ballroom were on them. She was a country bumpkin, child of a single mum, a kid from the wrong side of the tracks. Watching her, society's elite. She should be nervous, self-conscious, achingly aware of all the things she could do wrong.

But the day had blown away any last vestige of self-consciousness. She'd fought all day for the things that really mattered.

And here, right now, for this moment, was the only thing that mattered. Marc was holding her in his arms. Her steps were magically following his. His eyes were smiling at her, the music was all around them and the rest of the world faded to nothing.

'You do know how much I love you?' His words were a soft murmur, a background to the amazing music, maybe part of the music itself. 'What you've done today... I'm so proud of you, Ellie.'

'Don't,' she begged. 'I can't stay.'

'I'm not asking you to.' He swung her around, his arm encircling her waist. The silky folds of her skirt brushed her legs. *We might just as well be making love*, she thought, in the tiny part of her brain that was still available for thought. 'Ellie, it was unfair of me to ask. But we have tonight. It ended at midnight for the Prince too, remember?'

'Cinderella, huh?'

'I'm thinking they were both blasted out of their worlds. In fairy tales they get to fudge the ending—happy ever after. But in real life...'

'In real life the Prince has to get up the morning after, put on a suit and tie and discuss the state of the country's... I don't know...sewer system.'

His lips twitched. 'We do have to discuss that.'

'There you go, then. Where's the romance?'

'Here, tonight.' The turn of the dance brought them close again, and his lips brushed her hair. She could hear a collective gasp from around them.

'Marc, don't. They'll get the wrong impression.'

'No,' he said strongly and swung her again. 'They'll get the right impression. Josef talks of me finding a wife. I did find one. She's free to return to her own life and I understand the reasons she's going, but there's no need for me to find anyone else. Ever.'

She didn't last until midnight. Cinderella's Prince might have danced with his Cinders to the exclusion of everyone else, but this was no fairy tale, and after a full set in Marc's arms Josef was casting them anxious looks. Royal noses were being put out of joint. They both knew it, but it was Ellie who tugged herself out of Marc's arms and forced herself to break the moment.

'You know you should be dancing with someone else.'

'Some*ones* else,' he said ruefully. 'Josef's given me a list.'

'And I'm asleep on my feet.' Though it hadn't been true until now. It was only now Marc had released her that she felt like sagging.

'I wish…'

'We both wish.' She managed to smile. 'I should have excused myself tonight.'

'I'm glad you didn't.'

'It felt…important. To come.'

'It was.'

Josef was looking directly at Marc. Marc was ignoring him but Ellie saw the look. It contained a hint of desperation.

'I won't say good luck tomorrow,' she whispered, speaking fast, knowing this was the last time they'd speak in anywhere approaching privacy. 'You won't need it. You'll be a brilliant king.'

'Thank you for bringing Felix.'

'He's told me all about tomorrow. He's going to look as "bee*yoo*tiful" as you, apart from riding on a fat horse.'

'She's not fat.' Marc gave her a lopsided smile that said he was under as much pressure as she was. 'When Felix comes back next year without the brace he can have quite a different mount, but for a kid with no riding experience, with his leg in a brace, in a royal procession…'

'Hey, you don't need to convince me. I'm his mother.'

'And I'm his father. I wish I could…'

'Don't wish.' She took his hands. She would have raised her face and kissed him—every ounce of her wanted to—

but in this place, under the eye of the world's media and royalty…maybe not. 'Just be,' she told him. 'I'll be watching you from my place in the cathedral. Josef's arranged for Felix to be escorted to join me after the procession. We'll both be cheering for you like crazy.'

'And then going back to Australia.'

'Yes,' she said and smiled at Josef, a wide, encompassing smile that said she was done, Josef could do his worst. 'Yes,' she said again and pressed his hands hard, just the once, and then released them. 'Goodnight, Your Highness, and goodbye. Tomorrow you'll be too busy to see me, and the day after that I'll be gone.'

And she turned away, made sure her smile stayed pinned to her face, and walked away.

Through the glittering throng. Out the magnificent entrance. Down the steps to the waiting car.

And I have nothing to leave behind, she thought, and even managed a feeble smile. *Not even a glass slipper.*

CHAPTER ELEVEN

ELLIE SLEPT BADLY—okay, she hardly slept at all—but some time before dawn she fell into an uneasy doze. Her dreams were troubled, a jumble of royal impressions—the ball, the palace—plus the day she'd had treating burned kids. And interspersed amongst it all was Marc. Marc, looking at her with troubled eyes, hungry eyes. Marc, who would have held her, but who understood too well why she couldn't stay.

Marc was just down the hall. He was as far from her now as he'd always been. But, strangely, she seemed to know him better now. She knew the man he was—the honour and duty that would hold him to his lonely course.

It broke her heart, but to follow his suggestion, to re-marry... To let herself fall again...

Except hadn't she already? Would she once again break her heart as they parted?

When a knock at her door finally roused her, for a wild, half-asleep moment she thought, she hoped, it might be him. She glanced at the bedside clock and it was after eight.

Yikes. She sat up with a start, practicalities overtaking dreams. Felix had to be in his uniform and ready by nine. Hopefully, Hilda had woken him and given him breakfast.

And the knock couldn't be Marc. She could only imagine the list of formalities he'd be required to complete this morning.

'Yes?' she called.

It was Hilda, opening the door a crack to call through without intruding, 'Good morning, madam.' Her tone was apologetic. 'We let you sleep as long as we could but Felix is needed. Felix, your father's valet wishes to see you dressed...'

What? Ellie sat bolt upright in bed. Hilda thought Felix was here? 'Hilda?'

Hilda's head appeared around the door. 'Madam?'

'Felix isn't here.'

The door opened wider. Hilda stood, plump and perplexed, staring at Ellie's bed as if it were trying to play tricks on her. 'He always comes into bed with you in the mornings.'

'I couldn't sleep,' Ellie stammered. 'I mean, until early. Yesterday, it was so big, and dancing with Marc...' *Oh, for heaven's sake.* She was stammering like an idiot.

'That's why we let you sleep.' Hilda gave a half smile but it didn't last. 'But I checked on Felix an hour ago and his bed was empty. I assumed he was with you.'

'I tucked him in at midnight but he was fast asleep.' She was wide awake now. 'Maybe he's gone to the stables. Or to find Marc? He's very upset that this is our last day.'

'I'll find out,' Hilda said, and disappeared with such alacrity that Ellie realised she had indeed left it until the last moment to find him. And that the normally unflappable lady was close to panic.

She rose and tugged on jeans and a windcheater. The coronation dress made for her by the palace dressmaker, a dress fit for the mother of the future King, hung in state in its own wardrobe but it could wait until later. She headed to Felix's rooms and stared at his rumpled bed.

The bed was cold.

She walked to the window and saw the stables below. Felix loved this room. He'd spent hours sitting on the window ledge watching the stable hands walk the magnificent horses around the exercise yards.

The longing had been there since the first day. 'One day I'll ride a horse like Papa's.'

'When you come back next year you'll have the brace off your leg. Your papa will be able to teach you properly.'

'I don't want to come back. I want to stay now.'

Why did that conversation come back to her now? Why, as she watched Hilda talking to the head groom, why, as she saw men suddenly run, as she saw Hilda turn and look up at her window…?

As she saw fear.

And suddenly she was running too, taking the stairs two at a time, flying down and through the back entrance, heading for Hilda. Who was almost sobbing with fear.

'What…?'

Hilda stopped, couldn't get words out. It was up to the head groom.

'The lad—' he too seemed visibly upset '—he was down early, hanging round, helping the morning feeds. He's often here. He loves this place.'

'I know that.'

'And he's good with the horses,' the man said. 'He was going from stall to stall, feeding them the bits of carrot I always leave on hand because I know he likes feeding them. Usually I'd keep an eye on him but today… There are so many horses to get ready. I guess…' He was struggling, Ellie saw, trying to get his thoughts together. 'I called everyone into the tack room for a few minutes to collect the gear. It was last-minute polish, all hands required to give everything a last buff. And I had to ensure the right tack went on the right horses.'

He was wavering, almost wild-eyed, frantic. 'Just tell me,' Ellie managed.

'So…so we came out and the lad was gone,' he said,

catching himself. 'And I thought no more of it until Hilda came running. And then we checked.' And he stopped, as if he couldn't bear to go on.

'And His Majesty's horse is missing,' Hilda whispered. 'The great black stallion Prince Marc is to ride in the ceremonial procession today. It's missing and so is Felix. Oh, ma'am…'

And it was too much for her. Hilda put her hand on her heart and crumpled where she stood.

For a few moments Ellie had to concentrate on Hilda.

Her son was missing. He'd presumably taken Marc's stallion. Her whole body was suffused with panic but Hilda had crumpled and she needed to check it was a simple faint and not a heart attack.

But her pulse was steady. She regained consciousness almost as she hit the ground. She sat up and sobbed and apologised and went into frantic mode again and Ellie released her wrist and called one of the female grooms.

'Can you take Madame Bouchier to her room, please. No, Hilda, there's nothing you can do here. You've had a shock and you need to recover. Have you had breakfast? No? Stay with her,' she told the girl. 'That's an order. Hilda, you lost consciousness and we need to get you checked properly.'

'Felix…' she moaned.

'Is my responsibility.'

And then Josef came hurrying around the corner of the stable yard. Of course. The man was omnipresent in this place; he would have heard of this almost before it happened. He was demanding answers of the security guards, incredulous they didn't have answers. Then moving on.

'Claud,' he snapped. 'Take two of the lads. Ride the horses not in use this morning. Let me know the moment he's found.'

Three men. Ellie turned and gazed up at the great mountain that backed the castle. Three was all they could spare? But the coronation. The parade. Of course. This was a greater imperative than her son.

She closed her eyes for a millisecond, trying frantically to settle. And when she opened them Marc was there.

He must have been dressing, she thought, though her thoughts were close to hysterics. He was wearing skin-tight breeches. A voluminous white shirt, high-collared but not yet fastened. A crimson and gilt sash. High boots, moulded to his calves, glistening from hours of polish.

'We have things under control, Your Highness,' Josef said, stepping in to stand between Marc and Ellie. As if he knew what a threat such a connection caused.

But the threat was ignored. Marc took the man's shoulders and lifted him aside. His hands caught her waist and he held her, hard and strong.

'What's under control? What's happening?' He glanced around the gathered stable hands, and he got it. 'Where's Felix?'

So Josef had been told, but not Marc.

When Felix was Marc's son...

'We think he's taken your horse,' Ellie managed. 'But, Marc, the coronation...'

'Why would he take my horse?'

His voice was commanding. It was the voice of a king, she thought dazedly, but it was also the voice of a surgeon, a doctor facing drama, a surgeon who needed facts now. It brought her up short. This was how she had to respond.

Triage.

Tell the surgeon the facts.

'He hates riding the mare,' she managed. 'Everything about his feet, everything that's restricted him, he's fought every way he knows how. He knew the mare was chosen because of his leg. And...'

'And?' Marc's gaze was fixed on hers, urgent and compelling. 'And, Ellie?'

She'd only had moments to think what Felix would be doing but the knowledge had suddenly slammed home. 'You told him, at the start, you said you couldn't be crowned unless he was here. And I told him as soon as the coronation is over we'll go home.' She was struggling to keep her voice level. 'He'll have figured it out his own way. He loves it here.' And how much did it hurt to say it, but there was no way of saying it gently. 'Marc, he loves you.'

She watched his face change. She watched his shoulders sag—and then straighten. Turning to imperatives. 'So he's taken my horse?' He turned to the head groom. 'Is he saddled?'

'No, sir,' the man stammered. 'Just the bridle.'

'Reins?'

'I'll check.'

Ellie almost whimpered. For Felix to balance bareback, with only one leg available to grip… And he could barely ride.

Someone must have heard Felix ride away, Ellie thought numbly, but on this frantic morning hoof beats in the stable yard could well go unmarked. Felix had been lucky.

Or unlucky. The stallion was huge. How had Felix ever managed him?

He was smart. He was brave.

Just like his father.

'He'll have gone up the mountain,' Marc snapped. 'When I rode with him last week I showed him how the gates could be unlocked from the inside. I want every person who can mount a horse up that mountain now. Ring Commander Thierry. He has more mounted men readying for the parade. I want them here too. And saddle Theo for me.'

'Sir!' Josef's was a cry of bewilderment. 'The royal reception starts in thirty minutes. The parade starts in little over an hour. You can't just walk away.'

'I'm not walking away,' Marc said grimly. 'I'm asking them to wait.'

'But for how long?'

'For as long as it takes,' Marc snapped. 'I abandoned my family once for my country. I won't do it again. My country's important but my wife and my son come first.'

She'd been a child when she'd last saddled a horse. She did it now, instinctively, and so fast she was mounted as Marc prepared to lead the first group up the mountain.

His frown intensified as he saw her. 'You don't ride.'

'I chose not to ride. I'm riding now.'

'You'll be needed here. If…when he's found.'

'I'm coming. If anyone else finds him there are radios to let me know.'

He wasted no more time on arguing, just nodded and turned his attention to his horse.

She fell into the tail of the party. The mare she'd saddled was quiet, docile, one of the few not primped for today's ceremony. She seemed to sense Ellie's mood.

She also looked to Marc's horse as if it was the natural leader, and Ellie thought, *You and me both.*

The police commissioner had joined the search on his own mount. His face was as grim as Ellie felt. He fell in beside her and practically glowered. This was her fault?

'You realise we have thousands of people already lining the route. Every detail has been planned for months. For His Highness to disappear…'

'Marc hasn't disappeared,' she retorted. 'He's looking for his son.'

'Yes, but…'

No! She wouldn't listen to him. She wouldn't think about the beautiful uniforms of the searchers, uniforms worn for ceremonial occasions, not for bashing their way up narrow forest trails.

She wouldn't think of Marc, urgent, dark, commanding, seemingly almost one with the horse under him, throwing orders like the commander he was.

And she wouldn't think of Felix.

But that was too big an ask. All she could think of was Felix, small, wiry, braced leg, heading into the wilderness bareback on a stallion he'd never ridden before.

This wasn't a wilderness, she reminded herself, casting for comfort. It was part of the same medieval precinct that encompassed castle and village.

But no one would be up here today. Every soul would be lining the streets or glued to the television to watch the pageantry.

Except the searchers.

How many troops had Marc called in? It must be only half an hour since Felix's absence had been noticed but there were already calls from all over the hillside.

If you lose a child in the forest, do it on a day when half the country seems prepared to mount a horse, Ellie thought, and rode grimly on.

The group divided and divided again as the searchers fanned out, but she stayed behind Marc. Two bodyguards stuck close. Plus the police commissioner. Ellie wanted to talk to Marc but the grim-faced men by his side had her staying back. And what would she say to him anyway?

A man riding beside her gave a surreptitious glance at his watch and winced.

'What?'

'It's half an hour until the procession, ma'am,' he told her apologetically. 'My wife's there, with the kiddies. I'm wondering if they've been told.'

She winced. A whole nation's celebration...

How had she let this happen?

She urged her mare forward and the men around Marc reluctantly gave way to her. The track here was wide enough for two horses. This was the logical way he'd have come, Ellie thought, the widest track leading straight up. But there were cliffs at the side. She couldn't bear to think…

'If he's slipped we'd see the stallion,' Marc said grimly, hardly acknowledging her presence. 'My horse looks intimidating but he's gentle enough. He knows this mountain and he knows his way home. Dammit, where is he?' The last words were an explosion, a fury so fierce it made the horse he was riding start back. He swore and settled him and Ellie saw the rigid control descend again.

'Marc…'

He cast her a look she'd never seen before. Anguish? Fear? Anger? 'What?'

'I'm so sorry.'

'It needed only that,' he said savagely. 'Don't you dare be sorry. You think this isn't down to me?'

'If I'd agreed to stay…'

'Why would you agree to stay?' He shook his head. 'Ten years ago I made the wrong choice. I was conceited enough to think I'd make a difference.'

'You did make a difference,' she said, struggling to keep her emotion in check. 'I've heard enough of your work during the war. How many people you saved. And afterwards—the health system's flawed, but how much more so would it be if you and your father hadn't fought for it?'

'I can't even keep my son safe.'

'That's my job.' She took a deep breath. 'Marc, stop.' It nearly killed her to say it but it had to be said. 'You have searchers all over the mountain. I know… I know the procession will be smaller without them and I'm not generous enough to send them away, but you, Marc…your country's waiting.'

'You think I can be crowned without my son?' And he

cast her another of those looks, with such depth, such despair it almost killed her. 'Without you?'

'Josef would say...'

'Damn what Josef would say,' he muttered. 'Damn what the world will say. A man can be driven only so far. Ten years ago I walked away from you because of imperatives. Those imperatives have only become more urgent, but today, for this day, the imperative of my son, and of you, Ellie, take precedence over all. We'll find him, Ellie,' he said grimly. 'We must. And until then... Until you have your son again, the country can wait.'

And then they found the horse.

They heard a whicker ahead and Marc was off his horse in an instant, holding up his hand for silence. If Felix was ahead, struggling to stay on his mount, the last thing they wanted was to startle him.

They listened and the whicker came again. Close.

Ellie was off her horse too. She didn't think consciously of dismounting. She only knew she had.

'Stay,' Marc told the group around them. 'Silent.' He reached for her hand, imperious, in command. She hardly noticed. She slipped her hand in his and held on tight, and he led her forward.

The track here was steep and treacherously rocky, the climb to the peak rising in earnest. The ground fell sharply on the left, the cliff face too close to the path for comfort.

There were trees, stunted by snowfall, clustered to the right. The bends were sharp and sudden.

'Watch your feet,' Marc told her, but his hand held her, strong and sure, and she knew she couldn't fall. Not while Marc held her.

Oh, but Felix! To try and ride up here...

They edged forward, up and round the bend. And there was Mer Noire, Marc's magnificent stallion. He had his head bent, grazing on a patch of alpine daisies. As he sensed their presence he lifted his magnificent head and whickered again.

He was bareback. No rider.

She had sense enough not to call out, but oh, she almost did. *Felix!* Dear heaven, if he'd been thrown near the drop from the cliffs...

Marc released her hand. He edged forward, speaking softly to the great horse. Mer Noire let him approach, rearing his head at the last moment and trying to back away, but Marc had him by the bridle and held fast.

'So where's your rider, big boy?' he murmured but he was looking upward. 'Not so far, eh? He'll have been trying to make it to the top.'

'He'll have come off.' She was trying not to sob.

'I imagine so,' Marc said but he said it so matter-of-factly that she found herself illogically reassured. As if coming off was no big deal. 'These bends are tight. Mer Noire doesn't know the meaning of slow or caution and, without a saddle, any stumble could have seen Felix fall. But Mer Noire knows where home is. He wouldn't have kept going up after Felix came off. He'll have been coming down. He'll have stopped because he couldn't resist a snack.'

'But the cliff...'

'The steep drop's behind us. It's only a ten-minute climb to reach the top from here. We'll leave the horses and walk. Come on with me.'

He gave a 'Hoy!' and the rest of the group edged into the clearing. 'We're going up,' Marc told them and received a groan from the police commissioner.

'Sir, the time...'

And Marc told him where he could put his clockwatching. 'Stay here,' he told him. 'Ellie and I will go on alone.'

'But why?' The man was almost sobbing.

'Because he may be on the track, hurt, in which case we'll call you. But it's likely that he's come up here for a purpose and that's to stop my coronation. He knows what pain is and it won't stop him.'

'You think he could be hiding?' Ellie asked, and he put his arm around her and gave her a swift, hard hug.

'That's what I'd have done at his age,' he said dryly. 'And I'm starting to think my son is very like his father.'

So they climbed steadily, hand in hand, towards the peak. It was an extraordinary climb, an extraordinary view out over this beautiful country, but Ellie was in no mood for sightseeing. As they neared the peak she was close to collapse.

'You must be wrong. He must have come off near the cliffs. Oh, Marc...'

But he was looking intently at a branch broken beside the path ahead, at scuff marks and hoof prints in the dust.

'Something's happened here. It has to be a fall, which means he can't be far. He must be hiding.' He tugged his hand free from hers, cupping his hands and started to call.

'Felix, you've done it.' His deep voice echoed out over the mountain, seemingly all the way to the town below. 'You've done what you set out to do. You need to come out now and face us.'

No answer. Marc nodded, as if he expected no less, and started walking further up the track. A hundred yards on he tried again.

No result.

But fifty yards on, third try...

There was a sound very like a sob from the undergrowth. 'I... I can't.' A child's voice.

'Oh, Felix!' Ellie had almost given up on breathing she

was so afraid, and for a moment she couldn't believe what she'd heard. 'Felix!'

Marc was already on his knees, bashing his way through the bushes. 'Where are you?' His voice was demanding. 'Felix?'

'I can't come out.' Felix's voice was a sob from behind dense undergrowth. 'The coronation hasn't even started yet. I wanted to get to the top and wait but the path was too skinny and the tree hit me in the face. And I fell. And I tried to crawl higher but I can't. And I think I've broken my other leg.'

What should you do when a child's been so wilfully disobedient that he's disrupted an entire nation's plans for a coronation?

You hug him, that's what.

Only Ellie couldn't get near because Marc was before her, gathering him into his arms—carefully, though, so as not to disturb either leg—and holding him tight. Putting his face in Felix's hair. Saying things that Ellie couldn't hear as she fought to get through the undergrowth to join them. Things that silenced Felix's sobs and had him crumpling against his papa.

And then Ellie was with them and she was gathered too. Marc had them both in his arms, holding with a fierceness that was a declaration all by itself. And Ellie was weeping as she hadn't wept for years, giving herself this moment, this one precious sliver of time, to let go of her precious control. To give herself over to the knowledge that Felix was safe and Marc had him in charge, and he had her too, and she was where she was meant to be.

Or not, but that was for the future. For now, there was this one wonderful moment before the world broke in. One moment of stillness.

One moment where her heart knew all the answers, and they were right here with this man.

He kissed Felix, and he kissed her too, lightly, almost a kiss of wonder, but it was enough. It had to be enough.

For then the world broke in, in the form of Marc's bodyguards, bashing their way to them, looking frantic—they'd let their liege lord out of their sight and they were suffering. And the police commissioner was behind them. And more searchers were behind them.

And Marc was settling Felix, lying him down again, turning his attention to his legs.

Another broken leg? Reality was sinking back. *How bad?* After that first glorious moment of exultation Ellie's heart was sinking again. With the bad leg not yet recovered, it'd be back to the wheelchair, back to months of frustration, back to…

'Can you wiggle your toes for me?' Marc asked and Ellie hauled herself away from the other end of the pendulum. Bliss to panic in moments.

'My foot, I can't move…'

'Then don't move.' Marc's voice was still commanding. He was unlacing Felix's boot, easing it off. He set his hand hard against Felix's heel. 'Press. Just a little.'

There was a moan but Felix tried and Ellie thought the moan had been in anticipation of pain rather than pain itself.

'Now the toes,' Marc ordered. 'All the weight's on my hand, Felix, so you won't be moving the leg at all. Just a faint wiggle to let me know you can.'

And Felix gritted his teeth—and wiggled. And Ellie could see them wiggle.

Better and better.

'I need a knife,' Marc snapped and the police commissioner glanced at his watch and groaned with more agony than Felix had displayed. But in unison the bodyguards produced two wicked-looking knives, blades that had been cleverly disguised as cudgels.

And Marc even grinned. 'Let's hope that's the last time these are ever used,' he said and took one and slit Felix's jeans from hip to ankle.

Displaying the whole leg.

'You're sure the braced leg is okay?' he asked Felix, and Felix managed a nod. He was clutching Ellie, sweating with pain and effort.

'When I felt myself fall… I twisted so I'd land on the good leg. But I was trying to hold Mer Noire, 'cos Louis said only the worst horsemen ever let go. And there must have been a rock 'cos it was super hard and it hurt like crazy.'

'I can see that.' Marc was doing a careful examination of the leg, all the way down. Hip. Thigh. Knee. Calf. His strong fingers gently probing.

Ellie watched. This was her role, she thought. She was the doctor.

Not now. The coronation was forgotten. Marc was all doctor.

'It's your ankle,' Marc said and he lifted his hands away so Ellie could see. He'd sliced away Felix's sock. She could see the whole leg now. There was a shallow gash and scrape on his ankle, and the entire area was red and swollen. Marc probed with care while Felix bit his lip and held her hard. He was still a little boy.

And brave.

He was so like his father.

'It might only be sprained.' Marc flashed her a relieved smile, knowing she needed reassurance more than her son. Felix wouldn't have started to think of long-term consequences yet. Marc slit the second trouser leg as well, checking under the brace. Looking relieved. 'Felix, is there anything else? Did you hit your head?'

'No.'

'You're sure?' Ellie was already checking. Never believe a child. In truth, never believe anyone after trauma. The mind did weird things. If Felix's ankle was the major pain then 'minor' trauma could well be overlooked by the neural pathways, meaning lack of pain where pain was needed as a warning. But there was nothing to see. She gave Marc a reassuring nod and she saw him relax.

They'd come out of this so much better than she'd feared. She felt almost sick with relief and she watched Marc's face and knew he felt the same.

'Felix, we're going to have to get you off the mountain, down to hospital where we can X-ray that ankle and see what's what,' he said. 'But if I had to guess, I'd say there's no fracture. But I bet it hurts. We'll find something to help that now.' He turned to the police commissioner. 'We brought medical supplies—they're back at the junction. Could one of your men...?'

'Go,' the police commissioner barked at his subordinate. Then, almost pleading, 'Sir, the time...if the boy only has a sprained ankle... It's not just the dignitaries I'm thinking of but everyone lining the route, everyone about to turn their television on. We could take over from here. Sir, please...'

Marc looked at her.

He was obviously torn.

But Ellie's mind was clearing. This wasn't the decision he'd made an hour ago—coronation or a son in peril. Nor was it a decision as hard as the one they'd made all those years ago. To walk away from each other.

This might almost be a decision made by parents throughout the world.

My son has sprained his ankle but I'm needed elsewhere. The hospital facilities are adequate. My husband/wife can stay with him.

Need was weighed against need.

Here the decision was obvious and it wasn't heart-rending.

But still Marc gave her the choice. He rose and looked down at Ellie, who was still holding Felix in her arms.

'If you want me to stay I will,' he told her. His gaze met hers and held. 'Nothing's more important to me than you and Felix.'

'Tell him to stay,' Felix said urgently. 'Mum, tell him. I don't want him to be a king.'

'Felix, we don't have a choice.' Her eyes didn't leave Marc's. 'Sometimes there isn't a choice—and there's no choice for your papa now. Your papa is the King, and he needs to accept his crown. The people are waiting. Go, Marc, and go with our love.'

He rode down the mountain, trying to come to terms with what had just happened. Trying not to think of what he'd left behind.

The medical kit had arrived before he'd left. He'd injected morphine and seen Felix turn from hurting to sleepy. Ellie was staying until the stretcher bearers arrived. They were both safe.

He ached to stay with them but there was truly no need—apart from his desire.

Desire... He wanted them so much it was like a physical hurt. To walk away from Ellie...

To be crowned. To accept a life she'd want no part of.

The police commissioner was barking orders into the phone as they headed down the mountain. 'Notify the Royals at the reception. The parade will start fifteen minutes late. Have the PR people brief the media on what's just happened—no, the boy didn't run away; he obviously went for an early morning ride and his mount got away from him. Brief the security contingent. Let the cathedral know. Have His Highness's clothes at the stables—there'll be no time for niceties.' The orders seemed endless.

Riders were emerging from the forest, men and women in full ceremonial garb who'd been diverted to search for one small boy. There'd be some urgent brushing, removal of twigs, fast grooming of horses, but smiles were everywhere.

The drama was over. Marc could take his proper place.

Except it didn't feel like his proper place.

He knew what he was leaving behind.

They were clattering into the stable yard. The household staff emerged as a fast, efficient team. Brushes, soap and water—this was efficient chaos. The coronation would go on.

As Marc's personal valet, Ernst had time with him. He looked Marc over with a critical eye. 'There's blood on your shirt. No matter. I have another.' He started helping Marc strip it off. 'Sir, is the boy indeed all right?'

'He is,' Marc said gruffly and Ernst gave him a sharp look. In the midst of the fuss around them, he found time for a little reflection. Maybe he sensed Marc needed it.

'It must have been hard to leave him,' he said thoughtfully. 'His place is with you at the coronation.'

'It can go ahead without him.'

'I know that, sir,' Ernst said gently. 'But, if I may say so, it's a lonely role you're taking on. A man needs his family.'

'I can get by without one.' Ernst was helping him into a fresh shirt, followed by his magnificent coat. 'I have you.'

'Yes, sir, you do,' Ernst said softly. 'And you'll manage the role with skill and with honour. I've served you less than two months and I already know that about you.' He stood back and eyed his handiwork and then tutted as he saw a twig caught in Marc's dark hair. 'But even I have a wife, and I need her.'

'Ernst?'

'Yes, sir?'

'Don't make it harder than it already is.'

The old man's face softened. 'No, sir,' he told him. 'But

my heart goes out to you. As, indeed, do the hearts of every person in the country.'

And isn't that the crux of the matter, Marc thought as he finally mounted and readied himself for the parade to begin.

Too many hearts...

I just need one, he said to himself but there was no time for regrets.

The leaders were ready. A slow drumbeat started. The massive gates of the palace were flung open and Dr Marc Falken turned his face to his country.

He turned to become the King.

X-rays had been taken. The ankle was indeed sprained. Felix would have a few uncomfortable days but there was no drama.

Normally he'd be sent home but, in deference to who he was—and at the insistence of the bodyguards still with them—he was wheeled into a private ward to sleep off the effects of the painkillers.

A ward which just happened to have a television. A large one.

So Ellie watched as Felix slept. She watched the interminable parade. She watched as Marc rode at the head of the vast contingent representing every section of this country.

He wasn't on Mer Noire but on a horse almost as grand, black as night, as regal as its rider.

Marc looked magnificent. There was no other way to describe him.

He also looked regal. Imperious. Breathtaking.

Solitary.

And she thought of his face while he'd searched for Felix. She thought of his agony.

He'd known Felix for barely two months. How could he love him?

And yet that decision made all those years ago was suddenly all around her. That email…

'Do you want your name on his birth certificate?'

And his answer.

'I can't be there for him. I have no right to be his father.'

Adoption had been a decision they'd made together, but blessedly she'd been free to change her mind. Marc, though, had been given no choice.

And now she watched the cheering crowds acclaiming their King, embracing him, taking him as their own, and she knew Marc still had no choice.

But maturity had made her see the cost.

'Felix, you need to wake.'

For the procession had stopped and Marc was entering the cathedral. The trumpets sounded out their triumphant blast. The coronation had begun.

This would be watched in millions of homes throughout the land and recorded a thousand times over. Felix would be able to watch it time and time again. But right now it seemed important—no, it seemed imperative—that they both watched this in real time.

That, wherever they were, Marc knew his family was with him.

As Felix woke and watched, as Ellie held her son and knew that one day he, too, would kneel where Marc was kneeling and have the great crown placed on his head, something settled inside her.

Family.

Once upon a time she'd made the decision to have her baby adopted. She'd changed her mind. Life had been hard in consequence, but she wouldn't give away a moment of what she'd had.

And if she changed her mind about Marc? If she took on a royal role?

There'd be imperatives she'd hate—she knew there

would. There'd be moments, days, maybe even years where choices weren't theirs to make.

But what was the alternative?

'He looks like a king now,' Felix breathed as Marc rose, crowned, facing the future, facing his country. 'He doesn't look like my papa.'

'But he is your papa,' Ellie whispered. 'And maybe, maybe, if we had the courage, he could be so much more than just the King.'

The day of the coronation was a day of dignity, pomp and splendour—and reverence.

The pre-coronation ball the night before had held all the pageantry any right-thinking royal could desire. Tomorrow there would be receptions, banquets and a series of lesser balls which Marc would be required to attend, if only briefly. After that, there was a list of regal appointments stretching as far as he dared check his calendar.

For tonight, though, there was a moment of peace. At ten, the dinner for the most important dignitaries was over and Marc was escorted to the chapel.

For this was in his diary as well. Ten to midnight, chapel royal, time set aside for royal reflection.

Actually, Marc hadn't checked his diary this far ahead. He'd been acting on autopilot ever since he'd left Ellie. Oh, he'd demanded updates of Felix's progress through the day. The ankle was indeed sprained, Felix was safely in bed in the hospital and would stay there overnight on the off-chance there were any after-effects. His mother was with him. They were okay.

He'd even been given a message from Ellie herself. *Tell His Majesty that Felix and I watched the coronation with pride. And with love.*

Now, at ten o'clock at night, he was in the chapel staring at his bodyguards.

'Tell me why I'm here.'

'Orders are that you're supposed to be here,' the older of the bodyguards told him.

'It's custom,' Josef said, coming in behind them. 'The coronation programme has stayed the same for hundreds of years. This two hours is scheduled time for reflection.'

'You're kidding.'

Marc stared around at the exquisite palace chapel, the private place of worship for generations of royals, and he thought at another time he might have been glad of this respite.

The silence was almost overwhelming. All day, the shouts of the crowds, the music, the trumpets, the drums, the amassed bands, the noise at the reception, they'd battered him. But here in this place was silence, prescribed, ordered, and he knew what he'd do with it.

'Take me to the hospital,' he ordered.

'Sir!' Josef sounded horrified. 'The agenda…'

'Does it say anywhere that I can't be King if I don't follow the blasted agenda?'

'No, but…'

'But what?'

'The media's gone home,' Josef moaned. 'This is your prescribed quiet time. If you go to the hospital now, the nation will miss it.'

There was a deathly silence, a silence that rebounded over and over from the walls of the ancient place of worship. And, at the look in Marc's eyes, Josef took a step back.

And so did his bodyguard.

'My life is not prescribed by the media,' Marc said, in a voice so low it was almost a whisper. It wasn't a whisper, though. It had the men taking another step back. 'Nor is my life prescribed by any agenda. My life is prescribed by priorities. *My* priorities. My first priority today was my son. Then it was accepting the throne. But now—'

'But if you go to the hospital the media will learn of it.' Josef was still struggling to hold line. 'They'll say the palace held information back.'

'And so it did,' Marc said, and he tugged the great ceremonial sword from its scabbard and handed it to Josef. It had no place in the chapel anyway, and it certainly had no place where he was going. 'But there was no failure. The palace gave the media everything it needed to know about His Majesty, King Marc of Falkenstein. But the King has just decreed he's off duty. Agenda closed. Take the sword, Josef, and put it safely away. I'll take it up again when it's required, but now my need is to be Felix's papa. My need...'

He hesitated, but why not voice what his true need was?

All he could say was what was in his heart.

'My need is to see Ellie.'

The junior nurse assigned to sit by Felix's bedside was almost asleep. She should have been off duty hours ago but people were celebrating, doing dumb things, and patients kept streaming in.

She'd been due to leave at eight but the nurse manager had pulled her aside.

'I know you're exhausted, but we can't leave the little Prince alone. He's such a high-profile patient. Could you stay for a couple more hours?'

So here she sat, watching a child sleep. A child who'd one day be King.

Who'd have thought? she asked herself. She'd been sad to be rostered to work through the coronation, thinking she'd missed the chance to watch the procession and see real royalty. Yet here she was, watching royalty—although this pale-faced, bruised little boy sleeping soundly didn't seem the least bit royal.

And then the door swung open to reveal...her new King!

He looked at her patient, at the little boy curled up in the big bed, and something in his face seemed to twist. 'Sleeping?'

Somehow she found the courage to reply. 'Y…yes, sir.'

'How is he?'

'Obs all good, sir.' She was struggling to get her voice to work. 'I mean… Your Majesty. Blood pressure ninety on fifty. Temperature normal. He had paracetamol an hour ago when he woke. He also had fruit and custard and asked for his mother, but he wasn't anxious when I told him. It seems he's used to it, sir.'

'So where's his mother?'

'She's…she's in Emergency, sir. When Fe… When His Highness went to sleep someone told her how busy we were and she offered to help. That's why…that's why I'm here.'

And Marc smiled. 'I might have known,' he said. 'Once a doctor, always a doctor. Thank you for taking care of my son.'

And then he tugged off his beautiful coat, rolled up his sleeves and he turned to the man who'd come in behind him. 'Okay, Josef, let's go do something else the media isn't going to see.'

There'd been no major drama, but the day of celebration meant the emergency department was filled with a seemingly endless stream of minor injuries. Ellie had seen them on the way in.

Felix was shaken and sore, but he was essentially fine. The drugs he'd been given, plus the fact that he'd woken before dawn to creep to the stables before anyone was stirring, had him fast asleep.

Ellie thus had time to herself, and sitting by herself while Felix slept had been doing her head in. After an hour of Felix-watching she asked if she could be fetched if Felix was needed. She headed for Emergency and that was where Marc found her.

She was in the cubicle at the end of the ward. She heard a stir of people arriving and hoped it wasn't yet another drama. She'd had enough for one day, as had the entire staff.

But then the curtain was pushed aside—and it was Marc.

He was back as she'd seen him this morning. Breeches, dress shirt with full sleeves rolled to the elbows, boots...

He was the same Marc and yet different.

This was the King, she thought, and her patient's mother let out a whimper of shock.

'Ellie,' he said and it took a great deal to smile back at him as if he were a colleague.

'Felix...'

'I've just seen Felix,' he told her. 'Fast asleep. I've come to find you.'

'I'm dressing Lisle's leg,' she managed. 'Your... Your Majesty, this is Lisle Betier, and her mother, Madame Betier. Lisle decided she wanted her dog to watch the Coronation Parade. They have a tiny attic balcony and their dog is big and very old. Lisle's papa is one of your soldiers. He was in the parade. As you can see, Lisle's mama is very pregnant, so Lisle decided to carry the dog upstairs herself. Sadly, she fell. She came in with concussion, but her obs are looking good. I'm fixing her leg now. We can't put plaster on until the swelling goes down but we're bracing it to hold it steady.'

Even though she was telling Marc what was happening, she was also talking to Lisle's mother, doing what she did every day in her medical life. Informing and reassuring. It helped Lisle's mother and it also helped her. It made it almost possible to pretend Marc was nothing more than a colleague.

'Lisle will need to stay in overnight, because of the concussion,' she told Marc. 'But she's going to be fine.'

Marc nodded. He drew the curtains closed behind him, effectively blocking out his entourage, but he too was focused on Lisle and her mother.

'This happened while the parade was taking place?' he asked. 'That was hours ago.'

'You've been…everyone's been busy,' the woman faltered.

'And my dog's been in the car all this time,' Lisle whispered to Marc, as if he alone was responsible. 'By himself. And Mama says we have to worry about me, but I'm sure he's hurt himself. There was blood on his paw.'

'Where's your husband?' Marc asked Madame Betier and she cast him a look that was almost wild.

'He's still on duty. He won't be home until midnight. I didn't even have time to leave a note. I just put Lisle in the car, but she insisted on bringing the dog.'

'He's hurt,' Lisle said stubbornly and Marc lifted an eyebrow at Ellie.

'Has Lisle's leg been treated?'

'It's stable, dressed and braced. Greenstick fracture of the tibula.'

'I want to see my dog,' the little girl whimpered and Marc grinned.

'Well, seeing as your dog—and you—were injured because of my parade, the least I can do is check out your dog. Is he in the car park?'

'Yes.' Lisle's mother was bemused almost to the point of gibbering. 'He split his pad and there was a lot of blood but I did run out and check…'

'But Lisle needs to check too, and this is an imperative.' He tugged back the curtains to reveal Josef and his two shadows. 'Can you find a wheelchair?'

'There isn't one,' someone called from the far side of the ward. 'The nursing home borrowed them to take the oldies to the parade and they haven't returned them yet.'

'There is indeed a lot I'm responsible for.' Marc sighed and looked at Ellie again and smiled. 'But priorities must be maintained. We have an injured dog in the car park, Dr Carson. No other priorities?'

'I don't think so,' she managed.

'Then could you find disinfectant and bandages?' He turned back to Josef. 'I'll need a chair if I'm to work out there, and a decent torch.' He turned back to Madame Betier. 'There have been priorities all day, but maybe this is the last. I, madam, propose to carry your daughter out to the car park. Dr Carson and I will attend to your dog, so Lisle can see for herself that he's fine. While we do that, I'll send word that your husband is to be released from his duties…' he eyed the lady's very pregnant bulge '…for the foreseeable future. On full pay. Starting tonight. Right, team, let's get this priority sorted.'

Which explained why Ellie was standing in the hospital car park at midnight holding a flashlight while Marc assessed the injured pad of one ancient golden retriever. He treated the dog as he'd treat a child, with all the care in the world, cleaning its split pad, making sure there were no foreign bodies, then carefully padding and binding—and all the time chatting to the dog, to Lisle and to Madame Betier, as if he had nothing more important to do but this.

The bodyguard and Josef were still in the background, but to Marc they might as well not exist. He was totally focused.

He'd been focused all day, Ellie thought. One thing after another…

'There,' he said softly, patting the old dog's head. 'You'll be going home soon.' And then he looked thoughtful. He grinned at Lisle and lifted the old dog out onto the grass verge nearby. He lowered him onto the grass and held him by his collar. The dog didn't put any weight on his injured paw but promptly did what he'd obviously needed to do for hours. And everyone laughed.

Marc took the dog back to the car and then went to pick up Lisle. She needed to be carried back to the ward.

'Marc?'

Ellie's voice made him pause. 'Yes?'

'Could one of your bodyguards carry Lisle back? Lisle, would that be okay? I'm afraid His Majesty has another imperative he needs to deal with.'

'I do?'

'You do,' she told him and took a deep breath because some things were blindingly obvious. Maybe if they'd seen things this clearly ten years ago they would have saved themselves a whole lot of heartache, but sometimes sense took time.

But now…

Sense was all around her. She just needed to shake off his entourage and make Marc see.

They weren't allowed to stay in the car park and talk. That'd be too much for the security contingent to swallow. 'Go back to the palace and have your talk in private,' Josef urged, but some things were too urgent to wait. So Ellie grabbed Marc's hand and led him through the first door marked Staff Only, which happened to be the door through to the scrub room.

No one was there. The row of metal sinks, the bright white lights overhead, the sterile, scrubbed environment, it lent a sense of unreality to what she had to say. And yet it made sense too. She'd met Marc as a doctor. That was what they both were under the trimmings.

And because that was how she felt, stripped bare, in a place where only essentials mattered, she turned and faced him and said the thing that had been pounding in her head for hours. When she'd watched a lone figure take the crown.

When she'd seen past the glitz and pageantry to the lone man, solitary, taking on a burden that was surely far too heavy for him to bear alone.

As she'd watched him face what he must face and she'd known she couldn't leave.

'If you still want…' The words had been forming in her head for hours and yet they were still hard to say. But they were the right words. 'If you still want, then I'll stay,' she managed. 'Marc, if you want to make another go of our marriage…'

And there was such a blaze of hope on his face that she took a step back. Almost as if she was afraid.

But then his face stilled. 'Make a sacrifice, you mean?' And how to explain this?

She was tired, overwrought, overwhelmed by the emotions of the day, yet she still had to get the words out.

'It's no sacrifice. I love you.' The hope flared again but she held up her hands, as if to fend off any interruption. She had to get this right. 'You know I always have.'

'You know I've loved you. But, Ellie, I have no right…'

'And I thought I had no right either,' she told him. 'Ten years ago we stood in that airport and knew what we were both facing was impossible. We saw no way to be together so we parted. But, Marc, we were married. We loved each other. Surely we could have done it better.'

'Forcing you to join me in a war zone, you mean?' How many times had he thought this? 'And you halfway through your training. With your mother ill.'

'And me? Forcing you to return to Borrawong with me because that was where Mum needed to be? Both were impossible. So we did the only thing that seemed possible. We ended our marriage. But these last few weeks, I've realised… Mark, you can't end a marriage. Sure, a marriage can end if two people fall out of love. If two people should never have married in the first place. A marriage can stop being a marriage, but has ours?'

'What are you saying?'

'I'm saying…' She took a deep breath because she wasn't sure. It should be the guy, she thought, the man who went down on bended knee, but Marc had already done that. He'd already married her in all honour and then he'd walked away because that had been the honourable thing to do too.

He'd asked her to stay now. That had taken courage, she knew, but what had taken more courage was his acceptance of her response. He wanted her. She could see it every time he looked at her. And Felix was his son, and he had a right to be here for him, as he'd had the right these last ten years.

So say it.

'Marc, we haven't been able to be together for most of these last ten years,' she managed. 'And yet…and yet…do you still feel married?'

'You know that I do.'

He was past exhaustion too, she thought. Up at dawn, riding to search for their son, then going through surely the most demanding, emotionally overwhelming day of his life. He looked almost grey with tiredness. There was a trace of blood running down his sleeve. That'd be from washing the dog, she thought, and she looked up into his tired, careworn face and thought, *Of all days, to be carrying an unknown little girl into the car park and caring for her dog…*

'There'll always be other priorities.' She said it surely now, the sudden remembrance of Marc's tenderness towards Lisle and her dog almost overwhelming her. 'And…and we need to accept that. But if we decide that being married is a given, something that can't be revoked just by getting on a plane, then won't everything else fit in around that? And maybe, maybe we can work on priorities. Not accept them as given. Like your boxes…'

'I don't—'

'Marc, you've been told they're a priority,' she said, urgently now because this was important. This was at the heart of who he was. Yes, he was now Falkenstein's sovereign, and maybe he was also her husband, but part of Marc was also a surgeon. A fine surgeon. He'd told her once he couldn't even remember deciding to be a doctor—he just knew he would be one. So that was a given.

'We can work on this,' she said, urgently now. 'Together. But you need room for your medicine because that's who you are. Tonight you came in here exhausted, and yet fixing a little girl, fixing her dog…it's who you are and I love you for it. And your country has to learn to love you for it too, because they can't ask you to ignore what's part of you. Marc, maybe for now the boxes take precedence, but there's another priority as well, and that's choosing people we trust to share—'

'We?'

'We,' she said, firmly now because this was in her heart. 'If you want me, I won't leave you to face this alone and it can't be a sacrifice because I love you. Marc, if you'd still like me to stay, to share the burden…'

It was as if the room was suddenly super-powered, pierced by a jolt of something so strong it threatened to blow them both away.

Or blow them together?

She couldn't remember moving. She couldn't remember Marc moving, but suddenly she was in his arms. Her face was somehow thrust upward to meet his and his mouth claimed hers, with all the power of a long line of ancestral kings, with all the power of a man who'd hungered for his wife for ten long years, with all the power of a man who loved her.

How had she ever thought her marriage was ended? She knew as she melted into his arms, as she felt the heat, the strength, the longing, as she felt the absolute knowledge that this was home, that this was priority number one.

Or maybe it wasn't a priority. Maybe it was simply what was.

Ellie and Marc.

If she thought of the future it might well overwhelm her. She didn't want royalty. She didn't want media attention. She didn't want the baggage that would inevitably distract her from her medicine, even from Felix.

But some things were not arguable. She'd fight for what she needed, she thought, but, as Marc's arms held her close, as he lifted her high and swung her, his face ablaze with joy, she thought she'd never need to fight for this.

This was Marc. Her husband.

Hers.

Three months ago Felix had missed out on riding in his father's coronation parade. This parade was just as good. Actually, Felix thought as he rode his beautiful grey mare beside the great golden carriage containing his mother, this might even be better.

A royal wedding.

His mum had been horrified when the idea was first mooted. 'Marc, no. Let's just do it quietly at the council offices.'

'There's no such thing as quiet when you're the King,' Marc had said cheerfully. 'Josef said the coronation did wonders for the economy. How much more so a royal wedding?' He'd smiled, and he and Ellie had shared one of those goofy smiles they did so often, the smiles that Felix was learning to live with—and even like. 'Besides, I'm proud of my wife. We had a registry office wedding once before, if you remember, and we didn't take our vows seriously enough. Let's show the whole nation we mean business.'

So here they were, heading for the cathedral with all the pomp and pageantry the country could possibly crave.

And Felix was on a horse of his choosing. The mare wasn't quite as magnificent as his father's Mer Noire but she galloped like the wind. His leg was good—almost back to normal—and by normal they were saying it'd stop him doing nothing. Which meant when his mum had asked him to be in the carriage with her, there'd been negotiations.

His first idea was to ride behind the carriage in his new car. Or sort of new. For Marc had presented him with an ancient, battered hulk of a 1922 Austin Seven for his birthday. They were doing it up together. Half an hour a day was all Marc could afford, and sometimes there were gaps, so it wasn't nearly ready—for which Ellie seemed profoundly thankful.

'Then I'll ride,' he'd declared. 'I'll be an outrider.'

She and Marc had considered. 'If it's important to you,' Marc had said at last. 'Do it.'

There'd been a bit of that over the last few months. Discussions as to what was important, and what wasn't.

It had seen Ellie sitting up late at night helping Marc sort through interminable boxes, working out priorities.

It had seen Marc insist on a slab of time three days a week, three hospital sessions where he abandoned his royal persona and operated as the surgeon he was.

It had seen Ellie fly out to Borrawong and arrange for locums to become permanent, funded in part by the Royal Household of Falkenstein. 'It seems crazy when there's so much need here,' Ellie had told Marc but Marc had kissed her and hushed her.

'It lets you stay with me without worrying,' he'd told her. 'And that means Falkenstein has a stable government. It's a small price.'

So Ellie, too, was working whenever she could. The hospital was accustomed to the bodyguards now; in fact the junior nurse who'd cared for Felix the night of the coronation was now wearing a diamond, and Ellie's chief bodyguard was never without a great, goofy smile.

More mush, Felix thought, but he grinned as he kept careful pace with the carriage. He couldn't get distracted. He was accompanying his mother to the cathedral to marry his father, and that had to be priority number one.

And then they were there. The trumpets blared forth their *Ode to Joy*. Someone held Felix's horse as he dismounted because he had an even more important role now.

'Who'll accompany you down the aisle? Would you like bridesmaids?' Josef had asked Ellie, and Ellie and Marc and Felix had stared at him as if he was dumb.

'No one else accompanies me but Felix,' Ellie had decreed. 'My son will take me to my husband. On this day of all days, all I need is my family.'

He'd stood in this place three months ago and accepted the crown and he'd never felt so alone in his life.

What a difference three months could make.

What a difference one woman could make.

He stood and watched her walk steadily down the aisle. Josef had suggested full bridal—*the public will love it!* She'd considered and finally she'd not only given in but she'd actively enjoyed choosing. She was therefore dressed in white, with slivers of crimson netted through her veil and around the trace of the hem of her gorgeous billowing train.

'Because I need a bit of crimson,' she'd told Marc, laughing. 'I've slept in your bed for the past three months, Your Majesty, and me a divorced woman. Scarlet doesn't begin to cut it.'

Her laughter, her candour, her honesty—as well as the work she continued in the hospital—was endearing her to the nation.

And to him. Every day he loved her more.

Felix was walking before her, carrying the ring that'd been back and forth between continents in its quest for its true home.

He'd wear a ring from this day forth too. Some things were imperative.

Dear heaven, she was lovely.

Her dress was exquisite, the antique lace bodice skimming her figure to perfection, the skirt billowing like a cloud, a mass of silken embroidery. She looked young, happy, beautiful.

Felix was wearing the insignia of the Crown Prince of Falkenstein. He looked proud fit to burst.

His wife. His son.

Could he be any happier?

His thought briefly of that appalling morning when he'd learned he'd be King, when he'd thought the life he valued was over. But now he had his medicine. Things were happening in this country that most people had thought would never happen in their lifetime. And he and Ellie, what a team.

He and Ellie.

She was almost to him now. He reached out his hand and she came to him, putting her hand in his. With perfect trust.

She smiled up at him and he thought, *It can't get better than this.*

Who'd want to be King of Falkenstein? No one, he'd thought all those months ago. But now, with this woman by his side...

He smiled at her and then, dammit, he stooped and kissed her because one kiss at the end of the ceremony was never going to cut it.

She smiled mistily up at him. The hand holding his tightened and they turned together to say the vows they already knew by heart.

And, right there and then, the King of Falkenstein decided he was the luckiest man in the world.

The King of Falkenstein had finally sorted his priorities and found his happy ever after.

* * * * *

*If you enjoyed this story, check out these
other great reads from Marion Lennox*

*FALLING FOR HER WOUNDED HERO
A CHILD TO OPEN THEIR HEARTS
SAVING MADDIE'S BABY
STEPPING INTO THE PRINCE'S WORLD*

All available now!

MILLS & BOON®

MEDICAL ROMANCE™

THE ULTIMATE IN ROMANTIC MEDICAL DRAMA

A sneak peek at next month's titles...

In stores from 2nd November 2017:

- **The Spanish Duke's Holiday Proposal** – Robin Gianna *and* **The Rescue Doc's Christmas Miracle** – Amalie Berlin

- **Christmas with Her Daredevil Doc** *and* **Their Pregnancy Gift** – Kate Hardy

- **A Family Made at Christmas** – Scarlet Wilson *and* **Their Mistletoe Baby** – Karin Baine

---

Just can't wait?
Buy our books online before they hit the shops!
www.millsandboon.co.uk

Also available as eBooks.

1017/03

MILLS & BOON®

EXCLUSIVE EXTRACT

Dr Hayley Clark and Sam Price's holiday romance was
unforgettable – and unrepeatable! Then risk-taking doc
Sam arrives at her hospital… Could their fling become
something more?

Read on for a sneak preview of
CHRISTMAS WITH HER DAREDEVIL DOC
the first book in the MIRACLES AT MUSWELL HILL
HOSPITAL *duet*

'Hayley, meet your replacement, Samuel Price. Sam,
Hayley's just been promoted to senior registrar and you've
taken over from her. You'll be working together.'

Of all the places…

Sam hadn't told Hayley that he was about to start a new
job in London, and she hadn't told him where she worked.
London was a massive city with quite a few hospitals. What
were the chances that they'd end up working together? The
way her pupils expanded momentarily told him that she
was just as shocked and surprised as he was.

This was going to make things awkward. They'd had a
fling in Iceland, agreeing that it would be nothing more
than that, and they'd said goodbye. What now? Would she
want to see if their fling could be something more, something deeper? Or had he just been her transition person,
the one who'd helped her to move on after her partner's
death, so she wouldn't want to pick up where they'd left
off?

The problem was, he didn't know what he wanted, either.
He'd really liked the woman he'd started to get to know
in Iceland. But then again he'd liked Lynda, too—and his
ex-fiancée had let him down so badly. Could he even trust

his judgement any more? Would he be making a huge mistake if he started seeing Hayley?

She recovered first, holding her hand out. 'Welcome to Muswell Hill Hospital, Dr Price.'

Don't miss
MIRACLES AT MUSWELL HILL HOSPITAL:
CHRISTMAS WITH HER DAREDEVIL DOC
THEIR PREGNANCY GIFT
by Kate Hardy
Available November 2017
www.millsandboon.co.uk

Copyright ©2017 Kate Hardy

Join Britain's BIGGEST Romance Book Club

50% OFF your first parcel

- EXCLUSIVE offers every month
- FREE delivery direct to your door
- NEVER MISS a title
- EARN Bonus Book points

Call Customer Services
0844 844 1358*

or visit
illsandboon.co.uk/subscriptions

* This call will cost you 7 pence per minute plus your phone company's price per minute access charge.

MILLS & BOON®

Why shop at millsandboon.co.uk?

Each year, thousands of romance readers
find their perfect read at millsandboon.co.uk.
That's because we're passionate about
bringing you the very best romantic fiction.
Here are some of the advantages of
shopping at www.millsandboon.co.uk:

* **Get new books first**—you'll be able to buy
  your favourite books one month before they
  hit the shops

* **Get exclusive discounts**—you'll also be
  able to buy our specially created monthly
  collections, with up to 50% off the RRP

* **Find your favourite authors**—latest news,
  interviews and new releases for all your
  favourite authors and series on our website,
  plus ideas for what to try next

* **Join in**—once you've bought your favourite
  books, don't forget to register with us to rate,
  review and join in the discussions

Visit **www.millsandboon.co.uk**
for all this and more today!